GODLESS WATERS

GODLESS WATERS

Walter Brettingham

The Book Guild Ltd
Sussex, England

This book is a work of fiction. The characters and situations in this story are imaginary. No resemblance is intended between these characters and any real persons, either living or dead.

This book is sold subject to the condition that it shall not, by way of trade or otherwise, be lent, re-sold, hired out, photocopied or held in any retrieval system or otherwise circulated without the publisher's prior consent in any form of binding or cover other than that in which this is published and without a similar condition including this condition being imposed on the subsequent purchaser.

The Book Guild Ltd
25 High Street,
Lewes, Sussex

First published 1996
© Walter Brettingham, 1996
Set in Meridien

Typesetting by Keyboard Services, Luton, Beds.

Printed in Great Britain by
Antony Rowe Ltd.
Chippenham, Wiltshire.

A catalogue record for this book is
available from the British Library

ISBN 1 85776 076 X

A Sailor

He knew the icy loneliness and saw
    The dread affinity of sea and sky,
Close grey upon him, heard the weird wind's cry
    Shrilling mad descent to the brass of war:
The cold white latitudes of despair that freeze
Blood, dreams, enlightenment in the Arctic day
Called down the corridors of spray,
    His flesh of youth bruised by irreverent seas,
No fame or ribbon sing of those whose graves
    Like his litter the ocean though he flung
The sea his breath and had no more to give
    Only immortal and unfeeling waves
Moan his wild threnody. He was so young,
    He died before he began to live.

                D S Goodbrand
                January 1944 Russia

From 'JACK'S WAR'
Chapter 5 G G Connell
William Kimber – London 1985

1

A naval rating stood in the dimly lit corridor of a train that was just passing from the countryside into the south-eastern suburbs of the capital. He was only aware that it was doing so because the stops became more frequent, and usually a porter called out place names as well. It was still dark on this midwinter morning and there was only an occasional glint of light in the blackout beyond the windows. The corridor was full and when somebody had to get on or off there was a hurried kicking of cases and kitbags by servicemen as they tried to rearrange themselves and settle down to the next irritatingly short stage of the journey. He turned his gaze from yet another reshuffle in the corridor and surveyed those who were vaguely discernible, seated in the compartment beside him. A mixed lot, he thought. The war had certainly upheaved the population out of their accustomed routines. At this time of the morning, he recalled, this would have been the workmen's train taking dockers and labourers, still dressed in a working-class way, in mufflers and hobnailed boots, to factories and warehouses beside the river. It would have been befogged in a particularly odious variety of cheap, shag tobacco combining with a certain odour of damp clothes or bodies not over-washed, depending upon the season of the year or state of the weather.

Now, however, the compartment contained a man in a bowler hat which half hid his thin pale face. He was wedged in the far corner by the window, his umbrella behind him on a hook under the luggage rack. He wore a winged collar with his shirt and a black tie was secured with a golden ring. He endeavoured, unsuccessfully, to shut himself off from the other passengers with his paper, for it was necessary to hold it at an awkward angle to catch the meagre light from the masked bulbs in the centre of the carriage ceiling. His tight black overcoat and striped trousers suggested a civil servant, stirred from the comfortable hours of a peacetime ministry by the indecencies of war. Opposite him, in the other window corner, a khaki greatcoat, collar turned up, concealed the slumped figure of a soldier heavily asleep. Next to the soldier was a middle-aged workman, cloth cap wreathed in smoke from a hand-rolled cigarette which sagged damply from his lips. With an occasional quiet cough, just audible above the click of the wheels, he read a tabloid newspaper which carried large headlines seeming to suggest that a murder in the car-park of a south coast cinema was of greater importance and interest than a particularly nasty hill in Italy which had stopped the Allied advance. Beside the workman a woman of some bulk was knitting, tugging the grey wool from a hold-all on her lap. From time to time she glanced at her fellows and, as the workman turned to the inside sheet, took a fleeting interest in its contents. In the near corner, just below the rating, a youngish woman, head shrouded in a scarf, leaned back with eyes closed, but quietly awake, her black gloved hands firmly clutching both folded newspaper and handbag on her lap. Across the compartment from her was another civilian, a young man in dungarees under his overcoat. Despite a pallor that might have been engendered by night work he was apparently quite healthy and a little on the plump side. He tried to read from time to time from an orange coloured paperback book which, by its title, set in large black letters in a white centre band, was about the Soviet Union.

In the middle seats sat two sailors, outdoing the older workman in smoke production and passing an occasional quiet remark to each other. The rating was on draft with them, in a group of nearly a hundred naval men who had left the barracks at six that morning bound for the far north of the country. They represented nearly all ranks and branches of the lower deck, from a hoary chief gunner down to a very young ordinary seaman. Cooks, sick-berth attendants, torpedomen, coders and other branches too, they were liberally scattered along the length of the jolting, peevish train.

The naval rating turned back to the corridor and on the other side of the closed compartment door stood Johnny, the telegraphist he had first spoken to in the cockroach-infested kitchen of the barrack block in the small hours of that morning. They had considered the breakfast haddock together, still swimming, apparently, in its pungent greasy water, and the cocoa, so thick it could almost have been eaten with a spoon. Now his sallow face, narrow below ravenblack hair, gloomily thought about the passing of the stations. At one stop he stirred from a slouch to say, 'I feel like getting off.'

'Why?'

'This is my station.'

Then, as though to clear up the ambiguity, 'My home's here. In fact I used to work in that bloody booking office.'

Jabbing a blue gloved hand at the window he cleared an area of mist and in the faint blue light of dawn the rating could see the yellow patch of the ticket office window, silhouetting dark forms that moved back and forth before it. A sudden jerk and the clatter of wheels conducted Johnny back into his unutterable thoughts.

The dawn, changing from blue to cold grey, revealed the innumerable chimneys and meanness of the streets behind the riverfront and the jerking of the train, the clatter across points and its slackening speed warned of the approach of the terminus. Slowly the platforms came into view. As the passengers alighted the civilians sifted themselves from the crowd and, lightly burdened, disappeared quickly through the ticket barrier. Servicemen were sorting themselves into little groups with the help of an occasional loud command. The two sailors, yawning from a stuffy compartment, joined the other two on the platform. Leisurely they made their way back to the luggage van and found many of the draft there, retrieving their bags and hammocks. The rating found his gear and lugged it out of the van.

The very sight of the hammock filled him with intense annoyance. The intricacy of its clews and lashing seemed to be a thing he would always have to learn afresh. The rough canvas and abrasive rope, its very banana-like form filled him with loathing. He could not understand why this relic of earlier times had survived into the machine age, any more than the absurd fancy dress uniform in which they had to garb themselves and which had been such a joy to his late fellow adolescents in training. Somehow he felt that it was a conspiracy of the admirals to keep the lower deck firmly in place. Perhaps the very abasement he felt whenever he handled it was by design. Wherever he had gone, from his earliest days in the service the journey had been clouded by a sort of neurosis, aggravated when he took it from lorry to truck or from truck to luggage van. Most detestable it was to carry it along passageways and on escalators in full view of the population of the capital. It was his cross to carry through the war. He wondered if soldiers and airmen felt the same about the equipment they carried around strapped to their persons. Many times he would have gladly lost the preposterous thing or presented it to a museum as a genuine piece of Nelsoniana.

As he heaved it after his kitbag onto a truck Johnny had brought up his spleen nearly made it shoot off the other side, to the mild irritation of his companion. Coupled with his hatred of his hammock was the way he was addressed as 'Jack' everywhere he went. Somehow the two things were synonymous. He could hardly be civil to well-intentioned people who spoke to him using the word. Feeling ridiculously self-conscious he went his way through civilian crowds, a kind of folk-clown, Jack and his hammock.

A procession of trucks piled high with their belongings trundled down the platform, through the concourse and out into the road in front of the station. Two lorries were waiting and the whole enormous collection of baggage was loaded for transport across the city. Their own means of transport had not arrived and the middle-aged gunner who had charge of the group called everybody together and told them not to wander from the immediate vicinity. The loading bustle having subsided, the rating became aware of the traffic going across the bridge just outside the station approach, and it drew him on, a few steps at a time, slowly towards the river. Office workers, managing to keep smartly clad in war economy clothes, stepped out briskly for their workplaces on the other side. He stopped when he came to a familiar view of the river downstream.

It was a quiet scene in spite of city noises behind him. The grey light came from low, still clouds, taking colour from the scene, and all the riverside buildings, the wharves, the market and the crenellated walls of the medieval fortress were apparently deserted. Save for a few tethered barges so was the silver-smooth water. The hostile coasts opposite the estuary had severely limited the mercantile traffic in and out of the port for three years and the dockside cranes stood idle, not as he remembered them, nodding back and forth as they gathered up the produce of distant lands. A few seagulls, white blurs, swung aimlessly across the barges.

The chill air penetrated his overcoat and jersey and with a shiver he recalled the draft, shook off his dark mood and strolled back against the flow of early morning blank faces which still issued from the terminus.

As he entered the concourse two dark blue coaches with everybody on board save the chief gunner, standing sour-faced, paper in hand, at the door of the second one, told him he was not very popular. Quickening his pace, he came up diffidently to the chief.

'You silly little sod,' the older one exploded, 'we're waiting for you. Where've you been? I thought you'd done a bunk. Get in before I shave off!'

Considerably humbled, the youth entered the coach to a chorus of derision, the particulars of which were unclear, except that as he sat down he heard Johnny rhetorically grunt, 'Not a party at this time of day?'

The chief got in, slammed the door and turning to the driver, growled, 'That's the lot,' and went back to sit with some other ancients, two of whom had removed their overcoats to reveal, with a plentiful supply of stripes and anchors, the blue, white-edged ribbon of the long service and good conduct medal.

The engine roared and they moved slowly away behind the leading coach. The rating, in a gangway seat at the front, looked out on the passing buildings, pedestrians and traffic as though at a film of another place. Those things so familiar to him, day by day in the last year of peace and the first years of war, were invested with a curious nostalgia. The blast-walls, painted white at the corners, of neatly stacked and buttressed sandbags before doors and windows; the cross slits on the masks of the traffic lights; white marks on kerbstone and lamp post were suffused with a new significance. He looked into some partly boarded office windows, criss-crossed with sticky paper strips. Blackout curtains or panels removed, they revealed the homely glow of welcoming electric lights. It was curious that when in such circumstances he had thought of national service as a release from boredom, that particular ennui which seems to be the lot of the adolescent. Now as he caught glimpses of the Guildhall, the great dome of the cathedral, the markets and familiar offices, he began to feel that affection for the capital which the naval townee summed up in the word 'Smokes'.

The gaps in the old streets were grievous. Some had just been levelled and the sides of adjacent buildings supported with great timbers. Others with basement areas had been converted into emergency water supply tanks, impelled by the memory of the second great fire only three years before. Yet all in all, despite the bomb damage, the general run-down unpainted seediness of wartime, the vital throb of its antique pulse continued, cheering the spirit of many of its departing sons.

When the coach finally drew up in front of the departure station for the next stage of their journey and the door was opened by the driver the rating got out quickly. He did not care to listen to a succession of comments on his tardiness as his fellow draftees passed by. He went in search of a trolley and after a brief look in the circulation area found one and trundled it back to the baggage. It gave him an oddly boyish thrill to push it along through the hurrying throng and out to the lorries. Piled high it soon was, with kitbags, hammocks, large green suitcases – these last the privilege of petty officers – and the ubiquitous little brown attaché case which was the one democratic article in the service, one which all ranks possessed from ordinary seaman up to the highest level at which a person was obliged to handle his own belongings.

The awe-inspiring chief gunner had meanwhile been in search of the departure platform and on his return sent the trolleys along to it and ordered everybody to await him there and not – a baleful glance at the rating as he said this – not to stray, go adrift, get lost or otherwise be a bleeding nuisance. A last sad momentary look at the busy metropolitan scene behind him and the rating helped to push his trolley into the main station.

The soaring cast iron arches of the gaunt, chill Victorian structure disappeared into the billowing smoke which rose from several steam locomotives at various platforms, projecting from the labyrinthine main circulation area, crossed by walkways and staircases. The engines occasionally grunted, bellowed and hissed, sending echoes back and forth across the roof of blackened glass and sheet metal.

The passengers at this station seemed to consist of a greater proportion of servicemen. Soldiers and airmen, razor-sharp creases to their trousers, wearing well-pressed tunics and battle-dress blouses, passed by, some in neatly blancoed webbing equipment, carrying packs, haversacks and rifles. An occasional American, generally an airman, strolled by, sometimes looking a little bemused as though not knowing the puzzling ways of a familiarly strange country. Civilians there were, but fewer suburbanites now. Most seemed to be carrying cases bent on more distant travel. Perhaps some were off on their last journey as a civilian for the duration, voucher paid, on their way to a service training camp.

However it was the navy men who caught his eye. Many of them, officers and ratings alike, lacked the new pin spruceness of recruits and the rested, tidy casualness of the experienced barrack veterans on his draft. Their uniforms, number ones though they were, had a rumpled look about them. Gold badges had a greenish bloom; blue raincoats and overcoats a slight patina of white in places among the creases, and shoes, though rubbed joyously to be presentable for leave in the capital, had an unresponsive dullness. But it was their faces that made him wonder. Some had a red, raw, beaten-looking countenance, whilst others seemed drawn in; grey and haggard of features. Individuality of years was wiped from them and it would have been difficult telling twenty years from thirty-five.

As they approached the departure platform, which was almost the last, a deep sigh issued from a leading stoker helping to push the trolley. Observing the trellis gate as an old familiar, 'Now for the wild life of sheep and the Fleet Canteen,' he breathed. Although only two or three years older than the rating, the lines about his mouth and eyes and the self-mocking tone of his remark made him appear old and extremely experienced. It was obvious he had been this way before.

They had been waiting ten minutes when the chief gunner hurried up with a regulating petty officer from the transport office. The gates were opened and they pushed their baggage along the platform to two coaches that had been reserved for them. After a momentary upheaval in the scramble for seats, the rating found he had managed to get a corner seat on the window side with his back to the engine. This had been accomplished by closely following Johnny who, with body blocks and other dexterities, had got there first and claimed the seat facing the engine. He had obviously decided not to spend this part of the journey at a disadvantage.

'Look after the stuff, Dave,' he said to the rating, 'I'll go and help the others.'

David suitably arranged his overcoat, their gas masks and cases so that the four would sit together. A radio mechanic poked his head through the door from the corridor and enquired if there was room. 'Help yourself,' said David. The mechanic called a friend and they took the corner seats at the opposite end.

A few minutes later Johnny and the other two ratings came back and a rearrangement of the cases, overcoats, gas masks and packet lunches was made on the luggage racks. All this accompanied by only an occasional terse remark which was indicative of the very early start that morning.

David decided to leave the thickening smoke of the compartment and strolled along the train to the guards van, the doors of which were still open wide. He went in and was satisfied only when he saw the labels on his gear. Strolling back to his compartment he noticed the extremely long train was filling rapidly and the proportion of servicemen to civilians was great, there being a great deal of dark blue to be seen through the windows. He had just stepped into the compartment when a sergeant in an infantry regiment appeared and asked if there was a spare seat. As all the draft was by this time accommodated the sailors, in a momentary babble, welcomed him and after he had arranged his pack, kitbag and greatcoat on the cluttered rack sat down on the corridor side by the radio mechanics.

There was a quiet, somewhat awkward period and only the sound of hissing steam, conversation in the next compartments and footsteps on the platform made a background. Then talk picked up and began to flow in the easy way of service chat and David learnt that the other two ratings were special telegraphists with much the same background as Johnny and himself from initial training camp through wireless schools to barracks.

The bustle and concern of crossing the city and getting the train had temporarily muted the pensiveness in his mind, but in these final long minutes before the departure whistle it began to grow and he was glad of the almost absent-minded conversation that appeared to indicate a similar doleful vein in the thoughts of the others. Only the sergeant seemed different. His lean features carried a tan that was now more parchment yellow than healthy brown. Beneath there seemed a real face, one of stone grey hardness and age not suitable to a man still in his twenties. He leaned back in the relaxed manner of a person used to the company of men, but his sight was inward to other places than towards those around him. Over the left breast pocket of his battle-dress blouse was the ribbon of the Africa Star, on the upper part of his sleeve a tartan patch and the red flash of the infantry, and below, on his cuff, the slim golden bar of a wound stripe. The khaki of his uniform, against the dark blue surrounding it, had a yellow-like intensity.

There were shouts on the platform, whistles blew, the engine barked and the train eased out of the station.

2

The long, slow draw up the gradient of the northern slope of the metropolis enabled David to look at the crowded, mean streets, grey but rather intimate and friendly now. Through cuttings and tunnels, over and under bridges, the train gathered speed and the cramped terraces gave way to larger, Victorian houses of dull brick and slate, set in their own gardens with the smudges of bare trees between. Patches of green splashed the greyness more frequently and at last the suburbs of trim red brick or whitewashed houses, roofed in ochre tiles, along spacious tree-lined roads, gave promise of open country. Speeding at last, with a roar and in a swirling cloud of smoke and steam, the train raced through a clean modern station and out into green fields, brightening greener as weak sunlight filtered through the thinning cloud.

Johnny, too, looked out on the countryside and for some time talk ceased as all the occupants sat absorbed in the passing scene. Eventually, however, the spell was broken by the appearance of the chief gunner in the doorway, once more checking his list of draftees, closely followed by the ticket inspector who looked at the sergeant's travel voucher and murmured a few words to the chief, who said it was all right, before they moved on.

One of the radio mechanics reached up and took his lunch packet from the rack and this reminded the others that it was a long time since breakfast. Soon the sailors were examining the contents of their own brown paper bags: corned beef sandwiches, processed cheese, apples and small fruit pies, square in shape, a product familiar to customers of city tea shops, were in turn selected rejected, criticized, exchanged or eaten.

The special telegraphist next to Johnny was a large-boned

youth with blue eyes and blonde hair already thinning. With his pink oval face and large rough red hands his features suggested an authentic Anglo-Saxon countryman. His mild, slow rural accent, as he offered a sandwich to the soldier, confirmed this impression. This comradely gesture, repeated by the others from time to time in the course of the journey, drew the sergeant into conversation, prompted occasionally by a quiet remark from his neighbour.

The sailors lapsed into attentive silence as, without embellishment, perhaps to reciprocate their generosity or perhaps moved by an inner compulsion to give form to his thoughts, he told his story. He mentioned that he was going to his home town for the first time since he had arrived back four months previously, during the autumn. He had been in hospital and convalescent in the south, but was now on his way to his regimental depot. He was not keen to go, for in the town were relations of men with whom he had gone abroad, men of his platoon. Most of them were dead, he was alive. People would want to know what happened to them; in a small town everybody knew everybody else's business. That was why he had been content to stay in the south when he had landed.

The sergeant, observing that willy-nilly he had become the object of much interest, fell silent and his listeners turned somewhat shamefacedly to each other. The small talk continued. His neighbour offered David a cigarette and, oblivious to an unintended impression of moral rectitude, he primly refused with 'No, thank you, I don't smoke.' It had been his little gesture of independence since entering the service and wherever he had gone, on duty or off, he had refused offered cigarettes in a manner that had become an almost thoughtless ritual. He noticed the wry grin on the refined but pimpled countenance of his new friend. His grey eyes twinkled with amusement and beneath a crinkly shock of dun-coloured hair a wrinkled brow took the superior refusal in good part. It was an expression that he was to know well in the coming weeks and one that was oddly comforting in uncomfortable circumstances.

Johnny, who had been reclining in his corner, stirred himself to pick a cigarette from the same freely offered packet, accepted a light and through patterns of smoke enquired. 'Did you get the draft at the signals' camp or were you in the barracks? Incidentally my name's Squires, Johnny Squires and he's Dave Freston.'

'I'm Fred, Fred Windenham. Came up to the barracks from the camp. Rotten luck missing Christmas leave.'

'Wasn't it just,' agreed Johnny moodily.

The ensuing exchange of remarks confirmed David in his opinion that Fred Windenham was a townee and, as coincidence would have it, lived only a short bus ride from Johnny's home. He had worked as a junior in the newspaper business before he was astounded to find that his country needed his insignificant self for war service. He was the most unservice-minded of naval ratings and it was obvious that he had managed to avoid complications with the authorities to date only because he was not particularly obvious in stature or presence. Indeed his thin face was excelled by his body in thinness and even through the blue serge of his uniform it was obvious that he consisted chiefly of skin and bone. When cornered by the enforced social pressures of the navy, his engaging grin and friendly nature, expressed in an accent with a slight metropolitan twang, eased his way through local difficulties.

Very soon he was deeply involved in the merits – as he saw them – of the Palace soccer team. Johnny, in lugubrious tones, seemed to differ, preferring the local allegiance of the Riverside eleven. As they moved from the austere present to golden past achievements of cup and championship, Fred exhibited a phenomenal memory for facts about victorious games, superlative players and villainous referees. Not a football enthusiast, although he had quite recently played again after many years of abstinence – two games at the signals camp, which left him limping not from bruises but mere activity – David let the talk fade from his attention. He looked out on the bright fields and woods bathed in the clean low shafting sunlight of midwinter. The sky was a clear dark blue, reflecting on the windows of trackside houses as they flashed past and in the shady parts of stark forest and dell.

As the hours passed the landscape changed to a clean simplicity, not familiar to his southern eyes. Little towns, compact, grey and squalid, muted in a smoky veil, became more frequent and rail lines united from all directions in accumulating complexity. Then the great wheels of coal mine lifts joined the increasingly crowded scene and in mid-afternoon the train began to slow down. Clicking its way through a maze of diagonal tracks and points, it drew into the dark shelter of a northern station.

The chief gunner came along the corridor, telling everybody there would be a stop of twenty minutes, and as the train came to a standstill Johnny got up, opened the door and stepped onto the platform. A draught of chill air swept into the fuggy atmosphere of the compartment and precipitated everyone into hastily going in search of a cup of tea. As they wandered along the platform David, finding himself alongside the sergeant, mentioned he had a relation with the gunners in Italy.

'Och, I didna get onta the mainland,' the soldier replied in the clipped tones of a Lowlander, 'I stopped at Catania.'

They had come to the brown-framed, grimy windows of the restaurant which, no doubt from the elegant old style lettering and design, had seen more opulent times. Inside, electricity cast a feeble light over the dank, crowded sleaziness, combating the artificial twilight of the station roof. Three middle-aged women, wrapped up in overalls and turbans, sloshed a hot weak beverage indiscriminately into cracked cup and metal tray, keeping a wary eye on the few spoons available to stir the hint of sweetening added to the brew on request.

The sergeant and David moved away from the main throng and put their cups on a shelf along one of the misted windows. His thoughts still on the sergeant's remark, David intimated that the relation had written that there had been a noisy few days in front of that Sicilian town. The sergeant lit a cigarette, sipped his tea and said, 'I was hit there.'

David drank and waited.

'We were just outside the town. In other directions our lot were copping it, but although we were the first wave, got off lightly. We had moved up through these olive groves, along a road into the town, to an old factory. It was on the bank of a river that was dried up. There was a bridge where we reached it; we were supposed to hold and wait for 2 platoon to go through us, across the bridge and up the road. It was this time of day and the sun seemed hotter even than we remembered in the desert. More sticky in Sicily. As we started we could see our air bursts over the factory and our heavy MGs were spraying the area from both flanks. We moved up through the trees and along the road, expecting trouble any moment. Nothing. We got to the factory, the only Jerries dead ones. Our officer placed the platoon along the river bank and the Jocks tried to find every bit of shade they could, but the trees were chopped about a bit.'

The sergeant's listener looked out on the murky station and finished his drink.

'Then 2 platoon came up with the major and they went on towards the town. As they reached the next buildings, the first streets, the Spandaus and mortar racket showed they had run into it. A lad came back, hit in the arm, and told the officer the major wanted him to come up with the tanks he had called for on the radio. Then the tanks came along, kicking up a dust, and some of the lads came from their positions to watch them go in. I was sitting under a tree and didn't even get away from the dust. My legs ached and my head; I was feeling the heat worse than ever before. I should have stopped them, I would have done before for less, but I didn't. The little buggers were making themselves cooler in the dark corners of the factory, amongst the rubble.'

Insensitive as he could be at times, David nevertheless grew aware that this was more than mere chat. Somehow because there were no more listening, the sergeant seemed to be exploring as much for himself as his listener the events on that scorching afternoon not so long ago. He had gone back to those places that were in his sightless gaze as he sat in the train. His listener was a mere anonymity; the fact they would never meet again, that he was a no-person, a mere sounding board, had made the sergeant pour forth those turbulent memories that swirled in his mind untouched as doctors repaired his injuries.

He drew deeply on his cigarette and continued. 'Then it came over like an express train. An 88. It slammed into the grove behind the factory. I started to get up but it was as though I was in a dream, leaden-footed, intending to go across the road and get the lads out, and that's the last I knew until I felt someone stuffing a dressing in my chest. As I came round I saw the officer leaning over me; the poor wee bastard was almost out of his mind and kept asking me what had happened. There were ten blokes in there apparently and not much worth collecting up. But he faded out and all I could feel was a lump of lead on my chest and the roaring in my ears.

'I've not seen any of the battalion since, either at the dressing station or the field hospital where they took out a chunk of metal the size of an egg.'

'Rotten luck,' said David inadequately, the spell at last being broken by some of the draft moving towards the door. 'I suppose you'll be on home service from now on though, won't you?'

'They reckon I'll be quite fit again by the spring,' replied the sergeant, '... and there's always the Second Front they're going on about.'

By the time they had returned to the coach the sergeant appeared, strangely, to cheer up and when two land girls asked if there was room he took charge, indicated the spare seat between Fred Windenham and the radio mechanic and assured them – to a general infectious giggle – that they could squeeze the other one in on his side. He made room on the racks for their cases and they all settled down. The girl next to Fred broke the momentary silence by turning her buxom figure to fling her hat up on her case and, patting her ample auburn curls, beamed at everybody through horn-rimmed spectacles and said, 'I'm Pip, this is Helen.'

Helen, a blonde, open-faced, with gentle grey eyes, strong-boned and of ample bust, pushed from between the sergeant and the other radio mechanic and said in mock, infantlike tones, 'Hello, ev'rybody,' which had them all laughing and enjoying the girls' simple good nature. In their heavy brogues, corduroy breeches and green woollen jumpers they were not the picture of elegance but the servicemen loved them for their banter, which eased the tension underlying their apparent nonchalance, and as the mournful twilight emphasized the increasing bleakness of the passing scene David was glad to listen to the girls lightly word-fencing with their neighbours.

At last the reading that most had been doing spasmodically during the day became impossible and although a dim light was cast in the middle, the figures were only general shapes, identified by their voices or by a face thrust forward when the perpetual cigarettes were offered and taken. During the late evening the border town was reached and most were glad to stretch their legs and drink a watery beer in the buffet. Yet soon enough, with a last precautionary check of numbers by the chief gunner, their train headed out of the bleak stone city into the mountains.

After pulling down the blind over the window beside him, David wedged himself hand on chin, elbow on armrest, into a position whereby he might sleep. Johnny pulled down the blind on his side and also the one over the door. Quietly the conversation died away and everybody was dozing if not quite asleep. Outside the slowing click of the wheels and the laboured puffing of the engine told of gradients being climbed and sometimes, with a clanging bell and echoing roar, a small town station was passed. The compartment grew colder and overcoats were gently taken from the racks for use as blankets. When David got up from his jolting corner to get his own he saw that the blonde land girl opposite had fallen asleep on the sergeant's shoulder and he had put his arm round her. She seemed so like a child, relaxed and innocent and, glancing along at her friend Pip, he saw that she too leaned on Fred, asleep, but he sat primly upright, hands spread on the overcoat covering his bony knees. Before he settled down to sleep again, peeping through his blind, David was surprised to see the white blur of a snowclad landscape.

It was in a sticky-faced, dry-mouthed half-wakefulness that seemed only a few moments later when he felt the train rumbling slowly into a station as a distant, metallic voice echoed emptily the name of the place. Sounds of activity were few and over his coat he had just seen Johnny push his wrist out to glance at his watch and mutter it was one o'clock, when the door was violently pulled open and a blast of icy air swept in. It had them all stirring and to their astonishment a tall man of middle years, with thin grey hair, spare of frame, cadaverous of face, clad in the short jacket of a porter, stood before them in the dim platform light. It was not the sudden cold or apparition which shook them, but the hard, wild eye of the railwayman and his brittle, self-righteous voice saying. 'Now I know what you evil folk are about, get these blinds up.' He simultaneously released the door blind, which sprang up, and turned to pull up the one on Johnny's side.

In the few moments of their indecision this fanatic, in person and accent, seemed a latterday, beardless materialization of the John Knox he had read about at school and had seen portrayed on the cinema screen. The initiative of their accuser was soon lost, however, as the amazed look quickly left the face of the sergeant and the stone-like mask settled in its former mould. Deliberately he rose and as the others drew their legs under the seats he stepped forward to the door as though about to strike the porter.

'Man, you're a blethering fool,' he growled, 'get about your own business,' pulling the door shut so abruptly the porter was obliged to step back nimbly to avoid being struck. The sergeant pulled down the blind and Johnny did likewise on his side and after moments of silent wonder everybody settled down for a few more hours of dozing.

In the small hours of the morning the girls and sergeant got out at the great northern city. David caught only a glimpse of a tenemented skyline and heard the grind and clatter of the tramcars over cobbled streets, taking the early workers to dock and shipyard. The naval ratings, feeling strangely alone, went back again to their fitful sleep in the fuggy atmosphere.

3

The sound of the door on the corridor side being slid open roused David from his deep, unrestful slumber and he saw Johnny leave, rolled towel in hand. The train was slowly and steadily making its way between snowclad mountains which were bathed in the same low-angled sunshine that poured in by the corridor windows. All the others were astir; yawning, scratching and beginning to tidy themselves, brushing off cigarette ash and crumbs. David pulled up the blind in his corner and the one over the door, the one on Johnny's side being already up. For a time he watched the great humps of the mountains slide past, the white scene broken here and there by the grey mass of a small wood or croft. The sky was cloudless, a brilliant blue, and he was raised just a little from the profound depression that encompassed him, a product of apprehension, disturbed rest and the usual early morning gloom.

Johnny returned to the compartment. 'No bloody water,' he spat morosely, sliding the door shut too violently. He put the towel back in his attaché case and sat down in his corner with a sigh. David felt more stickily uncomfortable than ever as the last, long hour of approach to the northernmost point of the mainland passed. At the cost of disturbing his apathetic companions he at last got up and went into the corridor. Glancing along into the other compartments he saw that the same crumpled figures in dark blue lolled back, some still apparently asleep, others contributing to the stale odour of tobacco smoke in every part of the coach. There were no other passengers, civilian or service, but navy men. He went along to the lavatory but the stench was so appalling he decided to wait for the terminus.

Fred came out of the compartment and together they watched the sea come into sight beyond the port as the train wound down the slope from the mountain. The clear sky and bright blue water flecked with white horses seemed so attractive that David really felt that the little drabnesses of service life were fully compensated for by the sense of adventure that began to tingle in his veins.

At last the sea disappeared from sight behind the grey roofs of the town and, clattering leisurely across the points, they stopped at the town station to let off a few passengers, and then continued on behind houses and sheds, emerging onto the quayside where steam rising from the funnel of the island ferry intimated that he would soon be making his first sea journey.

'Been to sea before?' he asked Fred.

Fred grinned easily. 'On the Free Ferry,' he replied.

The gangway onto the steamer rested almost opposite where their coach had stopped and the chief gunner busied himself getting his draft into a group near the end of it, but not so as to block access for assorted passengers, service and civilian, running the gauntlet-scrutiny of papers and person by company officials, civil and armed military police. He detailed a few ratings to go and unload the baggage and it was brought along the quayside to the group, where each claimed their belongings. Since its twenty-hour sojourn in the guards van, his hammock, David noted, had acquired an even more disagreeable smell of stale fish, this mingling with the atmosphere of ice, fish and steam which assailed him when getting off the train. The lashing, too, seemed to have worked loose and the blanket was in full view and he felt he had been indecently exposed. Would he ever learn? He kicked it petulantly, to the surprise of a short coder with the wide eyes of a child who waited by him.

The chief, having conversed with the collection of gangway officials, told them he would call the draft list and they would pass up into the ship in that order, all other passengers having already gone aboard. Wondering how to achieve the impossible David took his cue from senior ratings and saw how to carry both kitbag and hammock, the latter hanging over the top of the former, balancing them on his left shoulder with the aid of his left hand which grasped the attaché case. This method left the right hand free to grasp the handrail and avoid the distinction of falling between quay and ship. So at last the junior ratings were called and, balancing his goods, he wobbled past the inquisitors and up the slippery ramp onto the already crowded upper deck of the vessel.

Edging along from the gangway he found a space of deck still clear of baggage and the tall country boy stacking his gear up against the superstructure. Clearly marked on the hammock, in regulation one inch letters, was 'G. Corder Tel.C/JX 404496'. They joined forces and as Johnny and Fred came up, made a neat little domain of their own in the surrounding chaos.

'Got a drag, George?' asked Fred, 'I've run out.'

George pulled off one of his home-knitted blue woollen gloves and took his cigarette case from his inside pocket and, the usual ritual being completed, they both sat on the baggage to recover from their exertions. They uneasily noted that although the vessel was still tied up in harbour she rocked perceptibly.

With very little fuss the gangway was pulled onto the quay and the steamer moved quietly across the sheltered waters, the rocking motion increasing as she neared the lighthouse at the end of the mole. The town receded, its greyness losing the particulars of house, church and warehouse and becoming general against the white hills. As they passed the exit and headed north into the bay a brisk wind whistled over the superstructure but moderated as she began to follow on her port side the lee of grim, towering red cliffs. High up on their face lonely seabirds wheeled and their distant plaintive calls descended faintly between lulls in the screaming of dozens of gulls flapping and gliding in the thermal from vents and funnel. The awe-inspiring grandeur kept the southerners dumb with astonishment. Such a coast came as a shock to those brought up along the gentler shores of the south-east. On the choppy water that merged from dark green under the ship to deep blue on the horizon the bright sun glinted, its brilliance reflected, too, in the foam and on the fine spray that ran along the vessel as she butted into each wave.

David noticed that several passengers were beginning to find an urgent necessity to take a place at the rail and half an hour after their departure a plentiful display of slumped bodies clad in khaki grey and, shameful to observe, navy blue, hung onto stanchion and handrail, examining with dulled sight the wonders of the deep. He stood for the three hours of the crossing, disdainfully regretting the weakness of other flesh; his companions reclining on the baggage, did not desire to push to the rail but seemed rather quiet and thoughtful. The more the little vessel bucked and rolled the more vainglorious became his thoughts. He had always wondered if he would be a good sailor and remembered those little trickles of doubt that had crept into the back of his mind in training days, but here he was astride a pitching deck and others were the weaker brethren. Not even the sight of the escorting destroyer meeting them off the great headland, as she sliced and wagged her way to the port bow, gave him any sobering thought. Strong in his youthful vanity he felt this was far superior to the stuffy four walls of a city office.

So at last the islands came into view, low-lying, unspectacular humps of undulating, snow-covered turf, the sea abating as they entered their sheltered waters and passed the boom defence vessel. A few preliminary calls were made at isolated jetties to disembark service personnel and the island ferry then went directly to the large grey bulk of a ship that had been once a queen of the southern ocean. They slid alongside and through a double-doored scuttle in the side of the liner a gangway was thrust onto their deck, over which the whole of the draft eventually made its way.

After the crowded ferry the former liner was capacious and although the draft caused some confusion on transfer, regulating petty officers and leading hands soon allocated and directed all arrivals to various parts of the depot ship. The telegraphists found themselves one deck down a broad companion-way ladder in a scrupulously clean and spacious area. There were tables and benches secured on both sides of the mess deck but much free space between, broken only by simple pipe-like stanchions connected to each other by overhead horizontal bars with hooks to suspend hammocks.

They dumped their baggage against the bulkhead opposite the

companion-way and at once began rummaging for toilet gear and towels. While they took turns to go and freshen themselves, the others took care of the baggage. The washplace, roomy and clean, was behind the stairway and a plentiful supply of hot water made a shower and change of linen possible, lessening the weariness of the travellers. They shared the mess deck with a few others, the radio mechanics appearing again, two signalmen and the wide-eyed coder who had come down with three other practitioners of his mystery.

The guard on their belongings was occasioned not so much by their companions in transit, but rather through the reputation of the care and maintenance ship's company who, perhaps slanderously, were rumoured to be exceptionally light-fingered even by the indifferent standards of the lower deck. The draftees tended to regard the depot ship in the same way as the barracks from whence they had come; that is, as a den of thieves where an unguarded, blind moment whilst pulling a jumper over one's head could cost a careless rating wallet, wrist watch, money belt, prophylactics and possibly virtue.

Be that as it may, when all were refreshed they went in search of the meal they had been promised in the general dining mess. Some wrong turns along alleyways and flats and up and down companion-ways brought them at last to a trestled space which, in former days of grandeur, had been a dining saloon. Taking plates, mugs and cutlery, they collected sausages, mashed potatoes and baked beans, syrup pudding and coffee. These expeditiously consumed, they relaxed, elbows on table, and the ritual of a social cigarette began. When David was offered one by George Corder the silver elegance of his cigarette case seemed oddly out of place.

'No thank you, I don't smoke,' he replied.

They passed an hour or so in a conversation which, under the enthusiastic direction of Fred, consisted mainly of opinions and expressions of taste concerning the current popular music compared with the earlier and more traditional style of jazz-music. The gulf between George and Fred was wide. The former advocated the superiority of the present forms, no doubt influenced by his proficiency as a dancer, usually exercised at his home town corn exchange where it would seem he was an object of admiration among the young ladies; and Fred quoted the authority of a weekly publication – pulled from his jumper – specializing in comment on the gramophone-record and dance-band scene, to support the superiority of the oddly-named jazz practitioners of yesteryear.

Johnny's normally severe countenance seemed to deepen with what was most likely a bored expression, but from time to time he interposed a modest remark which might be freely interpreted as 'A plague on both your houses!' On the other hand David was absorbed by the intensity of the views held, impressed to find that people could hear melody in something. Although subjected to it as a familiar background, on and off for many months, he considered it was usually quite discordant.

The topic had been thoroughly pulled to shreds, or so it seemed, and Fred was folding the manifesto of his doctrines and returning it to his jumper when, to their surprise, several names of ratings, including their own, were called on the speech-relay system and ordered to report to the regulating office immediately. Once more they searched and at last came upon that fount of official wisdom and saw that most of the others called had been spoken to and were going away as they arrived.

David had wondered if there was such a naval animal aboard, not having seen one since coming on, but he was not disappointed for out of the office doorway there emerged a chief master-at-arms. Dazzlingly bedecked with the gold crown and wreath on his lapels, a set of ribbons which suggested he had a similar office in the Ark, an inhumanly white starched collar and silk smooth black tie, above a stocky generously-fleshed frame, he had a face crumpled and lined by the seas of time. It was strangulated pink, with blue eyes of diamond hardness set in watery halos, hinting that his tot of rum had been generously long in losing its effect since the forenoon.

'Who are the sparkers for the *Watchful?*' he demanded quite unsociably.

'We all are, Chief,' replied Johnny rashly.

'No you ain't,' breathed the nautical dragon ominously.

'That's what we were told on the draft chit,' persisted Johnny even more heroically.

The crumpled visage began to quake; the others thought that there was definitely a hint of steam rising over the thinning hair of the ancient mariner.

'Did you believe everything what you was told about your parentage, son?' rumbled the stirring volcano. At last something of the state he had put the master-at-arms into began to penetrate Johnny's introspection.

'Has there been some change, Master?' darted in Fred with his most placating grin, hoping to soothe the ruffled monster.

'Change, sonny, change?' echoed their senior, not really euphoniously. 'There has been a regular balls-up down where you come from. At least a dozen ratings misdirected.' He paused, looked at their bemused expressions and added, 'But you can't expect anything else can you? We always say you're "chatty but happy".' Which revealed he was not of their port division, but most likely from that which had been a favourite of Lord Nelson, if not, unlikely, that refuge of West Countrymen and Welshmen, the one further west still.

'Who's Squires?' he demanded. On being informed, he went on, 'Well laddie it's with great pleasure that I tell you that you're not going to the *Watchful* but to an even smaller and vastly more ancient bucket called the *Obstinate*. 'Tis rumoured she rolls like a bastard.'

Trembling with anticipation the others feared the worst.

'Who's Windenham?'

Fred grinned nervously, 'I am, Master,' he said, apparently ineffectually.

'Who's Corder?'

'Me Chief?' murmured the Saxon boy.

'So you must be Freston, if my low-class logic is correct.'

David only risked a vigorous nod.

'Well, young gentlemen of the communications branch,' he went on, with mock patronage, 'you will go as directed aforesaid, to the *Watchful*, which is more than you deserve for she is a new ship by our standards here.'

Their relief was almost tangible.

'Right, at 1400 hours tomorrow you will leave here in the tender for your ships. Be ready. That is all,' he said in a brisk and conclusive fashion.

They turned and began to go away when he called 'Freston!' David came back tremulously. The dragonlike face had softened. 'Have you got any relatives in the Andrew, son?' he asked.

'Yes,' said David reluctantly. 'An Uncle Frank.'

'What branch?'

'I think it was the engine room.'

'Engine room? He was a bloody stoker, like me. We're like a couple of minstrels in a photo I've got of us coaling the old *Seagull*. That was before Jutland. He was a good messmate but wasted his education. See you don't.'

'Yes, Master,' said David, 'Thanks.'

The chief made to go into the office, but he turned and the weatherbeaten mask was relaxed; a trace of a smile was at the corner of those steely eyes.

'Oh – and – son; good luck,' he said.

In an abstract mood, partly occasioned by consideration of a relation only known by hearsay but also by thoughts of the morrow, David lost his way, returning to the mess deck, and found himself on what had been the promenade deck. He looked out on the anchorage where the light waned fast, although it was hardly gone mid-afternoon. It was a cheerless prospect, the low hills fading darker grey into the luminous grey of water and sky. In front of them the hard silhouettes of battleships, aircraft carriers and cruisers indicated the big ship area, with the low beetle-like forms of the picket and liberty boats moving between. It was utterly impersonal and difficult to apprehend that thousands of men worked, ate, slept and did countless personal chores within those floating communities. All the time, however, the silent masses spoke to each other. Some, confidential whispers, flashed privily between ships by the twenty-inch signal lamps on their flag decks; others more authoritatively, by a red light visible all round at the foremast top, addressed the gathered company. For a while he exercised his aural knowledge of the Morse code by endeavouring to read the visual flashes. Managing to get a few letters, with practice it was an accomplishment he brought to some degree of usefulness.

He walked on, and in another direction saw smaller vessels gathered together. It was the destroyer anchorage. They, too, talked to each other, but here there was movement, the long, low shape of a destroyer moving down the lines of tethered ships and disappearing in the passage between two islands into the encompassing greyness. There was still something of a wind and the clouds yet scudded across the darkening sky. Solitary gulls, winging past, called mournfully as though anxious to be with their fellows before nightfall. The cold did not encourage him to linger above and he went down to the warmth and light below.

Everyone was quietly absorbed in their own concerns when he arrived on the mess deck. George sat at the table on their side, large pink hands backed with blond hair spread over a small notepad, busy with a close-lined, lengthy letter he was writing. Johnny, a little apart, as though they had come already to the parting of the way, was rummaging through his kitbag, pulling out crumpled articles, shaking them and neatly folding them before diving into its interior to rearrange them. Fred, along the table from George, read an illustrated film magazine or rather looked at it, for he was stopped at a page which was all photograph of a well-known Hollywood anatomy in something rather like a bathing costume, fishnet stockings and high-heeled shoes. On the other side the coders and signalmen quietly employed themselves in similar activities.

'Darken Ship' was announced on the loudspeaker and, removing his collar, David sat down at their table, feeling relaxed for the first time in weeks, ever since he had gone with shaky knees into the drafting office at the signals camp to learn his fate. Many who had trained with him had gone before. Returning from the office they held the acute attention of their listeners as they told of what they had drawn in that lottery of name lists. The drafts with party or job numbers met with most uneasiness, unless, rarely, it was known what was involved. Otherwise it could be a step into the unknown, either a new ship with several weeks of running-up trials in and out of home ports; a battered veteran, revamped and battle-prone; or, surprising joy, a welded escort awaiting them in the bright lights and fleshpots of the United States. Only the young and the innocent were disappointed if it was a stone frigate or shore station. Older, seaworn men were glad to have, for a time, terra firma under their feet.

'That's a new one,' the one-eyed leading signalman had declared, sitting on the bunk above David's when he returned to the hut under the thinning foliage of late autumn trees. 'She was commissioned in the summer, a destroyer, not a bad number, but me I prefer big ships.'

Next to the black patch a good eye had looked down at him, perhaps with a hint of regret in its intense greyness; whether for the loss of its fellow, the imminence of discharge from the service or for bright blue, sunlit days of conflict the previous year it was difficult to ascertain.

'Me and the yeoman were in the Med together,' he explained.

Then followed the upheaval and boredom of draft routine; trudging from one end of the main barracks to the other to get a collection of rubber stamps on a piece of paper. It seemed that the whole depot – drill-shed, parade ground, blocks, sheds and alleys – was a disturbed mound of scurrying ants criss-crossing each other. It was here that he had first struggled to come to terms with his hammock, in an effort to sling it in the foul-aired bomb shelter burrowed under a hillside, where hundreds of ratings were nightly obliged to sleep for fear of the old red brick barrack-blocks being hit by an enemy attack. In this unhealthy warren, on his first night in depot, he recalled the dream-speech of a rating close at hand whose hammock twitched and jerked as he relived the nightmare of a sinking ship. Struggling with his blanket he kept saying to a shipmate, 'The ship's sinking, Bill, the ship's sinking,'

Fortunately the time spent in the main depot, heartily loathed by most, was always short, signals ratings usually being accommodated in a camp in pleasant countryside, but coming and going the depot was always a brief, unwelcome interlude.

After the ritual of draft routine came leave and this too had been a sort of limbo with people so familiar and intimate, placed, as it were on the other side of an invisible wall. Conversation was always on trivialities; perhaps folk were interested, but few seemed so. As was natural, they too were immersed in their own particular problems, complicated by the difficulties of wartime, and the larger aspects of the struggle presented to them by the press and radio. Or, perhaps what was so important to oneself, to them, so often had they seen it in previous years, was just a case of one more young fellow going away.

The artificial, seedy gaiety of the metropolis was no more attractive than the blasted-out, boarded-up austerity of suburban public houses. The theatres were tawdry and lacklustre shadows of their former selves; only the cinema was a window onto a sunlit world. True, some of its presentations were only too reminiscent of the strife which had darkened two large areas of the earth, but there were musicals and comedies, some in glorious colour, which spoke of happiness and peace somewhere.

As he emerged from his reverie he found himself gazing at the large well-scrubbed deck space and wondered how many naval boots had come up and down the companion-way and paced across those boards before them. A vague chilling thought almost too elusive of admission wondered what had become of them. He smothered it quickly, but what had been a mark of relative luxury had suddenly taken on a sinister quality as though it were electrified or might suddenly collapse.

Concluding his escapist studies, Fred yawned, scratched philosophically and regarded the growing epistle George was scribbling. 'Who's going to wade through that lot?' he enquired.

'The most beautiful and darling creature I know,' replied George in a tone balanced on a knife edge between hopeless sentiment and mockery. He leaned back against the bulkhead and rubbed his spreadeagled hands vigorously on his thighs as though trying to increase the shine which was developing in the blue serge of his trousers. He wore, curiously, as he was unmarried, a gold signet ring on the third finger of his left hand. A smile pushed itself slowly on his ruddy countenance and waited for the inevitable retort.

'That's what they all say,' observed Fred, his grin hinting perhaps that it was impelled by theoretical rather than practical knowledge of the subject.

'Never mind,' persisted George, 'she's a cracking little piece.'

'And where...' interjected Johnny, pausing in his housework, 'did you meet this model of perfection?'

'Don't tell us,' chimed in Fred.

'At the Corn Exchange,' they all affirmed.

Johnny, having padlocked his kitbag, sat down with the group at the table and managed in his lugubrious but apparently authoritative way to keep up the talk on the reliability of girls whilst their young men were away on national service. He was of the opinion, it became evident, that not many were to be trusted implicitly and that absence did not necessarily make the heart grow fonder, let alone more faithful. He pursued this argument with examples from his neighbourhood where no sooner had a young lady kissed her soldier boy goodbye on his way overseas than she took up with those idols of man-starved womanhood, the American allies, who were starting to arrive in comforting numbers.

From this mean and unchivalrous opinion George, in his rural simplicity, differed vehemently. Just because, he, that is, Johnny, came from the capital where the girls were generally known to be amenable, he should not think that all their countrywomen were the same.

To the other two, largely passive members of this debate, it seemed, although they would hardly have been likely to express it in such terms, a confrontation between the romantic and realistic views of the world. Fred, with such a variety of grins passing over his countenance, need hardly have said a word anyway, his conflicting thoughts on the subject swaying back and forth from one viewpoint to the other. The meagre quality of his experience on this matter hardly tended to confirm him one way or the other. Anyhow, it was a change from football and so did their present idleness pass that they were surprised to hear the pipe of 'Hands to tea' on the loudspeaker system.

When they sat down in the dining mess with their tea, bread and jam, they were next to the young coder. So youthful was he that there was still only a light down on his chin. A close mop of gold, curly hair contributed to his immature appearance, but it was his manner which was the most innocent. There was a perpetual air of wonderment about him as though everything were utterly new. His fellows were men of mature years, some quite staid in their domesticated ways, pipe-smoking and reserved, and therefore, perhaps, he felt even more solitary than he would have done anyway.

'Are you, by any chance going to the *Watchful*?' he asked them in a voice which, in its gentility, verged on the contralto.

'Yes, sonnie,' answered George for his companions, in a quite avuncular fashion, although the difference in their ages might be measured more in months than years. 'Are you?'

The coder nodded diffidently. 'Do you know what it's like?'

'No idea except that it's a new destroyer. What about your mates?'

It appeared they were destined for the cruiser *Northumberland* and considered her something of a soft berth, but their friend had been changed in his draft, as Johnny had, and was not too uplifted by the novel prospect. Furthermore, he did not care for the way the authorities raised and dashed hopes so impersonally.

'It's the Andrew,' explained George, the ancient mariner coming out in him.

'Andrew?' queried the coder, with a more puzzled expression than ever.

'The Andrew,' went on the elegant rustic, 'is what the Navy calls itself. How long have you been in if you didn't know that?'

'Twelve weeks,' whispered the golden youth as though admitting a great shame.

It was the turn of the telegraphists to be surprised. After a training period of nine months and more for themselves, that people should be ready for active service in under three months was extraordinary. Perhaps the nearness of civil life explained the circumspection and sedateness which was part of the aura surrounding practitioners of this section of the communications branch. And so it was with different eyes they looked upon these ratings with one foot still almost in that other world now becoming remote, who were with such abruptness thrust into the fleet machine.

The time between tea and supper was comfortably spent browsing in a small recreation space discovered by them, on the way back to the mess deck, furnished with magazines, newspapers, books of all varieties, wall charts and maps. Such was the nature of their situation that although the reading material was mostly dated, even the current numbers had begun to have an irrelevancy about them. It was true that some film reviews or articles on the more exotic aspects of the war held some interest, but most seemed to lack any sort of substance. Certain glossy publications of quality continued to show the social activities in city and shire of the higher social levels of the nation, albeit modified to war causes or charities, and they continued to be married, baptized in or buried from the best churches. Alongside this elegant reading material were more vulgar publications: papers which feverishly concentrated on the more bizarre aspects of human nature, or near hysteria, propounded the things for which or against which 'we are fighting...'

In spite of the variety of reading stuff, David might well have dozed at the table, in spite of the excruciatingly uncomfortable folding wooden chair, but for the arrival of their prospective shipmate, the refined coder.

He sat down near Fred and it was only a little while before the affability of the latter naturally flowed in a conversation about music. The coder obviously had an unusual knowledge of the finer points of music and it seemed Fred was not so lopsided in his tastes, for he soon adapted himself to the novel field of discussion and names of great composers flowed from his lips as they exchanged comments on the works of the masters. It was surprising to find that Fred had been a patron of those classical performances under the great Victorian dome in the capital which had become such a popular entertainment for so many young people. That they were both collectors of gramophone records was not, after their immersed discussion, surprising, but Fred's chameleon-like ability of adapting his conversation to all kinds and levels of person continued to be remarkable.

After supper which, for the convenience of watchkeepers, was a meal early in the evening, David returned to the recreation space and after a spell there, went prowling the depot ship in her remoter corners, in some parts of which he probably had no right to be. The general quietness, however, encouraged him to stroll back to the mess deck and on the way he noticed that many draftees had already slung their hammocks and were in process of turning in. It was the same on his own deck. On the other side most of the hammocks were up and some ratings were in them, reading or talking quietly. George was just unlashing his slung hammock, Johnny was in his and Fred was busy slinging his own. Selecting a place some distance from the others, there being spatial luxury unknown in hut, barrack block or tunnel, he went back to get his hammock from the baggage and dragged it over to his chosen place.

It lay below him, passive in its mischievousness. He bent down and unloosened the lanyards at both ends; then, lifting it up, tied both ends to their respective hooks. Gingerly he put his weight on it to see if it held. It did. He then leaned over it and took his feet off the ground and slowly and gracefully it lost height and it was only with the greatest agility that he recovered his balance before his knees were on the deck.

'Damn the bloody thing!' he muttered in vexation, kicking it so its supposed banana shape looked even more irregular.

He tried again. This time it apparently held under both tests so he thrust his weight on it, and it promptly plummeted at one end to the deck with a thud, shooting him painfully on to the hard boards.

'You sooner,' he moaned, disentangling himself from it, stiffly getting up and rubbing his knees, 'you bleeder,' his chafed hands symptomatic of his mentality.

Deciding on a pause in hostilities, he pulled his jumper over his head, rolled up the sleeves of his jersey and was about to recommence the struggle when George, a few steps away, leaned over his own hammock, neatly arranged for sleep, to watch proceedings as a sort of entertainment. He was not the only one amused by the contest. Nevertheless, in the lulls in the fight David had observed that the others, too, were not exactly expert in the speed and dexterity with which they had secured their own. Yet none had suffered his indignity as a victim of their sleeping gear. David looked at the absurd shape suspended at one end and steeply curving to the deck boards in a manner that needed no comment on its suggestiveness.

He was just getting the lower end when George stepped over and in his best air of sophisticated practicality said it was easy. Look! Up, over the hook, back and through the metal ring, round over the top of both lines, under and through, a quick pull and presto, it was done,

'Haven't you done it before?' he asked somewhat arrogantly, or so it seemed to the victim of the hammock.

'No,' replied David. 'Never, except to learn how to use it in seaman training.'

'Not even in the Tunnel?' enquired his benefactor.

'No, I always got down early and claimed a bunk and spread it out on that.'

Under instruction he retied the good end, although he thought he had done the same thing before. It was put through the three stages of effectiveness. It worked. He positively grovelled with respect for his companion, who rather smugly returned to his stolid but pernickety toilet before he retired.

David unlashed his hammock and was preparing to go to the washroom himself when George, ready to turn in, grasped an overhead bar and pulled himself off the deck and plumped into his hammock. The neatness with which it was done drew forth a gasp of admiration from others who had in their various ways, climbed, wrestled and fallen into their own. The general acclaim had polished the smug expression on the countryman's round features but of a sudden it changed to one of surprise, mingled with disbelief, for there was a very obvious jerk as the lanyard at the foot end gave way an inch or two. It was decidedly unsafe and its occupant reached up to haul himself out, when, aggravated, it went again and let him down a further few inches and so continued in fits and starts until he was sliding on the mattress too far to clutch the bar, and then quickly and smoothly he slid down as though on a chute and was deposited a tangled angry mass on the deck.

'Effme,' snapped he, as David vainly tried to muffle a laugh in the depths of his bedding.

'Couldn't have been too secure could it, old man?' said Johnny from the comfort of his hammock, observing the mishap over the paperback novel he was reading.

Fred looked on George's misfortune at first with an amused grin which, as it probably dawned on him that he too might be dropped similarly on the deck, changed to a nervous grimace of foreboding. He hung on and tugged at his hammock to ensure it was not likely to give way, and carelessly remarked, 'I wonder what you did wrong, George?'

'What did I do wrong? What did I do wrong?' he repeated almost melodiously. 'I joined the effing navy, that's what I did wrong! I joined the effing navy where I have to sleep in an effing hammock six effing inches too short for me and where I have to listen to silly bloody remarks from a lot of half-witted city prats who can't tie a knot properly to save their effing lives. That's what,' he concluded, 'I did wrong.'

Before the slow-burning Anglo-Saxon fuse reached the powder barrel David, with his ungrateful mirth, retreated to the washroom, leaving George, countenance pinker than ever, bent down sorting out the wreckage of his sleeping gear.

When he returned, fortunately all was once more quiet and George, at rest in his reslung hammock, was reading a well-thumbed letter which had apparently soothed all irritation away.

4

They were blasted out of their slumber by the loudspeaker system relaying a recorded bugle call of reveille. The first notes, so distant and coaxing in camp and barracks, on the mess deck were too strident and near, the urgency of the last notes merely an additional vexation. Half turned on his side and wrapped in the depths of his blanket, David became aware of his feet uncomfortably wedged in the clews, and the stirring of others. He emerged from his woollen cocoon, peeped over the side of the hammock to the deck far below, and was at first depressed by the sight of those familiar, clean boards; then amazed he had come through the night without crashing on them. Owing to the space and ventilation he did not feel at all that dry-mouthed muzziness which had been usual after a night spent in the deplorable Tunnel and as the ratings moved back and forth between washroom and mess deck there seemed no early morning grumpiness, although they were, for the most part quiet.

Having managed to get to the deck without mishap, he removed his uniform which, wrapped up with his valuables, had done service as a pillow, lashed his hammock, as it seemed, to his agreeable surprise, efficiently, unloosed the lanyards at each end from their hooks and tied them into the lashing. Washed and shaved, the latter hardly still necessary each day and really required not more than twice weekly, he commenced the rather uncomfortable and to the uninitiated, mysterious process of putting on his uniform. Even as he did so he glanced over with envy to the radio mechanics who were getting into a civilized rig of white shirt, black tie, ordinary navy blue trousers and jacket. It was true that this outfit was called a taxi driver's one by the square rig or sailor-type ratings, but perhaps there was an underlying jealousy for the ratings such as writers, sickberth attendants, stewards and others who were authorized to wear this rig, for it gave an impression of maturity in contrast to the irresponsible retarded adolescence of Jack Tar.

So he pulled on his blue jersey, then bell-bottomed slacks with a system of front buttons generously portrayed in old time prints of Portsmouth Point and other seaports and their lewd denizens of waterfront low life. Socks and boots followed; why not barefoot still? Then the blue collar, complex, with tapes to be threaded through loops and tied in front of the high waist of the trousers; then pulled the jumper on over the head in a struggle that did no good to the early morning glands. The best, or number one suits of some ratings, particularly the princes of dance halls and public houses were immensely wide at the bell-bottoms and asphyxiatingly tight at armpit and waist. Resplendent in gold badges, arms bent in ape-like curves, enormous flapping areas of cloth below, in buckled shoes, they would waddle across dance floors exceedingly self-assured of the irresistible sexuality of their appearance. Now, however, was the time for the regulation issue with sober red badges, but still an outfit hardly suited to the times. Then finally a silk band to put under the collar and secure with a tape at the bottom of the open front of the jumper; black silk, it was said, in memory of Lord Nelson. How appropriate; but once of use as a head band to keep perspiration from running into the eyes of seamen in the height of action. Taking his paybook, wallet and handkerchief from his cap and putting them into the inner pockets of his jumper he went back to the washroom to comb his hair.

In the outer darkness the air was sharp in their nostrils as they drifted along to breakfast, and on entering the humidity of the dining mess they saw that nearly all the junior ratings of the draft were there and considered that soon the motor boats would, in the course of the morning, start to collect draftees for units in every corner of the anchorage. The conversation, a low murmur that was easily dominated by the clatter of cutlery and dishes, came through the blue smoke beginning to blur the figures spread around the tables, some in their overcoats, surprisingly, as though expecting an imminent call. David had no real appetite for the scrambled egg, made from powder, piled soggily on a slice of fried bread, beside the narrowest slice of streaky bacon, fried to a brown curl, he had ever seen. He had a slight feeling of nausea from nervous anticipation rather than any physical cause and as he champed heartily on the unappetizing fare he glanced at his prospective shipmates and was a little relieved but ashamed to think that he was not, like Johnny, going to a ship by himself. Indeed, as he looked across the table at those sallow features with their early morning moroseness he began to feel a real pity for his erstwhile companion.

It was Johnny who broke their silence. 'Make the most of it lads,' he uttered mournfully, adding unnecessarily, 'You might not feel like it tomorrow.'

The childlike coder had, whilst they had been silent, sidled up to the cheerless four and sat beside them. He looked startled by the remark and could not forbear to blurt out enquiringly, 'We won't go to sea straight away will we?'

A lacklustre Anglo-Saxon eye drooped down in his direction and the heavy frame of George stirred perceptibly as he replied. 'And why not, son?' Drawing on his reserves of knowledge garnered second hand from the men of the seaman-training establishment near his home-town, he added, 'The ships we are going to have been commissioned for some time.'

'Could they go without us?' the coder asked, almost hopefully.

'Maybe,' answered the rustic oracle, 'but unlikely. They are almost definitely going to wait for the pleasure of your charming company.'

''Itinit,' said the one-time booking clerk before he went back into his shell.

The idle hours of the morning were at first enlivened by the calls on the loudspeaker system, summoning men to the motor boats that were coming alongside at first light, and quite early the coder saw his friends off to their majestic three-funnelled billet. With the departure of the signalmen and radio mechanics the mess deck was curiously forlorn. The spectacle of the boats calling and embarking the draftees soon lost interest for them and the fresh

37

sunlit anchorage, though lively with seabirds and an occasional passing vessel became so familiar under their keen and impatient gaze that when 'Stand easy' was piped they were glad of a hot drink as a diversion. They returned yet again to the mess deck to see their baggage had been moved and a seaman from the depot ship crew was busy with scrubbing brush and cloth, kneeling down, absorbed in what was obviously a task of pride for him, improving the lustrous quality of the deck boards. As they clumped down the companion-way he turned to wring out his cloth in the bucket.

He was somewhere in his late twenties, but verging on plumpness for his age, with thinning light brown hair very short at the neck and around his ears. His features, although smoothed by a layer of fat and closely shaved, carried lines which hinted at an underlying weariness contrasting with his present apparently rested well-being. His bulky frame was clad in overalls washed to a light blueness and neatly patched in several places. On his right arm was his gunner's rating. To the blue canvas buckled belt securing his overalls at the waist and from which hung a clasp knife on a lanyard, he was every particle a long service man of pre-war vintage.

He raised himself onto one foot and said, 'Had to shift your gear, lads. Got to get this lot done by tot time.'

'That's all right, mate,' answered George for the others, 'We won't be here much longer anyway. We're getting bored hanging about, you must find it dull on this thing.'

The others, embarrassed by the country boy's familiarity with a man who seemed so senior to them, were rather alarmed as he pulled himself to his feet and hung the cloth over the rim of the bucket.

'Dull nothing.' He was quiet in his rejection of George's presumptuous remark. 'I've got two here,' indicating where his long service stripes would be on his left arm. 'It's not long to the third. Then that's my lot. When the war's over, goodbye Andrew. I've got some good ideas and I want to be around to try them out. I may not have risen to the dizzy heights of cross hooks but I'm still in circulation which ain't the case with some blokes I've known. This old packet may be sitting on tins but its steady and quiet, it's all night in and not too much work. Time to think and that, sonnie, is a luxury.'

Even the slow imagination of George apprehended that here was a man who knew what he was about, when he was well off and actually made plans for the future.

The half circle of youths lounging around the ladderway gazed passively at the two-badge seaman who, now he was upright, could be seen, somewhat surprisingly, to be of only medium height. The aura of experience affected them all. He was disconcerted to have been the cause of such an impressive effect and asked them where they were going. Yet, in spite of himself, as though mesmerized by his own line of argument, he said, 'Dirty work. You're going to get all the dirty work.' David's heart missed a beat and seemed turned to stone. 'If there's any crap you'll find it. You won't swing round the buoy for long, lads! I was,' he nodded at Johnny, 'in your old bucket in the Med. Off Malta a small one dropped right on X gun so you can say it's been somewhat remodelled in its time. As for yours,' looking at George, 'I wouldn't care to exchange my berth on this old girl for your brand new metalworks. It's a long way to Jago's from here, but I get there often enough. My missus says she's sick of the sight of me after my other drafts and that's a bit of a laugh actually.'

He had spoken quietly and slowly but somehow did not know how to stop and get on with his scrubbing and Fred broke in at a hint of a pause with, 'How long have you been up here then?'

'Since February. After survivor's leave I came up here, and I hope to be forgotten now.'

'Bert!' A voice from above broke in on their conversation and, looking up, they saw a petty officer peering down at them. 'Bert, this just came over on the Lynewall boat,' and he flicked down a telegram envelope. 'Don't know what's special about you.'

The gunner managed to catch it and thumbed it open. Slowly a grin came on his face and the petty officer went on, 'What is it?'

'It's a girl,' Bert called up.

'Goodo, wack,' exclaimed the petty officer. 'Didn't know you had it in you. When you've finished down there the chief crusher wants to see you at the regulating office.'

'Thanks, Stan,' said Bert with an easy familiarity which hinted at many years' acquaintance. 'Reckon it's a few days down south.'

The spell broken, the draftees went and sat at their table, although they could have picked any of the others, and the happy father briskly completed his work. They watched him scrub and dry the remaining area and as he collected up his bucket, brush, soap and cloth and went into the washplace he burst into song:

You are my sunshine, my only sunshine...

The dirty water splashed into a basin, the bucket clattered on the deck.

You make me happy, when skies are grey...

There was the sound of running water as he rinsed the sink and utensils.

You'll never know, dear, how much I owe dear...

Then a thump as they dropped into the bucket. He emerged, bucket clanking, absorbed in his own pleasant expectations and as he ran up the companion-way continued:

Please don't take my sunshine away...

A figure of optimistic vitality, actually planning a future, oblivious of those he had left below with the haunting echoes of his own past.

The area was desolate in its emptiness.

Fred, as though moved by a desire to recall past pleasures, from his jumper pulled out yet another film magazine, unfolded it and, chin cupped in hand, retreated into his own world, observed by George who gently massaged, with spreadeagled fingers, his thighs. His gaze had something akin to envious wonderment in it as his large pink hands stopped rubbing and lethargically began the process of getting out the silver case to light a cigarette; but, unsure of his culpability if discovered smoking during working hours, although obviously in need of some diversion, he tucked case and lighter in his jumper pockets.

The coder got up and, going over to the baggage pile, got a little book from his attaché case. As he returned to the table Johnny, curiosity affording entertainment, asked the youth its title. He merely smiled and showed the front: *English Verse*.

'Blimey!' was Johnny's reaction, his hard black stare sparking with astonishment.

George, seizing on the chance of passing the slow hours as well as of reconstructing his self-esteem, cracked by the events of the previous night, put in banteringly, 'And what do you want to be when you grow up?'

The coder sat down again, opened the book at a turned down page, then pressed it open on the table with his knuckles. It was remarkable how odd those hairless, white, dainty hands looked at the end of the rough blue sleeve. He ignored the question for a moment, regarding the text then replied without taking his eyes off the page, diffidently, as though aware he was making matters worse, 'I'm going to write.'

'Write what? Poems?'

'I don't know yet. Maybe. Maybe prose.'

'Prose?' The word was not one George had remembered or noticed from his schooldays in Arcadia.

'Ordinary writing, dimwit,' uttered Johnny sepulchrally, 'not poems.'

'I reckon I could do this song-writing lark,' pronounced the country boy, forgetting his original intention of a little quiet sport at the coder's expense. It was all too unusual for him and not on his ground.

'You should bloody well be able to, the writing you do to your party. I don't know what you find to say,' remarked the gloomy one.

'Never you mind,' cooed George, a smirk hinting that his assumed prowess with the girls, superior to that of his companions, once again to the fore, rehabilitated that well-rounded surface of his amour-propre, which had been dented, if not holed, by the unfortunate rash assumptions on his part.

'I wish I could write a proper letter,' Johnny admitted, 'I just don't seem to be able to find the words.'

'Do you do much reading?' asked the coder.

Johnny shook his head and it occurred to David that in all the long waiting hours from the depot till now, save when in his hammock the previous night, Johnny was a spare reader. He sat, smoked, slept and ruminated but hardly read, whereas Fred would snatch the most unlikely moments to read.

This thought soon fled before a low moan which came from

George who was reclining against the inner hull of the compartment, his hands eventually having come to rest tucked half in the high waist of his trousers. This restful arrangement had been attained by pulling up his jumper in folds round his midriff. At first the others thought he was not well but as he rocked his head back and forth in a motion which was not quite a nod but more of a twist of the neck, tortoise-like, words oozed softly forth in what might be taken by the generous-hearted as crooning, indicating that his mind still echoed the carolling of the seaman:

Last night, dear, as I lay dreaming... A twisting jerk of the head. *I dreamt that you were by my side...*

'Oh, Gawd,' groaned Johnny, failing to hush the sound.

Then I awoke, dear, was disillusioned... A grin of pain minced its way across Fred's countenance as his eyes were caught by the dull blue glance of his tormentor.

You were gone and then I cried.

The coder was unable to read the lines before him in the face of this mighty competition and he waited patiently for the dim visions in George's mind's eye revolving hot masses of couples under the glittering light of the Corn Exchange, to lose their strangulatory effect upon his larynx.

He had certainly attracted their attention. Going the rounds of their stunned faces, he roused himself slowly and folding his heavy arms on the table explained, 'One of my favourite foxtrots.'

'Spare us the pleasure,' Fred pleaded as he pushed up his left cuff and nervously scratched an itchy place on his thin pimpled forearm. 'You aren't exactly Bing.'

Which only exacerbated that obstinacy which impelled George, against the interests of his companions, to continue the refrain which had been rendered with such panache by the happy gunner. But his smugness was abruptly despatched by the click of the loudspeaker and the pipe of 'Up spirits'.

The recollection of this ancient naval ritual of the issue of tots of rum to ratings in the morning just before dinner had the effect of depressing George's ebullience. For he sank back in apathy, and even a charitable observer might have thought he perhaps contemplated that at nineteen years of age he was still, as it was marked, callously to be observed by all and sundry in his paybook,

'Under Age'. His wealth of experience with the girls, on the dance floor and in and out the offices and factories of his home town, the impressive knowledge of life and human nature accumulated from the superior vantage point of a post office motorcycle, in county and borough, so effective in his handling of these wall-bounded townees, was, in substance, for the naval authorities, nought; for these absurdly callow youths would, in due course, not a month or two later than he, draw their tot.

The forenoon spent waiting had made David fidgety with boredom and he disengaged himself from between the bench on which he was sitting and the table and rose to look out of the side scuttle, opened to help dry the deck and thoroughly ventilate it. He leant against a rib girder of the ship's side and, looking out on the anchorage, saw the water surface ruffled into silver patterns by the gusting wind and felt the cool draught on his warm face. He realized it was heated by an apprehensive heart beating heavily in spite of his inactivity.

Behind him George was now humming and Johnny and Fred were discussing a musical film going the rounds whilst they were on draft leave, which dealt with a carefree snow resort in the United States. It had appealed to Johnny but Fred pointed out its meretricious artificiality beneath the acknowledged slickness of presentation. As it featured the renowned exponent of the groan who was as near to a patron saint and hero figure as the provincial was likely to recognize, he was soon involved in the recollection of the film and helped to lower the tone of debate to a spinsterish bickering. However, this did afford them some respite from his musical attempts. David ruminated on the sunshine in his life, the girls he had taken out when on leave and appreciated that it was all very superficial and none had left an abiding impression with him. There had been a gulf there too. Somehow across his life and thinking there lay a barrier, formless, lacking detail, but substantially cutting him off from all contemplation of the future and real communication with people he would have liked to reach; but then, as though the sparkling water had exploded in his mind, he realized what it was.

He had come through the pleasant groves of carefree training days and stood on the edge of the Reaper's field. Time had run out.

Fortunately the click of the loudspeaker and the pipe of 'Hands to dinner' broke in on his doleful thoughts and the scrape of bench and clump of footsteps brought him back to the lads as they went off in a rush to break the monotony. He followed them up the ladderway, feeling he lacked their seemingly thoughtless appetites. But as they walked to the dining mess the coder dropped back to enquire, 'What's your name by the way?'

'David Freston. What's yours?'

'Edward, Edward Meecham... Well Freston,' the coder went on, 'I feel this is one meal I really do not need.'

5

As though anxious to bring to a speedier conclusion the state of limbo in which they had been for the previous forty-eight hours, shortly after dinner the few remaining draftees began to assemble their baggage on the flat by which they had entered the depot ship and from which the earlier replacements had gone. After finally collecting his attaché case and gas mask David looked back from a few steps up the companion-way ladder and those empty white deck boards renewed the uneasiness he had felt the previous night; but now it was mixed with a familiar nostalgia to which he had grown accustomed when moving from any of the billets he had occupied in his months of training. No matter how uncomfortable or brief his stay, when everything was packed and the move imminent the most gaunt metal bunks and austere furniture had a beckoning homeliness equal to the cosiest of lodgings. A deep atavistic longing for the known pervaded his mood.

Alone, he went up onto the promenade deck and strolled its length again on both sides, seeing the distant movements of the anchorage but not really absorbing it. The swift passage of cloud shadows across the agitated surface of the haven and the increasing number and size of the scudding clouds in the bright sunlit sky eased his spirit but did not suppress the apprehension in his thoughts. The gentle balm of sight endeavoured to soothe the abrasions of knowledge and the struggle was unresolved when he saw the low dark shape of the motor launch emerging from the generality of distant warships and move directly, getting larger every moment, towards the old liner.

Almost simultaneously the loudspeaker system clicked and

ordered 'Ratings for *Obstinate, Watchful, Foxglove* and *Masai* muster on the embarkation flat,' and he went below to join the others.

There were about twenty of them waiting by the baggage when the master-at-arms arrived to superintend the transfer himself. He ordered the double doors unclipped and opened and the launch was plainly in view coming alongside. The gangway was lowered onto its deck and as the chief petty officer called the ratings he ticked the names on a list fastened to a board. Encumbered with their belongings they made their way down onto the motor boat.

As David's name was called he tottered to the head of the gangway where the chief gave him a covert thumbs up sign and, strained with exertion, he grimaced and nodded as he stepped on the slightly unsteady gangway. At the bottom he dumped his kit and looked back up into the hulk as George staggered down in his turn. Down thumped his baggage on the top of David's and when he had brushed his greatcoat and recovered his composure he turned and said rather enviously, 'What's special about you with the chief crusher, chum?'

'Friend of the family,' was the laconic reply.

The last man came down into the boat and as the engine spluttered the high grey side of the depot ship slid by and they were off in a direct line to the destroyer anchorage. Soon the hulk was in the distance, beginning to lose its form in that of the low hills behind and in a light that was no longer strong they were passing down between the small ships. The tubby shape of the corvette was their first call and with some difficulty a group of artificers got their baggage over the bulwarks and themselves up the ladder onto deck. Hardly had the last leg been pulled out of the boat than they were on their way towards a two-funnelled destroyer smart in apparently new paint. This suggested a thorough refit and the large number of draftees going up into it a fairly recent recommissioning.

Absorbed in the passing scene the remaining five suddenly realized the boat was nearly empty and was now turning towards a low-silhouetted destroyer which appeared deserted at first; but on their approach two men strolled along the iron deck to the ladder that hung down the side. The height of the men was more than that from waterline to deck. Probably shocked by this observation, Johnny exploded with self-pity, 'I'm not supposed to go on that bloody thing, am I?' And indeed, closer inspection did not make his billet more attractive. The deck fittings and equipment, impeccably stowed and secured as they were, had that worn grey look of hard and frequent usage and in contrast with the *Masai* the paintwork generally was battered and dull and scored with rust tracks round side scuttles, stanchions, anchor hawse-pipe and hatches. The whole effect, in sum, was not likely to rouse Johnny from his dismay or encourage him to go up into the vessel with confidence.

The boat slowed down and he gathered his stuff together, then turned to his erstwhile companions. 'Good luck, mates,' he said, prompting an effusion of well-wishing from them, which hinted, perhaps unwittingly, that he was more in need of that commodity than they; and maybe the lively and energetic help he was given in getting his baggage on board and steadying his way aloft was some kind of guilty compensation on their part.

Looking back over the water as they swung away, he raised his hand in farewell, a lonely figure.

The remaining four turned from the diminishing *Obstinate* and looked in the direction the boat was headed and at first were puzzled as they ran out of the lines of small ships moored to buoys and towards a large square shape looming up in the softening light. Their quizzical glances to each other were answered in a shout from the seaman at the tiller.

'The *Watchful*'s in floating dock,' he nodded ahead, 'you're going to have a bit of a climb with your gear.'

Whilst the giant rectangular mass soared over them, this latter remark might have been considered the understatement of the year. Up reared the sheer sides, hung with green marine growth and propped and secured over their heads, all of sixty feet, was the hull of their ship. The two gleaming brass screws thrust towards them from a bottom still relatively free of accumulation and in which ribbing and rivets were plainly seen.

The launch gently bumped up to an apron protruding from the open end of the dock which was some three feet above the water surface. The whole was covered with a slimy bright greenness and a repellent smell compounded of rust, stale salt water, oil and drying seaweed did not augur well for the state their baggage and greatcoats would be in by the time they achieved the deck of the airborne destroyer.

They missed the bark of impotent anger which such a prospect would have drawn from Johnny and in silent dismay heaved bag and hammock onto the platform, where they landed with a disagreeable squelching thud. Only a short step over the side of the boat brought them onto the apron, where they discovered the footing was as treacherous as it was repulsive to the eye and nose. Hardly daring to turn they heard the launch revving its engine in reverse and when at last they managed to change their cautious stance, saw it impersonally turning away, having already forgotten its chores of the day.

The search for a means of ascent among posts, stanchions, cables and blocks was a difficult one, made more tiresome by the large drops of water falling from above. Then there was perceived, half-way along the hull above, a circular metal ladderway of perforated metal steps constructed round a centre post, and a handrail with posts enough to hold it in position and far fewer to prevent a fall to the loathsome bottom of the dock.

It proved to be a task done piecemeal, three careful and wearing journeys up and down, perspiring in spite of the growing cold of the long twilight, with bumps, halts for breath and muttered curses. In the end the narrow gangplank that connected the top platform to the destroyer was crossed and together, damp and uncomfortable, in a pile of smelly baggage, they found themselves on the iron deck beside the midships gun platform.

This effort had not gone unobserved and waiting for them, fair hair unruly in the wind, was a tall petty officer telegraphist, probably in his mid-twenties. His face was rather pallid, but clear-skinned, with few lines but those around the ends of mouth and eyes, which hinted at a good-humoured disposition, an impression not belied by the soft grey of his eyes. He was in regulation dark blue trousers and jacket, the latter carrying two good conduct stripes with the crossed anchors of his rank, but underneath wore a white roll-necked sweater which gave, oddly, an impression of refinement. It was their first, but not last example of the informality of dress aboard a little ship.

'Welcome aboard, lads,' he said, adding with a gesture to the dock, 'but aboard what exactly I'm not sure.'

They had come on board on the starboard side and, turning right, followed him, carrying only cases and gas masks as instructed, down the iron deck, forward past the funnel to the break of the fo'c's'le and in the door under a ladderway there. They crossed an empty area, diagonally, to the port side on the afterside of the deck space of which, very much in evidence by its smell, was the galley. It was in a housing forward of the funnel. On the forward side of the flat a ladder went aloft to the bridge superstructure. Beyond the ladder, going forward on the port side ran a passageway. The first doorway off this on the starboard side was that to the wireless office.

The office itself was not much more than fifteen feet in length, fore and aft, by nine feet athwartships. The opposite side from the door had a heavily constructed dark brown wooden bench at table level running the length of the room. On this were radio sets. The first on the right was a squat, blue metal box with a long narrow rectangular tuning dial and below this a round, red tuning control. The fourth and fifth were also of this model and to the right of each on the bench was a Morse transmitting key. However, the second was a tall grey intership speech transmitter and next to it a receiver, smaller, but similar in colour and appearance. It had a black telephone handpiece secured half-way down its side.

Coming down through the deckhead and against the wall to the left of the radio telephone and opposite the doorway, were three voicepipes. At this time their ends were closed with hinged brass caps.

Behind the door to the right was the man-high, black metal bulk of the transmitter, connected to the passageway bulkhead with cables which ran aloft, through and along the deckhead to a control panel near the voicepipes. Also overhead, running fore and aft, were lagged steam pipes, cables and air ducts and between them the metal plating of the deck above was seen to be covered with sprayed yellow limpet asbestos for insulation.

The deck was covered with a thick dark brown glossless

linoleum and in front of each set was a brown wooden swivel armchair with blue plastic upholstery, secured to the deck by a metal post.

It was comfortably warm, the air free from the more pungent shipboard odours, except for a faint hint of warm dusty metal and varnished wood. Save too for the pervasive beat of Morse coming from a pair of headphones on the bench before number one set, the space was comparatively quiet, in contrast with the clattering activity in apparently every corner of the ship. The whole was brilliant with electric light, there being no outer scuttles, and as they entered, the only occupant was a red-cheeked lad of about nineteen years who lolled in the chair by the busy headphones, idly tapping his pencil on the message pad as the transmitter sent out an extraordinarily long message for some other unit.

'Right lads,' said the petty officer briskly, 'first here are your station cards.' He handed them the little coloured cardboard booklets in which they would detail their name, rating, official number, mess, watch, religion, last unit and home address. The top item, their ship's book number, had already been entered. 'As to your watches,' he continued, 'I don't know quite how you're going to fit in; your presence is something of a mystery because we already have three huff-duffers. I've been told by the flotilla HF-DF officer to reserve set five for you and until further notice employ you on general duties.' As a hopeful afterthought he enquired, 'Have you any idea what it's all about?'

'Not a clue,' said George for the others.

Whilst the petty officer was dealing with Meecham, a leading telegraphist, dressed in overalls washed to the pale blue which seemed almost a point of lower deck etiquette, had appeared in the doorway. He was of medium height, about twenty-one or twenty-two years of age with a round, open face and fairly close light brown hair.

'Here I am, Pots,' he said.

'Oh, all right Robbie,' the petty officer replied, 'take the lads along to the mess. When they've got their gear in and had tea, I'll see them again.'

'Righto Pots,' said the leading hand.

The trio followed their guide forward along the passageway,

passing the heads and washroom to the left and a mysteriously illlit cabin to the right next beyond the wireless room. The passageway ended in an open deck space almost the width of the ship, except, on the left, for a small cabin which had a door and a large roll-shuttered window. This latter proved to be the canteen store where the day to day requirements of the crew such as toilet articles, stationary, confectionery, tobacco and other sundry useful articles might be purchased.

The space was limited by a bulkhead which divided this mess deck off from the next mess area forward, well under the fo'c's'le. Up against this dividing wall was an enclosure fenced by a metal mesh about four feet in height in which, stowed upright, were the hammocks of the two messes who shared the area. On the aftermost part of the deck a large round metal obstruction some eight feet in diameter ran from deck to deckhead. This was, they surmised, the support to B gun turret above. On its starboard side a ladderway came down from the deck above, which was the petty officer's mess.

Beyond this ladder the outer, starboard hull of the vessel was evident by the row of scuttles, all open, airing the compartment. Below these, along the whole length, ran seating, covered with black plastic-covered cushions under which were, as it was presently discovered, the lockers of the crew. There were two long mess tables also lengthwise to the ship, one of which was well up to the forward bulkhead near a watertight door which was closed, and the other, in line with it, further aft and behind the ladderway.

Beside the tables were long wooden forms; they, the tables and the brown deck covering were impeccably clean. The rest of the interior was painted a light grey except for various metal fixtures, which were in their natural colour, and the white lagged pipes and cables running overhead. Bright electric lights were in round, glass-domed fixtures protected by a metal grill, but a fair amount of daylight still came in at the ports.

Robbie went across to the forward mess and turned, saying, 'Well this is home, lads,' and, showing each their locker, suggested they get their heavy gear stowed right away whilst things were clear. Meantime Eddie Meecham had been brought along and for an hour or so they were busy stowing everything as compactly as possible in the limited space available. They still felt very formally attired compared with the variety of garb worn by the old-stagers of the crew, but by some unspoken agreement, probably due to the fact they might be called to see higher authority any time, they continued in jumper, collar and silk.

During this time the rattle of mess kettles and cups was heard throughout the fo'c's'le and the cook of the mess returned with a steaming can of black tea to which he added copious amounts of condensed milk and sugar. The loudspeakers announced, 'Darken ship' and some of the ratings who were beginning to filter back to their messes busied themselves closing the glass ports and securing the metal lids over them.

The bread, butter, jam and heavy fruit cake were out and already being demolished as most of the remaining members of the mess arrived shortly after the call, 'Hands to tea', was given. The signalmen, coders and telegraphists were curious about the arrival of more special telegraphists and it was apparent they had only the vaguest idea of what their colleagues aft did in their little cubicle; indeed, as the three HF-DF telegraphists messed there, with the practitioners of a variety of esoteric duties in the ship's office, sick bay and other places, it was better not to know too well and they were spoken of as though on another ship. Meecham was soon acquainted with his opposite numbers and learned that his predecessor, a fellow in his thirties, had been found unfit for sea through the development of a stomach ulcer.

The conversation, after the initial curiosity had been dispatched by the knowledge of the new arrivals' origins, turned to the novelty of having spent the day perched up on the floating dock and all the multitude of snags the dockyard workers and artificers had found to rectify.

The next mess, they observed, was occupied by radar operators and seamen who were concerned with the direction of firepower. This mess seemed rather more boisterous than the communications mess and indeed, when they gained the entree to the area forward of the bulkhead, the gunners and seamen who dwelt there, and the stokers on the deck below, were a rather more animated bunch in the scarce periods of recreation.

During tea the telegraphist who had been on watch when they entered the wireless office had been relieved by his successor on the first dog watch and on coming back to the mess told Fred that the petty officer wanted them back there at 1630 hours.

Their mentor and guardian was busy probing the interior of the main transmitter when they stepped once again over the bulkhead threshold into the wireless room. He firmly closed the inspection panel, screwed it tight and nodded up to the fifth set.

'Seen one of those before?' he asked.

No, they had not. All their training had been on a transatlantic model with frequency change coils which plugged into its base.

'Nothing much to it,' he went on. 'Come over and I'll show you. Simple little job really.' Indeed it was, and they had no trouble in handling the refinements of tuning at once. It received on both high and medium frequencies and the selectivity between them was quite wide.

'Until such time as we hear from the huff-duff officer, you'll be day men on general duties, and at action stations I'm putting you on the damage control station aft in the sick bay flat and double banking the huff-duffers if things drag out.' He mused for a few seconds, then went on, 'The way things are shaping I reckon we'll be going to sea any time now so get out your lifebelts and keep them on night and day. It's standing orders and you're in the rattle if you're caught without them on.'

'Even in the heads, Pots?' Fred ventured flippantly.

'Even in the heads, lad,' affirmed their superior with a tolerant glance that suggested young Windenham had a lot to learn, 'and now, chaps, I want you to go straight aft and stand by the phone point and listen to me buzz you. I'll send DCl and to call me you send MWO all right?'

'Well sort of, but where's the phone?' asked George rather cautiously.

'Can't miss it, just inside the starboard entry under X gun on the for'ard bulkhead. You'll hear it all right, so off you go.'

The galley flat was now dimly lit by blue lights and the tarpaulins were back over the doorway which led to the iron deck on the port side. This area had reeked of fuel oil as they entered it when first coming on board, as well as of the more homely aroma of cooking from the galley. As they stepped out into the open they were surprised to see that during the time they had been occupied below the ship had left the floating dock and was now at rest on the glassy surface of the light vessel anchorage. There was still sufficient light in the late dusk to see the rest of the ship before them and the dim shape of the nearest neighbour in the line.

Going aft, they first passed on the left the boxlike housing of the galley and on the right, under its davits or derricks, and fitting snugly in crutches, the motor boat. Beyond this was the funnel, radiating warmth as they passed, and on the right was the cutter, in shape rather like a ship's lifeboat and secured in the same fashion as the launch. Abaft the funnel a superstructure carried the powerful searchlight, forty-four inches in diameter, and beyond this the deck was open, save for the low silhouette of the four twenty-one inch torpedo tubes. The set of tubes was topped with a flat pillbox housing for the torpedomen. Then the midships superstructure carried twin Bofors guns capable of firing two-pound, forty-millimetre calibre explosive shells at the rate of two a second. This armament was flanked by port and starboard gun positions of twin Oerlikons which fired small explosive projectiles of twenty-millimetre calibre with machine-gun like rapidity. On this platform rose the mainmast, crossed with a yard that carried the aerials which came from the foremast. The foremast, in its lower part, was a slim tripod, the legs of which were connected by a metal latticework of struts. The upper part carried a variety of aerials, radar and radio and the wireless yard. Where upper and lower mast joined another yardarm was located to which the signal halyards from the flag deck were attached. The whole rose up behind the bridge structure and above the galley.

Beyond the midships gun platform was another set of torpedo tubes, then the after deck housing. On top of this was another, smaller tripod mast crowned with a curious diamond-shaped aerial rather like a bird cage and X gun turret, mounting as did A and B main armament forward, a four-point seven-inch gun. Aft of the housing, at iron deck level, was Y gun turret. At the stern there were mortars on both sides to hurl the cylindrical depth charges well clear of the ship and the crates and rails right on the stern from which they might be rolled. A lifeline, they noticed, had been strung the length of the iron deck from the break of the fo'c's'le to the entry into the after superstructure, and from it hung ropes with looped hand grips.

Pushing aside the tarpaulin curtain, they entered the area known as the sick bay flat, the most prominent and central feature of which was the support to X gun turret above. It was not a large area, being in width about eighteen feet by about thirty fore and aft. The forward part of the flat was lit with the same kind of blue light as in the galley flat, but across on the starboard side, just aft of the support, the bright light of the sick bay cast a warm glow on the deck and they could see the two-tiered iron cots made up with the embroidered light blue coverlet of the sort that was common to all sick bays throughout the service. The faint hospital smell of ether and disinfectant left one in no doubt as to the purpose of the compartment.

The trio had only just taken in their surroundings when a buzzer emitted, 'Dah dit dit, dah di dah dit, di dah dah dah dah' and they moved across to the other side and saw the black telephone handpiece in a grey boxlike fitting, secured about four feet up on the forward side of the deckhouse.

Their move across to the instrument was more determined than their desire to use it and three hands wavered, groped and then retreated as they endeavoured to cajole each other into picking it up.

'You do it Fred,' suggested George, circumspection beginning to raise its cowardly head in his disposition.

'No, you, George,' replied Fred with a grin that hinted at his inferiority in technical experience.

'Hurry up George,' urged David, standing well back.

'What about you, then?' snarled the countryman desperately.

The thing repeated its deplorably insistent signal.

'Oh, Gawd,' breathed Fred, through his wide-spaced teeth. The bony hand clutched at the handpiece and then let it go as though it were red hot.

'Go on, you silly nit,' growled George and used his own great, blunt-fingered paw to push Fred's hand down again. The latter clutched it, went stiff and pulled it as though it were a loaded revolver to his ear.

'Hullo.' His thin voice rose on a wave of terror. 'Hullo' he reiterated all aquiver

The voice of Pots at the other end was not only easily identifiable to their apparent spokesman but to the other two as well. It was not amiable.

'Who've we got here then, Aggie Weston's?' And although that famous hostelry was not unknown to him, it was evident that Fred's numbed brain was losing its grip.

'To what or whom am I speaking?'

A brooding pause. 'Say what you are, you silly little bugger.'

'What are we?' Fred enquired in an agonized stage whisper, surely audible in the main wireless office.

'Aft damage control,' offered David.

'Damage control point one,' contradicted George, well back in his usual cantankerous mood.

Fred not only tried one, he announced both just to be on the safe side.

'All right. Now listen,' ordered Pots, speaking slowly, perhaps deciding he had cretins to employ. 'When I put down my handpiece, you buzz MWO. Em, double yew, oh, do you understand?'

'Yes, Pots,' mumbled Fred.

'Right then, replace the handpiece and transmit.'

Fred required no urging to do this and with a gasp of relief flung it back so vigorously it might have been shattered on its hooks.

The bickering recommenced.

'My hand's shaking too much,' whimpered Fred.

'I'm not used to such a funny little key,' George slyly excused himself.

'You do it,' they flung at David allied in their extreme reluctance.

He tentatively reached out to the little black knob on the front of the equipment and timidly tapped out, 'Click-click; cl-click-click; click-click-click.'

Back came the response and he picked up the handpiece, 'Aft damage control.'

'Main wireless office. Who's that?'

'Freston.'

'Right lad, now tell the other two that is the way I want it done always, got that?'

'Aye-aye, Pots.'

'Now look behind you. Can you see a circular hatchway beside the gun support?'

'Yes.'

'Well, go down there and at the bottom is the HF-DF cabin. Have a talk with the huff-duffers and tell them I want to see them up for'ard at 1800, OK?'

'OK.'

'Secure then.'

Fred was thoughtless in his relief. 'As an important official of the post office you weren't too anxious to use the phone, were you, old man?' he ventured carelessly.

'And as a pillar of the newspaper business you weren't very competent on the phone yourself were you, son?' was the growled riposte.

Fred smirked triumphantly. The complacent air of superiority usually habitual in George had been evaporated by the realization that he had no part in the episode.

'After all,' went on his tormentor, rather uncharitably, as he followed David over to the hatchway and peered down into the depths, 'it's only a bloody telephone.'

At the bottom of the vertical ladder was a brown linoleumed deck space of only a few square yards. The ladder was close against the after bulkhead on the port side. Opposite, forward, there were two open doors which revealed the two-tiered bunks in the cabins for the engineer officers. To the left of the ladder on the port side was another door, closed at the time but which was later to be established as being the entry into the washroom and heads of the same officers, whose duty, of course, was mainly centred aft. The whole area was yellow bright with electricity, insulated from the general hubbub of the ship and its variety of pungent odours, but it was a claustrophobic place, a sensation not alleviated in them by an upward glance at that one small exit at the top of the ladder.

One of the two huff-duffers came out to meet them from a doorway, the brown wooden door of which was slid open, next to the ladder on the starboard side. He welcomed them genially and they gathered round the entrance to a cubicle, a miniature of the main wireless office in general colour and furnishing but no more than a large cupboard space able to take a fitted bench and a swivel armchair. On the bench was secured a large grey direction finding set and built into the bench, at an angle, was a metal cylinder some ten inches in diameter and about two feet long which pointed up towards the side of the receiver and connected to it by a complex of wires, all of which gathered up behind the cylinder. These wires went up to and out of the deckhead above and, as the ratings knew, continued up to connect with the diamond-shaped aerial atop the mast on the after superstructure.

The front face of the cylinder had two calibrated degree markings around it. The outer was through 360 degrees and turned with the gyro compass of the ship, giving bearings relative to the world's surface. The inner, stationary calibrations, divided into green for starboard on the left and red for port on the right (the operator faced aft) had up to 180 degrees on both sides and gave the bearing relative to the vessel. In the centre was a black tuning knob, two inches in diameter, with a pointer bisecting it to touch the calibrations on each side. This whole device was a radio goniometer and turned coils within the drum, which were an internal arrangement obviating the turning of the whole aerial system, which had been the method in earlier models of direction finders.

The practice was to listen to a radio transmission which came down the aerials, turn the control until a fading of the signal was noted; then, if the signal remained dipped when a switch was thrown it was the true bearing. A signal of renewed strength meant it was the reciprocal or opposite direction.

It was equipment with which they had been familiar in training days and it was an easy matter to practise on the longwinded messages transmitted by enemy shore stations. However, the U-boat signals, as they knew, were extremely short and snappy, consisting of a dozen letters at most and some very quick operating was required to catch the bearing of a submarine transmission.

The other huff-duffer, seated and busy tuning the receiver, turned to nod to them, one headphone on his cheek to hear what they said. He explained that they had received orders to open watchkeeping on the operational area between the fleet base and the Island and it gave a hint as to the general direction they would be taking when they went to sea.

The two huff-duffers exchanged meaningful glances when given the message from Pots and their comments confirmed the new arrivals in their impression that sea-going was imminent. However, the faint atmosphere of apprehension which to some extent gathered on delivery of the message rapidly evaporated when they began to talk of their experiences of training schools in towns on the south coast. They were of very much the same age and had passed through their wireless training in golden summer days. They had enjoyed the free evenings and weekends, of which there had been many, for the authorities spoilt them and kept most necessary duties and routine to an absolute minimum so that they would be able to come fresh to the concentrated training. Of course, George spoke with affection for all the dance halls that he patronized so often, even those filled with an explosive mixture of Allied servicemen and good time girls, and which were out of bounds to the wireless trainees.

But more serious times had come and the three novices spent some time going over the controls and practising their direction-finding on the enemy coastal stations. In their quiet corner they grew quite oblivious to the crowded ship around them until they saw it was nearly 1800 hours, switched off, clambered up the ladder and made their way along the iron deck to the fo'c's'le.

The black water reflecting the occasional lights and signal lamps was no longer glassy smooth but rippled under wind gusts of increasing vigour. A faint glow over the island to the east of the anchorage foretold a rising moon. They were glad to regain the odiferous warmth of the galley flat.

Baked beans on toast was the not particularly attractive, if familiar, wartime repast being prepared by the cooks for despatch to the galley when the trio arrived back at the mess. They helped prepare the table, rolling out the white oilcloth cover and stacking plates, mugs and cutlery in readiness.

On the other side of the hammock net the canteen was open

and doing a brisk trade in cigarettes and other requirements of the ship's company coming and going from distant messes. The canteen manager could have been serving in the local corner tobacconist's in his methodical routine and it gave a homely touch to still strange surroundings. It was curious that whereas in everyday civilian existence the commonplace happenings and setting went almost unobserved and exotic uniforms and new types of military transport or aircraft excited notice, here, in a completely novel experience, one excitement following closely on another, it was these occasional reminders of more uneventful days which soothed agitated nerves.

During the wait for supper they had taken off collar and jumper, packed them away, put their lifebelts on top of their clothes and hung their duffel coats on the hooks fixed to the stanchion nearest their mess. In these activities they were joined by Eddie, returned from the wireless office where he had already started work in his cryptic art.

Once more, whilst the members of the mess were gathering for supper, he soon demonstrated his ability for being immediately friends with strangers and furthermore showed a talent, hitherto unrevealed, for being able to entertain fascinated listeners with his amusing anecdotes. This particular story was inspired by the serving of the glutinous, orange heap of beans on very dark toast, accompanied by steaming but greasy cocoa, which no doubt was meant as a lubrication. His delicate, if buttonlike nose, wrinkled with distaste and he recalled to the generality that less than a week ago he had been invited to have lunch with a wealthy maiden aunt at a luxurious hotel in the capital, the patronage of which was extremely select. A table had been reserved in the restaurant which, although rendered somewhat threadbare by the war, was still a place of respectful service and some gentility.

Eddie, with flapping dainty hands and an agile voice able to mimic timbre and accent with extraordinary ease, watched by messmates, quiet save for clatter of cutlery and crunched burnt bread, related the upshot of events.

Auntie had arrived before him and, balancing his known favourites with the practicalities of rationing, had ordered already. She explained to the head waiter – an old familiar – that she expected her nephew who was in the Navy. Undoubtedly he had a different image of this relation of one of his regular patrons for when the young gentleman appeared at the entrance not only did eyebrows over many a long face rise up, but so also did those of the majordomo when he saw the pale-complexioned youth in an ill-fitting, stores-issue, lower-deck rig. Self-consciously, Eddie passed through a barrage of stares which came down by way of tilted noses.

'You were always a good boy, Edward,' Auntie had said, patting his arm affectionately, 'for being punctual.'

He confessed to feeling not very comfortable there, owing to his very junior status. However, Auntie would not see this for apparently she did not know the difference between service ranks and actually he looked very sweet in his sailor suit. Whether it was gospel truth that she did not know his almost contemptible position or she had artfully feigned ignorance he could not judge at that instant, but he pretended to be absorbed in rearranging the contents of his jumper pockets, though not so much he did not apprehend the majestic tread of the approaching head waiter.

'Edward,' Auntie murmured, with admirable coolness, 'whatever you do, do not get up or apologize. Leave it to me.'

'Perhaps, madam would prefer to take a side table over by the palms?' smoothly hinted the hotel functionary, hands clasped in a complacent manner.

'Why for heaven's sake, man? I have sat at this table for many a year, and so, frequently has my nephew.'

'You might find better service over there, madam.'

'What! Half hidden behind those bushes? You might think it better.'

The voice of the head waiter was suddenly hard. 'There is no service at this table, madam.'

Eddie, crouching low over the tablecloth, reared up as though to go.

'Edward,' he was commanded, 'sit down if you please. We remain here.' His aunt looked squarely into the eye of the bully. 'Are you aware that Admiral Trumpington-Shovell is a personal friend of mine?'

'The Admiral?'

'The Admiral...' the inference being that he was responsible for naval affairs of an administrative nature in the metropolitan area. 'And how would you like this establishment to be put out of bounds to all service personnel, whatever the rank?'
'Out of bounds?'
'Out of bounds.'

The head waiter was in retreat. Faced with the prospect of disagreeable publicity in those newspapers which had a preference for large headlines, there was no option. These rags, strident propagandists of popular causes, were defenders of the minuscule rights of the downtrodden faceless ones of the services, the other ranks, a particular specimen he had before him now.

'I think, madam, as a special favour to a patron of longstanding I will be able to arrange service at this table.'

After the defeated but still unbowed back had faded once again into the distance and he had a restorative transfusion of very clear vegetable soup, Eddie ventured to ask Auntie if she indeed knew the eminent Trumpington-Shovell and whether it likely he would close this awe-inspiring establishment to service personnel.

'Oh I know him all right, Edward,' she had replied, 'indeed I've known him since he was a disagreeable little snotty. In fact, dear, I know him too well, much too well, but as to his doing anything about this place if I asked him, that is quite unlikely. He was an intractable little beast thirty years ago and from what I've heard and seen of him since, age and experience haven't improved him.'

The communications mess was stunned. The relating of the story, so entertainingly done, by a person who was, as they had observed, a type of character they had not encountered before, was impressive, but the intimation that a relative of this callow recruit personally knew an admiral compounded the shock it experienced.

'She actually knows him well?' growled George suspiciously, his ego fighting an irresistible urge to be impressed.

'Awfully well, Corder. She would never deceive one over that kind of thing. You see, I know it's terribly bad form to mention it, but she really knows so many important people, what is one more or less?'

A red-haired telegraphist, two or three years senior to all

present except Robbie, pulled a cigarette packet from the breast pocket of his US Navy-type blue overall shirt, lit it, fanned away the billowing cloud of smoke and remarked, 'Old Shovell was in charge of our base in the Med. No matter what kind of a bashing you'd had, him and his Gestapo checked through the ship every bloody item for repair or replacement as though they were paying up themselves. Even arguments about pencils in the wireless office. Had to show how much we'd sharpened them per day.'

'Gertcha!' was the response from the others. 'Pull the other one, it's got bells on,' and other, similar comments. Robbie, quietly and in an abstract frame of mind as though he were elsewhere in spirit, said, 'Swing that lamp, Ginger.'

Ginger grinned, a sudden ray of light on what was basically a wan, sad countenance. 'But tell you the truth,' he said, 'the old bastard never failed to come up with the goods and we never went short.'

While Eddie had been relating his story the loudspeakers had commenced relaying a broadcast on the Forces Programme of requests for records on behalf of servicemen and their next of kin and friends. This, with the loud babble of conversation largely contributed by the next mess and the rattle of mess traps, completed the bedlam echoing through the forward mess decks. Through the claustrophobic uproar came the bo'sun's mate, his whistle cutting the smoking air and his voice monotonously chanting, 'Fo'c's'le men on the fo'c's'le.'

A little group of seamen in duffel coats and sea boots passed through going aft. There was a sense of imminence as several others as well as the cooks, who had collected a steaming dixie of hot water, helped to wash, sweep and tidy the mess area. The signalmen gathered an enormous amount of warm clothing, consisting of several jerseys; waterproof, kapok-lined overalls, colloquially known as zoot suits; sea boots; long woollen stockings; brown canvas, fur-lined mittens and hats of black, brown or white fur, with turned-up peaks, ear and neck flaps. The canteen manager added to the clamour by noisily rolling down the window shutter, turning out the light and slamming and locking the door of his store.

The broadcast continued in its diversified way. Swing, classical and light orchestral strains followed each other with democratic indifference and were hardly noticed, save when a familiar ship was mentioned, by the crowded crew spaces growing increasingly humid despite the humming air-circulating system. Then the too familiar sentimentality of *You are my sunshine* once more had an airing and George, helping to dry the dishes, became somewhat morose as he moaned the lyric, the disapproving comments of his comrades unheeded.

As they finished clearing away Pots came down the ladder from the petty officers' mess abaft B gun with the chief bo'sun. The bo'sun was an impressively corpulent man of medium height in his mid-forties, whose red face was more an arrangement of convexities, fleshily overlapping each other than easily related features. His nose, flattened in some distant boxing tournament or liberty fracas, was just one slightly more prominent bump on the craggy mass. Two very crumpled ears defined the limits of the undulating contours and appeared from below a generous amount of greying, once black hair, through a thinning area of which a pink crown was appearing. His bulk was made greater by a very thick, dark blue, roll-necked jersey under his single-breasted jacket, which was adorned with three brass buttons on its sleeves. Under the jacket a grubby white life-belt was comfortably secured around his midriff. His trousers were tucked into black leather sea boots which were apparently, without stockings, unless worn inside his trousers, and he had not in the slightly raffish style of many of the younger members of the crew, turned the tops of the boots over to reveal the grey-white inner side.

He murmured a few private words to Pots and clumped heavily down the alleyway by the wireless office. Pots came over to Fred, about to open his locker and, pushing up the seat cushion, said, 'I'll see you in the office for the forenoon watch, 0800 hours.'

Plaintively the whistle of the bo'sun's mate was making its rounds again and this time it was, 'Special sea dutymen to their stations' that was passed along. An occasional metallic clank and running of hawser motors carried through from over the next compartment forward, confirming that the vessel would soon be on the move. The hands were beginning to disperse from the mess as they hurried off to sea stations or went to the washplace to freshen up before settling down for the evening. A slight vibration from the deck underfoot told of slowly turning propellers and no doubt their ship was under way.

6

Stepping out of the washplace which was adjacent to the heads or lavatories, David, stripped to undervest, towel round neck, passed along the alley and noticed that the door of the mysterious dark room, later known to be the TS or transmitting station, was wide open. Radar ratings were to be seen closed up to their sets, an eerie green glow from the screens reflected in their faces. He glimpsed a chart table illuminated from below and a large vertical glass screen marked in concentric circles from which radiated lines related to bearings from the ship. He then comprehended that this was where all information received by observation, signals, HF-DF, radar and range finders was collated into a pattern of intelligence easily digested by the captain. On one circular radar screen he could see a faint beam, rotating from the centre like a lighthouse, and as it brushed other ships in the anchorage and the edge of the protecting islands, smudged traces of green luminosity over the screen surface, indicating the position of the ship relative to them. Otherwise, as far as could be ascertained in the dimness, the room was largely the same as the wireless office with its complement of telephones, voice-pipes, air vents and cables.

After he had stowed away his toilet gear and was putting on his jersey and life-belt, which he noticed was absolutely de rigueur among all hands, Fred covertly beckoned him over to the stanchion behind which he tried ineffectively, guilt-ridden, to hide. George too had been included in this invitation and in a whisper, hardly necessary considering the emptied state of the area, offered them a little black tablet from a very small tin. 'Want a sea-sickness pill?' he enquired of them.

David was doubtful of accepting one but as George did so

readily, so he, to be sociable, took and swallowed it without ado, on the principle that if it did no good it was unlikely to do any harm. It had a bitter and salty taste and minute particle though it was, it was to grow larger in significance. Following this clandestine episode David put on his duffel coat and gloves and suggested they should go and see the last of the islands. Fred, similarly clad, was agreeable, but George, a general enquiring imagination not one of his strong points, declined and slumped down on the outboard side of the mess table and looked rather broody as though he might be contemplating reading some letters again. The music was interrupted by a brief 'Red watch to cruising stations', a command that was reiterated by the wandering bo'sun's mate.

The port door at the break in the fo'c's'le was already securely closed for sea and they crossed the galley flat and went out by the starboard side by which they had first entered. They found another couple of ratings standing by the galley-housing, smoking a surreptitious cigarette. The engines were gathering power and the vibration, which gave an animal life to the ship, was much more pronounced as the land slid past. The coast was a dark silhouette against the light of a low moon, frequently masked by clouds moving far too quickly for ease of mind. The water was rippled by the receding washes not only of the *Watchful*, but of other ships ahead and astern. Looking round the curve of the fo'c's'le plating, they could see a destroyer ahead, a faint grey in the moonlight, against which the blue station-keeping light was hardly discernible and to its right the smaller shape of what materialized as the boom-defence vessel, opening a gap in the line of anti-submarine buoys and nets. An adjustment of course swung the stern so that in the other direction they could perceive the fizzing wake and, following in it, another destroyer which they guessed from its general appearance was probably the *Obstinate*. So Johnny was still with them.

'I wonder what old cheerful's doing now?' speculated Fred in the murk.

At that particular instant Johnny sat, a prey to self-doubt, in the cabin high up in the bridgework, behind the wheelhouse, in the following vessel. He was concerned at being thrown, with only a couple of hours' preparation, into taking the first watch on the high frequency direction finder. He sat writing down preambles of the routine messages of the enemy coast stations, took an occasional bearing to make the operation of the set second nature to him and at the same time uneasily felt the growing sea motion through the seat of his swivel chair. Being required instantly on operational work after formalities had been completed, he had been saved the embarrassment of joining alone. Moreover, he was relieved to find his place of duty was in such a comparatively pleasant part of the ship, away from bad air and odours and not below decks aft as in some of the destroyers. By some quirk of the service the direction-finder before him was the latest visual type where a click of a switch gave light-green luminous blobs on a cathode ray screen, related to bearings from the ship. On a sad, weather-beaten, tired ship, it was surprising to find such an up-to-date model and he assumed that the earlier type had gone wrong and had been replaced. Furthermore it was just the thing to beat the speed of U-boat transmissions and although he had been told about it in training, the school had not actually had a working model. He felt a shade more confident of being able to catch a bearing on this than the aural type with the goniometer. Still, it had all been something of a rush and he could not believe he was sitting there listening for enemy submarines and the whole thing was in deadly earnest.

Although they were in the lee of the land at first, the changes in course as the line of destroyers curved round south of the islands caused wind changes which blew warm air from the funnel or chill blasts around them erratically and so the telegraphists followed the example of the two smokers and, after a sympathetic glance at the solitary look-out perched up on the starboard midships oerlikon platform, they retreated in through the tarpaulin flap. The deck in the galley flat had grown more animated in its rolling and the smell of cooking had ceded its place to the throat-gripping acrid smell of fuel oil, which was more pervasive now the ship was on the move. As they shakily walked forward past the wireless office and TS they were obliged to grip at handrails to steady themselves and by strength of arm try to compensate for the increasing inability of their legs to deal with a movement which was not the simple rolling they had experienced the previous day, but was in fact, although it was only through bitter experience they were able to appreciate it, that combination of pitching, or rising and falling of stem and stern, and the simple athwartship roll which is called a corkscrew motion.

Eventually, stiff-legged and dizzy, they attained the mess where George sat at the other side of the table, smoking and talking to a leading radar hand. The drift of conversation was on George's home town, for which so many seamen retained fond memories from their training days. Very soon the seaman got up and went over to his own mess and George unfolded some loose sheets of paper, rather dog-eared but obviously another letter from his apparently inexhaustible stock.

Fred had lifted the kapok cushion of his locker and was just rummaging inside when the ship lurched, bringing the moderate action they had experienced up till then to an abrupt conclusion and drew a gasping 'Ker-ryst' from him to suggest it had caught his stomach at an awkward angle to the perpendicular.

The vessel shuddered and the motion increased in pace and vigour. They both sat down and gripped the edge of the table and George, unable to concentrate on his loving girl's epistle, hurriedly folded it and stuffed it in his trouser pocket. 'Eff me,' he breathed, the beginnings of a halo of corpse-white skin forming around the dull blue eyes. 'I don't think,' he murmured querulously to Fred, 'that your marvellous bloody pill is going to have much effect.'

For once David was ready to subscribe to one of George's opinions for the table in front of them, seemingly infused with that spirit of cussed revenge of all slavish inanimate objects on their human creators and nominal masters, pushed and thrust at them, ready to drive them from the very mess deck.

At the end of the spiteful table Fred, fallen back on his locker, arms rigidly forming a bridge to the table edge, grasped it, bony knuckles white with tension. Beads of perspiration were forming on the pimply forehead and those thin jowls from cheekbone to jaw tautened and whitened in a grimace of chagrin.

'It appears to be getting worse,' he remarked, the midriff of his spare frame involuntarily jerking upwards.

A dull boom echoed through the next compartment forward to signal greater motion still. This pulled the deck and furniture from under them, leaving them curiously weightless, then, in the next instant, pushing up to give them unnatural and excessive bulk.

Fred broke first. The white on his face deepened to a sour yellow and spread downwards to his neck below his ears. There was a sort of internal convulsion, accompanied by a choking squawk and he jumped up and staggered, duffel coat flapping loosely, as quickly as the insurgent deck would permit across to the passageway and out along the TS alley.

The heavy form of George, at first humped morosely over the table, had slumped log-like back against the locker seats. Plain to see was the advance of the whitening skin across his usually rubicund features. Creeping round the end of his cheeks it intimated to David that the country boy would soon be lurching his way aft to the iron deck. Only too cruelly and hardly necessary, it recalled to him that a tingling sensation was beginning in that area of his own face in conjunction with a certain numbness of the ear, which were finding the hum of vents and clatter of machinery too upsetting to their growing sensitivity.

The boom of waves thudding on to the fo'c's'le quickened and, in malicious conformity, the deck was now eschewing any pretence at a roll or corkscrew motion and was just rising up and down like a maniacal lift. After one particularly long, heart-stopping fall, the rustic youth stirred up and flopped rather than stepped out from behind the table and with weak, paralysed, land-lubberly legs, managed to reach the hammock net in the middle of the deck space. Here he clung, struggling to avoid an utter disgrace by soiling the hammocks of his messmates. A few more infantile steps towards the passageway were made before he became stuck in an open space empty of any means of support. He tottered and groped like a drunkard, sawing at the air in a vain search for stability. Then a particularly severe lurch to port projected him across to the canteen store and thankfully grasping the handrail along that side, he clawed his way aft to the fresh air.

During this ignominious exit Robbie had come back from the

washplace stripped to his vest, towel in hand. He took out the mess waste bucket from under the metal locker which secured all the mess gear and casually pushed it out so it was up against the hammock net. Then, knees wedged against the locker seats he packed away his toilet gear, put on an army khaki bush shirt and then replaced his lifebelt. Pulling a watch from his trousers pocket, he wound it, listened to it and put it on.

He looked down at David and smiling, asked sympathetically, 'How do you feel, squire?'

'Not too champion, hookey.'

'Never mind lad,' Robbie said, 'if you can stand one of these bleeders you can take anything. Meself, I prefer big ships, like the dear old *Persephone*. To think I used to drip about her at the time.'

So saying he pulled his hammock from the net and with no apparent effort slung in the position of honour with a white-lagged steam pipe on one side and a grey-painted air duct on the other.

Whilst he unlashed and arranged his bedding he added as an afterthought 'If you get worse, squire, I'd join the funnel club if I were you.'

Most of these remarks were heard by David through a sensation suggestive of the gathering of cotton wool in his ears and down the sides of his neck. His Adam's apple was slowly losing control of his swallowing power with growing tenderness, and an ominous gurgling began in his gullet. He involuntarily belched and into his mouth came a bitter regurgitation of the beans, toast and cocoa of supper and, most revolting, the taste of the pill he had taken.

He shut his eyes but the thudding deckhead, rattling mess-traps, clattering machinery, humming fans and general creaking and groaning of the straining ship pressed on his harassed eardrums.

He opened his burning eyes and the harsh electric light glared mercilessly on bulkhead, pipe and stanchion, locker and furniture, Their shapes were severe, metallic, comfortless, as they began to go out of three dimensions and took on a distant unattainable flatness. He was losing touch with substance altogether as his shaken body was increasingly ill-served by his defeated senses.

Tentatively, afraid that too agitated a movement would bring the nausea to crisis point, he stirred from the position astride the bench to which he had been clamped, and going to rise was astonished to feel himself still rising up in a disconcerting levitation as the deck fell away, Hardly had his feet touched bottom than the brown linoleum came upwards, doubling his legs so that the knees were likely to touch the deck. At last he tottered back against the ladderway to the petty officers' mess, hung there, trying to focus his painful eyes in the direction of the TS alley. Occasionally crew members passed by, staggering with various degrees of effectiveness about their business. Screwing up what remained of his determination he took advantage of a comparatively level period to make for the alleyway, but a sudden jerk to port threw him violently and with a clatter against the canteen shutter. His spinning brain failed to grasp the significance of the prostrate bodies on lockers and deck and the ready buckets glimpsed through the door into the forward mess decks. Looking back along the bright, slightly curving passageway disappearing into the twilit galley flat he lamely wondered if he could reach fresh air. Those of the crew, passing by, whether coming or going, hardly touching the rail or clawing along yard by yard, had to struggle to reach their objective. At last, however, he made an effort, but as he moved, first his legs pedalled at thin air and he felt sure he would hit the deckhead, then he slid to the bulkhead on one side or the other, apparently walking fly-like on the side. Then again would come that unfortunately now familiar sensation of pushing through the deck under the sudden tonnage that he had acquired.

Past the open door of the dim TS, a bucket in there too; past the closed door of the wireless office through which penetrated the steady beat of Admiralty signals; past the heads, where somebody was hanging on to the handles over the basin urinals, hunched up, and looking for what the almost extinguished mental state of David did not permit him to guess, and at last to the familiar emptiness of the galley flat where the fuel stench hit his throat, twisted his stomach and rocketed him through the tarpaulin into the outer cold, where, whilst gripping the metal curve of the fo'c's'le break, beans, toast, cocoa, dinner and probably breakfast burst in disgusting vomit over the side.

In that bludgeoning instant, glazed eyes dimly appreciating the closeness of the black, hissing, white-flecked torrent that rushed so perilously near, David instinctively realized that this was the advent of an experience that would take for ever from his essential being that slack, passive, juvenile innocence, which in his years of adolescence had been masked by a bogus sophistry.

Vaguely, as black shapes formed against the dark greyness of the funnel and galley housing, other crew members were perceived. Growing chill he moved over to them and through a shell of numbness heard Fred's thin voice say, 'You too, Dave?' and he realized that the doleful band gathered round the funnel was not just enjoying its warmth and the passing billows but had been or was desperately trying to stave off the shattering indignity of sickness. In a state of stupor, senses battered by the throb of engines, humming vents and power units, washing seas and moaning wind, he realized now that there were many established members of the ship's company who had as yet to discover the knack of remaining unaffected by this miserable existence.

With baleful regularity the tipping of the ship to starboard brought a torrent of foam sluicing over the iron deck and it disappeared in the darkness aft, washing and splashing heavily through post, pipe, stay and stanchion. It was no place to spend a night and David resolved to try and put up with the mess deck at any price. So leaving the wordless and demoralized gathering he tottered to the door and braved the disgusting reek of fuel oil to reach the TS alley.

An effort of will helped him into the heads where the odour of sickness was very evident, but propping himself against the screen to the showers he managed to gather some water from taps that only trickled, owing to some suddenly developed fault of shipboard plumbing and splashed to cool and clean his aching face.

Reeling into the mess area he saw that Robbie was in his hammock, a peaceful blanket-shrouded mound, and that a few more hammocks had been slung, particularly in the radar mess adjacent to his own. The tranquillity that emanated from Robbie's swaying hammock possessed David to try at all costs to sling his own. Being the latest arrivals, their places were the outermost from the mess corner, there being only Fred's between his own and the gangway into the fore part of the fo'c's'le. However, it meant there was no distance to the hammock storage net; in fact he was almost alongside it. The petty irritation he had always felt for his sleeping gear had evaporated before the brutal reality of this clattering, bucking and clammy mass of metal and his physical weakness. Summoning up minute reserves of strength from where he knew not, to drag out his hammock, at last hanging over the edge of the enclosure he paused, dizzy with nausea, and enfeebled by his tortured stomach.

Sliding down beside the net he fumbled to unpick the lanyards; then, after moments of tension verging on hysteria, managed to tie them to the overhead bars. Completely forgotten were his months of enmity and distrust of hammocks as his deadweight hung on it, gathering willpower and any last vestiges of strength to unlash it. Though he was beyond caring it was obvious that he had at last mastered the trick of securing it.

A seaman, in full topside gear, blundered into him going aft, as he staggered to and fro gathering the rope into a coil which carelessly he threw in at the foot of the mattress. By now he was at the end of his resources and haphazardly, boots and all, he flopped in on top of his folded blanket, in duffel coat still. He did not fall asleep but collapsed, as it were, into unconsciousness.

During the night he was roused slightly from what was almost a state of anaesthesia by the sad whistle of the changing watches and the hint of seamen and stokers passing to their cruising stations. However, when he emerged finally from his state of utter exhaustion, for a few blissful moments before he opened his eyes he imagined the ship was in calm water, It was an illusion engendered by the hammock taking the sea movement and his fragile senses observing the oscillation of the deckhead and hearing the growing storm din outside, rapidly disabused him of this deception.

Looking over to the mess area through an undulation of slung hammocks he saw several messmates struggling in difficult circumstances to prepare a simple breakfast of tea and toast. The thick slices of bread were toasted on the electric radiator secured to the forward bulkhead beside the closed water-tight door. His stomach, at that time flaccid, murmured in rebellion at the thought of food, but recalling the view generally expressed by many of his acquaintances that one ought to keep eating in spite of sea-sickness, he resolved to swallow something to pacify its rumbling emptiness. He got out of the hammock, and as his feet touched the deck, the bucking motion, no slighter than the previous evening, jerked up his stiff joints and again aggravated the queasiness in his vitals. Gritting his teeth, so that he feared the muscles of the jaw might become locked, hanging onto his bedgear, he lashed it into the familiar banana shape, pausing and struggling from time to time to force down the sour bile that spouted into his throat, and shutting his eyes to keep at bay the dizziness that threatened to overwhelm him again. The securing of its lanyards into the lashing and placing of the hammock into the stowage net was a great trial, for he had to bend and heave, agitating the already erratic movement caused by the ship.

Ducking under several hammocks to get over to the table, he collected both a fork and slice of bread and began toasting it, wearily holding onto a stanchion as he did so. He noticed that Fred was flat out on the seat cushions but George, down by the petty officers' mess ladder, had got his hammock up and the waxen yellow features that protruded from the blanket at one end were far from the homely pink which had given such a complacent effect formerly. As David looked at him he opened his eyes, which painfully darted about as he tried to regain his composure.

For security the large tea kettle had been suspended from the deckhead by a hook and wire and Ginger busied himself making the powerful and not very appetizing beverage. Besides a large amount of brown sugar, he poured in the contents of a tin of condensed milk, turning the tea an unpleasant bright orange hue. Meanwhile David had made his toast but could not face the butter or marmalade available and having obtained half a mug of tea, propped himself back against the hammock net, awkwardly trying to keep the tea from splashing out as he sipped and nibbled cautiously, miserably aware of the experimental nature of the snack.

Managing to consume most of the tea and toast, he saw Fred

rousing himself on the seat. The crew were turning out and there was less room on the lockers as he dragged himself to a sitting position. Tottering over, David asked if he wanted a drink. At first he refused but on persuasion sipped a cup of the reviving brew.

Now the mess areas were crowded with people struggling to secure hammocks, collect and put away toilet gear and reluctantly taking mouthfuls of breakfast before going on watch. Most, already, were as grey and tired-looking as David felt and, it was plain, fighting in much the same way against pangs of seasickness. He contrived somehow to collect towel and soap, waves of nausea and dizziness flooding up towards his numbed brain, whilst he knelt to open his locker. He could have screamed with irritation as he rummaged in the jumble of his belongings.

In the washplace, deteriorating rapidly as far as cleanliness was concerned, he freshened himself a little, rather than washed, in the trickle that came into the hand basin. Soapy water was beginning to slop over the deck and the urinals and water closets were foul with the stench of vomit.

George was out and stiffly lashing his hammock when he returned to put away the toilet gear. One of the signalmen was garbing himself in layers of woollens and zoot suit, to which he added duffel coat and knitted balaclava hood. The bo'sun's mate was going the rounds, calling 'White watch to cruising stations,' whilst David combed his lank dark brown hair in the mirror fixed to the bulkhead. He could hardly take the haggard, wild-eyed creature he saw as himself. He looked a stranger. The too brisk clang of eight bells on the sound relay system told him it was time to go to the wireless office, whatever the state of the others.

It struck colder as he reeled down the TS alley and the outer roaring of the sea was more apparent as he opened the door of the office and stepped inside. Robbie, as quiet and composed as though he were on a mill-pond, was just handing over responsibility for the eight to twelve stint to Ginger and an ordinary telegraphist was already engaged on the signals coming from the Admiralty transmitter. Shortly after, Eddie came in to relieve the red watch coder and finally Pots arrived.

The relative quiet, warmth and odourlessness of the office was some relief but it was still a fight to avoid slipping into physical collapse again. When Pots enquired, rather pointlessly as David thought, as to his condition, he replied he felt bloody awful. A little work to take his mind off things was the prescription offered and he was ordered to tune into the frequency covered by HF-DF to see if there was anything interesting afoot.

After wearily and clumsily going through the wave band he at last came on a long signal being sent by the enemy high command headquarters in the tidy, characterless, methodical style of transmission to be expected from a tightly controlled operational network, It was evidently the routine that came up on the hour when important messages transmitted in the previous sixty minutes were repeated and signals from operational units were repeated back for general information. David listlessly began to take down the messages for practice and to occupy himself. Mercifully there was no trace of U-boat activity in the whole zone, perhaps owing to the foul weather that was presumably continuing to deteriorate.

Along the bench Eddie, at first busy with his grid and table, had decoded messages in hand and Pots prepared them for delivery to the officer of the watch. Now he was bent over, propping his head in hands and obviously the worse for wear. He fell back and pulled a neatly pressed handkerchief from his jersey sleeve and patted his perspiring white jowls.

'I have to go, Petty Officer,' he whispered, choking, and without a by your leave shot from his chair and out of the door. The spectacle did not improve David's debilitated condition, but when the hourly routine finished he just lolled back and the remnant of judgement wandering unhappily in his racked body considered it was just as wise to stick it out there as in the increasingly foul-aired dampness of the slippery, noisy discomfort of a chilly mess deck.

The two hours up to the forenoon stand-easy, a mockery of the term, he spent almost as a passive invalid rather than an alert watchkeeper, but Pots, who had nursed Eddie along in his duties and excused his lapse, had a considerate attitude and as he came and went on a variety of tasks obviously kept a fatherly eye on his charges. About ten o'clock he asked David to go and collect the cocoa being made in the mess and as he made his way forward it was quite plain the ship was more violent than ever. The thunder of waves breaking over the fo'c's'le was incessant and noisier than the previous night and although everything was now stowed away and tied up, the mess area relatively empty, there were still many men prostrate on deck, benches and seats. In particular, one seaman he had noticed before through the portside door to the forward mess decks, sprawled out on a bench, lay in exactly the same position, fully clad, a great bundle of damp, suffering clothes, unable to muster the strength to remove an article of apparel.

Robbie was helping the cooks prepare the cocoa. Possibly because it was much nearer to the boiler room there was no shortage of hot water in the galley, but whoever had been responsible for getting the kettle back had performed an act of great skill and near heroism. Watching the evaporated milk and sugar go into the thick fluid to give it an additional stickiness, David pondered that getting jug and mugs to the office would be beyond his diminished capabilities. There were so few present he wondered what had become of his colleagues as he collected three mugs, each on a separate finger, and grasped in his left hand the small jug Robbie had almost filled. The idea was to leave the right hand free for steadiness.

Now came the testing moment and pausing at the hammock enclosure to await a favourable instant, he darted across to the canteen. He waited there for another suitable pause in the motion of the ship and started off briskly down the TS alley. Whilst he did so the steepness of the slope increased formidably and he was set fair by the rising bows to be shot all the way to the galley flat. However, just beyond the office door the deck changed rapidly from downhill to upwards and he was obliged to turn awkwardly to grasp the rail on the office side with his right hand. This put him into a distorted if not dangerous tangle with the jug threatening to empty itself over his crouching lap.

Stranded on the wrong side of the closed door, not wishing to let go his grip on refreshment or handrail, he waited for inspiration or something miraculous to happen. The miracle came in the form of a distraught-looking Eddie, who staggered out of the heads and hand over hand came up to the office. Opening the door he stepped through and prevented it slamming with his own slight-boned, sagging form.

The undisguised pleasure the arrival of cocoa gave Ginger was some reward for his exertions and after his senior had prudently half filled the mugs David was glad to go back to the set and, sipping a little, half listen to the atmospheric inactivity of the frequency.

When Pots looked in later, he said it was all right to go off the frequency, as there seemed to be nothing doing, and meander across the wavelengths. On medium wave he crossed a musical breakthrough and turned to telephony to hear a concert coming in clearly from somewhere. Then he noticed Eddie flopped back in his seat, eyes closed, but a momentary peace on his drawn features, fluttering his hands in the air before him. The surprised apprehension in the faces of Ginger and the ordinary telegraphist at the other end was comical.

'Are you all right, kidder?' exclaimed the former anxiously.

'Quite all right, thank you, Ginger,' Eddie softly replied.

'What in hell are you doing then?' persisted the senior hand of the watch.

'Conducting.'

'Conducting?'

'Yes; conducting the music Freston has found.'

'Dave,' said Ginger, 'find something else before we have to lock him up.'

David did not care to go off this music, which he enjoyed, although it could not be claimed he really understood it.

'What is it, Eddie?' he asked.

'Wagner,' the coder replied, 'Overture to *The Flying Dutchman*, I think. Let's keep it on a bit, Ginger. Yes, that's it, *The Flying Dutchman*.'

The piece ended and there was the unmistakable voice of a German-speaking announcer. It was very clear and loud.

Ginger was peremptory. 'It's a bloody Jerry. Go on Dave, switch it off. We don't want to listen to that bastard.'

He addressed Eddie. 'Who was this flying Dutchman feller anyway?'

Rousing himself from his weakness, Eddie condescended to

explain. 'He was a sea captain who sinned and when he died he was condemned to sail the seas for ever or until redeemed by the love of a good woman...'

'Christ,' interjected Ginger, 'in this weather.'

'...and Richard Wagner wrote an opera about it,' Eddie concluded, as wearily he sank back.

Pots came in again and told David he could close down and should report next day at 0800. Taking the opportunity, David enquired as to their destination and Pots said he did not know himself yet, but at present they were generally on a north-west course.

'I bet it's the Island,' put in Ginger.

'Too soon yet,' said Pots, 'could be Newfie.'

Outside in the alleyway it was much colder and the noise of the storm was astounding. David thought he would go and look at the cause of the tumult and at the same time maybe fresh air would pull him out of the sickness which hovered, ready to seize him again. The mess deck was beginning to take in water that seeped in from the incessantly crashing waves above. The atmosphere was now a distinct foul-smelling haze and all surfaces were damply cold to the touch. He found that his duffel coat, left hanging on the stanchion with many others, was tied with cord to prevent them flapping loose or falling on the deck. While he tottered and struggled to free it from the bundle and get it on he noticed that Fred, wrapped in his duffel coat, was again stretched out on the cushions, bony fingers clasped on stomach, his thin face whitely skeletal. How he managed to keep on the heaving locker was a mystery. He was not the only prostrate one; there were some in the next mess and the usual collection of fully-clad figures in the seamen's mess through the bulkhead door.

He shivered, crossing the wet bleakness of the galley flat, and when he pulled back the tarpaulin on the starboard side, the port exit still tightly clamped, he was astounded at the sight that met his inexperienced eye.

Somewhere on the port side to his right a cold sunlight brightly pierced the scudding clouds and illuminated the foaming watery surface in light green patches. They were headed mainly into the wind and as the shredded fleece raced aft so did the sunlit patches on the water. The waves thumped against the bows, showered spray to topmast height, then, lined with spume, rolled angrily past the stern and on savagely towards the following destroyers. Continually, as the ship, already beaten to a starboard list, lurched over even more under a particularly heavy wave, the crest of the billow swept inboard and frantically battered its way aft through the intervening superstructure. It was an apparently suicidal thing for anyone to move along the iron deck at all and the moaning wind of the previous night had risen to a steady roar in the mast above, silencing the throbbing great heart of *Watchful* as, like a living thing, she struggled with the ferocious elements. Yet he could feel her vibrant life through his feet despite the frenetic motion of the deck.

Propped in the doorway, hood of his duffel coat over his head, gloved hands deep in pockets, David felt chilled, utterly miserable and alone. He did not care to go back to the increasingly disagreeable mess deck but it was evident he could not spend all his idle hours where he was. Seemingly drained of all willpower and physical strength, it appeared likely he would be rooted to the spot indefinitely. Then his painful eyes perceived two figures clad in black oilskins appear in the starboard entry to the aft superstructure, pause and then, using the lifeline, make their way forward.

From time to time they left the line, disappeared behind torpedo tubes or other structures and it was then that there was a particularly bad jerk and a wave rolled and hissed its way aft. Then they would reappear, advance a few more paces, casually examining the security and state of all movable equipment as they came.

They were behind the searchlight platform somewhat longer than usual and, when they came round by the funnel, shouted something to people David could not see. They dodged a particularly abundant shower of spray and staggered into the galley flat, stamping and shaking off the water on their clothes. The first lieutenant and chief bo'sun had been making a round of the upper deck.

The taller of the two, a thin-faced tired-looking man of about twenty-eight, stared hard at him and snapped, 'Who are you?'

'Telegraphist Freston, sir.' It was no casual assumption that he was addressing an officer for the sufficient reason that there was a gold laurel wreath, anchor and crown of an officer's badge stitched to the upturned peak of the black fur hat the first lieutenant wore.

'Oh, one of the new sparkers, eh?' He removed the hat, shook it free of droplets and pushed back his thinning brown hair. 'Cheer up laddie, remember you're not the only one. The captain will be speaking to you at a convenient time.' Then as an afterthought, 'There's one of your unhappy chums round behind the galley.'

The stockily built bo'sun had been removing his oilskin and fur hat meanwhile and his red, coarse but kindly visage widened in a grin as he realized, like David, all too well, the implications of the remark. 'If you join him, take care,' cautioned the first lieutenant. 'I don't want to have to write to your next of kin. It's no weather for taking liberties.'

'Aye aye, sir!'

Warily David gripped the handrail along the galley-housing and edged along to the funnel. Round the corner, among a confusion of pipes, stays and racks, several ratings were sitting, standing or wedged in awkward positions which would not exactly come in either of those descriptions, between fittings. George, propped between a boiler room vent and a vertical pipe, stood hunched up, balaclava pulled right over his head so that only a small area of greeny-white face was exposed. The one feature of interest in the part visible was a very red nose.

'Hello, George,' David gasped, the futile words snatched away on the wind that gusted erratically even on this lee side.

The blue eyes, watery and weary, glanced at him and the muffled head just nodded.

David found a little space into which a silent, dejected figure had not been fitted and leant back against the galley wall. A faint warmth reached him from the funnel and he gave his attention to the wild scene before him. Down the starboard side of the ship the water rolled in sunlit crests towards the horizon. From the mainmast the ensign of the ship, stiffly flying in the wind, was a brilliant white patch with its red cross against the darker sky. It was already fraying at the trailing edge, yet through his weakness and depression the flag brought a perverse sense of pride which conceived in him a feeling of purposefulness that after years of aimless adolescence he was out here in the forefront of the war effort of his country. The line of ships astern rose and fell, dark patches against light, then changing to light against dark. Curiously, the counterchanging rhythm of their movement released a memory of the music he heard during his watch and which, like a refrain of madness, was to well up again and again in the ear of his mind. He noticed a change in the ship next astern. It was not the *Obstinate*.

'What's that one?' he shouted to George.

'*Stavanger?*' he replied curtly, 'Norwegian.'

'Where's Johnny's tub?' David persisted.

'Dropped back. Lookout told me she can't manage the weather.' George was not conversational. It was likely he opened his mouth at the risk of being sick.

'What's it like in the office?' he enquired, after a long pause. 'I'm on at 1200.'

'Best place, I reckon,' shouted David. 'It's warm, dry and no smells.'

The effort of conversing above the gale was having an upsetting effect on his nerves and his ears and stomach became more painful. Somewhere on a distant loudspeaker muted by the wind there was the wailing whistle of the bo'sun's mate and the call, 'Red watch to cruising stations.' The clang of eight bells contributed to the call to duty. George lethargically extricated himself from his roost and, without acknowledgement, teetered round the corner to the office. There was a reshuffle of crew members; some went and some came, the new arrivals always lighting a cigarette as soon as they were established. A haggard-looking stoker, shivering in his thin boiler suit, evidently only up for a quick cigarette, offered David one. 'No thanks,' he said, 'I don't smoke.' Wondering what the dinner was, the thought impelled a constriction in the back of his throat. However, he would try to eat, as he had been able to do at breakfast.

His attempt to repeat the modest success of the morning was a failure. Although Robbie presided at the serving of the shepherd's pie and showed an unconquerable appetite it was evident that most of the other members of the mess who had decided to fight their weak flesh were not over-enthusiastic in consuming their share of the meal which, in spite of the tossing ship, had arrived miraculously hot and well-cooked. It would not have been unwelcome if David had helped to clear up at the end but the sight of Fred still slumped on the lockers in the space between the radar mess and their own, and the taut, thoughtful look on the faces of most of his curiously silent messmates had a demoralizing effect upon his stomach already turned by the slimy scraping of plates being done at the end of the table. Ignominiously he withdrew to the heads where he was quickly relieved of the small amount consumed. Only foul gastric juices now gurgled in his throat and lay bitterly on his tongue. The hateful, clattering soulless interior of the vessel span, sound and sight hopelessly confused in his disorientated mind.

When in mid-afternoon the light faded, he left the funnel club and chilled to the innermost painful core, went into the galley flat and sat on a low step of the ladderway to the bridgeworks. In the faint blue light, lone, struggling figures came and went, their garb showing whether they had duties above or below decks. The motion, so violent previously, drove to new extremes of height and depth and the frenzied ship was shaking, sliding, jerking and reeling as she ferociously fought like a giant she-animal, her natural enemy, the hateful sea. There was no doubt about it. Befuddled though he was David knew the impossible was happening. The storm was getting worse.

Stiffly, bone-tired, he eventually came back to the mess and sat down near Fred, once more prone on the lockers He looked up and weakly muttered, 'Pots wants me in the office at 1600.'

'George is on now,' David informed him.

'I don't reckon,' Fred mumbled, 'I can get there,' a ghost of a wry grin hovered in his spectral face.

'Of course you can.' David tried to be encouraging, but felt it sounded hollow somehow. 'It's better in there than out here.'

Eddie propped up between seat and table tried to read a book. It looked like the poetry. 'Eddie managed it this forenoon and he's pretty grim.'

The indefatigable Robbie had appeared with a kettle of hot

water and with much clatter and a little muted cursing made another brew of strong, sweet tea.

'Who's on the wheel?' he querulously demanded of an off watch signalman, as a particularly irritating shudder threatened to demolish all his carefully done arrangements for dispensing the beverage.

'Effie off the *Albemarle*,' the signalman replied.

'No wonder,' was Robbie's petulant comment, 'he couldn't cox a boat on the Serpentine. He treats this heap as though it was a bloody battlewagon.'

In spite of his natural interest in a smoother passage and the probable inability of his body to distinguish any difference in nuances of motion, David felt that under the circumstances, even allowing for the superior knowledge of ship handling that his years of seatime had given Robbie, he was being somewhat unjust in expecting any helmsman, however proficient, to overcome the particularly odious weather they were experiencing.

Ginger, who had staggered into the exchanged remarks, voiced this opinion. For he, no doubt, seeing he had spent part of the afternoon in the seamen's mess where he had card-playing cronies, took their viewpoint.

'You don't half expect a lot, hookey! How would you like to spend your watches standing up there getting flat feet?'

Robbie took the rebuke in good part, smiled and having second thoughts, perhaps, amiably splashed the stomach-twisting brew into the jingling mugs.

Fred had, meanwhile, managed to pull himself up to hold onto the rail of the petty officers' mess ladder and obviously wondered where to go from that position. David had taken a partly filled mug of tea and, although blundering up against the bench, reached him and gave it to him. His grey eyes were sunk right back into greyer hollows and the usually unhealthy complexion was stark white, the pimples being more dirty grey than pink. Yet through his obvious suffering there emerged a smile of spirit and gratitude. He sipped a little, forcing it down in spite of its, for him, repulsive taste and whispered, 'What about the Free Ferry now, Dave?'

David nodded lugubriously. He took back the cup and finished the tea, which had been likely, because of Fred's limp grasp, to end on the deck.

They staggered and swayed, exchanging no words, the whistle and call of white watch to cruising stations penetrating the continual pandemonium of the shuddering ship. David shrugged encouragingly in the direction of the TS alley. Letting go the ladder for an instant, his companion in misery shook himself up inside his flapping duffel coat. He shivered as much from weakness as the coolness of the mess deck, grimaced faintly with probably a hint of reproach and, pushing at the ladder and the B gun support, slowly worked his way round its curve, making for the office.

Sitting down on the lockers midway between the two messes, David hunched up, hands in pockets of his duffel coat, grew more aware of the sleepiness which had been a concomitant of his malady. He began to go into a doze which was to sap his willpower as the sickness had not managed to do. He did not notice as he slipped away into an unwakeful condition, still aware of the violence of the ship, that its oscillation was growing in fury and that even the minor chores of the mess were becoming impossible for those ratings, diminishing in number, who were sufficiently fit to carry them out.

In mid-evening he emerged from his half-sleep to hear the call of blue watch to cruising stations and sensed the staggering, swearing watch keepers coming and going and dimly he was surprised to find supper time had come and gone and he had not been disturbed from lying full length on the lockers. He did not know that the galley had at last ceased to be usable and, except for cocoa and tea, nothing hot would be consumed thenceforward.

He next came out of his torpid state at the change in the first and middle watches at midnight. The whole compartment was in semi-darkness, a few lights left on for people to move about. He raised himself precariously, on one arm, to look around and saw no hammocks slung and many people full length on the deck as well as the lockers. Fred was prone on the deck just by him. Over yonder, with his back against the gun support in an attempt to get stability, George, his inflated lifebelt as a pillow, was curled up in a strangely childlike posture.

The roar of water pounding onto the plating next to him and overhead contrasted with the calm of the sleeping quarters. Internal noises of the ship were in comparison relatively quiet. He sank back into sleep, completely assured that the confidence and professionalism he had seen in the first lieutenant and bo'sun earlier in the day, typical products of the tight discipline and training of the regular service, would see them through any crisis the baleful sea might produce.

So through the lunatic night the flotilla battered its way north-westwards, the units spreading out and making fair or foul headway depending upon their overall efficiency. That part of the ships' companies, on duty, as vigilant and effective as their weariness and the elements would allow, counted the slowly ticking seconds to their eventual relief from purgatory. In every corner of the tossing vessels those off duty sat, crouched or lay uncomfortably rocked in merciful oblivion.

Far astern of *Watchful* the sea-weary *Obstinate* wallowed and rolled in a terrifying manner. At least, anyway, to Johnny, alone up in the HF-DF office, or alone, with his thoughts, in the bleak companionship of the mess, it was terrifying. The general debility of many of the crew, veterans though they were, his own sickness that made it difficult to comprehend the Morse he knew so well, these, with the sluggish motion of the ship recovering from extreme rolling ran, spiderlike, a thread of fear through the tangled thought web of his mind. He could hardly credit that it was only three days before he had glimpsed the office where he had spent many dark winter mornings punching workmen's tickets in the cosy warmth and quiet, broken only by the softly popping gasfire. Then he realized that in the years he had been quietly engaged in clerical routine there had been others out here before him, and many of his very shipmates had been serving then. He wondered how they had endured it so long.

In the menacing loneliness of his first middle watch there was but one cheering thought. So far the frequency was quiet. Not a hint of submarines was there anywhere in the zone.

Sometime in the small hours David was brought out of his virtual coma by a sense of impending trouble and was just conscious enough in a few swift moments to realize a prodigious list to port was about to roll him off the lockers and manage in time to grasp the table. From then on he had to sit up, resting his head in his folded arms on the table. For a while he was disturbed by the incredible motion but gradually sank again into unconsciousness.

Vaguely he was aware of somebody preparing the tea for breakfast but he was held hard in the grip of sleep. Sometimes his mind surfaced with little hints of what he should be doing, particularly that he ought to go on watch. However the leaden weight of his sleep-conquered body effectively prevented any real initiative.

Miles away somebody was calling his name and shaking his shoulder and that person changed with fleeting glimpses of the past in his clouded imagination. Then, rousing himself enough to fall back on the seat, he saw in a severely painful brightness the close visage of Eddie. Just returned from the morning watch he was trying to get David to his place of duty. That he had been largely in oblivion for the past sixteen hours was astounding and even in his almost eclipsed state a spark of energy impelled him to his feet and helped him on his numbed and tottering way.

Stopping at the ladder he leaned his head against it, the cold of the metal penetrating the numbness of his cheek and hands. He heard Eddie from the other side of the muffling, invisible barrier of sleepiness, urging him on with the fact that Pots awaited him. The general physical weakness and sickness was still with him but now it was slumber that mastered him and he could very well have dropped off, standing up, grasping the ladder.

Desperately yawning, oblivious of his unkempt appearance, only aware of his chronic desire for sleep, he blundered into the office. Pots had the personal supervision of blue watch and was sitting before the ship-to-ship transmitter next to the coder, a quiet, clerkish, balding man of about thirty-five who was something of a reserved mystery in the mess. David had felt, seeing him from time to time, that the whole business was a special trial for him. Not of fear, sickness or fatigue, but rather of disgust at the enforced intimacy of the lower deck, not the least with very young men, many not out of their teens. It was one of those occasions when the grip of intellect is lessened and it is the intuition that functions uninhibited. So he apprehended that because of the peculiar position of the coder, Pots had the tact to assign him to his own watch.

'Christ, Fres,' his equable petty officer remarked, 'you look like something the cat brought in.'

'I feel like it, Pots. Can I go to sleep?'

'No you bloody well can't. The huff-duffers tell me there is still nothing doing in this zone. What about the next one west? They've given me the frequency for this time of day.'

David was in no mood or state for conscientious watchkeeping, particularly as it was more out of curiosity than ordered necessity, so he sat reluctantly in front of the set, switched on and slowly moved across the wave band he had been handed on a slip of paper. No sooner had he crossed the frequency and caught the powerful transmitter of the enemy high command headquarters repeating back a submarine message, than he realized something was in progress.

Even through a haze of sleepiness the urgency of the traffic he recorded told of a pattern of action somewhere below and between the Island and the American shore. The U-boats hardly waited for one to cease its brief signal than another tried to jump in. During a brief pause he saw Pots taking a keen interest in his work.

'Someone's having a delightful early morning,' he remarked ironically.

David wondered what was happening to the south-west of them, hundreds of miles across the boiling wastes he had seen yesterday. Perhaps there were fellows he had trained with out there in the thick of it. It took him back to the training classrooms, where recruits grouped around long trestle tables learned Morse from nine till five each weekday. They had been warm days, cheerful days that had led up to the passing out photograph with their civilian instructor, chief petty officer telegraphist and commanding officer in the centre. Now they were all split up and very likely, on every part of the seven seas eavesdropping on the enemy.

'Well for one thing...' Pots broke in on his reverie, 'they won't be getting this weather down there.'

'How do you know, Pots?' the coder put in.

'Subs don't like it very rough. When it's really bad they dive deep and wait for it to moderate.'

There was some advantage in their present misery, anyway, reflected David.

Traffic with Admiralty being rather slack Pots, at ten o'clock, sent the coder for cocoa. He got it back to the office without mishap. Partaking of the hospitality of the communications mess, he enjoyed the drink too much for the tranquillity of David's stomach.

'There's nothing like a cup of pusser's kai to buck you up,' he declared to everyone. 'Settles the digestion, relaxes the nerves.'

Balderdash, thought David, he looks like a newspaper advertisement. Mine are beyond redemption.

'Do you want me to go on with this traffic, Pots?' he asked.

'Go back in an hour just to see if it's still busy, otherwise search around.'

The search was threatened by the sleep that was always likely to claim him again, but somehow at midday, very soon after eight bells, George appeared, clay-visaged, with Robbie. David told him he had been listening to the next area, showed him the frequency and the traffic preambles in the log book. He explained it was a whim of Pots, not a definite instruction from flotilla. He also mentioned the interpretation put on the activity by their superior. George showed no interest or enthusiasm, flopping heavily into the armchair without comment. He might have at least said thanks, David scowled to himself, as he picked up his duffel coat, left on the deck under the bench, and put it on.

Down at the funnel club the grouping was much the same as before but many of the constituents in it were changed. Some weary faces he had not seen before. Ensconced near George's vent was the blue watch coder, strangely incongruous in his navy blue overcoat and knitted grey wool balaclava pulled down as headgear over his ears but not over the rest of his face. It was an odd contrast of casual and formal attire.

The noise of the wind had now reached a disagreeably steady

shriek above in the foremast and even when, by turning close up to the galley housing, the smokers tried to light their cigarettes, they had the greatest difficulty in doing so. The sunshine had given way to a grey overcast below which lower clouds in shredded form, much the same as the previous day, still raced greyly. The sea appeared, in its pulverized light greenness, lighter than the sky and now the retreating crests had grown into an enormous swell in the troughs of which companion ships would disappear, save for their wildly wagging antennae. Then *Watchful* would descend into one of these great watery saucers between the ridges of the swell and high above her stern would emerge *Stavanger*, perched on the unstable skyline. Within the giant structure of these mighty billows there were innumerable lesser hollows and convexities and it was in these that the ship rolled and pitched as they poured the water over her side or splattered the spray along her length; the giant swell contributed merely a general inclination as the vessel struggled up one side and down the other. The salt water itself scarcely contrasted with the streaks of briny foam, so beaten was it into its effervescent light green.

The warships had long since abandoned their tidy line ahead formation and were in irregular staggered positions both sides of a general line from the convoluting stern of the *Watchful*. The air was now bitter, not merely chill. It did not have the earlier, rather mild salt tang but was almost liquid in texture and somehow mingled with the odour of fuel oil into a compound of almost demoralizing unpleasantness. It was not only the gathering dusk of early afternoon which made him go in quickly from the only tolerable part of the upper deck; the atmosphere actual and psychological was exceedingly depressing.

An attempt at the washplace, as he went along to the mess to rinse his dryly acrid mouth, was thwarted by there being only a scalding trickle in the hot taps and nothing in the cold.

Bemused though he was, curiosity drove him, as he came shakily along the TS alleyway, to look into the seamen's mess deck next forward through the compartment partition. The general appearance of this area was even more daunting than his own. Here the sides of the fo'c's'le started to move towards each other and the forward end was not more than ten feet in beam. There were the usual variety of pipes, cables, ducts, stanchions and furniture, but all were more gathered together with less spare room than in the canteen area. The two foremost mess tables were within arm's length of each other, with only a watertight door into the paint store and chain locker between them. Four groups of seamen messed here, and in front of A gun support and the hammock net a hatch led down to the stokers' mess on the deck below.

By the gun support the prostrate seaman noticed so often was once more flat out on the deck in his damp oilskin, fur cap and sea boots. There were others too sitting or stretched on the lockers, dozing or endeavouring to read books or magazines. The air was abominable. A light blue haze that had ceased to have purely an odour of tobacco, was laden with an organic heaviness of cramped, unwell humanity and unnatural fumes produced by the busy, straining, internal mechanisms and electrical devices of the fo'c's'le. The outer, raging ocean thundered, thumped and roared to a degree not experienced, fortunately, anywhere else.

He turned abruptly from this cheerless scene and looked for a place to sit. In the corner, formed by the hammock storage and forward bulkhead, just by the electric radiator, an area of deck space was unencumbered with his off-duty messmates. He sat down, finding it passably warm, though after a time the deck became uncomfortably hard. He dozed in a sitting position, legs doubled up under his chin, but gradually the thrust and sagging of the ship rocked him down to sleep horizontally on the deck. Here, when vaguely aware of his surroundings, there was a relaxing warmth from above and his beaten stomach, twitching and gurgling in its bilious emptiness, was a little less persecuted by the disturbance of the ship.

Deeper into blessed nothingness he slipped, ego already driven far into a suffering shell, unable even to assert itself in dreaming, lost blissfully in the peace of nowhere. To his messmates, struggling up to duty in the dulling reaches of the long night, as they stepped back and forth over his duffel-shrouded figure, it was just one of many, heavily breathing or eerily still, but all now rolled and shaken into surrendered passivity.

It was only by a clatter of tin kettle and mugs, as he emerged from what seemed a dreamless sleep, that he was aware that for an extraordinarily long time he had been sprawled on the deck. Attempting to stir, he realized that his bones had pressed down to the unyielding deck through his flesh, which had become so numbed that at first he could hardly move and trying to do so felt excruciatingly stiff and painful. Pins and needles probed in every corner of his anatomy, contesting with cramped muscles for priority in his torment. His neck was so stiff that as he tried to turn his head the muscles clicked and creaked. Slowly, combating a strong urge to swear aloud, he raised himself up in the corner to a sitting position, cautiously opening sticky eyes to see Robbie once again defying hell and high water to make the tea.

The inside of David's mouth had become so furred, his tongue so swollen and coated, the thought of a drink even of that sticky concoction did not cause much of an offensive sensation in his fragile stomach. That organ had indeed become so evident recently that he knew each corner and fibre of it, so if urged would have been able to draw such a reasonable facsimile of its area and dimensions on his tautened abdomen that would have been an efficient guide for exploratory surgery.

Creaking like an octogenarian, audible to himself if not others in the continuing pandemonium of the struggling destroyer, he managed to stand up. His resurrection caused Robbie amiably to enquire, 'Had enough sleep, Dave?'

David nodded.

'I should bloody well think you have,' continued the leading hand,' I nearly trod on your goolies coming off the first. You shouldn't get into dark corners.'

Hanging onto his favourite stanchion David drank deeply, even, in a perverse kind of way, enjoying what should, by all experience, have been nauseating. He felt odd; quite light-headed and relaxed. The sea movement was just as fierce as the previous day, the thundering overhead undiminished. He found he was letting the motion expend its violence in the looseness of his knees. The ship dipped and slid away or pushed up aggressively as before but now the trunk of his body balanced on an unseen vertical line and he drank his tea without great discomfort.

The forenoon was agreeably passed in the company of Robbie,

the red-cheeked ordinary telegraphist and the third coder. David went from their still quiescent zone to the one that had been so busy yesterday and although there was still some activity, it had lessened considerably.

Ginger and George came into the office together and Robbie very soon followed David along to the mess. Somehow the cooks had managed to produce a thick pea soup and a cupful of this and a couple of dry biscuits served to at least dampen the gnawing hunger which he was surprised to feel in his midriff. Several ratings still sat around looking rather miserable, Fred with them, but even he was beginning to take notice of things about him.

When everyone wanting sustenance had finished David even made himself useful by helping to dry and stack the mugs in the dresser locker up against forward bulkhead. Then he went back to sit with Fred who was actually smoking again.

Just after 1300 Robbie came back from the funnel club and told them they were off the Island. They were not too battered by the past few days to have lost all curiosity for their first sight of foreign land. Managing a little more expertly to move with the ship, they swayed and reeled down to the galley flat.

Going out of the door they were surprised to see that the *Stavanger* had closed up to the starboard quarter, being only 200 yards away. Her signal lamp began to blink as they accommodated themselves in the funnel club and David, mildly exhibitionistic, started to call out the letters to Fred. The early letters did not make sense and subsequently he decided they must have been flags or abbreviations for words or sentences, but the concluding letters, also incomprehensible to them, A - K - U - R - E - Y - R - I, made some sense to a muffled up rating beside them.

'Akureyri,' he said.

'Akureyri?' Fred was puzzled.

'Yes, Akureyri. It's on the north side of the Island. You can get Yankee rabbits there. We were up in September. Reckon we're going there now.'

The two greenhorns did not think to enquire diplomatically as to why gregarious North American mammals were so memorable, for the *Watchful* was turning to port, her curving wake just visible on the foaming slope of the swell. Following suit, at the ten knots the flotilla had only been able to maintain through most of the journey, *Stavanger* slid down the rim of the giant watery hollow. The still shrieking wind was now gusting in from starboard, bringing hard particles of snow that melted as they dashed on the deck near the funnel. As one, the loungers moved over to the port side which was now the lee and, like a fearful apparition, the grim ice-clad ramparts of the north-east of the Island rose up from the tortured main. Sheer cliff walls soared hundreds of feet to disappear in the racing blanket of cloud that flickered every variation of grey over the topmost snowy masses.

Such was the terrible impression of these giant rocks that it was impossible to imagine this could be the home of living human beings. It was easier to feel that in their timeless suffering they had crossed the ancient legendary River Styx to arrive at the dreaded shores of the Underworld, inhabited only by the forlorn spirits of the dead.

The funnel club, mesmerized by the awful prospect, hardly noted the tangle of cable, canvas and splintered wood that had once been the ship's whaler or the motor-cutter knocked askew in its davits. It was not the clamour of the tempest in his ear that David really heard in his tired brain as the ship soared and plummeted, but the powerful strains of the music in his headphones which conceived a mental apparition of a ghastly captain sailing the seas of the dead for ever.

7

Through the later hours of an afternoon hidden too early by the shroud of night, the flotilla pounded its way westward along the north side of the Island. Towards the end of the second dog watch at eight o'clock, the lessening violence of the deck told those below in *Watchful* that calmer water was being reached and when red watch was piped it was not for cruising stations but for entering harbour.

Fred and David, this time joined by George, once again interested in a cigarette, went out to the funnel by the port door to the fo'c's'le. The darkness was not so omnipotent that they could not perceive the darker mass of the sheer cliffs closer at hand. From time to time a lone speck of light suggested that people managed actually to exist on the edge of these inhospitable shores.

The water was now smooth, the air stirred only by the progress of the ship. Thumps, clatters and thin shouts forward indicated preparations for anchoring. A gentle glow from the starboard bow direction began to illuminate the scene, showing up the white cliff walls, the wake of the ship and the following *Stavanger*. Taking advantage of better visibility, they went round the funnel to the other side and saw lights strung like a necklace up the steep slope of the opposite side of the haven they had entered, glittering diamond bright in the bitter air. Lone snowflakes caught the glow as they danced down.

Fascinated they gazed, after four years of blackout, on a town fearless of air attack, with its streets, homes and shops brightly glorious in an uncanny peace. They had forgotten that the Island, in a vital area of sea war, was adamantly and resentfully neutral.

Several merchantmen and warships were silhouetted darkly against the town light, but they passed by as humming machinery signalled the presence of another vessel very close by; then high on the port side, deck lights ablaze, a tanker slowly loomed as the destroyer gently eased alongside.

In the forward mess decks the established hands off duty were grasping every precious minute of stability and peace to achieve all those personal requirements which were battered out of accomplishment during seatime. Coming back to their mess the convalescent trio saw most of the seat cushions up and lockers being rearranged or searched for toilet gear. There were a lot of people about with much the same idea, a shower and shave.

The lockers, damp from seepage and condensation, had not improved their jumbled contents and David spent some time shaking his belongings, folding them and, after wiping the lining of his storage space and letting it dry, rearranged the articles in an order of priority he was learning. He left out a change of underclothes and socks and closed the metal lid. The undergarments were too damp for comfort or health and he sidled over to the electric radiator and as inconspicuously as possible aired them; not that a little steam from his clothes would be noticed in the still clammy atmosphere.

Fred had gone quickly to and from the washplace and cheerily said, 'It's like a poxy rugby scrum down there just now. I'm waiting.'

Determined to see for himself, David went down and looked through the doorway. About fifteen naked bodies, crammed in a space that might have taken five decently, and glistening with soapsuds, stood under apparently scalding water, in rolling clouds of steam. Each washbasin had its incumbent, busy scraping away the growth of several days. The whole lot, under the showers and out, was shouting, laughing, singing, if efforts in the last instance could be honoured with such a description, and making bawdy remarks and gestures, all of which suggested that their morals were a great deal worse than actually was the case. Right in the middle of this disgusting, infernal scene, his voice mirthfully squeaking above the general hilarity, was Eddie, a glossy white-skinned imp conjured up from nether regions in his own cloud of splashing water and vapour.

Back at the mess David agreed with Fred that his observations were not overstated and the sight of Robbie slinging his hammock inspired him to do the same.

'Reckon there'll be divisions tomorrow,' the leading telegraphist called over to him. 'You'd best get your number ones out, squire, and air them.'

'What's special tomorrow then, hookey?' interrupted George, hardly looking up from beside his locker where he fastidiously patted his gear back in place.

'Sunday, mate,' was the reply.

A day of the week, thought David. He had begun to forget that there was a larger pattern to the slow passing of time than a cycle of watches. 'And on the seventh day God ended his work...' Would they be allowed a respite from the buffeting of their metallic purgatory?

'If we're alongside the jetty,' Robbie went on, 'a quick inspection, then back here for psalm bashing.'

Later, when he could get into the washplace and had showered, changed his underclothes and was shaving at a mirror that would stay unmisted only for a few seconds at a time, he ruminated on the fact that less than a week ago, about this time, he had done much the same thing in preparation for the early departure. The divisions in the main barracks that morning had been extremely formal. Everybody had been carefully inspected by the commodore and with a large band playing *Hearts of Oak* and *Middy* they had marched off to the barrack church. Its red-brick architecture did not inspire, and the solemn, tattered battle ensigns hung reproachfully over the heads of some very apprehensive junior ratings.

Before returning to the mess he visited the heads and through the open scuttle, standing at one of the stalls, could see through a larger porthole into the oiler. The bright glimpse he got of spatial luxury in the crew quarters gave him a twinge of envy until reminded of the uneasy cargo the merchantman carried, when he decided it was probably not worth even the substantial bonus money this branch of the mercantile marine was supposed to collect.

Quietness had fallen on the mess deck when he returned and most hammocks were out of the net and slung. Eddie was standing in the entry to the forward mess, talking to a seaman of emaciated appearance who was just about identifiable as the bundle of clothes to be glimpsed generally prostrated when off watch just inside the door. He was well wrapped up in an enormous roll-necked jersey and was still wearing his sea boots and stockings.

Robbie, up by his steam-pipe, was quietly reading to Ginger items from the agony column of a magazine for women. The quiet mirth and comments of the latter suggested that this was a not unusual practice for them and that they read a great deal more between the lines.

David tied his boots to the clews at the head end of his hammock, doubled his inflated lifebelt to use as a pillow, over which he laid his folded trousers. Pulling himself up onto the blanket he wrapped the edges over himself. With the hum of ventilators and the murmur of quiet conversation from other hammocks he sagged bone-weary down below the canvas sides and was swiftly lost to his narrow world.

Several miles away to the north-east Johnny, on the lockers of his mess, lay quietly swearing and trying to keep from falling to the rolling deck. Still fighting sickness, he was cold and even more miserable than he usually felt. It was fortunate that he had not been called upon to excel himself at watchkeeping in his present state. The frequency had continued to be very quiet. The puzzling, erratic changes of course which he had noted on duty in the early evening had been explained by the senior HF-DF telegraphist when he relieved him for the first watch. They were acting guard to the haven entrance, patrolling back and forth to keep any submarines at a distance.

Just their luck, he fumed, after being knocked to hell on the way up. The others would be tucked up very nicely by now, but another night at sea was their own stinking lot. He speculated how long his stomach would be able to take the punishment. His predecessor had finally succumbed to ulcers. Most of those limp bodies, snatching fitful sleep around him, had been with the ship for eighteen months. Their constitutions must be very remarkable; personally he did not think he was capable of lasting the round trip.

There was a casual air of Sunday morning about the mess decks when David awoke considerably refreshed with stiff but rested limbs, a more settled, if tender, stomach and a clearer mind. Fellows were lashing their hammocks and starting to go to the washplace as he hauled himself out. Breakfast had arrived and he quite relished the sausages awash in very fluid tomatoes which the cooks were preparing to serve.

He quickly lashed and stowed his sleeping gear and as he took his place in the line for a washbasin Eddie informed him that there was divisions at 1000 hours. A little signalman, between brushing his teeth, speculated on the possibility that as they were now alongside the jetty, having shifted just after midnight, there might even be a run ashore.

George and Fred had obviously regained their appetites, although still drawn and white, as indeed everybody was, except those whose topside duties reddened and chapped their features. Most had quite recovered their natural ebullience and good-natured banter darted back and forth the length of the table. Robbie supervised the work of the cooks and the meal went forward in a manner that might almost be described as genteel.

After washing up and sweeping and mopping the deck, in which those present lent a hand, everybody began to get into their best uniforms. Much polishing of boots and brushing of cloth went on and as they discarded their diverse working gear the crew began to take on a most formal appearance.

Robbie looked impressive in a suit cut at the front of the jumper and in width of bell bottoms in a faintly exotic fashion which hinted of Kingsway, Valetta or some other more desirable place of service than the present. The good conduct badge, leading rate's hook and second-class telegraphist badge with its three stars all in gold wire, increased the aura of experience, confirmed by the solitary blue and red ribbon with its silver rosette that indicated seatime in the earlier years of the war. The impression was not deceptive. The formal attire was, as had been amply demonstrated in the previous few days, the man. Age in calendar years had no significance here. Older than their messmates by no more than a score or so of months Ginger and he had, their casual youthfulness notwithstanding, grown ancient in their time at sea.

Not having noticed his opposite numbers in camp or depot, it was surprising to see them also in their number ones. George had cautiously edged in the cut of his uniform, made in a material less coarse then the standard issue, towards a low U front to his jumper and wider bell bottoms. A collar, scrubbed to make it appear a venerable light blue, a black silk of an almost feminine texture and sheen endeavoured to complete an effect of considerable service. In spite of the effort made it did not seem really authentic. From somewhere or other he had managed to obtain a gold telegraphist's badge which was slightly larger in size than official.

In contrast, Fred apparently still had the suit thrown across the store counter to him at the first training establishment. A narrow V front to the tunic and modest bell-bottoms, it hung on him loosely and although neatly brushed and clean in his appearance the total effect was far from impressive.

Eddie, specially ordered to divisions, should have been on the forenoon watch. He too was in an outfit of more or less standard issue, but in his case he had made, or had done by somebody else, alterations, so that whereas Fred's stark boniness was hidden in folds, with Eddie the opposite had been achieved. At waist and ample buttock the folds appeared to have been miraculously eased away so that the undulation from the former to the latter was only too obvious. The tightness of his jumper round his shoulders emphasized rather than disguised their sloping narrowness and he contrived to show too much neck, even allowing for the informality of square rig. Both Fred and Eddie had unashamedly dark blue collars, but whereas that of Fred was flat and crinkled to the point of it being doubtful whether it would pass inspection, Eddie's was very neatly ironed into four unnecessarily spectacular folds. Considering he had been as badly laid low as the rest of them he contrived to appear very clear-skinned and fresh compared with the haggard greyness of the others.

As people finished sprucing themselves up they sat or stood around waiting the call to the formalities of the morning. David at the end of the bench, best cap, much the worse for its brief spell in the locker, in hand, sat thoughtfully picking stubborn pieces of fluff from its crown.

At last the order to fall in on shore was given on the loudspeakers and the whole ship's company, except for a skeleton crew of watchkeepers, made their way out and over the gangway onto the wooden jetty. No order had been given for overcoats as rig of the day and most found it extremely chill but the cold expedited the formation of the crew into their divisions, the four new members being hurriedly placed among the communications ratings by Pots. They faced out over the anchorage, the steep white cliffs forming a background to the metallic angularity of their ship, which still pointed up the fiord. The town was at their backs. Called to attention by the first lieutenant, he, assisted by the coxswain, quickly checked the dressing of the ranks. The whole tone set was to get the business over as quickly as was decent and efficient and return to the relative shelter of the destroyer.

Over them the air was covered by racing clouds but the wind down between the high mountains was only moderately fitful, continuing to bring sparse petulant snowflakes reluctantly to the thinly drifting snow on the boards on which the waiting men stood. The tanker was still in the middle distance with an escort vessel both sides. Approaching slowly from the extreme left and waiting its turn to refuel, came the *Obstinate*, modestly, seemingly embarrassed by its weather-beaten appearance, as though it were someone caught in greasy overalls when all around people were in Sunday best.

For a few minutes, which were quite long enough, they were stood at ease and then the captain emerged from the starboard fo'c's'le entry to their right, briskly walked along the iron deck and onto the jetty followed by the heavy, rolling figure of the bo'sun, strange in his number one uniform. The first lieutenant called the ship's company to attention, saluted the captain who reciprocated the compliment, and began his tour of the ranks, pausing to say a brief word to a rating before him or over his shoulder to his following deputy and the two senior members of the lower deck.

As he passed along the sound relay system broadcast a tune which David thought was far from martial and, he suspected, might be from a musical comedy that was vaguely familiar. Its quaint Victorian daintiness was quite at odds with the stark realism of the setting on which the notes quavered thinly.

The bulky form of George to the right of David at the end of the front rank of the communications group attracted the close scrutiny of the captain as he passed by. He paused to ask him a few questions about his training, experience and background and David had an opportunity, out of the corner of his eyes which should have been looking straight ahead, to notice the appearance of the man who up till then had been a remote mystery and in whom paradoxically he had reposed a great deal of confidence. He was of more than medium height but not obviously tall. Probably about thirty, he was rather slightly built, lighter than would seem appropriate for his height. He had a penetrating, but impenetrable grey of eye and under a hat, oddly large for his head, a face waxen of hue, which was surprising, considering he spent as much time above decks as the three ruddy-faced men who followed him. His pallor was emphasised by his hair, which was of that soft yellow-grey which is usually described as ash-blond. He then came to David and asked much the same questions and further down the line stopped to talk to Fred and Eddie.

The short but chilly time they were on the jetty was quite long enough. Whilst they filed back on board David looked back across the waterfront to the town where a few curious locals had stopped, dark figures against the snow-covered street, to watch the divisions. Forward of the destroyer, a liberty ship, large in comparison, was also tied up, and a few of its crew stood near the stern watching the antics of the Navy. Astern, another escort vessel was just about to have its own muster and its crew were being organized in their ranks.

Everybody went into the fo'c's'le and in the communications mess area benches collected from other messes had been arranged fore and aft. Those who were able to do so sat down; the rest stood crowded up to the canteen side. A lane was cleared by the bo'sun through the press and the officers and senior petty officers moved up to the starboard side and sat on the lockers to face the ship's company, putting their hats on the tables before them. It had been impossible to call everybody to attention properly, but as the captain rose to commence the proceedings an expectant hush overcame the slight murmur of the compulsive talkers.

David, never very attentive at devotions, on any occasion, was more interested in the novel manner of the service than its content. The crowded mass of heads and faces, some interested, some obviously bored, longing for stand-easy and a cigarette, others shut up in their own minds, perhaps hundreds of miles away in spirit, but all directed towards the captain as he loudly proclaimed: *When the wicked man turneth away from his wickedness that he hath committed, and doeth that which is lawful and right he shall save his soul alive...*

Fred, leaning against B gun support, stifled a yawn and covertly scratched his back. It was hardly likely that his nervous itch was guilty in origin. George, perched just in front of him on the edge of a form, muscular shoulders roundly hunched, head tucked in, had probably tuned out of the proceedings as they droned on:

...and darkness was upon the face of the deep. And the Spirit of God moved upon the face of the waters...

Too many readings, too many services had made divine worship a largely meaningless ritual, yet somewhere behind it all there must be an ultimate reality, a design, or so they had been led to believe from infancy.

The coxswain was reading a lesson. He was a shortish, slightly framed, dapper man, lean and leathery of face, somewhere in his late thirties, with still very dark, smooth, well-brilliantined hair. He had an air of tightly controlled explosiveness. He piped through his nostrils rather than spoke through his mouth

The same day went Jesus out of the house and sat by the seaside. And great multitudes were gathered together unto him, so that he went into a ship and sat; and the whole multitude stood on the shore.

And he spake many things unto them in parables, saying, Behold a sower went forth to sow...

David's legs were beginning to ache. He was still very much aware of the beating his body had taken in the past few days, but then was vaguely comforted by the prospect of dinner. It brought to mind Sunday dinner at home, even on rations, but it was not very nostalgic; there was a real blockage between that life and now. His thoughts were quite objective, passing recollections without feeling, people and places, coming and going, the indifferent images of boredom.

But now the captain was standing again and the familiar words of the Navy's own prayer he spoke, thrilled away David's ennui, with a significance he had missed ashore, although their poetry had not gone unnoticed then:

...Lord God, who alone spreadest out the heavens, and rulest the raging of the sea; who hast compassed the water with bounds until day and night come to an end; be pleased to receive into thy Almighty and most gracious protection the persons of us thy servants, and the Fleet in which we serve...

Surely the people who first approved these lines knew the sea themselves as well as the seafarers they were supposed to comfort. He never could hear them, without being spirited back to the olden days when their colourful, short-lived forebears, amoral but devout, grasped at a few sentences to ease the combat of great odds against elements and foe.

...Preserve us from the dangers of the sea, and from the violence of the enemy; that we may be a safeguard unto our most gracious Sovereign Lord King George, and his Dominions, and a security for such as pass on the seas upon their lawful occasions...

He wondered if the convoy they had heard embattled had got out of danger: *...and that we may return in safety to enjoy the blessings of the land, with the fruits of our labours, and with a thankful remembrance of thy mercies to praise and glorify thy Holy Name; through Jesus Christ our Lord.'* Amen, they said. These last sentiments were ones of which he whole-heartedly approved and produced his most emphatic and aware response in the course of the proceedings.

At the end of the service the captain announced there would be shore leave for as many as could be spared and this enlivened and cheered the messes at their dinner. Eddie, it was revealed, had high church tastes but had been charmed by the unusual setting of their morning ceremony and said as much, to the evident disgust of George who, it was surprising to learn, had ill-formed opinions of a generally atheistic nature. They were a surprise for it might have been thought that a countryman, a provincial, might have been expected to have a reverence for creation that debased city-dwellers could have lost. It was not a good difference of opinion to the other diners, for George was a lightweight in debate and Eddie, after at first making rings round his opponent, from sheer generosity, or – quite unlikely – from fear of a black eye, eased out of the discussion. Meecham obviously preferred to charm rather than antagonize his messmates.

His discomfiture had evidently been forgotten by George, however, when he joined his opposite numbers on the way along the iron deck, across the jetty and out onto the street. They felt the ground move giddily under them and exchanging remarks about it realized they were doing the rolling and that, in a few days, they had acquired the traditional reeling gait of the sailor ashore.

To eyes accustomed to years of blacked-out towns the main street, littered with electric cable and telephone posts as well as lamp standards, seemed as bright as full daylight although the long and early northern dusk had set in. There were a few cars of American manufacture to be seen cautiously moving over a roadway surface of packed snow.

With other libertymen the trio moved along on sidewalks swept clear of snow and ice in front of business premises and shops and gradually the crowd thinned as individuals and small groups went their own way in sidestreets. Several of the byways at right angles to the main thoroughfare were well lit, and occasional lights, placed even on the bleak bare slopes of the outskirts, were visible from the centre. By the standards of more densely populated lands it would be correct to say the town was no more than a large village, but shopping amenities seemed out of proportion to its size. Whether this was owing to a wartime boom or to being the only emporium in the vast emptiness of the northern side of the Island, was unknown to the visitors. Yet they considered there was more of a North American flavour to the place than a European one. Most of the houses were of a brown painted wood with white door and window frames, and the articles for sale in the shops were mainly of transatlantic origin. This was quite understandable with the Continent cut off by hostilities and their own embattled island having little to export in the way of luxury articles. The seamen, therefore, naturally took advantage of shore leave at this aggressively neutral port to buy things unavailable or scarce at home.

New nylon stockings were only a rumour to their womenfolk, and this was what mostly they bought, although, no doubt, some would find their way into the hands of traders in all kinds of scarce commodities at home. George was to the forefront in the haberdashers and it was to be wondered how he could buy so many on his meagre pay; but then there was always a moderate air of affluence about him as though a multitude of rural uncles and aunts saw that he did not go short.

They had climbed well up the slope of the main street in their stroll and although it was cold, somehow amongst the lights it seemed less harsh and for a time their purpose in this remote land was forgotten, but as they saw they had reached the town limits and all beyond was a murky grey wilderness, they turned and as they descended saw below them the fiord and the lights of the shipping and winking signal lamps.

Pausing to cross the slippery surface of the roadway they were attracted by a shout from the side street, on the corner of which they stood. It was Johnny, they rather tardily recognized, for his narrow features seemed even more drawn and peaky.

'Christ!' he exploded. 'You're still standing then!'

'You don't look too brilliant yourself,' growled George, probably not caring to be reminded of his time of humiliation.

'Is it nice on your lot, Johnny?' Fred asked, the grin furrows asserting themselves around his mouth as though he thought the whole business was a ghastly joke.

'It's effing grim, chum. Effing grim. You know,' Johnny complained. 'It's like that chief crusher said. She really does roll like a bastard. One of these days it'll tip right over. Mark my words.'

'Yes, it must be dodgy,' admitted George magnanimously, 'the way you dropped back like. Still it wasn't happy for us either.'

'Were you sick?' Johnny eyed them hopefully.

'We all were,' Fred informed him, as though it were the height of fashion, 'even some of the old hands.'

This last seemed to make the matter respectable. 'Were you?' he enquired of Johnny.

'Like a bloody dog, and trying to keep watch at the same time,' was his frank reply.

'We haven't started round the clock yet,' David put in. 'We're still daymen.'

'Lucky sods!' Johnny's envy was forthright. 'What are you supposed to be doing then?'

'That,' George mumbled, 'is a mystery to everyone.'

By now Fred was very cold and still looking weak from their common ordeal, so he suggested going into a milk bar they had passed on the way up. Their brief hours away from the metallic nightmare of the destroyer were already much wasted and they hoped for warm drink that would help their recuperating stomachs.

They came to the misted windows of the café and George led the way. Inside the damp warmth was pleasant and Fred generously ordered creamy coffees from a far from welcoming assistant. Near the door a small group of merchant seamen, rather a curious sight in their wide range of civilian apparel, were laughing and joking loudly in a cloud of smoke.

The naval ratings took their drinks to a corner table far from the door and by the window and sat down wearily. By the counter a fine specimen of nordic womanhood, tall, blonde and clad in the most attractive fur coat and hat, sat on a high stool, drinking a milk shake and chatting to the sullen attendant. Resplendent in his immaculate white overall and white forage cap, he muttered something to her and she looked in their direction. Being considerably sea-battered, they were not in any state to take an active interest in such a remarkable creature and could only admire her fair attributes in an objective sort of way.

David revelled in the relative peace of it all and was aware again of the curious relaxed sensation of his body conditioned to the motion of a ship. His chair seemed to be heaving as though alive, but it eased rather than agitated his mind. The door opened and a stocky, wrapped-up figure of an Islander entered with a blast of cold air. He joined the conversing pair at the counter for a hot drink and was soon casting looks far from amiable in not only their direction but that of the merchant seamen as well.

George consulted his watch and said it was time to go. Collecting up their packets they went to the door and were about to go out when the daughter of Norsemen said, 'Yes, go; the U-boats for you are waiting.'

The other two Islanders burst into laughter, which stopped Johnny in his tracks, causing the others to pile up in the doorway, and nettled to the point of aggression he shouted, hoping for a reaction which did not materialize, 'Yes and it's a pity they didn't occupy this bastard hole in 1940 too!'

During this disturbance the merchant seamen broke off their conversation and started to get up quickly. David had turned back too, angered by the remark, but the foremost seaman came up to him and said quietly, 'All right, mate, get your chum out of it, you're in uniform. We'll set these bastards right, it won't be the first time.'

Fred and George, fearing an impending uproar, pushed Johnny out on to the inhospitable pavement of a self-righteous and insular town.

David felt warmer than he had for sometime as they trudged down the hill. The libertymen were gathering once more into little groups and making their way on board the ships alongside or to various liberty boats awaiting them. They went and saw Johnny off in his boat, for the *Obstinate* was still in the middle of the anchorage, and walked along to their own gangway. The pattern of town lights had lost the welcoming mystery of yesterday. Now they were merely an amenity, not a symbol of hopeful days to come. Spite could flourish just as well in a lit world as in the darkened mass of the Continent. There was, apparently, no escape from the ingrained, pointless malice of the human race.

Once on board the oil and fume reeking fighting machine, in whose crowded nooks they found the totality of their world, they collected their station cards and were making their way forward past the wireless office, when Pots looked out of the doorway and called 'Wait a minute!' The tone of urgency stopped them abruptly and they went inside. The red-cheeked telegraphist, whose name they had learnt was Rowe, was busy with the

Admiralty at the far end, the steadily nagging Morse providing a demoralizing threnody to the turn of the conversation. The oldest coder, relaxed from his charts, watched in anticipation, probably hoping for a little diversion from the tedium of his watch but not wishing to appear too interested.

'Yes, Pots?' enquired George.

'Where've you lot been?' demanded the petty officer telegraphist, in a tone which suggested he asked more in sorrow than anger, and which he answered for himself. 'Who said you all could go ashore? The flotilla huff-duff subby came over specially to see you.'

A visit from the person responsible for the whole of the intelligence work throughout the group of escorts was an honour that they were perfectly willing to forego, especially as their value as naval operators was considerably in doubt after the past few days. Furthermore, for David anyway, there were growing misgivings as to the amount of knowledge still remaining after weeks of waiting at the signals camp and drafting barracks. However, they perceived the situation and hoped for the best and prepared for the worst.

'Who said you could all go ashore?' reiterated their superior. 'Do you think you can walk off at any time?' In his outraged earnestness he looked touchingly younger. Half a dozen years had dropped from him and perhaps it was to some extent caused by the higher pitch of indignation in his voice.

'Who's blue watch?' he demanded.

'I am, Pots,' George reluctantly confessed.

'Blue watch, laddie, is duty watch. It's about time you knew the Andrew's routine.'

'We weren't watchkeeping and the others said it was all right,' said George morosely, some feeling emerging from his rustic phlegm.

David hoped he was not suspected of leading George astray, but thankfully saw that Pots had weightier things on his mind.

'Anyway, enough of this argy-bargy, lad,' said he, reverting to his usual urbane self. 'Next time always clear with me before doing anything daft.'

Whether he would permit them to do anything daft was not

clarified. 'Here is an envelope from the subby.' He thrust it into Fred's hand. 'They are your duties until further notice,' he concluded.

Fred looked down at the small buff rectangle thoughtfully, as though dubious of its safety, perhaps suspecting it of explosive properties.

'Well, open it you big nit,' urged George, fully coming into the round as a concerned being.

Slowly Fred ripped the top edge with a bony thumb and pulled out a folded piece of signal paper. The coder peered round the petty officer; Rowe removed the headphone from his nearer ear and leaned over from his seat. The standing four were close together in the middle of the office, all eyes down on the unfolding paper. The thin hands shook as he read painstakingly in a quivering voice: 'From 1800 hours this day, a watch to be kept on a frequency of so and so kilocycles with usual changes of waveband from hand book as required. All enemy transmissions, unit and shore to be carefully taken and UNUSUAL PREAMBLES PASSED TO ESCORT COMMANDER. Where possible bearings to be recorded. This until further notice, etc.'

'What does that mean exactly?' asked Pots.

'I don't know, I can't remember offhand, it'll be in the book,' said Fred.

'I do,' said David, surprised at his memory producing anything worthwhile at all. 'It's the Arctic Series.'

'Christ,' moaned Fred, 'the Norwegian coast.'

'Eff me,' murmured George.

'We were up there in August.' Pots sounded as though he was protesting. The coder gasped inarticulately. Rowe, diminished, sank back to his Admiralties.

They felt drastically in need of relief and paid a communal but brief visit to the heads. When they arrived back on the communications' mess deck they were assailed with questions as they attempted to pack away overcoats and purchases.

'Is it true?' everybody asked. 'Is the buzz correct?'

'What buzz?' asked Fred.

'That we're going to Russia,' someone said.

'It looks,' he answered cautiously, 'bloody well like it.'

8

A barrage of outspoken remarks of extraordinary variety confirmed the three telegraphists in no doubt whatever as to the sentiments of the crew on hearing their likely destination. Indeed, not directly, but by unthinking innuendo, it might seem they were considered a sort of multiple Jonah, but this embarrassment was quickly gone if any of the others had even been aware of the effect of their comments.

As it was, between tea and supper, the preparations for leaving harbour involved so many people that their probable destination was forgotten in the innumerable and complicated tasks to hand.

At 1800 hours David went along to the office and tuned in to the required frequency and found that all was very quiet, the routine transmissions being rather distant compared with U-boat control but quite readable. He pondered on what could be so special in this area that was not covered by HF-DF anyway, and required the instant attention of the escort commander. However, it was a comfortable beginning to watchkeeping and they at last fitted properly into the routine with their shipmates.

Beside him Eddie was kept moderately busy, but had a fair amount of time for comments on their run ashore. He had been very enterprising in purchases he had made and he inferred it was important to keep on the good side of his aunt. It was an interesting thought to consider what the police at the dockyard gate or the customs would think of his colourful goods if by chance he should be stopped and asked to open his case. Unlike most of his contemporaries he had travelled on the Continent before the outbreak of war, perhaps rather young to appreciate it at the time. His reminiscences enticed Ginger, not too involved in his clerical and supervisory duties, into talking about his days in the Mediterranean.

He and Robbie had been together on and off since their training days and had had much the same experience. David was left with the impression that his time between Gibraltar and Alexandria had given Ginger a conflicting and turbulent collection of memories with which to come to terms. He spoke easily of golden days and balmy nights ashore and some off his remarks about the bizarre customs of local inhabitants as seen by sailors or involving them, were droll. Yet sometimes unuttered thoughts momentarily glimpsed in a strained expression caused him to stammer, before going on to something more agreeable.

Towards the end of the second dog watch, increased activity – people moving and voices – outside the office door told them departure was imminent and soon after, blue watch was called. George came in to take over and his intimation that they were on the move was not really necessary. A slight vibration of deck and bench told them the engines were stirring.

David collected his duffel coat and went down to the funnel. They had cleared the jetty and were well out in mid-channel, slowly turning towards the exit. The wreckage of the whaler had, of course, been cleared and from near the motor boat, stowed securely again, he watched the passing town lights in the distance. Now they represented not an exotic landfall but a dreary outpost of provincial boredom. A slight turn in the fiord and they went out of sight and very soon after, as the throbbing engines pushed up the speed of the ship, even the glow on adjacent snowy cliffs had disappeared.

Remembering he was on duty at 0400 hours for the morning watch he went forward over a deck that was beginning to heave and prepared to turn in. The other white watch ratings were the last to sling their hammocks. Doing this, he noticed Fred reading a film magazine. He accidentally bumped his hammock and Fred, jarred from his escapism, said confidentially, 'I wish I was up homers.'

'Don't we all chum,' grunted David, experiencing a faint sneaky feeling of humbug as he thumped his mattress and blanket into an acceptable arrangement.

'No, I mean, Dave,' his opposite number went on, 'next week.'

'Oh? Why? What's so special about next week?' David hauled himself up, at expense of further disturbance to Fred's bedgear. 'Have you got a date with a party?' An unlikely thought was this.

'No,' said Fred wryly. 'There's a bloody good musical on at the Regal.'

David was slowly roused from slumbers, which he was discovering were far more deep than anything experienced on land, to that liverish state of hatefulness of the small hours. The bo'sun's mate was making his blundering way under hammocks, calling white watch to cruising stations, while fellows were turning out onto the cold and lively deck to lash up and stow.

The morning watch was, he was finding out, if anything a more disagreeable time than expected. Four o'clock in the morning, the time of least physical resistance, the time when death frequently claimed its own, was a strain on the senses. No matter the civilized apportionment of night and day did not exist at these dark latitudes, the biological clock, ticking on, put an extra burden on the tired watchkeeper. With a dry mouth and a strange dragging sensation at his face and neck muscles, and a woolly, half-asleep brain, he tottered down to the office.

In his chair, with enough reading matter for a library, Fred had combated the drowsiness of the middle watch. It had been quiet, only the routines on the hour. David, apprehending it was likely to be the same in his spell, the main problem being to remain awake, decided to write a letter. Like Johnny it was not a strong point with him, but for other reasons than mere disinclination. If he wrote about personal things he did not care to have somebody, the censor, probably a member of the ship's wardroom, sharing his intimacies. On the other hand it was obvious he could not write about the ship's activities or his own, in the former instance because it would have been blue-pencilled and in the latter as it could so easily seem like self-indulgence. The substance of a letter, then, would be very thin and barely worth recording. Still, the drafting of even a letter of such uninteresting content kept him awake until Eddie went and made the cocoa.

Soon after 0800 hours George rather grumpily came and relieved him and he went back to a simple breakfast of tea and toast. By now the *Watchful* was bucking and shuddering well up to the old style in violence. Those who were able to help, among which number, David was amazed and delighted to find himself, tidied up the area. Ginger then set himself to prepare a stew that he called a pot mess. He got all the ingredients into a metal dixie and staggered off down to the galley.

The next task in hand was preparation of the mid-morning hot drink. All the mugs had been arranged on the table and a jug placed ready, then an almighty crash above the general rattling, thumping and humming of the storm-battered vessel indicated that a large amount of the mess crockery and cutlery had got loose from the locker and cascaded onto the deck. Knives, forks, spoons and bits of plates shot in all directions. One dinner plate marvellously unbroken rolled across to the hammock net, spun a few times and settled base upwards.

Most present began cleaning up the debris and Robbie bent down by the locker and sighed, 'Roll on the Rodney, Nelson, Renown...' and was capped by Ginger leaning against the forward bulkhead, gathering fragments with a dustpan and brush, saying, 'This one-funnelled bastard is getting me down.'

It was some time-honoured cathartic ritual between them for they both burst into laughter which took the frustration out of the others present.

Robbie said with a resigned air, mainly to himself, 'I wonder sometimes how I get through to tot time.' It was an interesting thought that there were only four in the communications mess eligible for the daily issue of rum.

Just before dinner Fred, who was again not very well, and David went down to join the funnel club. Taut and queasy though the former looked and admitted to be, it was evident that he too was not going to succumb totally, as before, to seasickness. He was not comfortable, but then there was no comfort for anybody on this steel-walled bedlam. He was quite well enough to smoke and offered a cigarette to the thin-faced stoker David had met before.

There were still the giant, saucer-shaped troughs and crests, and although the wind was howling steadily it was not forceful enough to beat lesser billows into the depressions of the great waves. The destroyer majestically tipped and dipped up and down the watery slopes of a sea pulverized to a fizzing milky green.

Beyond the ensign, more shredded than ever, the stern housing ascended to the sullen snow-laden grey overcast or descended to a foaming mound of salt water. Moving generally eastward, they were not in formation with other warships, but far to the south-east a two-funnelled destroyer, possibly the *Masai*, tiny on the horizon, was dark against the weak glow of an unseen sun. South and west, which were usually on the starboard quarter, the terrible ramparts of white headlands, shrouded in low cloud, passed by one after the other. Closer towards them, dwarfed into toy-like shapes by the mighty rocks, cargo vessels, scattered by the storm, were struggling east. The wind continued steadily from the north-west and a quick glimpse out of the protection of the funnel revealed the great ridges of water rolling down on them out of a dark grey vagueness where sea mingled with sky. A point of light, flashing, indicated another vessel somewhere in that sinister murk.

The remaining hours of poor daylight were spent, as indeed had been the dark hours, in searching waters adjacent to the Island for merchantmen of a convoy scattered by high seas. An occasional visit to the iron deck showed much the same picture. Distant escorts, sometimes blinking secret lights, and freighters being informed of the rendezvous, acknowledging briefly, then turning to plough along sluggishly on an easterly course.

During this time primary considerations were not of human foes but of the battle with natural forces. Life aboard the tossing ship descended to that of mere existence, where a desire to conserve essential body heat, a wish to avoid injury from some butting piece of malicious wood or metal and a need for food and drink to keep at bay a persistent damp cheerlessness were uppermost. For ratings employed below, however, there was not the additional tribulation of the freezing wind and wet discomfort suffered by those at cruising stations topside. With the exception of the seaman, still sprawled out when off duty in the mess forward, most had now come to terms with, or conquered their sickness, and could doubtless take the worst the ocean had to offer.

So into the second long night they passed, in the blackness continuing the search with the electronic eye of radar. The signalmen, damply chilled to the bone in spite of phenomenal layers of clothing, tottered down from the bridge and told the others it was all very much routine; looking for strays and telling them to go to Seydis Fiord.

Seydis Fiord, a place of ill omen to the experienced, was a long narrow inlet on the east coast of the Island. It pointed north-east. There was no escaping the implications. It was a favourite starting point for convoys to Russia. Here ships could be collected from transatlantic convoys bringing American war supplies and arranged with others from home, laden with hardly spared military aid. Here last minute repairs, victualling arrangements and conferences took place.

During the middle watch, not a busy one as far as David was concerned, he had to resort to the device of standing up to avoid falling asleep. Ginger, Eddie and the ordinary telegraphist were just busy enough to keep them awake. The quiet rushing sound of static was hypnotic and as the hands of the clock crept intolerably slowly round each sixty minutes he was afraid of not logging the hourly routine, which was an indication, by serial numbers, of any traffic missed or unheard. Ginger was amused by this expedient. About cocoa time he became interested in the work of the special telegraphists.

'What are you supposed to be doing, Dave?' he enquired.

'Listening to an area which both subs and surface units off Norway use,' David explained.

'Why?' the senior hand persisted. 'You don't seem very busy and the HF-DF is covering us here anyway.'

'No, it's a mystery,' admitted David, 'but I expect there's some reason for it. They wouldn't waste time or money on it otherwise, would they?'

This youthful trust in the omniscience of the civil and naval authorities was not shared by his young, old too soon, superior. 'Wouldn't they, squire?' he questioned cynically.

Towards the end of the watch the sea motion abated, suggesting the approach of sheltered waters, and it so happened that by six o'clock they were entering Seydis Fiord. Of this David was unaware for he was stretched out on the lockers, blissfully surrendered to sleep at last. His rest, deep but not long or refreshing was ended at eight o'olock by the clatter of capstan and motors that indicated mooring was in process. With the muting of sea noises, those sounds in the ship, people stirring, hammocks being taken down, breakfast being prepared and the ever humming vents brought him up to a strained, glandular wakefulness.

Up to the forenoon stand-easy, all those off watch, and this was the greater part of the ship's company, were busy with those tasks of cleaning themselves, the living and working areas, repairing or securing equipment that went by default when in a heavy seaway and tiring continuous watchkeeping. The TS was shut down and so were most other operational parts of the ship but for the communication ratings, except the HF-DF operators, it was business as usual, with watches in the office and on the bridge.

That peculiar air of levity which pervaded the mess decks in these respites from the grinding weariness of seatime began to increase as the morning progressed. During stand-easy the canteen was opened and with a background of cacophonic music from the General Overseas Programme the Forces' Programme had faded with distance; the whole flat became a place of social intercourse. A popular topic of conversation was the run ashore in Akureyri. David backed away, with chocolate and soap, from the scrimmage at the canteen window and found himself crowded against the bulkhead door beside which Eddie was chatting to his acquaintance, the seaman-gunner. They were exchanging comments on mal-de-mer. Eddie mentioned his predecessor, the man who had developed stomach ulcers.

'Lucky bugger,' exclaimed the cadaverous seaman with surprising envy. 'Three months on this gash bucket and he's put ashore. Me? I've been sick every trip for bloody years. Never get a battlewagon, except for a stretch at Whale Island, always these little bastards. Somewhere somebody hates me.' Almost plaintively, he speculated, 'Why don't I get ulcers?'

Eddie was horrified by this revelation. 'Why don't you go sick?' he clucked solicitously.

'I have,' said the unhappy seaman, 'even went for a medical. Trouble is, a day or two ashore and the quacks can't find anything permanently wrong with me. Roll on my effing doz.'

Having had a few days of it, David was astounded that anybody could have put up with it so long without becoming a complete physical wreck. Yet here was upright evidence of what the human organism could take.

Over at the table Ginger was superintending the making of coffee; he had had the enterprise to buy in Akureyri, to relieve the monotony of tea and cocoa.

'You been talking to Scouse Edwards?' he observed. 'Quite took our Eddie under his wing an't he?' He was not impressed by David's comment on his perennial sickness.

'Half his imagination, I should bloody well think,' he said inconsiderately. 'Always was a bit of a dripper.'

His junior did not care to question such dogmatic assertions but thought that if it were a case of mind over matter, it did a first rate job of demolishing a strong young man into a bundle of miserable clothes every time they went to sea.

After stand-easy George, Eddie and David cleaned the wireless office – 'shamfering' Pots had quaintly described it – washing the linoleum floor and dusting and wiping paintwork and furniture. Fred, on watch, sat knees up on the bench, giving unwelcome advice and George nearly kicked the bucket over twice and managed to stand on the soap once. Otherwise the job was so much to the satisfaction of Pots that before eleven o'clock he told them to get lost but not to stand around looking idle. David got his duffel coat and went out the break of the fo'c's'le.

On the port side they were tied to a supply ship and bundles and boxes were being dumped down by the aft torpedo tubes and – to the accompaniment of repartee and snatches of song – carried away by seamen for stowage. The interesting two-funnelled shape of the *Masai* was tied up to their starboard side and all three ships were pointing up the fiord away from the entrance. It occurred to David that he had not yet been on the fo'c's'le and he went up the ladderway by the break, then under the arch formed by the Oerlikon platform above and the life rafts on the outer side. These latter were secured in an almost vertical position to the girder supports of the bridge works. The metal door to the petty officers' mess situated abaft A gun and below B gun was open and clipped back. The place was being cleaned and aired.

Several upper deck men were scrubbing down paintwork and touching up places where rust was beginning to leave its brown streaky marks. These sailors too, like the storage party, did not work silently but with a staccato commentary on each other, other crew members, the Navy and any other person or thing which became the object of their cheerful ire or ridicule. It might have been a means of keeping the chill atmosphere out of their minds as well as bodies. Not only did the icy gusting breeze impose upon them but the unfriendly cliffs around them did too.

Up among the anchor chains, hawsers and capstans near the bows three artificers in oil and rust-grimed overalls were engrossed in some noisy hammering of metalwork. Beyond them, far up the anchorage, against a backcloth of spectacular snowy mountains, there were three cruisers. Two of them were three-funnelled and one of more recent construction had two. The *Northumberland*, for which Eddie had been destined, was one of the three-funnelled ships.

David thought that he had better not go too far forward and come under the critical eye of the bridge and, turning to go back to the ladder, encountered the bo'sun coming out of the doorway to knock the dust and particles from a large green canvas-covered suitcase over the side. He had noticed David looking at the cruisers. 'They're the covering force,' he said without elaborating on the matter.

Going down the ladder, David was now intrigued by the different layout of the *Masai* and, seeing a gangway connecting them and people casually coming and going, was moved to go across and explore. Its unfamiliar arrangement seemed more of a clutter than the *Watchful*. An earlier class than his own ship, *Masai* had probably to improvise when later models of armament and equipment were installed, whereas *Watchful* had been built with most of its equipment already in the mind of the designers.

He found his way to the starboard side to look across to the shore of the fiord. Here and there were jetties and Nissen huts behind them, each perhaps with a particular function. Alongside some there were merchant ships or escorts and others lay at anchor up and down the length of the stretch of water. The perpetual flashing continued and motor cutters moved back and forth everywhere. Quite close a big liberty ship eased to a standstill and a small, rusty-red cloud rose from its bows as the anchor splashed into the water. The rattling roar of the anchor chain came across an instant later.

Most of the merchant ships were of this type. A high, slightly curved freeboard, above which a low superstructure and squat funnel amidships or at the stern was the main shape, but the most distinctive feature of them were the short masts, usually four in number, to which were fitted elaborate deck cranes or derricks. It was presumed that these were required for the unloading of cargo in remote corners of the world to which the war had spread, where there were no dock facilities. Moreover, there were other places where docks and harbours could have been pounded into rubble and mangled metal. Another well known but dubious feature of these wartime vessels was that they had welded plates for speed of construction and a reputation for cracking at the seams in violent weather. The least agreeable rumour about them was that the authorities considered they had paid their way if they had done one voyage to a war zone.

Whilst he pondered and prowled around, a shrill whistle from forward startled him into looking up in wonder to see who had the nerve to break the naval taboo, let alone do it in the vicinity of the bridge. On the starboard side of the flag deck a muffled figure beckoned with a gloved hand.

'Fres,' the figure called, 'Dave Freston, here!' Puzzled and intrigued to know who knew him on the *Masai* he came down the iron deck and saw the same figure encouraging him up.

He went up the ladder from the main to the fo'c's'le deck. Then mounted the next ladder up past the Oerlikon platform and emerged slowly on the flag deck to see a familiarly cheerful face beaming roundly at him from under the dark halo of a brown fur hat. The ruddy, healthily glowing features of Signalman Spencer were just as he had last seen them in the hut at the signals camp. He had always called him, as everybody did, Spence, but thought of him as Old Spence, although he was still a blithe twenty-five or thereabouts.

'Well old bean,' Spencer enquired, enthusiastically shaking David's hand before he had pulled himself upright off the rungs of the ladder, 'how did they manage to get you out of the luxury of Hut D11 into this posterior of the universe?' It was his way of saying something that was, in other words, general naval coinage.

'A fortnight after you disappeared,' David explained, 'when I was on a Friday while, there was a regular epidemic of drafts. Pop Reeves the coder went for his cypher commission and that happy chap, whatisname, in the top corner bunk by the door went to an escort carrier, the *Vercingetorix*, I think it was.'

'Oh yes, I remember, the one who was always dripping about his wife's infidelities.'

'Well, anyway,' continued David, 'there were plenty of others, a real clear out. I got the *Watchful* and a great shock it is.'

'No doubt about it, old man,' Spencer agreed. 'After four months' delight in the fleshpots of Town it was bit of a shock for me.' Unsaid, but inferred, was the fact that before that well-earned rest he had in camp there had been a hard eighteen months rolling on the North Atlantic in a corvette until the commission was brought to an end abruptly by a torpedo.

'And how are the ladies of the Royal Forest Hotel?' David asked. For this was a subject which had brought the greatest interest and hilarity to the conversation round the red hot stove, roasting chestnuts collected from trees among which the camp was situated, as they passed the autumn duty nights in camp.

'All in tears when I was on draft leave,' Spencer told him. 'Didn't know what they were going to do without my weekend visits. There'll be many a forlorn grass widow this winter I fear.' Although he spoke flippantly, David really believed they would miss him in the Royal Forest. One wet and blustery October evening when half a dozen of the hut inmates had been gathered round the stove, which was roaring cosily on an abundance of fuel obtained by questionable methods over and above the official ration, one of his fellow signalmen, an individual whose person was as unkempt as his mind seemed to be, jeeringly enquired as to whom the old bag was he had seen Spencer with in the lounge bar of the Royal Forest Hotel on the previous Saturday night.

'The lady, to whom you disagreeably refer as an old bag,' he had answered with dignity, 'is a very great friend of mine, mature though she may be, whose husband is misguidedly serving his country somewhere in Italy. Who am I to deny her a little comfort in her dull colourless existence?'

Of a truth, he made it seem he was obliging his lady friends with a service and probably this was no exercise in vanity but the sober truth. His candour disarmed his hut mates, as it most likely did the ladies, and probably it was as much the way he expressed things as the facts themselves which made him so entertaining. In the course of long conversations up to lights out, he weaved his way with dexterity through a maze of dogmatic assertions that passed for argument on the part of most members of the group in a manner which educated and informed David not only in the ways of women but other affairs as well.

Pop Reeves, sedately puffing at his pipe, often quietly chided him when the subject was Spencer's amorous gymnastics, with the proposition that he should marry and settle down. This was usually met by a cheerful exposition of the snares of domestic life, based perhaps on his experience before the war when Spencer had been for a time an insurance salesman. One could not help wondering whether access to homes at all times and of all conditions had not given him rather a distorted impression of the pleasures of the hearth. Somehow David recognized, presented in Spencer's inimitable bantering spirit, certain observations he had read before in the interesting works of socially reforming authors writing at the turn of the century.

That Spencer was under-extended for his education there was no doubt. For three years he had remained steadfastly a plain signalman. He went to a great number of clever dodges to avoid courses or situations that could end in his being upgraded to leading rate. The bald fact was he would have made an excellent officer and that some called him Baron was as much a mark of the respect his fellows had for him as for the mysterious affluence that permitted him to travel to Town two weekends out of four.

When tackled about his apparent lack of initiative by Pop Reeves, who disapproved of his refusing responsibility, he had riposted with a surprising and ingenious argument.

'As I am now,' he had elaborated, 'I am a nobody. The war, the politics of it, do not concern me. I had no part in the making of it by default, being too young, and I see it now only as a gigantic aberration of the human race which drags down everybody willy-nilly. If I went up for a CW course and was commissioned, it would put me in the responsible class, not only technically but morally, for whereas now I can say I am only an insignificant cog in the war machine, then I would become a wager of war. I'd be morally responsible.'

'But you have a duty to do your best,' remonstrated Pop Reeves, the only one in the circle able to rise to Spencer's reasoned dissertation. Perhaps the thought of his own impending elevation to the upper deck laid uncomfortably on his mind.

'My duty is to my lady friends,' grinned Spencer evasively. 'If I took authority it would be to approve of all this futility.'

Now these unpatriotic sentiments surprised David, coming as they did from a person of so impeccably middle-class a background and district as Spencer. He was not sure, but they sounded rather subversive. Also he would have liked to know what Spencer considered a purpose in life. By this time people with a purpose, certain vociferous citizenry, approved heartily of the war. From an imperialist one it had become overnight a People's Patriotic War. He was reminded in particular of the time when an agitator with whom he had worked turned his war-opinion back to front one fine June day when Russia was invaded.

Of course, when tackled by senior ratings or officers, Spencer was more devious. Once, when down in the regulating office, where he was on duty as commander's messenger, David heard a gruff, commissioned, one-time yeoman of signals try, in turns, to bully and cajole him to take the third class signalman's course. Spencer was like a butler in his respectful demeanour, but adamant in declining these studies for promotion. His argument was simple and unanswerable and probably quite true. He explained modestly that he had private means, that his salary was made up by his company and that more pay would mean much more tax. Those nebulous currencies, duty and honour, faded before one so commonly understood, namely, hard cash.

'And you, Fres, how did you spend your draft leave?' Spencer broke into his fleeting memories.

'Oh, nothing much. Visited some relations, friends; took a girl out a few times, nothing special,' David told him.

'Not even a small port, old man?'

This was a reference to David's rather undeveloped drinking habits, which were something of a joke in the hut.

'One or two. A lady of my acquaintance nearly knocked me out with some of her home-made parsnip wine.'

'Some lady! Deadly stuff, old bean, you really should develop civilized boozing habits.'

Spencer broke off to peer round the anchorage for signals and, having satisfied himself there was not a clamour for *Masai* turned back reminded of their purpose in that place.

'Where are we taking this little lot then?' he enquired. 'Obviously they go somewhere from here.'

'I'm surprised you don't know,' David said. 'Have you looked at a map?'

'Not lately, Fres, not my kind of thing old lad. Why?'

'Well, one of the chaps in my mess has got one of those newspaper war maps and marks everywhere he goes on it. This neck of water points right in one direction, north-east. And that's not all. It's a wonder the buzz hasn't got around to you. We're listening to the Arctic Series. So one and one make two.'

A shadow flickered across Spencer's gentle countenance and after a pause, a little tersely he said, 'It'll be most enjoyable, I think.'

Somewhere on the bridge a telephone squealed and a seaman peered round the fire-director tower and called out, 'Bunts, the skipper's coming back on board.'

'You'd better be going, old bean, he's been nattering to your skipper,' Spence said, 'There'll be hell to pay if you're caught up here passing the time o' day with me. They'll be taking the plank away soon.'

'Cheerio, Spence,' said David, hurriedly starting to go down the ladder. 'Give my regards to the ladies.'

Spencer leaned down through the entry to the flag deck and said loudly, 'Listen, Fres, call me up. If we ever get leave together I'll complete your education at the Royal Forest, OK?'

David looked up, grinned and said, 'Righto, Spence, it's a date, see you in Smokes.'

As he went past the torpedo tubes he glanced back at the bridge and saw Spencer closed up with a colleague at the signal lamp, immersed in receiving a message from the flotilla leader on the other side of the fairway.

That afternoon David was unlucky for at dinner time the pipe was 'Hands to make and mend,' which meant a few hours of recreation. After dinner a quietness would descend on the living quarters, as hands washed themselves or their clothes or, most probably, tried to catch up on some sleep.

It was the afternoon watch for him and it was, as before, quite empty of wireless interest. Eddie was luckier; there being a lack of messages Ginger had, with Pots' indulgence, let him off half way through the watch. About 1530 hours the quietness was broken outside by the movement of people and their chatter as they went along forward. David got up quickly, opened the door and, looking along the passageway, saw a gathering in the seamen's mess. Another service? he wondered. Well, he was better out of that. He had never cared for mass worship although he had not questioned the belief in which he had been brought up. Even so, in this respect it had never been possible to make things fit together. The theoretical sat uncomfortably with the realities of existence as they had been materializing for him.

Shortly after the hubbub even Ginger disappeared and David and the white watch ordinary telegraphist were left to look at each other and twiddle their thumbs. There had been no occasion for them to talk to each other much since he had joined the ship, but David did not care for this youth in that irrational intuitive way to which he was subject. There was, moreover, a sour tenseness about him which recommended that he be left alone.

It was extraordinary how, David contemplated, even his features suited his likely disposition. The proportion of the face seemed longer from ear to ear than from forehead to chin. The main distribution of prominences were corrugated and lateral. A bulging forehead gave way to a concavity of sunken eyes emphasising the sockets; then, below this, a flattened, broad-nostrilled nose moulded into prominent cheekbones under which a wide mouth was set back behind a prominent cleft chin. The skin had a roughened greyness about it, generously mottled with something apparently more permanent than adolescent pimples. A mass of dark brown, wiry hair was cleanly trimmed at neck and ear. Yet it was rather full by naval standards and fell down over those eyes, too deeply set for accurate assessment, but of an uncertain green-brown hue, and was repeatedly pushed back over the forehead with open fingers. In fact the movement was an aggressively nervous habit.

David had given no thought to a subject of conversation, but the awkward silence was not long. Down the length of the office, with the delicacy of a cannon ball and from sardonic lips that spoke with a disagreeable, grating accent that might have been North Midlands, came the topic for discourse.

'Your oppo Corder fancies his luck with the birds, don't he?' exclaimed the ordinary telegraphist, not without a great deal of envy in his unfriendly tone.

The veracity of this remark did not pique David so much as the hint, perhaps unintended, that somehow he was responsible for the vaingloriousness of George.

'So it is generally accepted,' David replied warily.

The thickset little body of this rather unpleasant fellow watch-keeper swung the chair abruptly sideways to the bench, bare elbows firmly wedged on the arm rests. There seemed an indecent amount of dark hair in spirals round muscular forearms. Deep in their sockets, the beady eyes regarded him without charity.

'Ah don't believe a word of his bull,' growled the ordinary telegraphist, jabbing his pencil in the general direction of David. 'Ah've had more than he's had hot dinners.'

With this contention, David was privately ready to agree. There really was an aura of sexual experience about this repugnantly mature lout. Of course he was hardened to the great number of claims of erotic prowess he had heard during his time in the service and those of George had a rather threadbare quality through which it was possible to see a fair amount of wishful thinking. It was not so with this creature, who unfortunately brought David in mind of a toad.

'Yer know ah'm married?' asked the warty individual bluntly.

'No, I didn't,' mildly replied David, wondering why he was striving to be agreeable.

'Well, ah am. Last boiler clean. Two month ago. She were three month gone.'

It did not seem tactful to enquire as to the age of the young lady concerned for if she were younger than her spouse – husband seemed hardly the right thought – she would be very young, and if older he was surprised she could not take care of herself. Whichever way it was, she had, however, been no match for such a single-minded, ruthless embodiment of masculine aggression.

'She weren't the first, ah'll tell yer, an' she won't be the last,' he breathed, suddenly being drawn back to the distant call of Admiralty, leaving David to wonder whether he intended emulating the infamous example of Bluebeard.

David was relieved in more than one sense then George came to take over at 1600 hours. After having had his opposite number as a subject of conversation, he was diffident about talking to him at any length in the presence of the ordinary telegraphist, so he just enquired as to the nature of the gathering in the seamen's mess deck.

'Tombola,' said George enigmatically. 'I wasn't interested. Wrote a letter to the party.'

About then Pots and the oldest coder came in and as he went out David was thankful there was less possibility of there being friction between Bluebeard and George before the former's relief arrived.

The peaceful air of concentration encountered by David as he emerged in the forward mess area was quite extraordinary. The greater part of the ship's company seemed to have crammed itself into that triangular space forward of A gun support. Through a blue haze of tobacco smoke ratings were to be seen sitting on the deck, benches, lockers, standing against bulkheads and enclosures, all intent on a little rectangle of paper covered with squares containing fifteen varied numbers between one and ninety. Somewhere well inside the crowd, audible above the humming vents, numbered cubes were being rattled in a cloth bag and evidently drawn out one by one to an announcement that contrived to be reverent and flippant at the same time.

'Two little ducks, twenty-two.' It sounded like the bo'sun's voice.

One or two ratings stirred with joy and ticked off that number on their paper.

The devotions continued.

'Downing Street, number ten.' More anxious ticks were made. David noticed Fred on his knees up in a corner formed by the gun support and the adjacent bulkhead, using the curved metal wall as a writing rest. David leaned through the door and said, 'What is it?'

'Hush!'

'All the fours, forty-four.'

'Fred, what is it?'

Fred scratched tensely. 'Pipe down,' he whined. 'It's tombola.'

'Kelly's eye, number one.'

Fred was far gone in his addiction. By now his questioner was getting some nasty looks from others nearby.

'Legs eleven, number eleven.'

Sitting comfortably next to his seaworn chum on the lockers' side of the foremost mess table, Eddie was just visible through the concourse and smoke. He was being initiated into this ancient naval folk mystery. Enjoyably slumming, thought David rather meanly.

'The army number, nine with the spot below.'

The manager, evidently above this activity of the hoi polloi, came along the TS alley and unlocked the canteen door. The next number was missed by those close at hand as the shutter rattled open.

'I say again, top of the shop, ninety.'

There only being an occasional person at the canteen David took the opportunity to buy some razor blades. The ceremony was still going strong when he turned back.

'On its own, number five.'

'House,' shouted somebody obscured in the haze.

A murmur swelled into a loud chatter and it was apparent the session was over. Fred awkwardly stood up and stepped into his own mess area.

'Just my bloody luck, Dave,' he grimaced, indicating the slip almost complete. 'That's the second time I've been near.'

'Come and drown your sorrows in tea, chum,' said his not very concerned opposite number.

Whilst tea was in progress a few letters were handed to Robbie who was astonished that there should be mail at this unlikely place and time. Answering his demand as to how they had arrived, the postman said the cruisers had brought a few bags when they arrived the previous day.

'Well those three-funnelled bastards do something useful sometimes when they get off their tins,' he commented, forgetting conveniently he had been in cruisers once himself. The allusion was to the general opinion of small ship crews that the bigger ships spent so much time in harbour they eventually grounded on their empty food tins dumped overboard.

He handed or flicked letters to various people at hand, looked at a postmark closely and said, 'Happy days' and pushed it down to Fred, marking, 'This one is for your oppo, give it him when you go in for the second dog.'

Between tea and supper Fred and David went down to the after mess deck and talked to the HF-DF operators. For a time they discussed the ultimate purpose of their extra watchkeeping without coming to any conclusion. Fred, of course, did not allow the conversation to dwell too much on this matter and the time passed agreeably talking about music, films and something new, books. This was due largely to one of the operators being a great enthusiast for what he described as literature. From the light-weight reading Fred occupied himself with up till then, it was again a surprise to see him airing his knowledge about the books that were mentioned. Contemporary American literature held a high place in the esteem of both the chief participants, but they ranged far and wide beyond the rather narrow reading accomplishments of the others.

On the way back Fred remembered the letter and popped into the office to give it to George and then came on to get his supper before going on watch. He had been gone some time before

George came back to the mess. He showed no desire for a meal and sat down away from the others on the lockers near the radar mess. He looked very preoccupied, even distracted, and David sensed something was not right. The table had been cleared and a noisy game of ludo was in progress, Ginger being one of the noisiest of the protagonists. He had a habit of biting his fingernails and swearing hard as though his tension would turn the dice in his favour. All around people were engaged in all kinds of pastimes or conversation happy in the thought that for most it would be an all night in their hammocks.

Beginning to find the smoke-laden atmosphere oppressive David put on his duffel coat and went down to the iron deck. They were now moored alone and although it was extremely cold, with only the usual signal and navigation lights to look at, he found it quite a relief to be away from the crowd. There were several other people too, wandering about or smoking in nooks and crannies.

He went up to the searchlight platform and sat alone with his thoughts, which were mainly concerned with his recent experiences and an uneasiness about what was to come. A music programme, following the news, drifted up faintly from between decks. He remembered that unlike most of the others he had not longed for training to end and to get out on active service. In fact, he admitted to himself, on his entry into national service, although he could have avoided it – indeed he had been given the chance on two occasions of a reserved occupation – he had been drawn reluctantly by an awful curiosity. He did not relish the unfolding future at all but could not avoid being attracted by it and tremulously drawn on. Yet now, caught in the war vortex irrevocably, he did not mind; perhaps some camaraderie had rubbed off on his rather solitary nature and being among fellows all involved together provided some kind of easement of his foreboding. To anyone with an atom of common sense it was obvious they were not in a very desirable predicament but somehow, perched up alone in the icy darkness he would not have cared to be anywhere else.

Getting accustomed to the gloom he saw a figure walk slowly along the deck below him and stop, hunched up in a duffel coat. The shape looked vaguely familiar, perhaps George; he called out.

George's unmistakable country accent said, 'Who's that? Dave? Where are you?'

'Up here on the searchlight platform. Come on up, the ladder's just beside you.'

George's heavy figure rose up and leaned against the guard rail. He bent down and under the cover of its canvas screen and lit a cigarette. Its brief pungency was wafted away on the breeze.

'You don't want one I suppose, Dave?'

'No thanks, I don't smoke.'

'Yes, I'm remembering that by now.' There was a different character to his voice. The soft, superior, critical tone had gone. He sounded more natural, less of a poseur.

'Effing Yanks!' he confided abruptly to his astonished shipmate in the darkness. He drew on his cigarette and hand and face glowed redly for an instant.

'What's up, George?' David asked, unable to suppress his interest.

'That letter I just got. From a mate I worked with at the post office.'

Occasionally David knew when it was inadvisable to speak.

'He wrote and said the girl is seeing a lot of Americans from the airfield. Mum knows and she's upset, but won't say anything for fear of being thought jealous. My mate says everybody reckons I ought to know. It was going on even when I was training. They say she's out with somebody different every night. I said I'd marry her if she wanted.' Even in the dark it was possible to apprehend he had lost his superior airs. He was deflated. Almost demoralized.

'Does it really matter, George?' David asked, 'There are others.'

'Not a month yet since I saw her. Hardly turned my back and she started. What about all those letters she wrote, eh?'

'I expect she was not putting all her eggs in one basket – unlike the song. If you get my meaning.' David sensed that his comments did not mitigate a particle the feeling of desolation felt by his shipmate. He stood up, anxious to break the doleful conversation. A warship, indicated by a few shaded lights, glided up the fiord. She was making for the supply ship and as she slipped alongside the deck lights of the auxiliary vessel were switched on and she showed plainly that the *Obstinate* had arrived.

9

It was Ginger shaking his hammock that hauled up David from a sleep that seemed inadequate, for the forenoon watch.

'Come on, kidder,' he said quietly, for many were still asleep and regular watchkeeping throughout the vessel had not recommenced, 'rise and shine. I reckon we'll be putting out today.' This last was too blithely said for such an hour. The usual early morning depression deepened into a sensation that there was no bottom to his stomach as he turned out. A wash, shave and a hurried breakfast helped to allay this feeling before he went down to take over from a jaded and smoke-dried Fred. His watch had not been eventful and he had got through a great deal of light reading matter.

'There hasn't,' he intimated, 'been a bloody peep, except for the hourlies and they were only strength three.' For an afterthought he added, 'As far as I can see we're wasting our time, I could have been turned in.'

It was quite true. The forenoon watch regarding what came through the head-phones continued empty of incident. In the office and ship it was a different story and David was glad to be unoccupied.

Down at the far end Bluebeard was engrossed a lot of the time taking messages that Eddie was kept busy decoding and Ginger despatching or taking to the ship's office or the first lieutenant. Pots was in and out most of the time, unlocking and locking the safe and consulting confidential books and papers. He checked the tuning of the ship-to-ship telephone and there was a brief exercise of question and answer on the clarity of signals. He exchanged Morse and speech with various telephone points and had taken the panel from the main transmitter and inspected its interior again. The yeoman of signals called in and they discussed the code words for use between escort units and convoy. The code names were the product, maybe, of some mind endeavouring to escape the present bleak environment. A piece of card was neatly made out with the names and placed beside the radio telephone. Amongst the others David noticed that the escort commander was *Bluebell* and the *Watchful, Crocus*.

By now blue watch was closed up to its stations and the ship was in a state of preparedness for sea. Whilst ratings just off duty ate a hasty meal, 'Secure for sea' was piped and the scuttles were closed and clamped tight by those who had finished. People were going out to see the last of the Island.

The port exit from the galley flat had been secured so it was obvious that the weather was expected from that side. Down by the funnel there was a larger group than usual, drawn out to see what was in progress.

They were still well inside the fiord, its towering walls continuing to keep most of the storm force from them. The light exhaust from the funnel was blown in every direction by contending gusts. The ships were going out, rather haphazardly it appeared, in lines, escorts mixed up with merchantmen. Astern, on the starboard side was *Foxglove*, the little corvette they had last seen at fleet base. It was cheekily moving along with a large freighter, whose shape was not that of a liberty ship, but with a high superstructure amidships. From the amount of signalling it was doing, they deduced, quite rightly – it was confirmed later – to be the flagship of the convoy commodore.

As they cleared the two great snow-mantled headlands, thrusting like rocky supernatural fists into the uneasy waters, the low sun cast a long-shadowed, almost theatrical beam over the ships as they began to move into their positions. It was the first sunshine they had seen for days and it gave a fleeting beauty to the rocking vessels, briefly making their drab grey paint yellow brilliant against deep green, foam-flecked water. Signal flags, of which there were plenty, gave a bizarre gaiety to the scene.

Steadily overtaking them came the *Stavanger* with more signals displayed than anybody else visible including the escort commander in *Severe*. Her ensign, darkly exotic, streamed out bravely from her mainmast, as she drew abreast, then overhauled *Watchful*.

'There go the mad buggers,' said Ginger, leaning nonchalantly against the funnel. It had to be something unusual to draw him up to the funnel club.

'Why mad?' Fred was as inquisitive as ever.

'He's talking about what my mate said who's on her,' explained Robbie from the monklike depths of his duffel coat hood. 'He's the killick bunting tosser on her. Says that they do more signalling than anybody else.'

'What about the *Schleswig* do?' put in Ginger.

'Yes, he said he nearly wet his drawers. They went into less than a thousand yards before firing the sardines. He said the silly sods were jumping up and down with glee.'

The *Stavanger* moved on to the starboard bow and turned away in that direction. The commentary had given it a sullen, hateful air, despite the gay flags and bright light; an atmosphere of suspended violence. Its receding stern brought to David's mind a class of Norwegians, dressed in their strange uniform, which assembled to his right for divisions at the initial training establishment. There was already an aura of experience about them. The greater part of the group had not joined the easy way. Some had crept out of their occupied homeland in small boats or trekked across mountain fastnesses to get away from a regime they detested. They were on the outside now, ready to break into the prison of their nation. Their cause was not an abstract one, its animus was personal. Ancient berserk still lingered in their phlegmatic twentieth-century minds. It only required the catalyst of battle to let it forth.

'They always seem so bloody pleased when something's doing,' remarked Ginger peevishly.

'They're going home – almost anyway,' said Eddie, who had joined the spectators.

Robbie was sober. 'Almost but not quite,' he said.

Meanwhile *Masai* had come up abreast, and her port lamp was flashing. David wondered if it was Old Spence clicking away. He missed the preceding letters but there was a pause; then distinctly 'TTFN.'

'Tat-tah for now,' said Robbie censoriously, 'Such signals! Hardly pusser!'

She turned away too, following *Stavanger* to the southwards. It became obvious as she went further on that she was going to keep guard on the starboard bow to the south. *Stavanger* was centre in the forward screen and *Watchful* was to be on the port bow, to the north. They were approximately in position, slowly rolling along as the rest formed up astern.

Out of the conglomeration of ships at the mouth of Seydis Fiord, *Obstinate* emerged and dropped into a position immediately following. The merchantmen were sorting themselves out with the aid of the corvette which fussed in and out of the forming columns. The gleaming sunlight eventually ceded place to the more usual greyness, accompanied by a wind that increased in steadiness of force and direction, bringing thin snow flurries as they came out into the open sea.

The Island faded ghostlike in a gathering gloom that had a heavy almost purple, snow-laden quality to it as it came down from the north-west. The group around the funnel was thinning as people began to feel the cold and went below, but David remained doggedly to see the last of land. They pushed further out into water that was developing a very heavy swell. The wind whipped the tops of the billows and scattered spume along their fizzing, green concavities. The forward screen started to zigzag across the path of the convoy; sometimes the *Stavanger* closed so it was only a few hundred yards to starboard; then it parted company as it went out to converge on *Masai*.

The convoy did not promise to be a fast one.

During the afternoon the motion of the ship increased in violence as it moved steadily on to the north-east. Its speed was only half that which had been maintained previously, to accord with the crawling freighters. On the whole, people were less unwell, mainly due, perhaps, not only to having become habituated to rough weather, but also because the storm had slightly abated in fury. It was quite likely that the order for departure would not have been given unless there was a chance of less severe weather.

Off watch, most sat or stretched on the lockers, reading, writing or dozing.

At teatime during the change of blue and red watches the Overseas Service was being relayed on the loudspeakers when there was a click and 'D'you hear there? D'you hear there? The Captain will speak in a few minutes.' A hush fell through the mess decks and ratings stood or sat silently, there being only the occasional clink of cup and knife above the hum of fan and dynamo and the outer sea roar. The knot of customers round the canteen held up their transactions as everybody waited.

Then a nasal voice that sounded like the coxswain unnecessarily said, 'Keep silence for the Captain.'

A brief pause, then unmistakable clipped tones said, 'This is the Captain speaking. I want to let you know exactly what we are about to undertake, although I'm sure you have a pretty good idea of what is in hand anyway. We are helping to escort this convoy to North Russia. As most of you know we were up there in late summer, but that was a quick run up with supplies. This will be much more tedious. A long slow business. It's a large convoy, divided in two. We are in the vanguard with fifteen merchant ships. There is quite a lot of ocean between us and the second portion. Behind them will be the covering force, the cruisers you might have seen in Seydis Fiord. I've heard, too, that some heavier units are coming up to join it from base.'

'Hard graft for them,' breathed Ginger sarcastically.

'So although you won't be able to see it, we'll have lots of company. In fact with our fifteen charges and dozen escorts we'll seem very much on our own. I want to emphasize, we are not. We have some valuable cargoes for our Russian friends and it is up to every one of us to see they get through safely. It is stuff that is vitally needed.'

'Bolshie!' Robbie murmured.

'As members of my ship's company and the service, it is hardly necessary for me to remind you to carry out your duties diligently. We rely on other people, as they rely on us. That is all.'

'And highly appreciated our efforts will be,' growled Ginger.

'By whom?' asked Eddie.

'The Russians.'

'Well, they will won't they?' This was more of a rhetorical question from Robbie.

'You'll be lucky, hookey!' Why should they? They don't seem to have been before from all accounts.'

'We ought to appreciate them, Geordie, look what they're doing,' Bluebeard had to put in his say. It was a rash initiative. Ginger looked sidelong at him.

'What do you know about it sprog Reynolds?' For that indeed was Bluebeard's real name. 'You've only been in a dog watch!'

'Oh, but they're taking a hell of a lot from our side,' protested Robbie. 'Only because they haven't any option. Where were they in 1941 when you and me and the others were getting kicked to hell off Crete? It was a rotten capitalist war then, remember?'

It was apparent everybody had strong opinions on this and all wanted to air them. There was a babble of remarks, one of which emerged clearly enough at the end.

'Still it is to our benefit to help them now isn't it?' asked Rowe.

So the *Daily Reflector* says,' Ginger was sarcastic.

Throughout the warm discussion he had cleaved to his sceptical line of argument. He had his supporters, most of whom were less articulate than he, in their remarks. One thing was obvious. Whatever kept him at sea, efficiently carrying out his duties, it was not political motivation. Perhaps once caught in the discipline of the service, he could not do anything about opting out even if he had wished, although there had been individuals who had managed to do so. No, probably having got himself involved, he would rather put up with being disillusioned about the point of the whole business than recall in the future that he had deserted his friends. That he could have insinuated himself ashore and possibly out of the service if he had set his mind to it, there was no doubt. Others had managed it. Half-educated and tending to lapse into strong dialect when excited, a penetrating sensitive intelligence illuminated his most pithy comments, indicating clearly that properly educated he could have been a substantial personality. He would have been able to find a way out.

'Never mind, Ginger,' Robbie said sententiously, 'ours not to reason why . . .' Which remark hinted that the leading hand of the mess considered the debate had reached a suitable conclusion, for it might continue to his discomfort. In contrast with his old shipmate, Robbie accepted circumstances and the pronouncements of the authorities with an almost oriental fatalism. It had probably never crossed his mind to question the influences that had brought him to his present way of life. He was the perfect team member, doing what was required of him in a willing and efficient spirit, hardly thinking of anything but the task in hand and possibly, but not too expectantly, of the next boiler-cleaning leave. As time went on it became obvious that if present he would endeavour to damp down theoretical discussion with a deflating remark, so one wondered whether he was incapable of thought in the abstract and was uncomfortable unless talk was on the immediate and tangible.

During this brief but surprising foray into politics by the mess, Fred had reluctantly left such an entertaining scene to go on watch. George came back and sat eating and drinking stolidly, thoughtful, hardly aware of the debate around him. All was cleared away and Ginger was rounding up three others to play ludo and David reclined on the lockers midway between the two messes. George, pausing against the petty officers' ladderway to light a cigarette, came and sat beside him.

Soberly, he murmured, the last vestiges of patronage gone from his demeanour, 'A sub sent a sighting report, just before 1300. We were hardly out of the fiord. DF said it was Red 50, about five miles to the north of us. Pots reckoned it didn't matter one way or the other. He says the Island is supposed to be crawling with enemy agents, who'd let Jerry know what we're about anyway.'

But it was not this piece of disturbing news with which he was concerned. 'What do you think I should do about that letter, Dave?' he asked.

'What letter?' David found it hard to concentrate.

'From my mate about the girl. Do you think I ought to write to her?' This might have suggested he did anything but write to her.

David was naturally flattered to be consulted about something that George had apparently considered his own speciality up till now.

George,' he said, 'suppose it's true. She'll either tell you a lie or the truth. Neither will be pleasant or of use to you. If it's not true you'll offend her – quite rightly – and stand to lose her anyway. Why are you so stuck on her? There's plenty of time, she's not the only one. You'd best wait to see if she writes. If she doesn't, you'll know, and would you still want her after that?'

David, of course, felt this was not the last word in worldly wisdom, even if it had a certain primitive logic about it, but he was moved to say something in order to appear sympathetic. Yet George remained screwed up with jealousy and growled, 'Bloody Yanks. Why don't they keep in their own effing country?'

'Look here, George,' David was somewhat nettled by his opposite number's egocentricity. 'Some of those poor bastards haven't got very good prospects. Didn't you see them going out on those daylight raids when we were on the south coast nicely comfortable at training school? And coming back shot full of holes and belly-flopping all over the Downs? They've got very little future, can you really blame them for grabbing things while they can?'

Perhaps his recent experience had given some kind of broader dimension to his understanding for this last argument, quite a speech, delivered with some heat by David, appeared to console George a little. He stood up without replying and staggered over to the TS alley on his way to the heads. David was left to ruminate on the news he had brought back from the wireless office.

Above the ship noises, the sea could be heard thumping regularly on to the portside. The ludo game was descending into farce as the plastic counters slid out of their allotted squares. This led to a certain amount of sleight of hand and protests couched in good-natured swearing and fits of laughter.

Yet out in the darkness, beyond the canteen store and the thin, yellow-lit vulnerable steel plates of the ship, a black metal sea monster slithered up and down, hatefully keeping pace with them as they meandered uncomfortably through the neutrally violent night.

10

The first night out with the convoy, as the ships rolled on north-eastwards, was uneventful and David managed to get a comforting but hardly sufficient amount of sleep. The morning watch was free of incident and in the generally slack atmosphere Eddie chatted, tirelessly it seemed, with Ginger. This time a lot of talk was expended on the subject of fabrics. The topic had been initiated by a remark Ginger made on the desire of the ladies for nylons, such as those bought at Akureyri. Eddie was able to instruct him and David on the superior wearing quality of these synthetic fibres and informed them there would be other novel textiles in the not very distant future. His interest and knowledge was once more extremely impressive. He expressed himself well considering the dull hours of the night, and it helped much to ease the dragging watch.

Down at the far end Reynolds, when not writing in his log book, was occupied reading a magazine which seemed to be concerned with famous murders. In rapt interest his glittering little eyes flicked back and forth, just visible over the top of its limp pages, but his attention flagged towards the end of the watch and he sat stewing, abstracted, in his own thoughts. When George came in at 0800 to relieve him David was disturbed to hear Reynolds call out jeeringly, 'Who's the sex king of the Andrew now then?' George was remarkably indifferent to this sally. As was his custom he sat down heavily morose but stirred himself to look round Eddie, droop a heavy eyelid and say 'Rollocks', before taking down the hourly routine.

The poor opinion David had of Reynolds took an even more disapproving turn at this manifest triumph of the latter, hollow and immature though it was. As he opened the door he paused, hanging on to it, riding the lively deck. True it was no business of his, yet he looked pointedly at the ordinary telegraphist and said sarcastically to Ginger, 'I can do with a bit of fresh air.'

The object of his scornful remark pulled off his headphones and rose up threateningly.

'Just try it, said David coldly, clenching his fists in preparation.

'Bugger off, Fres, interjected Ginger testily, 'go and get your breakfast.' Then, turning to Reynolds, 'You keep your big mouth shut, sprog. We've got enough troubles without you stroppy juveniles.'

David's anger evaporated with breakfast and the usual forenoon chores. Indeed any kind of pugnacious spirit would have been hard, if not impossible to realize in action, owing to the struggling vessel.

Shortly before noon it fell to the lot of George to take down the second shadowing report from the U-boat. It was still out on the port bow, bearing red five zero, four to five miles. There was a likelihood it was using the *Watchful* as a marker and would have the convoy silhouetted against the southern glow of a sun, low on the horizons that broke fitfully through the racing clouds.

When David went out on the starboard side for a breath of fresh air, just after dinner, he observed all the neighbouring vessels were in the same position to each other, except that another destroyer had joined the forward screen between *Stavanger* and *Masai*. The freighters were in three lines abreast of five each and behind *Watchful* was the *Obstinate* and astern further still another escort bringing up the port quarter. In the distance behind everyone, the corvette was sometimes to be seen wandering about in an erratic fashion. *Foxglove* seemed to be a general factotum.

That afternoon David spent spread out on the lockers, dozing, as did most of white and blue watches. The two hours of the first dog-watch passed comfortably enough, still being quiet but for the routines, and the prospect of supper to follow was an attractive one.

After they had eaten and cleared the table Ginger got out his ludo board.

Fancy a game of uckers, Dave?' he asked.

When first observing this game being enthusiastically played David had confided to himself that it was all rather infantile. Since then, however, he had begun to comprehend that it was one of the artful ways the old stager kept an importunate environment at bay.

'Don't mind,' he nodded magnanimously.

Fred, never backward in these diversions, was already taking the red counters.

'My watch colour,' he explained.

At the behest of Ginger Eddie reluctantly closed a book he was reading and claimed the yellow counters.

'My favourite colour,' he informed them.

David took the green counters. He felt obliged to justify his choice. 'The colour we were a few days ago,' he murmured ironically.

'And a variety of other hues,' Eddie contributed.

'So that leaves me blue. My lucky colour,' said their senior hand as, with a complacent sigh, he sat down.

'Now,' he continued, 'we'll play properly. The counters shouldn't slide about like they did yesterday. The sea's not as bad as it was. Let's shake to start then.'

As was to be expected, Fred already had the box and dice. He rattled them nervously and shot. It was to no avail. Eddie, yellow being the colour next clockwise on the board, threw and came up with six to start off immediately. He enquired whether he was entitled to another throw. Fred said not, but was magisterially contradicted by Ginger exclaiming, 'Who's the uckers champion of the Home Fleet? Yes he does; go on Eddie.' Meecham obliged and rolled another six.

'Can I start another counter on that?' he asked. Fred said no again. Testily, Ginger said, 'Yes he can, don't muck up the rules.' The dice rattled to one. Unfortunately this brought out the worst in David who said, 'That's more like it.' However, if there ever was such a thing as natural justice, it manifested itself at that instant and for some to follow.

'Now Dave, said Ginger, 'see what you can do.' All he could manage was one and the remark, 'Bloody hell.' Ginger was beginning to work himself up into the competitive state of nerves that he usually demonstrated during these contests. He rolled a six. 'Goodo! he shouted, 'I'm off. I get another go.'

Fred was now, the second time round, calling on his watchword to steel himself for the tenseness of the occasion. 'Up the Palace!' But he rattled and rolled but one. The yellow counters of Eddie marched steadily onwards round the board. The language of David began to get more disgraceful as he continued unable to produce a six. Complacency settled on Eddie and Ginger which contrasted with the agitation of Fred and the glumness of David. The former, however, gave a triumphant upward jerk of his arms and to yet another utterance of his war cry rolled a six and shouted, 'Hooray I'm off!' That the four green counters remained contumaciously at their starting point was not any more the palatable for Ginger observing, 'Blimey, Dave you're in Queer Street,' but then even he gasped 'Hell' through a mouthful of finger tips as he failed to throw another six.

Soon after the first red counter had been launched on its way there had been, for a few minutes, a painful complexity of moves in which red, blue and yellow counters were within single moves of cancelling each other. However, the field extended itself and as most of the other counters, save green, came out, there was a steady move round the board with the occasional disastrous cancellation and return to starting point. This of course led to much bad language between the three fortunate contestants although Eddie managed to couch his disappointments in more genteel terms.

'Sorry, Fred,' said Ginger insincerely, '... back you go!'

'Effit. I'll get yer.'

'I tell you I'm the champ,' boasted Ginger. 'Eddie, I'll have you yet.'

'Never mind Ginger, I'll get my revenge.'

'Stand by.' Ginger was rattling the box vaingloriously. 'I'm the tops. Now what did I say? Six. I'm spifflicating you, good-bye Eddie back to base-ums.'

'It was all too good to be true at first,' Eddie meekly whispered.

All the time this frightful dogfight had been taking place David continued to throw anything but six. His remarks were down to an almost inaudible mutter. 'Hopeless,' he said.

'And helpless.' Ginger was not exactly sympathetic. Then at a time that might be considered the turning point in the struggle, David managed to throw a six, 'I don't believe it,' he said.

'Neither do we mate, go on, 'said the self-appointed champion. David threw another six. 'Incredible,' he whispered.

'Shattering!' Ginger was sarcastic.

Then he managed yet another six. 'Out of this world, uncanny!'

'If I hadn't seen it with my own eyes...' gasped Fred. To Eddie it was fantastic.

'It must have been the way the ship rolled,' David modestly suggested. Ginger warned him, soon after, 'Look out Fres,' the deadly moggedors are coming up fast.' This was a reference to red counters through the agency of which Fred had managed to get a distinguished record of regularly leaving base in time to cancel transients of other colours. He never managed to profit himself, because he was cancelled with equal regularity almost as soon as he had turned the first corner. He gritted his widely spaced teeth and growled, 'Never mind I'll get my own back.'

'You're quite successful enough now,' twittered Eddie.

With occasional setbacks the blue counters continued their relentless advance. 'Look at Ginger,' commented Fred, 'way out on his own. Still, plenty of traps yet, chum!'

Indeed, this was an accurate forecast of the turn of events, for hardly perceptible, though it happened, his leading position was eroded and although blue was the colour of the first and third counters home, unfortunately for the egomania of the champion so blue was the colour of the last two home. Moreover, such is the inscrutability of luck that the first set of four counters to complete the nerve-rending circuit was green. With relief David could say, quite justifiably, 'Green is not so unlucky after all.'

The other participants were so engrossed in combat that the reversal of fortune had gone largely unobserved. The language was quite deplorable even to ears hardened to the expressiveness of the lower deck, but out of the drifting smoke of histrionics Fred and his four red counters emerged, battered but complete and happy. When he had wiped his moist hands with a handkerchief something less than white he lit a cigarette. He drew smoke deeply down into that bony chest then, leaning back, let it trickle out through a sardonic grin.

'Well,' he said to David, with a suspicion of mutual congratulation, 'we buggered old Ginger up didn't we mate?' Naturally this was not well received by the senior hand, entangled as he was with Eddie in the struggle for third place.

'You're a bloody lot of city twisters,' he fumed.

His last remaining antagonist patiently rattled and threw, edging the yellow counters along the road home. Their early promise had been negated by the vindictiveness of the blue ones and the heavy-footed blundering of the red. Yet Eddie, probably resigned to ultimate defeat, now saw his counters sliding unimpeded for home, creating havoc with the remaining two blue ones as they went. Indeed, Ginger had to start them again at least half a dozen times. His aptitude for throwing sixes was ruined repeatedly by a hopping yellow counter coming to rest on one of the blue ones.

'You're a 'orrible little sod, aren't you, kidder?' he groaned after seeing one cancelled when almost on the home straight and his despair was not unfounded in fact for all the yellow counters came safely home while the blue ones, restarted, were winding their way between the green and blue quarters of the board.

'Must have a quick wash before I go on duty,' Fred started to get up. 'Thanks for a pleasant little game, Ginge.' He was enjoying the discomfiture of the erstwhile champ. 'We must have another round soon.'

'Not on my bloody board you won't,' Ginger grumpily said.

When Robbie came off watch at 2000 hours he staggered over to David who was busy slinging his bedgear.

'Don't forget you and Eddie are cooks of the mess tomorrow forenoon, Dave,' he said.

'OK Robbie,' David replied, in the same instant wondering that they would have to prepare. Fred and George had been lucky in having an experienced rating with them when they had done their turn and as he settled down in his hammock, gazing at the swaying cork-mottled deckhead with its tracery of pipes and cables, he wondered if Johnny had experienced any trouble in preparing a meal. Indeed he speculated on what he was doing at that exact moment, those few hundred yards back across the dark billows.

At that exact moment, it so happened, Johnny was on watch, enjoying himself, as much as was possible in his little wireless cubicle. He had nothing to do for most of the time and in the idle hours he had rediscovered an old pastime. On the reverse side of sheets torn from the message pad he had begun to draw. It was a recurrence of a practice which had annoyed his stationmaster in the old railway days, but his boss had never made a serious attempt to stop him, perhaps amused by the things he drew. During the quiet parts of the day he had sketched on any available scrap of paper. The subject matter was largely footballers or cowboys, sometimes a war incident he had seen in cinema newsreels.

Now the subjects were ships, or part of them, mainly from memory; it was hardly possible up till now to view other parts comfortably although he had taken to rendering odd corners or fixtures of the office. The light blob in the middle of the cathode ray screen was only stirred by the hourly routine from Narvik control, and although he too knew of the shadowing menace out on the port side, he had found a way of fighting the depression of the lonely night. His stomach was ceasing to be constantly aware of the heave and slide of the armchair; albeit reluctantly, he was beginning to live with the ship.

During the middle watch, David who, prior to it had dropped off to sleep comforted by the thought he could leave it to Eddie, was perturbed to hear the kind of cooking the resourceful coder thought he might accomplish.

'I'm quite good with vol-au-vent or lemon meringue pie or some other things Aunt has shown me,' he admitted.

'But they're not much good now with pusser's stuff as the ingredients are they, kidder?' put in Ginger scornfully.

'No I'm afraid not Ginger,' Eddie agreed.

Reynolds, unfortunately, not very busy either, had to put in his observation that he would not eat that muck even if it were available.

This was all too disappointing for David as he sat and listened sullenly to these exchanges and some more in a similar vein, particularly from the senior hand of the watch.

'So what?' David demanded, during a suitable pause in Eddie's exposition of his past culinary achievements and Ginger's interest in some of the more exotically named dishes he mentioned. 'Do you suggest we do in the forenoon?'

'Simple, Dave, simple,' he replied with an airy flick of his left hand in the direction of his questioner. 'We haven't had it for some time. The galley should be able to handle it now and you shouldn't find it too difficult to prepare!'

'What is it?'

'Meat and vegetable pie.' He paused, gloating, and visualized it. 'Roll a nice bit o' pastry, lay it on the bottom of the tray – empty a few tins of M and V into it – more clacker on top – take it down to the galley – lovely grub!'

Ginger had got them out of their predicament. David relaxed. It would be a simple job. Had he not seen his womenfolk make pastry on many occasions? Thenceforward he would pay more attention to what the others prepared and he helped to consume; that is, when he had been capable of doing so.

The swaying table of a damp, cold and fuggy mess deck was not the best platform for preparing a meal for over a dozen people however. Only half-recovered from a disturbed night, David, with Eddie, after cleaning away the breakfast things started to assemble the tray, cans, tins and containers necessary for the task. They sat at the dresser end of the table and peeled potatoes, helped magnanimously by Ginger who, prodding out the eyes of some ancient-looking vegetables, speculated on their origin. He was of the opinion they had been left over from Scott's expedition to the Antarctic, or alternatively had not been used as ammunition at Trafalgar.

When this was concluded he went off to talk to acquaintances in the seamen's mess forward and Eddie took it upon himself to grease the tray and open the tins of meat and vegetable concoction. Meanwhile David had managed to get some flour into a basin, added salt and powdered egg and was endeavouring to stir the mixture, adjusting to the pitching of the ship, his knees wedged under the table. It was unavoidable that flour tended to flick out onto table and deck. Adding water he gradually kneaded a reasonable lump of dough and cut it into two halves. Dusting the well-scrubbed surface of the table with flour he proceeded to roll it into a large rectangular flatness. This was accomplished, luckily, without it sticking to the table surface.

With the assistance of Eddie he gently lowered the pastry into the tray and they moulded it into shape and left the edge hanging over. He got Eddie to grease a mug which was placed upside down in the middle and joyously they emptied in the contents of the tins, smoothly spreading out the brown mush.

'Don't forget some salt and pepper,' said Eddie and he got the condiments and dusted the surface.

David left him to roll out the other lump of dough and together they laid it carefully on top. An aesthetic impulse asserting itself, David, with a knife, notched a pattern all round the edge and trimmed the overlap. The trimmings he rolled out and cut into diamond shapes as decoration. With a gesture as near that of a chef de cuisine as it was possible to conjure up in the poor circumstances he prodded holes in the pastry over the base of the mug.

For a few self-satisfied minutes they sat and admired the product of their labour.

'Not bad is it?' ventured David.

'Quite nice,' observed Eddie, 'quite professional really!'

David went further. 'I reckon it's top hole, old chap, top hole.'

'Let's take it down to the galley,' Eddie suggested. He picked it up carefully and with David bringing the dixie of potatoes they managed to get it down to and across the galley flat, noisy and bleak, and into the comforting warmth of the galley. The culinary efforts of the others' messes were also being brought along and secured to the cooking range. There was a cheerful roar from the ovens and grills and it seemed a most desirable place to have a duty. One of the ship's cooks, red-faced and perspiring, was quite complimentary. 'That's a nice-looking pie, wack,' he was kind enough to inform Eddie.

Its creators exchanged glances of mutual admiration and pride and blithely they ignored the giddy TS alley as they went back to clean the utensils and prepare the mid-morning hot drink.

Unfortunately their pride was not of long standing. Well before noon Ginger, anxious to see the meal he had inspired and no doubt to get things comfortably eaten before the afternoon watch, brought it back from the galley. David followed with the steaming potatoes. As those off watch assembled to eat, Eddie held the stack of plates steady and passed them over to David one by one for potatoes. Then they were passed to Ginger who had cut the pie into portions.

'This crust is a bit hard,' he murmured in a puzzled way.

The pie looked a delicious brown, but there seemed a certain rigidity about it and there was an ominous cracking and splintering as the knife divided it.

The plates, when complete with the meal, were passed to the other end of the table. Ginger put the duty watch share securely on the dresser and prepared to make short work of his ration.

'Funny,' said one of the blue watch signalmen cautiously. 'Clacker seems a bit solid.'

'Looks all right to me,' said George but then he had not started on it and was pushing a small potato round the gravy with the end of his fork.

'Oo made the clacker?' burst out Reynolds sourly from the end of the table.

'Dave,' said Ginger, 'I reckon,' he admitted, 'it's a bit hard.'

'Eddie helped me and he didn't say there was anything wrong,' said David in self-defence.

'Oh now,' said Eddie, 'I was busy with the tins and things.' He was determined not to share his colleague's culpability. 'It is rather hard!'

'Hard?' shouted Reynolds, 'Hard? If he was to make enough of the stuff and we was to nail it to the upper deck we'd be effing bomb proof!'

'You should bloody well criticize, sprog!' said Ginger looking severely down the length of the table. 'What about that so called pot mess you made a few weeks back? That wasn't so great!'

The older coder was having a tricky time with his dentures but managed to advise, 'If it is so bad just push it about in the gravy. It goes nice and soggy.'

Moreover, the truth was that although one or two others protested about its quality and there was the painful sound of crunching teeth, most ate the pastry, getting it down in the manner suggested by their venerable mess mate.

David was glad to get away from this uncharitable atmosphere and was very sharp in relieving Fred.

'It was,' he told him,' not a success!'

'What wasn't?' Fred, of course, required elucidation.

'The pie. If you eat it you'll have to soak it well in gravy.'

That wry grin forced its lines onto Fred's thin jowls as he got out of the chair and handed his relief the headphones. 'Never mind Dave, we must live and learn. The trouble is nobody's stomach is in much shape for experiments right now.'

The hourly routine began almost as soon as David was seated and there had been no significant change in the serial numbers since 0800 hours. He logged the headings and checked the carbon copies and had just turned the pad to a fresh sheet when a loud squalling sound burst forth and the first unmistakable letters of a U-boat message began. It was very close. Jotting down the few letters he was hampered by a cold shock wave down his back from head to bowels leaving a hair raising sensation of goose pimples. Ginger had looked sharply at him as he too heard the squeal of the headphones, asking in his eyes alone what it was.

His mouth having gone suddenly dry, David could hardly speak. He had known it would be his turn to hear a shadowing report one midday, but when it came he was still shaken.

'It's,' he swallowed breathlessly, struggling to draw up saliva, 'it's the sub. It's still with us.'

Narvik, repeating back the message with a serial number, drew him back to the message pad. It was an effort to steady his trembling hand as he wrote. When the only sound was static he sat tense for some minutes. Meanwhile the telephone to HF-DF buzzed. Ginger got up and answered it.

'OK kidder, thanks,' he said to the operator aft. Coming back he picked up the signal David had torn off and placed in the tray.

'Yes,' he said quietly, as he wrote down the bearing, 'the bastard's still with us red zero six five, about six miles.'

He turned up the brass flap over the bridge voicepipe mouthpiece, whistled and called up, 'Wireless office to bridge.'

'Bridge to wireless office – what is it?'

'U-boat signal bearing red zero six five range about six miles.'

There was a brief pause; the rushing sound of the wind was quite audible. Then, 'Thanks sparks – for nothing.'

During this activity David had looked beyond Eddie, sitting passive, wide-eyed, bland-faced, a silent spectator, to Reynolds. There was a puzzling look on his face. The eyes seemed larger, more protuberant, their whites visible. He had not recalled seeing the whites before. Round the sockets there was a puffiness and the lips of his long mouth twitched and grimaced damply. Surprising too was that he had remained silent, looking from David to Ginger and back again as the incident went forward.

Ginger, his job done, resumed his chair and the four watchkeepers sat brooding, the outer sea and ship sounds penetrating the quiet office.

Their senior hand, though, was not one to remain unoccupied for long and very soon he recollected the unfortunate dinner David had produced. It could not strictly be described as inedible because most of the mess had managed to eat it, but perhaps at a more fastidious time and place it would have been suitable only as pigswill.

'It's a wonder to me,' thought Ginger aloud, 'that pie didn't end up in the gash bucket. What our stomachs can take is remarkable. Dave, you let our watch down, I wonder what you did wrong?'

'Let us, Ginger, reconstruct the process,' suggested Eddie, exhibiting an uncharacteristic scientific turn of mind.

'All right, let's,' said David, 'perhaps I'll do better next time although I thought I knew how to make pastry.'

As their preparations were described Ginger jotted down each phase and when David and Eddie had recalled what they had done it was to the former that the great mistake was revealed at once. 'I know what it was, he exclaimed, glad to be the first to spot his error, 'it was the cooking fat. I forgot to put in the cooking fat. No wonder it was like concrete.'

'That was a bit wet, Fres,' admonished Ginger mildly.

'Yes, rah-ther,' said Eddie.

'Still I think you might have noticed, Eddie, you were using the cooking fat yourself weren't you?' complained David.

Only Reynolds was uninterested in the solution to the cause of the disastrous meal. He leaned back in his chair, listlessly, quietly scratching his hairy forearms. He could not have cared less. His mind was on something else, far away. It was a relief that, for a change, he was minding his own business.

11

Next morning, when David turned out, he was aware the temperature of the cold mess deck had sagged even lower in the night. It was astounding to find that, as he struggled to lash and stow the hammock, hard breathing produced a vapour cloud. The metal rim of the stowage net was icy to touch and he hastened to put on his duffel coat, below which he already wore trousers, jersey and overalls. He pulled out his long, hand-knitted grey scarf from the coat pocket and wound it twice round his neck before tucking it into his overall front. Thus clad he felt ready to cope with the delicate business of getting his tea and toast.

Over by the electric radiator, that was, apparently, reluctant to emit any real heat whilst he contrived to give a fair browning to the slices of bread from a loaf that was beginning to go hard anyway, he glanced up at the metal lids over the scuttles. His slow, early morning mind saw something odd without registering, then a second startled glance allowed the impression to sink in. The steel discs were gathering a surface of frosty rime similar to that to be found lining a refrigerator or cold store.

'Look at that frost, Ginger,' he said to his senior hand, who sat in a wrapped-up mound on the bench just in front of him. 'We'll be like a lot of frozen mutton if this goes on.'

Ginger, unfamiliarly clad in a dark blue roll-necked jersey over his more usual blue American shirt and overalls, and wearing boots instead of white plimsolls, looked up from the gamboge-hued tea he was stirring lethargically. Drowsily he said, 'Yes I know, Dave. Robbie says they're going to try out the Arctic steam heating today. We're bloody well going to need it if this keeps up. I'm beginning to feel like the Eskimo with the frigid digit.'

Down at the office, in spite of having just done the morning watch, Fred was quite cheerful. His face twisted into a masochistic smile.

'It's cold out there ennit mate!' he said exaggerating a low-class accent and dropping the headphones casually onto the pad. 'I trust your boss has made us a lot of that steaming poison he does so well.'

He had already got on his overalls on top of his blue jersey and trousers. Before he left the office he pulled a hand-knitted khaki jersey over these as well. 'My mother thought I was going in the army,' he explained. With his life-belt underneath he began to take on a slight appearance of bulk.

His balaclava was properly navy blue and this he pulled down over his ears. At last he put on his duffel coat and wound a scarf round his neck.

Robbie was just handing over to Ginger. 'You should be warm enough in that lot, Fred, when the steam heating comes on.'

'Never mind, hookey,' replied Fred, as he put his cigarettes, matches, writing pad, envelopes and magazines into his pockets. 'I don't want mine to drop off.'

In the relative luxury of the office the forenoon went by peacefully enough. In this heart of the ship it was comfortable to manage without a duffel coat. When Eddie brought back the cocoa a wisp of vapour curled in from the alleyway as though out of a bathroom.

'They're trying out the heating,' he told everyone. 'There are clouds of steam floating about below the deckhead and large unpleasant drops of water splashing down everywhere. It's rather like the Amazonia greenhouse at the botanical gardens.'

'This class was purpose-built with the system,' Ginger informed them, 'it ought to be all right. It's the first time we've had it on.'

'Well, Ginger, I regret to say it doesn't look at all satisfactory,' persisted Eddie. 'Everybody will be down with bronchial pneumonia or something if it goes on. The bulkheads are running with condensation and it's all very beastly.'

His observations were only too true as they discovered themselves when they were relieved at noon. Clouds of steam were wafted about by the vents and the whole atmosphere was stickily unpleasant. People were in doubt as to whether it was advisable to take off their extra clothing, and the upper deck men, such as seamen and signalmen, found the change all too upsetting.

It so happened that afternoon they were all upper deck men part of the time at least. For dinner had hardly been cleared by the white watch ratings than Pots came down from the office and, rather apologetically it seemed, told them all spare hands were required on deck to chip it clear of ice that was forming. They had noticed how deserted the living quarters were, although David had observed Scouse Edwards was sprawled out on the lockers next door.

So once again they clad themselves in the extra clothing just taken off and trudged aft to the galley flat where the first lieutenant and bo'sun were detailing ratings to various parts of the upper deck. Ginger was ordered to take his three watch members down to the midships gun platform on the port side where there were implements left by the departed blue watch.

The cause of the icing was very evident. The heavy, grey gloom still hung along the north-west and out of it the wind, strong but not fierce now, carried curtains of snow. They advanced stealthily across the heaving sea which, although still high, had nevertheless lost its broken appearance and was a simple pattern of dark grey humps washing onto the port side. The destroyer was rolling heavily but in a steady, predictable fashion. The waves rarely washed along the iron deck and when they did only skirted it. As the showers passed across they dusted the ship with a fine, almost powdery snow which, in the bitter air, clung to the superstructure and grew the ice which hands were busily hammering and chipping away. The snowfalls passed on southwards across the convoy and in the distance, on its far side, the sky was more broken and cold yellow sunlight flickered in the clouds. Although it was not yet one o'clock, the sun was as low as it would have been at four in the afternoon in more civilized latitudes. All the ships visible were black silhouettes against this weak light with the exception of *Obstinate* which, rising up and down aft, was an eerie yellow grey, shining ghostlike on the dark water.

The dusky and forlorn scene was suited to knock the cheerfulness from anyone present. Yet all over the upper deck there was a staccato clatter and knocking which formed a background to many a quip or happy vulgarity. Bending to pick up a crowbar, David saw the peaky features of Fred glancing up from within his duffel coat hood. 'It's bloody cold isn't it, Dave?' he grinned, tugging vigorously at a particularly hard lump of ice with the claws of a hammer, only to discover it concealed a large bolt.

'Cold, Fred; bloody cold,' he replied. This remark inspired Ginger from near the forward torpedo tubes to render theatrically to the elements:

'Cold, cold, bloody cold, As cold as charity and that's bloody cold...'

This poetry caused a muffled figure busy sweeping ice chips daringly close to the guard rail to call out in the unmistakeable voice of Robbie, 'But not as cold as our poor Tilly,' which a chorus rounded off with: 'She's dead poor cow and that's effing chilly.'

'We were at it in the forenoon,' Fred confided, clenching his jaw as he raked out a particularly clogged up corner between a stanchion and pipe. 'What the panic is I don't know!'

Ginger was now down against the gun support, pushing his iron bar forward rhythmically. This was giving him a great deal of satisfaction that might be called suspect. He paused in his task to wipe some lumps of ice from the bar with his gloved hand and, hearing the remark, instructed them in the urgency of the business.

'If,' he said sharply, like a schoolmaster putting a dull pupil right, 'we did not get it over the side before it got too thick, the stability – you ignorant seaman – of the vessel would be endangered by too much top hamper. First we'd roll like that miserable bastard back there, then we'd keep going and not right ourselves. That is why all fit hands from the highest to the lowest are hard at it. The buffer says that even the skipper was enjoying himself up on B gun platform. Anyhow it'll give you an appetite for tea and this is better than breathing that atmosphere that reminds me of a Mombasa knocking shop!'

'Oh! I see, Ginger,' Fred humbly said.

In the meanwhile, when they were busy, a merchantman had come up from behind the convoy and closed to the starboard side. Drawing near, its lines showed it was an oiler and the two ships moved close together and continued on a parallel course. A line was shot over to their fo'c's'le, and a group pulled first on a rope that brought across a cable along which a pipe was suspended to connect with a fuel intake on that part of the ship. The destroyer was topping up its tanks and their closeness to the galley flat accounted for the strong reek of oil in that vicinity.

By now the light was failing and the hands were being called off the deck. David pulled off a glove to wipe the irritation of sweat from under the top part of the balaclava near his eyes, then reached down to pick up the bar with his bare hand. On the instant he remembered what he had read about metal burning flesh in extreme cold as well as heat. He loosened his grasp and for a breathless second it was suspended, stuck to the skin of his open palm but fell, without pulling off skin, with a crash to the deck. He put on his glove, picked the bar up and went forward into the fo'c's'le where the tools were being collected.

Eddie went straight into the seamen's mess when they got back into the steamy fo'c's'le. There was a general mix-up as they took off their damp top clothes and put them on locker or deck. Nobody was too keen to put the gear away in case, as was likely according to the rumour circulating, the heating was to be turned off owing to leakages caused by heavy weather.

By the time tea came up the heating experiment had been brought to an end. Ginger was glad since he said it was unkind to remind him of service in more agreeable places.

'I recall to mind,' he said, spreading jam thickly on a slice of bread that was on the verge of staleness, 'the time Robbie and me had a run ashore at Alex.'

There was, he remembered, a member of their mess who was not very popular on account of the fact that he did not keep himself too clean, and the odour he exuded was not welcome in the warm, between decks atmosphere off North Africa. There was, it seems, not far from Ramleh Square in Alexandria, a Turkish bath which they frequented especially after a boisterous liberty. One night, particularly warm, still and sultry, a group from the mess had come across the odiferous one, very intoxicated in a side street, the surface of which, he had evidently come into contact with in his uncertain progress.

Quickly they devised a plan which they hoped would not only take care of the smelly one's present unfortunate condition but would perhaps be a forceful way of convincing him of his messmates' disapproval of his usual hygienic standards.

'First of all, under the pretext of helping him back to the ship, we got him round to the baths, and to the amazement of the attendants did a quick job, despite his weak protests, of stripping him rollocky naked,' Ginger related. 'We then paid them generously to give him the full treatment and tell him if he resisted he wouldn't get his clothes back.'

They had then gone in search of somebody who would wash and press his gear, which they found without difficulty in spite of the late hour, as one always could in those parts where people wake up at night. Then they had gone back to see how he was getting on.

'We waited outside and could hear him screaming blue murder, so we sent in a message to say if he didn't submit he'd go back to the ship in a towel.'

By then he was sobering rapidly and realizing his predicament. They asked an attendant if he was getting cooperative and when this was affirmed gave him the clothes and directions to see their mess fellow left in a presentable state. Then they strolled back across the square and down to the dockyard, enjoying the beauty of the night.

'And it could be beautiful,' said Ginger rhapsodizing, 'A large moon and the aroma of the East that comes out at night. Even some of the disagreeable smells had a romantic quality. When I think of the Middle East I think of smells. It was a combination of dung, petrol, flowers, the cooking and women. They pour scent on themselves. And mates...' Here he pulled up his jersey neck so it was over his chin and tucking his head down like a tortoise retreating into its shell, 'white fronts, shorts and socks. Happy days!'

'What happened after,' Fred asked, 'did he get stroppy?'

'He never knew who did it. He was well gone when he went in and by the time he got aboard we were all turned in and innocent like. I reckon it did him good. He's a killick now. But it was the last of the good times. A few weeks later was the Crete do.'

Hardly had Ginger finished reminiscing than Eddie, now returned for his tea, said, 'Scouse isn't at all well.'

This forced a burst of laughter from Ginger and, regrettably, sniggers all round the mess table.

'That's nothing now, Eddie, when is he well?' asked Robbie, who hitherto had leaned over his mug, quietly sipping his tea with a faint smile on his lips, abstracted, as though taken back by Ginger's narrative to more congenial days.

'Oh, no,' Eddie was more explicit, 'I mean more than seasick, he says he has a bad pain in his abdomen and severe headaches now and again. Not the same thing.'

'I suppose it's caused by it,' said Robbie, not wishing to speculate further on the condition of the seaman-gunner.

With the second dog watch nearing its end David sat, headphones pulled off his ears, quietly assuming that except for the usual sighting report from their portside shadower the day had gone in a reasonably uncomplicated manner, even allowing for the steam-heating experiment in which he had not been too involved. It was a somewhat premature assumption, for two reasons.

The first was caused by a gap in supervision by a senior hand when Ginger had gone round to the ship's office and Pots had not arrived to take over. Ordinary telegraphist Reynolds had been yawning with boredom for the last half hour and when George came to take over he afforded an opportunity for sarcasm in which Reynolds indulged himself, singing with a certain emphasis, fortunately not for long, *You were my sunshine, my only sunshine...*

This time George became rather nettled and moved towards his tormentor. Reynolds was hastily pulling off his headphones and starting to rise when Pots stepped into the office. The heat was taken out of the situation and although nothing was said Pots looked from one to the other, not voicing the puzzlement that flooded his face as he sensed the tension.

Rowe, somewhat dilatory, came on watch after David had left and so the friction which might have occurred if the white watchkeepers found themselves in the TS alley at the same time was avoided.

Having put up his hammock and prepared it, David went down

to the washplace to meet the final irritation of the day. About to step into the area, he saw a tidal wave of soapy-blue water in which unpleasant little bits and pieces floated, washing back and forth across the deck with the motion of the ship. When it rolled to port the water rushed away to the other side, past the showers, where it gathered to a depth of nine inches or thereabouts. Then as the destroyer heeled back to the starboard side, so the waste water poured furiously down, hellbent to slop over the bulkhead step into the TS alley. It was obvious one could not wash in the ten to twenty seconds the deck near the hand basins was free.

Somebody else came and looked over his shoulder. He turned and saw Ginger very petulantly say, 'Effit, bleeding bilge trouble again. It's a freeze-up.'

To a testy enquiry from David as to what they could do he nodded to the far side of the space. 'Those tin baths in the shower. Watch me.'

In the shower area were two oval galvanized tin baths with quite high sides, usually employed for washing the heavier articles of gear. David gave him plenty of room as he put his towel round his neck and steadied himself by the sides of the doorway to spring forward.

The ship, in a momentarily level position before lurching to port, Ginger leapt across the near part of the deck as it cleared, grabbed a bath and stepped back to the hand basins up against the alley bulkhead and nimbly jumped into it. He just achieved his refuge as the greasy flood came splashing back. Wedging his toilet gear and towel behind the taps and rinsing the bowl, cheerfully he called out, 'Come on Dave. Try your luck. You can only get wet feet!'

To be less encumbered by it David leaned through the door and put his gear firmly behind the nearest basin. Then, waiting for exactly the right moment, he emulated the example of Ginger.

He was congratulated on still having dry feet. 'Good work,' said Ginger, 'You know, Dave, this never happens on big ships.' He paused whilst he rinsed his face and groping carefully, released the towel to dry himself. 'Never; well, hardly ever!'

12

'I think, Dave,' yawned Fred through a cloud of smoke, 'I'm going to kip down here. That mess deck is getting like Omsk in January.'

Well, thought David as he began to take down the 0400 routine, if he's asleep he can't be smoking. All the same, if everyone decided to do it the place would be like a tube train in the rush hour. By the time David had checked the preambles – hardly any traffic had passed since the sighting report at midday – Fred was propped up in the corner behind him, head on knees, sound asleep.

The main concern of Eddie at this hour was the continued pain of Scouse Edwards. He insisted to Ginger that it was something unusual but the senior hand of the watch remained sceptical. After a time he managed to turn the conversation in a more entertaining direction and Eddie chattered on about his aunt and a host of other relations who would leave him very comfortably settled one day. David was perturbed at the way he was so sure of his eventual well-being. Under the circumstances it was really tempting fate.

Although Eddie and Ginger managed to keep awake by their conversation that only halted for the occasional business – so occasional it suggested that even the Admiralty had forgotten them – David had begun to struggle with an overpowering drowsiness and once more he could only fight by standing up and gripping the chair as a support against the heaving deck.

He managed to get through the first hour until he sat down again to log the routine. He blew away the ash Fred had left liberally scattered about, instead of putting in the old tobacco tin provided, and had slapped the message pad clean when he was electrified by the unfamiliar steady, high-pitched beat of Morse, loud and cleanly tuned. It did not have a U-boat preamble and at first he thought it was another shore station in the network, but did not recognize the tone and hand of the transmitter. Indeed, the other stations along the enemy coast were always weaker in strength of signal than Narvik. This was louder.

He wrote down the time, date and numbers of groups. Twenty. No serial number. The preamble was being repeated and as he checked, gave Fred a kick and shouted, 'Up, quick!' The others were astonished by this performance. Reynolds, Ginger and Eddie stared inanely.

Fred was groping his way, half sightless, to the bench as David jerked his pencil towards the telephone and shouted, 'Bearing, quick!' Ginger managed to grasp the idea and leapt over the telephone and buzzed the HF-DF office. 'Dave says to get a bearing on what's coming through – all right, I'll wait.'

Finishing the message, David waited for the repeat back by Narvik to check it. The control acknowledged. It made key taps to show it was preparing to check back and then started the preamble, adding a serial number. As the check neared its conclusion Ginger said, 'Green zero four two – thanks mate – no I don't know, but it had Dave Freston in a flap. Yes, I'll let you know.'

'What do you think, Fred?' David asked.

'It can't be, can it?' he replied enigmatically to the annoyance of the other three present. 'No serial number!'

'Control added it,' David reminded him.

They thought a minute.

'Would they broadcast it for our benefit?' Fred was wide awake now and with shaking hands lit a cigarette. They both paused and thought hard. 'A regular bloody mystery,' said David, in a break from whistling air softly but untunefully through his teeth, 'but I've got a creepy feeling this is what we're here for.'

'What are you here for, kidder?' Ginger was getting agitated.

'Anyway it's the kind of thing the escort commander wanted,' Fred remembered. 'We'd better see about getting it across.'

'What the effing 'ell is it then, Dave?' Ginger was getting

worked up into a suitable state as spokesman for the almost uncontrollable anxiety of the others.

'It's – I, er, we, think it's from a surface vessel.'

On their urging, not liking to call Pots from what was tantamount to an all night in, Ginger reluctantly took the message, wrote the bearing on it and left the office. Half an hour later he came back. 'You will be happy to know,' he said as though he had enjoyed ruffling a few roosting feathers, 'that not only has your poxy message got Pots up, but has also managed to turn out the yeoman and even the skipper. Jimmy was on watch and – fortunately – in his right mind.'

It was from about this time that the message became their personal property and responsibility. That is, of the three special telegraphists in the main office. Somehow, the HF-DF operators aft never did have to bear the same onus. Theirs was a strictly tactical job, involved with the defence of the ship and convoy. It was George, Fred and David to whom this mysterious and unnerving business belonged. That it was still a mystery to them was not a mitigating circumstance. It was 'That bloody message you took,' or 'That effing message wot you got,' and later as they multiplied, just, 'Your messages.'

When George came on watch at 0800 he did not need to have the situation explained. It was circulating around and away from the communications' mess. The trio discussed the best plan and Fred suggested it ought to be put to the petty officer that there always should be two of them on watch in order to see if there was anything similar and if so, whether it had the same origin. David rather suspected Fred desired to take out a lease on the warmer office, but when it was mentioned to Pots he was quite agreeable and somewhat relieved, it seemed, to have a particular line of action.

So through the forenoon watch David and Fred came and went for refreshment and other necessities. David was out drinking cocoa when the older coder came down to collect drinks for blue watch.

'Your message is up again,' he said gravely, 'came through at 1000 hours. Fred Windenham says it sounds the same. They got a bearing.'

'The plot thickens,' said Eddie flippantly.

It's nothing to laugh at, you blewdy prat,' snapped Reynolds, looking up from his steaming mug, which he clasped tightly with both hands. He leaned over the table, the picture of miserable coldness.

'Well, we can't sit and cry over it!' exclaimed Eddie, a flush starting on his usually ivory pale features.

Once more that sensation of being a pariah, experienced earlier, came uppermost and David was glad to be called out with the rest to clear the upper deck of ice. He was not allowed to forget the shadowing U-boat either, for just before dinner he had encountered the literary, minded HF-DF operator who, as they methodically knocked and chipped away at the ice, mentioned that another report had been sent. The bearing of the submarine was still to port, at zero five three degrees.

Crouched down by the after torpedo tubes, David raking away with a hook paused and looked out over the cylindrical forms to that part of indetermination where the blanket grey of the overcast fused with the black, glacial humps of the swell. He screwed up his eyes as though anxious to pierce the poor visibility to where the enemy boat uncomfortably but confidently rode the waves, secure in the knowledge that no escort could be spared to hunt it.

In that dreadful place, he thought, there was no life but the few thousand humans, seemingly forgotten, drawn there by the unending aggression of their own kind. It was a place shunned by all other animals, a lifeless world. Deeps empty of living things and air void of birds or other evidence of creation. It was a dead sea. A sunless ocean that resented life and joyfully clawed dead men and ships down into its freezing, lightless oblivion. It was hard if not impossible to cleave to the daydream of a natural cycle of creation and life-force. There breathed no spirit of hope or promise on the sullenly waiting surface of these godless waters.

With a clatter the hook he had been wielding dropped on the iron deck and shook him out of his sombre thoughts. He shivered not with the cold, but more from that primitive sensation of creeping flesh, perhaps inherited from an ancestry more remote than reason when the instinctive predominated. The operator gave him a curious look. 'What's up with you Dave?'

'Nothing much mate. I was thinking about the sub out there.'

'Yes, it's funny to think there are probably blokes just like us in it.'

That afternoon David spent partly in the wireless office, double banking Fred. At 1500 hours a long transmission of some twenty groups came through clearly, bell-like in its ringing quality of tone. The hand of the operator was the same. Fred was immersed in getting it down and shortly after he had finished, the telephone to HF-DF buzzed and Robbie took the bearing. 'Green, zero three eight.' He wrote it down on the message and when Fred had checked it from the repeat back and added its serial number, appended by Narvik control, left the office. Presumably he was going to see it was reported to the escort commander in *Severe*.

In the second dog watch those off duty, ludo and other pastimes neglected, fell to squabbling over the significance of the messages intercepted by the special operators. One could almost feel the unspoken, communal sense of impending crisis that was developing below everyone's casual words and activities. Robbie thought that whatever it was could not be very important because the enemy would not be advertising themselves.

'They do it with the subs,' Ginger objected.

'All right, get your map out, mate, and let's see where we are,' Robbie suggested.

At some inconvenience to those on the lockers nearest the head of the table, Ginger rummaged amongst his gear and brought out a map, rather dog-eared, which he lovingly spread out on the tabletop. A pattern of red lines straggled their way over the sea areas round the Continent and a particularly complex maze covered the Mediterranean area. One lonely line soared up from the base, round the North Cape to Murmansk.

'Now,' said Robbie, assuming an odd air of command as he reared over the paper, 'according to our good friend the chief buffer we're galloping along at the fantastic rate of six knots, which is six nautical miles per hour.'

'How much is that in real terms?' Fred was determined not to be hoodwinked.

'In dry land terms, Freddio, somewhere in the region of seven miles per hour.'

'Not very fast is it?' Fred sagely observed.

'Fast? If we go any slower we'll be at a bloody standstill.'

'That map is in land miles anyway, so don't baffle us with science. Let's get on with it,' grumbled Ginger.

'Let's get on with it,' mocked his old shipmate in a passable impersonation of the radio comedian whose catch phrase it was. 'Now supposing we are doing seven by twenty-four miles a day, that is, um, 168, say 170 miles for every day we've been out of Seydis Fiord.'

The others – except Ginger – were impressed by this exercise of nautical expertise. 'That's four days. Go on mark it up towards the north-east; 680 miles at midday.'

There was an unusual silence while Ginger, with a piece of cigarette packet as a gauge, took pencil marks of a hundred miles from the scale of the map and picked out a route due north-east from their departure point.

'That puts us about here,' he said, 'even if it's almost off the map.'

'Never mind,' said Robbie, 'it's only water there as we know too well!'

'Is that by the rhumb line or great circle?' Reynolds had slithered up to the edge of the group.

'All right sprog,' scowled the leading hand of the mess, 'we all know you were in the sea cadets.' He continued. 'Now then we can't allow for zigzags or diversions, as far away from the Norwegian coast – I hope – as possible, because the skipper hasn't taken us into his confidence. But we know from HF-DF both the ship's heading when the transmissions were made and their bearing from us.' Even Ginger was impressed now by his friend's learned exposition of the facts.

'Now say we were there at 0500 hours back about ninety miles. Mark it, Ginge.' He waited for Ginger to use the piece of card to mark off a tick back along the course line. 'We were headed 048 and the bearing from us was green four two. We haven't got a means of measuring angles...'

'Yes, I have,' interrupted Eddie, 'I've got a ruler in my writing case.'

There was another concentrated pause while he got it.

'Now, taking this bearing near enough across to the Norwegian coast, let's leave it a minute.'

'That's my map you're drawing on.' Ginger was asserting his rights.

'All right misery, you do it,' Robbie mollified him. 'Now, sir, will you kindly mark another point a quarter inch forward from our midday position to 1500 hours when the last message was intercepted. Thank you, your lordship. Now, our heading then was 043 which is more or less what we've got marked. Now from 1500 hours will your highness draw a bearing green zero three eight. Now look children, where they go. The latest passes north of North Cape and the other goes to here on the Norwegian coast. Measure the shortest distance between them from the coast northwards.'

Here for a moment, Ginger appeared not to know north from south.

'That way, you crun,' indicated Robbie airily.

'An inch and a quarter,' said Ginger.

'So,' pronounced Robbie, pausing a moment while he did some arithmetic on the piece of card. 'If the scale of this map is a hundred miles to the inch then that is 125 miles – at least – in ten hours. Therefore that ship, if it is the same one,' here he looked quizzically at David, who said, 'It certainly sounds like it, hookey,' '...that ship is moving at twice our rate, say about thirteen miles per hour on a course likely to converge on ours, somewhere between North Cape and Bear Island, depending on how far south the ice is.'

The gathering was morbidly silent when Robbie ended his dissertation. The ratings sat or lolled around looking down at the map. A curious few had even been drawn across from the radar mess. They quietly swayed in rhythm with the rolling ship, its humming and shuddering once more apparent.

'What time?' asked a red watch signalman, a thick-set young fellow whose youth had been wind-blasted from his chapped ruddy features.

'If it's moving towards us – that is, west-north-west and not due north – it would mean it's moving faster than we calculated, and so likely to meet us early in the morning.'

'So what?' snapped Reynolds. 'Yew're all getting steamed up over their poncy messages.' Not diplomatically put, it was, nevertheless, true. That nobody present could gainsay. Yet always it is the unknown which troubles and this was such an occasion. Their companion-enemy out on the port bow was an established fact to which they were becoming accustomed. Would it be more comfortable for them to have the mystery remain or at last know its significance? It was a debatable point.

A capital ship on a foray? David smiled inwardly that the idea had even fleetingly crossed his mind. But somehow the messages had an individuality about them that recalled the instruction of his wireless school days. Such a signal could have come from a battleship.

'Where does that first bearing go to Ginger?' he asked aloud, peering down at the fine print of place names on the coast.

Nose almost touching the paper, Ginger wagged his head from side to side to read the small letters. 'Let's see. Hammerfest, no. Tromso, too much south. Some place right between called Alt – Alten Fiord.'

'Oh no!' Fred exclaimed dolefully, 'I know.'

'And so do I,' said David as they caught each other's glance.

'Well what do you think it is then?' Ginger voiced the concern of the rest.

'You know. You mentioned it yourself. The *Schleswig*.'

'Yes, but it's sunk, you big nit!'

'Half a mo, Ginger.' Fred grinned nervously at his unenviable role of revealing bad news. 'There's another one. Even bigger. I've seen it on the news at the pictures. Whatitsname, begins with a T.'

'*Trebnitz*,' put in David.

'Yes, that's it Dave, the *Trebnitz*. Why wouldn't they like to have a go in revenge for the *Schleswig* going down?'

'And it could be a trawler,' Reynolds thought aloud.

'Making a hell of a lot of row if it is,' David contradicted severely.

'Well, whatever it is we'll bloody well know by this time tomorrow,' Ginger murmured unhappily as he carefully folded his map.

Not long after the inquisitorial group had dispersed George

came off watch to reveal there had been a fourth signal, louder still, just as he had been about to hand over to Fred. Its bearing was still to starboard, zero three two degrees. Whatever it was seemed steady on a course towards them and this did nothing to relax the tension and probably helped to exacerbate it. Feeling in dire need of fresh air, David went out to stand by the funnel. He gazed ineffectually out into the swishing darkness and wondered what was coming up to them from the south-east. He had not been on the iron deck long when the tarpaulin flapped open showing briefly the blue light, and he heard Eddie say, 'Is that you, Freston?'

'Getting some air,' David said by way of an explanation, 'before I try to get a little shut eye.'

'You can cut the atmosphere with a knife down there,' said Eddie confidentially as though any other person could possibly hear above the clamour of ship and waves, 'in more senses than one.'

'It may not be anything special,' David averred, contriving to be unaffected by the general mood.

'I'm not talking about your messages, Freston, I'm afraid Corder and Reynolds nearly came to blows just now.'

'Go on! What happened?'

'George sat down to write a letter to his girl and Reynolds made some remark about her being like Florence; all the troops would be going through her. Only Ginger and the blue watch coder, you know, the nice quiet chap, Streeter, kept them apart. It was all very unpleasant. I can't stand such scenes so I came out here!'

'Well, that's a turn up! Sometime, sooner or later, we're going to see a dust up and it's so pointless and useless. What the hell's wrong with Reynolds?'

'He's not popular.'

'Hardly sets out to be, does he?' observed David as, driven in by the freezing night, they slowly went back to their hammocks.

Whilst David prepared to turn in he noticed Ginger sitting over on the lockers side of the mess table, looking remarkably uninterested in snatching a little nap before midnight. He noticed David's curiosity and covertly shook his head and put a forefinger to his lips in a gesture of silence, then looked from George, swinging in his hammock over by the petty officers' ladderway, to Reynolds, sitting at the end of the table, very much awake, reading his magazine. An explanation would have been superfluous to the most unperceptive mind that the senior hand of his watch was taking care there would be no further outbreak of hostilities.

It only seemed a few minutes after David got into his hammock that the call of white watch to cruising stations was being made by the bo'sun's mate. Ginger was already down at the office when he arrived and Fred merely drooped from the chair down into his favourite corner. 'The way we've been getting those signals every five hours, there should be another one up at one o'clock,' he said. 'Might as well stay here and see it out.'

Fifty minutes later his forecast proved correct. Very loud, so loud David had to turn down the volume to make it less painful to his ears, even managing with one earpiece on his cheek, the message rang with beautiful style and the hand of the operator, the same one as before no doubt, had a metre that evoked a mental picture of elegant handwriting. The same keen interest was taken by the other occupants of the office and HF-DF sent through a bearing of green zero one five.

'The bastard sounds just on the other side of the convoy,' grumbled Ginger as he left the office. Fred, thinking his duty was done, stretched right out on the deck and was soon lost to the world.

When David had checked the carbon copy and tidied up the bench around his set he leaned back and glanced past Eddie, absorbed in his poetry book, to Reynolds. It was quite natural to do so for the ordinary telegraphist was continually fidgeting. He would swing his chair from side to side, tap his pencil on the bench or pad and nervously flick the corners of the message pad. In sum, he presented such a picture of imperfectly suppressed agitation that he began to unsettle David, and as the hour hand on the office clock, high on the bulkhead behind Reynolds, crawled intolerably round from one to four, he felt that any instant, in the next painfully anticipated second, the alarm bells would ring, simultaneously with the wail of huge shells falling into the convoy.

Ginger, however, had come back, saying he could elicit no worthwhile information from the yeoman and first lieutenant; Eddie had gone and made the cocoa and it had been drunk; Narvik control had started the last hourly routine of his watch and David was relieved to find the threat had still not materialized. Now the clock hands stood at nearly ten past four and the door opened and George stepped into the office.

Uncoiling from his swivel chair like a striking cobra, Reynolds reared up taking a wild swing with his right fist at George, who paused by the main transmitter to regain his balance and shut the door before he noticed Streeter following him. Instinctively his great arms went out in a posture of defence and with his long reach he easily pushed his attacker back, as though he were a punchbag. The aggressor slipped, fell back against his seat, failed to grab it as it treacherously spun round and slithered down, like a concertina, knees doubled under his chin and struck the back of his head on the corner of the iron safe. There was a horrid box-like crack and almost at the same time his lower jaw clicked shut, cutting off a ghastly moan, his arms falling limply on his doubled-up trunk.

In the brief seconds of the scuffle Streeter had stepped over the coaming into the office just too late to restrain George. He shut the door and, with Ginger, who had risen up despairingly, quickly got between George and Reynolds. They need not have bothered.

'Christ!' shouted Ginger, 'this'll cause it if Pots comes in. Quick Jimmy help me get the mad bastard up.'

George staggered back against the door appalled; Fred aroused by the disturbance stood irresolutely by him; Eddie recoiling in horror, got out of his seat and leant against the bench, hypnotized by what was happening but sickened by the violence. 'God,' he gasped, 'how horrible.'

Ginger and Streeter were having a great deal of difficulty getting the unconscious telegraphist out of the encumbered corner into which he had slumped. 'Come on someone, give us a hand,' snapped Ginger.

David had pulled off the headphones and dropped them on the pad. Now he pushed past Eddie and the three of them managed to get the extraordinarily heavy Reynolds into his chair. He was not just stunned. He was quite unconscious. His head lolled back so badly Streeter had to support it with his hands. He drew one away and the rest saw it was covered with blood. The sallow dirty complexion had gone a pasty white and the bone structure of the face was more prominently corpselike than ever. The jaw had loosened and the wide mouth was disgustingly agape with a trickle of saliva in its corners.

George, shaken to a white faced horror, whispered, 'Effing 'ell. He's bonkers. Raving stark bonkers,' as he shakily accepted a cigarette from an equally tremulous Fred.

The door opened. Pots stepped in and was looking as though he was going to make some humorously caustic comment about the unusual throng, when he saw Reynolds. 'What's up with him?' he asked sharply. After a brief embarrassed silence, Ginger said, 'He fell and hit his head on the safe.'

'Fell? You can tell that to the Marines. Is he bad?'

'Pretty bad.'

'Well don't just stand there! Ginger, get one of the stretchers secured in the galley flat.'

Just then Rowe came in. 'Get on that frequency quick. It's not the time for missing signals.'

This Rowe had to accomplish sitting on the metal box which had so effectively put his opposite number out for the count. Pots himself called HF-DF and told them to get the sick berth attendant up as fast as he could be turned out. Having done all that could be done for the time being he turned to David, Fred and Eddie and said, 'You lot had better clear off. We'll need all the room we can to get this silly bastard onto the stretcher.'

Unhappily they went back to a mess deck, quietly innocent of the drama in the W/T office. David took off his boots and hauled himself up into his hammock. Fred was manifestly still all aquiver as he finished his cigarette and turned in. He looked over to his messmate and said quietly, 'Bloody hell, Dave, what are we going to say if there's an enquiry?'

David pushed his partly inflated lifebelt down into the clews to serve as a pillow. 'The truth,' he said somewhat priggishly. 'I don't see that it can hurt George.'

At breakfast time the scandal was generally known in the communications' mess and rapidly getting to distant corners of the ship. When George came off watch he was his usual stolid self, but perhaps a soft core of worry was to be detected below his phlegmatic shell. He had some interesting news, however, when he told David, who had been earnestly assuring him he had nothing to be concerned about, that the mystery transmission had moved to green zero two four degrees. Perhaps this considerable change of bearing was due to the heading of the convoy, but George did not think so. Furthermore, much relief was experienced while David was at the office double-banking Fred at 1100 to hear a signal less powerful and a starboard bearing of zero four seven degrees. There was a general feeling that whatever it was had turned away sharply from them. It was to be hoped so anyway.

His extra duty done, David decided to take advantage of the brief daylight to join the funnel club for a spell before dinner. Whilst he was putting on his duffel coat the chief bo'sun came heavily down the ladderway from his mess above and was about clump down the TS alley when Ginger called over from where he was helping the cooks, 'How much longer before we get in, Chief?'

'About three days, Ginger, we're coming up to Bear Island now.'

David followed the bo'sun down to the iron deck and joined the group of loungers. He would have looked, to the casual observer, well integrated with his shipmates, one of the mob, but he was alone. Quite alone with his thoughts as he gazed over the convoy. *Stavanger* was on the port leg of her zigzag and was quite near. Taking advantage of her close proximity, she had quite a conversation with *Watchful* by lamp. Astern *Obstinate* rocked madly in the swell, which seemed of the consistency of molten lead, without its temporary quicksilver shine. It was solid-looking and grey, rose up in long, slow humps which rippled with tiny indentations. The ships were dark grey, formless shapes as though cut from cardboard, and they slid up and down, crest and trough in a gentle relaxing rhythm. The sky was now totally overcast, but the snow had ceased to fall. To the south there was a silver brilliance hinting at a sun somewhere shining, but above the swinging foremast the overhead blanket had a woolly quality about it, and as it fell away to the north it darkened into the deeper grey of the sea.

He went round the funnel and felt the wind still blowing from the north-west but it was now hardly more than a stiff breeze. It was not an interest in the weather that had moved him to looking over the port side, but the thought that he might glimpse the almost legendary Bear Island. It was a name that figured often in the conversation of those who had done this run before. It symbolised the discomfort they had experienced and represented the suffering. It was a vain hope on his part to see it. Few had. Those who had said it was a grim sight. A sheer, ice-clad rock; high, grey like a gravestone, the very embodiment of death. Indeed it was just that: the tombstone of ships and the bones of men, rearing out of the frightful black deeps which they littered. The remains of the ingenuity, skill, craftsmanship and love of many nations all gathered together in an awful, unseen rubbish dump of life and hope. A watery charnel house. It was very depressing. As he glanced back even the defiant white ensign had a forlorn quality in its raggedness.

In the office after dinner Eddie was smart in a black roll-necked sweater that he had not worn before. He explained it was his last resort. He had been leaving it as the final layer of clothing. He had every other wearable item of apparel under it. In fact, in or out of the office, they were all gathering odd-looking bulk as they stuffed extra clothing below overalls or jerseys. In the forenoon he had seen Scouse Edwards, who was no better, doubled up with pain, sickness and headache.

'I'm really worried about him, Ginger,' Eddie said.

'Well, why doesn't he go and see the tiffy?' was his somewhat acid reply. He was getting irritated by Eddie's solicitude for the seaman-gunner. 'Does he want you to hold his hand while he goes?'

It was not Edwards who became the main concern of the watch that afternoon, however, for when Robbie came in to do an hour on the Admiralty frequency – all the general telegraphists including Pots were doing an hour of Reynolds' watch – he mentioned that their erstwhile colleague had spells of consciousness and in one of them had told the coxswain he had been knocked down.

It was the central theme of speculation during the dog watches. Nobody was happy to hear that the incident had reached higher authority. This would most likely mean complications. 'If he hadn't opened his trap and told the coxswain what happened Pots might have been able to make it just another sea injury,' said Ginger.

'Still,' Robbie reflected aloud, 'with a skate like Reynolds you couldn't trust him to keep quiet about what happened. Sooner or later it would have come out. Pots would be in the rattle himself and he's got a lot to lose.'

'All the same I reckon he'd have hushed it up,' persisted Ginger.

'Yes, maybe you've got something there,' agreed his friend.

They were able to talk freely; George was not there. Blue watch was at cruising stations. Eddie was puzzled that a person could behave in such an irrational way. 'What on earth is the matter with Reynolds?' he asked rhetorically but which was productive of an answer.

'He was windy,' said Robbie quietly. He saw that there was a quizzical look on the faces of many around him. He felt obliged to explain. 'Of course we're all the same, when it comes down to it, but we try to settle it in ourselves. He had to take it out on somebody else. George was the most convenient. He was always a bit cocky in a quiet way about his ability with the girls and also had that solid way, as though he didn't appreciate any threatening danger. This niggled Reynolds, but it could have been any one of us; George filled the bill. I'm afraid he couldn't get at the Jerries for making him feel abject so George was a good substitute.' He turned to a perplexed Fred. 'If you'll excuse the expression your oppo was a kind of ersatz Hun. Reynolds is the type who has to relieve his own feelings at someone else's expense.'

'Never mind,' said Ginger, 'if it gets serious we'll all speak for George. I don't see why that little effer should ruin his prospects. It wouldn't be right.'

'By the way, how is our injured war hero?' asked Eddie.

'Pots says he's in a bad way. They don't know whether his skull's fractured or not. He still passes out. How serious it is the tiffy isn't qualified to say,' Robbie continued. 'The *Severe* has the flotilla quack, but as she's on the other side of the convoy he can't be put over to us. They'll have to wait till we get to Kola, we've got a hospital there now.'

After a cautious wash that was more of a cat lick as he did not care to expose himself to the cold more than absolutely necessary, David went down in a passably cheerful mood to do the first watch. Nothing had been heard of the menace since the forenoon and it seemed to have disappeared south beyond their ken. But the instant he stepped into the office he knew something had happened, for Fred was tremulous in a billowing cloud of smoke. Robbie had a faintly uncomfortable grin suggesting he was amused by Fred's agitation but not whole-heartedly. David did not have to ask what the matter was. 'A sub signal,' exclaimed Fred, as though it were a birthday surprise gift, 'on the other side of the convoy; came up a few minutes ago. It doesn't sound like Old Faithful.'

David took the headphones with one hand and wafted away tobacco fumes with the other. 'There isn't any need,' he said, 'to be so bloody pleased about it!' He decided his opposite number saw the wireless office as some kind of motion picture house, for he folded his duffel coat into a cushion and made himself comfortable in the corner formed by the alley and forward bulkheads. I wish, thought David, as he took down the routine, but left it unsaid, for Fred was such an inoffensive fellow, you would go and take your bloody cigarettes with you.

The ensuing four hours proved, however, that Fred's instinct for the diverting was reliable. For hardly had Narvik finished its routine than a submarine signal came up loud and clear. 'Green one four five,' repeated Ginger as he jotted down the bearing HF-DF sent through. 'There's another bastard on our tail,' he complained.

Control repeated it back with a serial number and followed it with a very long signal of many groups. Assiduously getting it down, David wondered what its content was or whether it was just a dummy. A bit pointless that, at such a time. Hardly did he get it torn off the pad, than another U-boat transmission came up. HF-DF said this one was also astern, this time red one two seven. Uneasily he recalled the battle they had heard in the area between North America and the Island. Behind him Fred vigorously scratched himself, fumbled for a cigarette and offered Ginger one. Their senior hand accepted it, put it on the bench in front of him until he had called the bridge and given the latest bearing, then begged a light from Fred before he sat down in his chair again. He sniffed, coughed and looked along at David. 'They're ganging up on us. I feel like one of those cowboys in a covered waggon train when the Indians close in,' he said lugubriously.

13

When he had turned in just after midnight, David thought he would not be able to sleep, so uncomfortably excited had he become. However, hardly had he wrapped himself in the carefully arranged blanket than he was fast asleep. He awoke considerably refreshed by seven hours of rest and breakfasted on tea and hard biscuits. All the bread had been consumed, the last being almost as hard as biscuit and not as edible.

Going into the office for the forenoon watch the uneasy sense of anticipation welled up again as he looked at the work of the preceding watches. The log book showed how busy they had been during the small hours with many more signals from U-boats on bearings all round the convoy and greatly increased activity by Narvik control. Long messages were being sent and for the first hour of duty he was concerned with the tail end of this business. By 0900 things were once more becoming quiet except for the hourly routines.

There was not much conversation during the watch. Eddie read a book, not being busy, and Ginger pottered in and out of the office when he was not doing a spell on the quiescent Admiralty wavelength. Eddie fetched the cocoa. It was drunk with only a laconic remark or two and it was extraordinary how softly people spoke to each other. There was an understood kindliness between shipmates and gone was much of the customary brashness. In the office the absence of Reynolds might seem to have accounted for the gentler atmosphere, but the same phenomenon had been noticeable earlier at breakfast and in the washplace, as with those who came and went in the office. It was reasonable to assume that perhaps they all looked with unpleasant foreboding to the coming hours and somehow, in the mysterious chemistry of the human spirit, it was productive of a heightened awareness and consideration for their fellows.

Pots came in whilst they were drinking the cocoa and confidentially informed David that if the ship went to action stations he was to go down to aft damage control. George was to take over his watch if he should happen to be on the set, and Fred was to double bank George. David would have very much liked to ask why they were being rearranged in this somewhat fussy way, but surmising it had something to do with the poor showing of his friends when first coming aboard, remained silent.

The morning wore on and the idle rush of static was, in its way, as disagreeable as the obvious intention of the enemy manifested in the earlier messages – no doubt battle instructions – sent out from their headquarters. David tried to divert himself with games of noughts and crosses: left hand was X, right hand 0. Eddie looked sidelong at him from his book: 'Come on, Freston,' he said, 'I'll play too!' They covered the back of one message sheet and had started on another with a game remembered from schooldays. This was where, by means of a pattern of dots, one tries to make little boxes and the initial of the player who constructs the fourth side to the square is entered in it to score a point.

'I thought you two weren't sporty types,' Robbie said, quietly amused, when he came in to do an hour for Reynolds. David looked over Eddie's shoulder. 'I'd even play cricket now if it was possible,' he smiled wanly. Robbie paid only fleeting attention to the remark for a message had started to take his attention. Below the twittering of the Morse Eddie murmured, to the not inconsiderable embarrassment of David, 'My mind isn't on this. You know, right now I'm praying hard to stop anything happening.'

'If it's going to happen, it will. There's nothing we can do about it. If you want to know I think we've been forgotten by God and the Admiralty.'

'No, we bloody well haven't, Dave,' shouted Robbie flinging the sheet along the bench. 'Here, Eddie, get stuck into that, it's "Most Immediate".'

Pots had the sixth sense of the veteran. He picked that moment to come back, going straight to switch on the ship-to-ship radio telephone, then breathed down Eddie's neck as he worked on the code. Before its content was in plain language the awful clangour of the action alarm bells stridently probed into the last fibre of their nerves and along the TS alley running footsteps pounded by. In burst Fred, narrow jowls drawn down, open-mouthed, his grey eyes glitteringly wide. He was closely followed by Rowe; then Streeter, breathing hard, George and every other off watch wireless rating.

'Here you are, George,' gasped David, through a constriction in his throat, 'I'm off!' He dropped the headphones, picked up his duffel coat, pushed through the crowd and rushed down to the galley flat putting on the coat at the same time. Emerging hastily on the iron deck, he heard the whooping siren of *Stavanger* out over the swell and glancing across saw her leaping forward, stern down in a beaten frothy wake, signals fluttering up to the halyards.

Prudence slowed David to a brisk walk and, grasping a lifeline loop, he moved aft. Passing below the starboard midships Oerlikons he heard the number one gunner call out to his partner, still struggling up the ladder onto the platform, 'Look at the mad bastards, taffy, they're effing well enjoying it!'

Even if the imminent air attack signals had not been flapping stiffly from the foremast, David would have had no doubt as to what kind of enemy assault was coming in. Over the stern housing, X gun was slowly rising up to a high angle, a phallic symbol of strife. Before he stepped through the starboard doorway, the door clipped securely open, he looked back and saw the Bofors and Oerlikons were all pointing skywards, the former moving round from side to side as though uncertain which way the enemy would approach. Atop the foremast the radar grid rotated, silently probing the ether for the oncoming danger.

Stavanger was now well ahead of them, slowing down to convoy pace, in a zone of fire unobstructed by her consorts, her armament thrust upwards, similarly unsure from whence the airplanes would come. The overcast was smooth and high, though its silver brightness was unable to soften the hard grey ripples on the slowly heaving water.

In the flat there was peace; underfoot the turning engines were comfortably steady but distant. The sick bay door was latched open and the attendant was carefully arranging surgical instruments, dressings, syringes and sundry other medical requirements. There were four cots and only the bandaged head of Reynolds was visible outside the coverlet of a lower one. The attendant turned round and said, 'What's doing, sparks?'

'Looks like an air raid on the way. How's Reynolds?'

'Under sedation. When he's awake he's in great pain. I'll only be happy when he's had an X-ray at the hospital.'

'Maybe,' mused David aloud, 'he's the lucky one being out for the count right now.'

As he spoke the droning sound of aircraft became audible above the muted noise of ship and sea. The attendant paid attention to his lifebelt. He tugged it close on his shoulders and tied the front knot more firmly. Then he half inflated it so that it would not be too much of an encumbrance. Going back to the doorway David, covertly, did likewise.

For some moments the aircraft droned above the overcast, the pilots probably unsure of their exact location or, if sure, steeling themselves for the dive through the friendly clouds. David recalled the clock in the sick bay was at eleven thirty-five. He wondered what they did in the galley about dinners cooking on the range. Did they turn off the heat? Just about now people in city offices would be thinking of going to lunch but they were more than hundreds of miles distant. He felt beyond all four dimensions. The person who had gone with others to restaurants, canteens or teashops was somebody else, not him. Yet he was not here now. There was a person standing there, in that freezing, uncomfortable and possibly dangerous place, but it was not him. He, that is, the thinking, feeling part of him, was disembodied and in some infinity light years away.

Then his stomach wriggled with a sensation familiar from the old days of air raids on the capital, for the engine sound of one of the airplanes changed to a shrill whine as it dived through the clouds. It appeared on the far side of the convoy, a dark speck, flew steadily, even whilst deadly little sparks that blossomed into white and black puffs of smoke flickered nearer and nearer, marking its flight. Then it turned upwards into the clouds and hardly had the changing sound of striving motors carried across to them, than several huge columns of water gushed up, soon followed by the roar of exploding bombs.

So the attack proceeded, haphazard, and, fortunately, it seemed ill-directed. An aircraft would dive through the clouds, hold steady as long as it was necessary to aim its bomb sights on a ship and release its deadly load. To the gunners it was a race to turn to another part of the grey sky and fire off a few rounds with the main armament. Even the guns on the merchant ships were participating in this larger scale parody of a grouse shoot. Tracer shells from Bofors and some Oerlikons curved upwards, more as a deterrent than with a hope of making a hit. It was the large calibre guns which roared angrily around the convoy as a competition took shape to get the first shot in on a new target. Ships seemed to have extraordinary luck. Up would sprout fountains of exploding water around some vessel or other and when the spray was gently drifting away it would emerge, rocking defiantly but none the worse, apparently, for the experience. It was all very casual; even, thought David, rather guiltily, somewhat entertaining. The forward guns had crashed out shells on a few occasions but so far X and Y turrets had been silent.

Unnervingly, several things then occurred so closely in succession as to be almost simultaneous. The guns above and abaft his post fired, the noise more of a metallic, crashing thud than an explosion. Between their repeated shots the descending whine of an aircraft merged with that familiar staccato, swishing, madly breathless rush of falling bombs indicating they were very close. The engines had been beating up furiously to full speed and *Watchful* rocked and bucketed on the swell. David, hanging on to the doorway, instinctively crouched, foolishly hoping it would render his body less vulnerable. Under an order that could only have been 'Hard a'port' the ship lurched wildly in that direction, almost wrenching him from his support. There was an ominously growing thunderous roar; the ship jerked as though punched by an invisible mighty fist and the sea surface all down the starboard side soared up out of his petrified sight. There were a number of peculiar rending, scraping thuds in the uproar and down came a deluge of salt water and an acid cold spray rolled in the entry stinging his bare face and hands.

'Christ!' he screamed to himself, rubbing at his burning face, 'that water's cold.'

Her racing engines throbbing fiercely, *Watchful* never took on a more living character than at that moment when, sympathetically, her thumping pulse kept pace with his own. This complex arrangement of metal, this floating factory became organic just as when he had felt her fight the storm. Recoiling from the bombs it was as though she strove to protect with a maternal instinct the men within her bosom. During those desperate minutes David conceived an affection and pride for her that was almost unbalanced.

The engines slowed their pace, the roar of guns and drone of aircraft faded, the sick-bay flat was once more its former quiet self. Nothing might have appeared to have happened but for the wet deck inside the entry and the faintest whiff of gunsmoke. David rummaged below his duffel coat for a handkerchief and, wiping his damp hands and face, looked out of the door. Then he had an odd recollection that in the tumultuous seconds of the bombing there had been only one thing that had flashed through his numbed mind. He laughed aloud at the absurdity of it. It was quite ridiculous. A girl he knew often wore a very becoming black dress with a low fronted V neckline. In its cleft between her breasts she pinned an artificial red rose. In that grim instant it had come before his mind's eye as clear as a lantern slide. He grimaced at his own embarrassment, blew his nose vigorously, put his handkerchief away and went outside.

From under the starboard aft Oerlikon platform he could see the merchantmen trying to occupy their exact stations after the straggling caused by manoeuvres to avoid falling bombs. Then again he heard over the swishing wash the growl of aircraft, low this time, and hardly was it audible than the main armament of the escorts on the far side flashed, followed quickly by thuds.

The telephone buzzed. Stepping back he felt the increasing revolutions as the ship built up momentum for action, that echoed again the increased thumping of his heart as the dryness of excitement rose in his throat. It caused a high pitch in his voice as he called, 'Aft damage control, point one.'

'This is Pots,' barked the petty officer telegraphist in unaccustomed exasperation. 'What's going on?'

'There are some more planes over the other side and they're shooting at them.'

'Well tell us then,' snapped the petty officer.

'Aye-aye, Pots.'

'Don't stand up there like a spare one at a wedding!'

'No, Petty Officer.'

'You're there to keep me informed.'

'Yes, Pots.'

'You buzz me!'

'Very good.'

Click.

Stepping back to the door he could see the smoke streaming away from the flashes and the growing pattern of anti-aircraft fire along the southern horizon. The irregular thunder of big guns was joined by the steady coughing of Bofors as the targets came in range and then the rapid crackle of Oerlikons completed the distant curtain of sound.

He jumped back to the telephone and rattled the buzzer. 'Wireless office.'

'They're all firing now,' he reported, 'at a low angle.'

'Torpedo planes,' said Pots, 'you'll be seeing them any minute.'

Back at his doorway he stared keenly at the rippling fire and tracers flicking up over the ships. Then he saw them, fast moving, darting between the oblong hulks of the cargo ships, soaring up and turning away from the zone of fire. Again he felt no fear; it all seemed so distant, film-like, only that guilty exhilaration aggravated when a great column of dark stained water, smoke and vapour shot up and the rending crash sped across the sullen ocean.

'One of the packets' been hit,' he reported.

'We heard it all right,' Pots answered soberly. But now he was apprehensively aware the aircraft noise was increasing and that movement and clatter on X gun platform above again presaged something disagreeable. Hardly had he returned the telephone to its rest when a crash overhead, followed almost simultaneously by a bang from Y gun aft and the swirling reek of explosive, sent him dashing across the sloping deck of the flat to the port doorway.

At first he saw nothing in the northerly grey fusion of sea and cloud but then, as the spiteful yellow sparks changed into anti-aircraft bursts, he saw the torpedo bombers fanning out, dropping down to sea level and almost disappearing as they skimmed over the swell. Now his ears were overwhelmed with the bellowing of A and B guns, joining the stern main armament as fast as the shells could be rammed home into the breeches. It was not an objective thing now and his mentality tried to take refuge deep inside his vulnerable flesh.

The engines were pounding up to maximum speed, shaking every atom of her superstructure as the destroyer began to zig-zag erratically to avoid a fatal torpedo. He was hanging onto a rail just inside the door, poking his head through to watch the smoke and flame belch from the forward guns and the wash hissing high up to the iron deck as they listed to port in sharp turns. The sick berth attendant had left his unoptimistic duties and staggered across to his side just as the aircraft came into sight.

'Look at the buggers!' he gasped, his eyes hard and bulging with anxiety, as in line abreast the attacking aircraft weaved from side to side, taking avoiding action as they hugged the deadly water. Tracer shells spat out from amidships as the Bofors guns added their quota of thumping to the bedlam. The sea was covered with wriggling and bouncing points of speeding light as the Oerlikons joined the shooting from all the port escorts. Astern, *Obstinate* came into view as she raced, with arcing bow wave, at a diverging course from *Watchful*, smoke trailing astern, her port side aflame with frantic gunfire.

Through the uproar and the daze of his retreated mind, dully he perceived that the tracer shells from the Bofors armament were darting methodically in one direction, hitting the water in front of one of the attackers, then bouncing upwards. At first he thought it was poor shooting, then realized that the intent was for the projectiles to hit the target on the broad underside. Almost in the moment of this realization the airplane bucked as the torpedo dropped into the water. It was meant for them. Then the aircraft, now obviously a two-engined one, soared, still weaving and was coming low over the ship. Both he and the attendant raced through the starboard doorway and out under the gun platform on that side, the furious guns on it clattering metallically, but not enough to drown the sudden roar of aircraft engines in the general cacophony. They saw the light green underside of the enemy flash overhead, its slim fuselage and broad wings large against the sky. The flaps, undercarriage doors and black cross markings were obvious in detail. Yet it turned astern as though afraid to cross the convoy and started to slide out of sight to port, so back they ran to the other exit to see it gliding down between *Obstinate* and themselves, turning parallel with the convoy, dropping lower and lower to hit the water ahead of them with a large white splash.

It was only then they remembered the torpedo that had been racing at them through the water. The ship moved up abreast where the bomber had plunged and there was not a scrap of wreckage visible, only a widening oil patch, silver light and smooth on the leaden crinkled swell. Awestruck they gazed at the spot a moment, then, as the din of battle subsided with the diminishing sound of aircraft and an occasional valedictory roar of heavier guns to speed the departing enemy on the way, they remembered their duties. The attendant went back to the sick bay and David went over and rattled the buzzer.

'They came in our side,' he told Pots. 'One hit the sea near us. I think our gunners got it.'

Replacing the handpiece he looked in the sick bay where the attendant was again busy over his instrument cases and bottles, and noted the time was about twelve twenty-five. The whole air attack had lasted less than an hour. It did not seem likely there would be a renewed onslaught for already the light was subtly weakening. He went back to the starboard doorway and looking astern could see the stricken freighter now low in the water, stopped, distant and apart from the convoy, the corvette moving slowly close by. The throb of the engines losing their urgency, the *Watchful* slowed and was soon wallowing at cruising speed. He went along behind the superstructure and saw the gun crews clearing their positions. Well aft the *Obstinate* had already dropped behind to her allotted station and was gently rolling in the old manner, rising up, then disappearing in a trough so only her superstructure and masts were visible.

Shapes were beginning to flatten in the deepening gloom. He shivered violently, whether outwardly from the intense cold, of which he was suddenly aware, or inwardly from a delayed shock of fear, he knew not. Glancing forward to the bear-like gun crews moving awkwardly about their cramped chores on the midships platform, the ragged ensign streaming out from the mainmast, he went into the flat and sat on a locker by X gun support. The only sounds that came to his still ringing ears were the occasional muffled clank of movement above, the steady engines and the splash of the acid-cold outboard. Gently he let the air out of his lifebelt.

He did not note, or care to mark, the time that passed, but at last the loudspeaker clicked, 'Secure action stations. Secure action stations. Blue watch to cruising stations.'

Going forward, he noticed a confused group emerge from the fo'c's'le entry and half way along the iron deck he stepped aside as it moved hurriedly past. He saw then, with an unpleasant turn, that in its midst was a stretcher and the whole business of getting the blanket-obscured body aft was directed by the chief bo'sun, looking somewhat uncharacteristically harassed. The bearers had difficulty in getting their burden through the entry to the sick bay flat but eventually they disappeared within.

Dinner, a shepherd's pie, was none the worse for being delayed and most in the communications and other messes were settling down when he arrived. The sharp hunger, of which he had been very conscious after the action, had been stifled by the sight of the stretcher party. When Robbie pushed a plate of steaming pie down to him, at first he prodded unenthusiastically at it with a fork; then, coming slowly out of his introspective mood, he noticed that the other ratings at the table were extraordinarily quiet. He thought that they might have been discussing the air attacks at least, but hardly a syllable was exchanged. Eddie could be relied upon to chatter sociably; he missed his prattle, looked around and saw he was not present.

'Where's Eddie?' he asked Ginger.

'He's had an accident.'

'Was he the one I saw on the stretcher just now?'

'Yes.'

'What happened?'

'He was daft enough to get up to secure the office door that was swinging open just when we took that hard turn. He went through the doorway at a rate of knots and laid himself out.'

'Bashed himself badly,' added Robbie.

'Eight green bottles,' mumbled Fred through some pie he was forcing down.

'Eh?'

'It's like the song – "...and if one green bottle should accidentally fall..."'

'Bloody cheerful,' growled Ginger.

14

During the afternoon most of those off watch managed to snatch some sleep and by teatime they had become, passively, a little more conversational. The relayed Overseas Programme was getting weaker and listening was complicated by atmospherics. Jim Streeter, when he came off duty, stood under the loudspeaker situated above the hammock net and, mug in hand, strained to hear the news. David, developing a curiosity to know what was happening beyond the freezing blackness up there at the top or the world, came over and joined him. It was near the end of the bulletin.

'Anything special?' he asked the coder.

'They're still stuck at Cassino,' Streeter replied. 'Sounds pretty grim.'

The music started again, but only for some minutes; then it was interrupted in order that the captain could speak to them about the midday action.

He said it was arguable as to who brought down the bomber, *Obstinate* or themselves, but he and her captain had agreed to claim half each. This occasioned some murmurs of disapproval by people who thought the honours should go entirely to *Watchful*. The signalmen present were particularly forward in disagreement. He went on to say that the usual efficiency of the enemy regarding time was not evident and they were probably disorganized by fighters from an aircraft carrier with the force coming up directly from base. 'We don't know what success they had,' he continued, 'but their presence must have upset the enemy's timing and grouping. The torpedo bombers, who timed their arrival punctiliously, were probably unmolested during their approach. On the whole, though, we can be pleased with the unseen support we've had. I'm impressed by the way my ship's company rose efficiently to the occasion and remain confident you will respond in a similar way in future contingencies.'

George was having his tea at the table and David went over to join him. 'All quiet,' he said, in response to an enquiry about the afternoon watch. 'If you ask me . . .' – David had not for he already suspected the reason – 'it's too quiet. Sinister like.'

'How's Eddie?' he asked at large.

'Laid out comfortably in the sick bay. The tiffy can't do much except wrap them up and keep them free of pain,' Ginger said. 'I reckon there's a jinx on the W/T office.'

'We're not much of an example to the rest, are we?' said Rowe plaintively. He was an earnest youth. With his soft, nicely unkempt light brown hair and red apple cheeks, he looked much like a keen boyscout. His grey-brown eyes gazed steadfastly, with honesty and interest, at all that passed before his round, frank features. His language was always moderate and somewhere in his background there was a hint of a tin-chapel, not narrowly Calvinistic, but broad-minded, charitable to weaker souls, and determined not to be soiled by those unfortunate but necessary surroundings. Moreover he was a steady, reliable rating even if he was inclined to be too inquisitive. It was doubtful if he ever exchanged more than a dozen words with his late unfortunate opposite number in white watch. David always felt a trifle uncomfortable in his presence. Not in a manner likely to raise his blood pressure – as with Reynolds – but as though at any time he would embarrassingly bring out a Bible or prayer book and read it; or worse, quote chapter and verse. However, although he perhaps tended to that air of hygienic superiority which was a degenerate tolerance typical of his kind, he was a civilized person and his utterances worthy of consideration.

'Most likely our local difficulties will be overlooked in the general emergency,' said Streeter, in a detached, rather avuncular manner, sitting down with the rest. 'Bombs landing close enough to knock holes in us make everything else of secondary importance.'

'What holes?' asked David, puzzled.

Ginger quizzed him with a faintly amused glance. 'You're the only one who doesn't know,' he said. 'In the funnel, bridgeworks and X gun turret.'

'Well, that accounts for it,' thought David aloud, recalling the peculiar metallic scraping thuds he had heard during the attack. It had not occurred to him that bomb fragments would hit the ship. He explained the remark, an enigmatic one, to the others.

'Oh, those few holes are nothing,' Ginger said. 'In the Med the *Persephone* got to look like a sieve. We weren't seriously holed, but the upper works were riddled, simply riddled. You ask Robbie if it's true. I'm not bulling. As a matter of fact, according to the buffer, the high level Jerries didn't seem to have the go they did in the Med, although he says the torpedo planes persisted more.'

'I don't think so, Ginger,' contradicted the little dark jowled signalman. He seemed more in need of a shave than ever. 'They didn't want to come in close before they dropped the tin fish and turned away.'

'Lucky for us,' said his blue watch colleague.

'Only the one that came after us went in close,' observed the dark one.

'Unlucky for him,' said blue watch contrapuntally.

'Well, the buffer wasn't all that impressed with their effort,' said Ginger.

I was, thought David.

'Still, let's hope that's the last we've seen of them before Kola,' said George.

'How do you account for their lack of enthusiasm, Ginger?' asked Streeter.

'I don't suppose,' the veteran replied, 'they fancy the thought of that cold water any more than we do.'

Not long after red watch had gone to cruising stations Robbie came along from the office and asked David if he would relieve Fred for a time. Walking back with the leading hand David asked what the matter was. 'Fred says he's going to be sick any minute,' was the reply.

'Not sea-sick?' exclaimed David incredulously, for the sea motion was now merely a gentle swell, the ship rocking steadily but nowhere near its former madly tumbling self.

'Just nerves I reckon,' replied Robbie casually, 'reaction after the air raid.'

Fred, an embarrassed smile jerking lopsidedly on his face, hurriedly rose when David took the headphones. He was not smoking and with no exchange of civilities darted from the office. It was rather pleasant to sit quietly and watch Robbie busy on the hitherto unused set. In answer to an enquiry he said he was tuning in to Polyarnoe W/T, that is, naval headquarters in North Russia. 'We were there in August. A right dump,' he said. 'We called it Dodge City.'

For some time the headphones lay heavily and hotly on David's ears, emitting the crackle and rush of atmospherics and a curious sort of twanging noise that seemed to be some kind of music and speech breakthrough and the indistinct chattering of Morse transmitters on the remote fringes of audibility. They suggested a happier place than the sinister zone of silence into which they had moved since the previous night of tediously long messages sent by nagging control at Narvik.

He examined his plain wood, austerity pencil, twiddled it in his fingers, idly swinging his chair from side to side. He had time to watch Robbie taking an occasional message from North Russia and pass it to the coder. Beyond him, at the other end of the office, the fourth watchkeeper was engrossed in traffic which was coming endlessly from the Admiralty. The steady beat of the Morse carried his thoughts soaring out of the ship, taking supernatural wings along some ethereal line to swiftly cross the darkness so that, in his mind's eye, he saw the busy streets and quiet fields of home bathed in a blessed gentle light of a late afternoon in midwinter. The trains would be crowded in the yellow, warm underground and buses would be trying to ease the patient queues. Familiar faces, late workmates, and friends, drifted back and forth in the unsubstantial world before him though his eyes looked on the yellow, pipe and cable-crossed bulkhead of the wireless room. Diffidently he wondered if Pauline would miss not seeing him as she walked through the tube station on the way home.

Pots came in, washed and changed into a clean, white roll-necked jersey, which made his life-jacket look grubby. He leaned over David and asked if there was anything doing. 'Not a thing,' was the answer, and he left unresolved the doubtful expression on the face of his questioner. He had a fair idea of what had been going on up to the forenoon watch but was puzzled by the present silence.

The instant that the petty officer turned away to examine the coder's output, a long, loud squawk that broke into a staccato flurry of Morse abruptly shook David into writing down the few letters of a U-boat signal that seemed to come from under the very keel of the destroyer itself. As he scribbled he hoped that aft they had got a bearing and other ships too. He was putting in the time and date when the intercommunication telephone buzzed and Pots went over and repeated what he heard. 'U-boat signal bearing red four five – about two or three miles.' Old Faithful was closing in. He came and took the torn-off message sheet, wrote down the bearing and stepped back to the bridge voice pipe, whistled and to the call 'Bridge' reported the interception. He then slowly sat down at the ship to ship radio bay and applied himself to the accumulated paperwork.

David meanwhile had recorded the shore station as it repeated back the signal for general information and accuracy, which sounded rather like an old, cunning wolf calming and encouraging an excitable but ferocious young warrior of the pack. He leaned back in the swivel chair, conscious again of the gentle rocking of the ship.

Just before the change of watches at 1800 hours Fred came back and said he was feeling much better and insisted on doing the second dog watch for David. At first the latter demurred but realizing he would miss supper, for which Fred showed no enthusiasm, he allowed himself to be persuaded into handing over the headphones.

Beans and bacon was the meal being served when he arrived and he recalled the first meal in *Watchful*. This recollection induced a faint sensation of nausea which was speedily overcome by the hunger that snapped at his stomach. It was extraordinary how, in spite of restricted exercise, he could grow so hungry. Perhaps it had something to do with the all pervasive cold that was never far from his innermost core. He supposed it was a psychological as well as physical well-being that the food induced. False security, of course, rather like, but unfortunately not as long as that engendered by alcohol.

Supper was cleared away and the hands off watch settled down to the pastimes that filled the gap between going on duty or turning in. It was pleasant to think of the restful undisturbed sleep for white watch until the morning turn at four o'clock and taking his cue from Ginger, who was at the net tugging out his hammock, he went over to do likewise. It appeared that Pots owed him time for doing an extra bit of Reynold's watch and had let him out early. He murmured, 'Dave, I've got that sinking feeling. I shouldn't take any gear off if I was you.'

Coming back from the washplace he remembered this advice and placing his towel and toilet bag on the hammock clews started to put on all his clothes, except for the duffel coat. There was peace on the mess deck; men were already turned in, or dozing on the lockers. One or two still read, waiting the call for blue watch. George was writing a letter at the table. The deck tilting gently and predictably to a shallow angle, and the quiet vibrations of the engines were a soothing inducement to sleep. Through the door, in the cramped forward mess, men were sprawled out in any available space but no hammocks were slung. Everybody was getting very tired; the first consideration and requirement was sleep and the ship herself was a lullaby.

David had just replaced his lifebelt over the two jerseys he was wearing when a rending explosion echoing across from the convoy side stabbed terror in his vitals. His startled gaze across to where Ginger had been leaning over his hammock arranging it, met the veteran's stare. Never before had he witnessed such a look of anguish in the face of another. It illumined deep wells of spiritual pain and horror that it was sickening to see. Men were already staggering up, sleepily groping, grabbing heavy top gear, tripping, grunting, running and swearing as the raucous, clattering bells called them to action stations. A stream of men poured through the doorway and pounded aft along the TS alley. Already the damage control parties were assembling and the dull clang of watertight doors and hatches being slammed echoed in the fo'c's'le. Grabbing his top gear David joined the rush along the alley. He opened the office door, the first off watch rating to arrive. The loudspeaker on the ship-to-ship telephone was on and to his dismay he heard a voice, disguising not a jot its desperation, repeating, 'Hello, this is *Sentinel*, this is *Sentinel*, we have been torpedoed – we have been torpedoed,' and already as Ginger, Rowe, George and the others tumbled over the bulkhead coaming, the depressing rumble of distant depth charges was plainly to be heard.

As they came in people changed places, slipping into jobs that had been obviously prearranged. Rowe sat down at number one, the Admiralty set, replacing Pots who had been doing an hour for Ginger. Meanwhile Pots had leapt over to the voicepipe and called the bridge to inform it of the distress signal. Ginger sat down before the radio telephone and flicking a switch acknowledged the call. Streeter took the coder's chair and the red watch telegraphist the Polyarnoe frequency next to it. In the end place Fred half turned as the crowd rushed in, a twisted grin of painful disbelief on his face. Unsure whether he was to go aft or not, David dithered. Pots gestured in his direction and turning from the voicepipe said, 'Wait, Fres, there's a huff-duffer down there. I may need you this end.' It was an order, at first welcome because the thought of groping his way over the iron deck in darkness had no appeal, but as the first hour of the battle dragged by David found it did not ease his tormented thoughts.

George sat down in the corner usually appropriated by Fred and David after standing lamely for a time by the door with Robbie and the red watch coder, settled himself in a similar manner. The perpetual thirst of Fred for the diverting could not have been more liberally, but uncomfortably slaked. The progress of the struggle was only too clear to those free to listen to the communication in plain language between ships that issued forth from the radio telephone.

Almost as soon as David had sat down, another crash above the continuous watery reverberations of depth charges indicated a torpedo had struck home. *Obstinate* called *Severe* and said it was a merchantman on the port side of the convoy between herself and *Watchful*. A voice broke in and ordered the latter to go and take off survivors and this was conveyed to the bridge. The deck tilted steeply and the engine vibration increased as a turn began to be executed, but a sharp order came across from the escort commander: 'Hello *Watchful*, this is *Severe*, do not leave position. I say again, do not leave position.'

'What are they effing about at?' growled Robbie tensely.

Relief in the office was very evident when the order was countermanded for although it had all the urgency of a battle order, within everybody there was a moral struggle. It was the chill realization that a ship hove-to, taking men from a listing victim, was itself an ideal prey, conflicting with the nagging thought that comrades in peril must be helped or they would not have an easy night till the end of their lives. Perhaps David shocked himself – that cheerful, lively group they had seen in Akureyri were out there struggling in fear, to get boats away, as the deck under them sagged down to the icy swell.

The ship was beating up to full speed and abruptly 'Stand by for depth charges', was called over the loudspeaker system. A thudding, jerking, rattling sensation shook them violently as the sinking drums of death exploded in the wake of the destroyer. 'C-C-Christ!' moaned Ginger, through his chattering teeth, 'it sounds like Judgement Day.' Rowe, his soft features aquiver with vibration, seemed to disapprove of the remark.

'Pick the bones out of that, you bastards,' murmured Robbie philosophically as he clung to the main transmitter. The bridge voicepipe whistled. The precise voice of the captain sounded high with excitement. 'Send a signal to flotilla.'

'Sir!'

'Am attacking U-boat on port bow of convoy. Turning about for a second run.'

'Aye aye, Sir!' said Pots, writing it down for Ginger to transmit.

'I only hope,' observed Streeter, as they felt the tight turn to port, 'that *Obstinate* isn't doing it in the opposite direction.'

The engines eased in pace as the asdic operators endeavoured to regain contact; then, as the speed went up again, a similar bone-jarring pattern of explosions was repeated.

Concurrently with these events, *Sentinel* slowed to a few knots, but mercifully, not in a sinking condition, was instructed to take up a position in the centre of the convoy. It left a temporary gap over on the starboard quarter of which the enemy took a swift advantage.

A torpedo struck home on another merchantman with a characteristic echoing roar so different from the grumbling depth charges. Again they were ordered to go and pick up survivors by a voice that came in unceremoniously. Once more the inner struggle between the instinct for survival and conscience welled up in their hearts. This time the captain was obviously reluctant to leave his position for the turn was unhurried, but before *Watchful* had gone far there was a transmission from *Severe* in a copy-book fashion which let their commander know in no uncertain terms that he was to hold his position relative to the convoy. There was confusion too for other escorts and Ginger said, 'There's something funny about the signals we get sometimes.'

Sombrely, Robbie looked down on the others. 'Sounds as though Captain D is up the creek without a paddle,' he said.

'Anyway,' Streeter remarked to Pots, 'why have a list of code-names if you don't use them?'

Pots, taking advantage of a pause in the action, was blowing up his lifebelt. Others were starting to follow his depressing example. David had felt that nervous sickness experienced by Fred, soon after he reached the office but now there was a cold numbness, rather like a lump of lead settled in his stomach and he could hardly find the strength in sluggardly limbs to inflate his own life-preserver. He was not excited or momentarily in terror as he had been at midday. Fear was beginning to tickle at toes and fumbling fingers, edging wormlike along nerves and arteries towards his vitals.

'Aye,' said Robbie, suddenly enlightened, 'they've used plain language since the do began. What a gift for the Jerries. If we're listening to them what's the betting they're listening to us?'

'Those ballsed up orders?' Pots queried in exasperation.

George was taking over from Fred when *Severe*, as though in response to a telepathic question, sent a coded message to all ships. 'Hullo *Bouquet*, Hullo *Bouquet*, this is *Bluebell* – Pick the flowers – I say again – pick the flowers – acknowledge – over.'

'What's that mean?' asked Robbie.

'We're to use code from now on,' said Pots, without looking away from the radio-telephone loudspeaker.

Obstinate got in first with its reply. Hullo *Bluebell*, Hullo *Bluebell*, this is *Daffodil* – Wilco – out.'

'Hullo *Bluebell*, Hullo *Bluebell*, this is *Buttercup* – Wilco – out.

'Who's that?' Ginger asked himself looking down the list.

Pots remembered. '*Stavanger*,' he said.

At last *Watchful* managed to get in its acknowledgement that *Crocus* would thenceforth transmit in codewords.

George, endeavouring to accomplish the feat of recording frantic U-boat and shore signals, at the same time smoking, accepted a light from Fred who, propping himself up in the corner and drawing his bony blue overalled knees up under his chin, pulled sharply at his own cigarette. His grey eyes gazed soulfully through lids that crinkled nervously with combat between overwhelming fear and an unquenchable sense of humour that threatened to make him laugh out loud at the incredibility of his present situation. The folds that ran from his skeletal cheeks to delicate chin flexed and twitched at the absurdity of it all.

'It's effing grim, isn't it, Dave?' he asked, in need of confirmation that it was not all a bad dream. All that David would permit himself in the way of a reply was a funereal nod. Fred thrust the palm of his hand across his face and jerked another cloud of smoke from his cigarette. 'It's effing grim, chum, effing grim!'

The enemy desisting from their passion for sending messages for the time being, George turned his chair to look down on them. He carefully drew on his cigarette and through the smoke faint watery haloes could be seen around the sad blue of his eyes, hinting that perhaps he wished he were hundreds of miles from this place of death, dancing perhaps with a girl in the dusty, scented dalliance of the Corn Exchange. 'I tell you what,' he murmured, his soft rural tones even milder. 'My Uncle Reuben said, "Never volunteer for nothing".'

Even as his body grew numbed with an all-consuming terror, more organic than he ever thought possible, David wondered whether it showed in his own eyes as he stared at his comrades in misery. Paradoxically, though his body was apparently without feeling, he was conscious of the texture of his surroundings. The cold brown deck, the pattern of pipes on clammy bulkhead and deckhead carrying the warmth and strength of their ship and outside, the blue twilight of the alleyway and the sealed, dim-lit compartments with their little groups of agonizing sailors listening to the rumble of battle beyond the flimsy outer plates. And outside that steel the waiting, deadly black water, so cold it was pointless to let go rafts for nobody would live long enough in its lethal grip to clamber on them. One would exist a few endless, hopeless minutes as the life heat was extinguished, leaving a mind clear with terror and regret till the final heart beat.

He saw the telegram fall on the quiet suburban front-door mat, the trembling, care-worn hands picking it up. The words read through a mist of tears: 'The Admiralty regrets to inform you that...' And over at the regulating office of the signals camp the card with his name at the top being taken from the index files and 'Discharged Dead' being rubberstamped on it. Please God that cannot be! Why should innocent kinsfolk suffer for the world's idiocy? Do not let us die, God, we want to see those hidden years. It may be coming straight for us now and prayer will not stop it. Oh God, please turn it away from us, I beg you let us escape. Make up your mind, mere words are no good here, nor anguished thoughts or prayers. What is special about you? Or the *Sentinel* or those merchant packets? Dear God, let us live to do something useful with our lives. Such as what? You are only another 200 ants to be trodden under the boot of time.

So all right then, if we are to die let it be quickly done. A rending gigantic explosion that blasts us mercifully to oblivion, please God let it be that way. No lingerings but quickly, use the scythe well, blast us instantly into the blessed unknown. This will not do. What use are prayers? There is no Thing, only Nothing out there in the eternal night. If the Reaper comes he will come, let him be quick that is all. All this is painful, futile thought, struggle out of the remote recesses of your cringing useless frame and command it. You are not the only one.

David shook himself and yawned loudly. It was getting on for 2100 hours. The fight was not yet two hours' old; he wondered if he would be able to do his work properly in his distracted state.

The others seemed to be able to manage. He wished he were busy, perhaps that would help. He had to do something about his abject mind, for it was fear that he worshipped. He had feared fear, and now it encompassed him. He saw it on the faces of his shipmates and heard it in their voices, changed, unnaturally gruff or strident, when they spoke briefly and in monosyllables. The creaking metal of the fear-ridden beast that was their living ship clammily oozed it, in vibrations of her uneven pace and the sudden lurches of her pounding heart.

He could not be more afraid and keep his mind. They stood waiting by the great, heightless, cold doors of eternity; one knock, one devastating crash and they would be through. God give him strength not to lose his mind's grip when the awful time came and the black acid cold clawed inwards, or in the freezing blackness they clambered for rafts that would delay the dread moment only seconds more.

His fear hurt physically, The great icicle plunged in his vitals, radiated paralysis to his stiffened limbs and yet he moved, he spoke. The constricted muscles of his face and neck did not prevent him saying to his grimacing companion after the passing of some time, 'Yes, Fred, it's a bastard.'

Yet in the distress of his comrades he found strength. To fear was not to be alone. It was the common, natural lot. What they could take he would also. It was not death he feared for had he not prayed to be killed by the explosion? It was the indignity of having to struggle hopelessly like an unthoughtful animal to avoid the inevitable that he feared. He had ever thought he was alone in this respect but he was not. Some, in lesser circumstances, dissembled their failing nerve, but here in this timeless reality no ordinary pettinesses of deception could mask their innermost torture.

Lucky were those who were really occupied, he thought again, although from time to time as they glanced up from message pad and cypher grid, he saw the hurt look in their eyes as the depth charges rumbled and growled near and far. That they apparently made no errors was a tribute to their instructors, some of whom in their time also had passed too near the gates of death.

Pots looked up from the code list he was reading. 'It's about time we had some kai,' he said to Robbie.

'Come on,' said Robbie to the red watch coder, 'let's get cracking. I'll take Dave too if it's OK with you, Pots.'

Passing the TS, the doleful call of radar contacts could be heard from operators and the information being repeated to the bridge.

'Dark object bearing red three five, range one five closing.'

The ship vibrated with increasing speed as the depth-charge warning was made and shortly after there was the shuddering rumble of another pattern exploding below.

On the mess deck every loose object had been thrown into the scran bag, spare top clothing lashed to stanchions and hammocks taken down and crammed in the net. Not a scrap of material likely to be sucked into the pump intakes and so block them was allowed to remain loose. The little group of stokers who had achieved this quick miracle of secure tidiness now sat along the benches between the two messes as glumly thoughtful as the group in the wireless office. They were totally cut off from their mess forward on the deck below by the doors clipped watertight. Having arranged the mugs and chopped up slab cocoa into a jug Robbie sent the coder for hot water. When the cocoa was ready the damage control party gratefully accepted his offer of a drink then the remainder was taken to the office.

'Dave,' said Pots, 'when you've finished your drink I want you to go down to the aft telephone. The huff-duffers are getting too busy with bearings.'

David put his mug on a shelf just inside the door and, picking up his duffel coat, saw Fred looking at him sympathetically. 'Sooner you than me, Dave,' he said.

'Thanks, chum,' said David, 'for those few words of encouragement.'

In the spacious gloom of the galley flat a handful of damage control ratings sat closely grouped on a closed hatchway at the foot of the bridge ladder. They glanced in mild curiosity at him as he went out of the port exit. It was now open not only in consequence of the reduced bad weather from that side but also to allow easy access in case of emergency. He paused against the galley housing and gripped the handrail, waiting till he was accustomed to the darkness. The humming of the funnel, hiss of sea and stink of fumes and oil and bitter air more acutely assailed his sightless faculties. He was reluctant to start the walk aft. Some minutes passed and fearing he would be missed and cause a disturbance, he began to grope along the rail, then, touching the familiar warmth of the funnel under his left hand, went on to negotiate the searchlight platform. By now it was possible to make out the slightly less dark sea from the dense blackness of the ship but it was not much help. He leaned over, seeking the forward torpedo tubes. The space between the platform and the tubes was not to be visualized and his hands could not find the reassuring metalwork. There was nothing. Starting to perspire, he groped on each side, finding only the freezing air. A wave of panic flooded through him, momentarily overwhelming the ever present fear. His feet were slipping on the damp, smooth plating as it swayed gently on the swell. In an act of desperation he threw himself away from the ship's side and hit his lower legs painfully on the tubes. He swore aloud with pain, surprised to hear his own voice in the darkness. The obstruction had been very near but lower than he thought. Thankfully edging along them he felt his way blindly through the complexity of the midships' gun platform and on across the next uncomfortably open area of torpedo tubes to reach the haven of the quiet sick bay flat. Pushing aside the tarpaulin curtain, he stepped inside.

Over by the telephone the HF-DF operator was sitting on the deck, a soft covered book unopened at his feet. He got up and put it in his duffel coat pocket. 'Hallo, Dave.' It was Collins, the bookish one. 'Too dark to read here. You can only sit and stew in your thoughts.'

'How do, Jumper. The main office is just as chokka,' David replied, going over to the light coming from the sick bay to look at his barked shins. Gently rolling up the bell-bottoms he saw that the skin was badly grazed. 'Did it on the iron deck,' he said by way of explanation.

'You'd better get it seen to,' said Collins. 'I'll hold on.'

Just then the attendant looked out. 'Here mate,' he said, 'that needs attention. Come on in.'

David went in and sat on a form just inside the door. He carefully folded up the trouser bottoms and the attendant first washed away the traces of blue fluff left by the serge cloth. Eddie was in the lower bunk nearest them. He turned a bland, white face and took a weak interest in the proceedings. He asked what was going on. David told him. 'We're beset by a U-boat pack' – he winced as the antiseptic was applied – 'still, it can't be long to Kola now. How d'you feel?'

'Not bad, could be worse.'

'He'll be all right when we get him into hospital,' put in the attendant as he applied lint and sticking plaster. 'How's that?'

'Fine chum, just fine, thanks.'

'Just as well to see to it. Might have infected. I'm busy enough in here as it is.'

Outside Collins was lifting the hatch to go down into the HF-DF cubicle. 'OK Dave?'

'Yes, thanks, mate!'

For some time there had been no depth-charging and fortunately no torpedoes had exploded. It was a menacing silence. He wondered what was going on. Deciding to let Pots know he had arrived, he buzzed the main office.

'All right, Dave?'

'Yes. Collins has gone down below.'

'It's all quiet here. Don't know what's going on. Let's know if anything happens.'

'If I can see anything, Pots! It's as black as Newgate's knocker up here.'

When Pots rang off David felt suddenly alone. He was uncertain whether it was better to be in the main office, fully aware of and able to worry about what was happening around the convoy, or to sit there in the half light and be in ignorance of events. He got up and glanced at the sick bay clock. It was coming up to midnight. He was getting very sleepy and sleep was a temporary retreat from the corroding fear that hung on him like a physical presence. It was becoming a struggle to stay awake.

The crack of a gun shattered his dozing reverie, just after he had sat down. He rose up half way and tumbled out of the starboard entry. The ebony night had changed to an apparently gently moonlit scene and whilst he gazed across to the *Stavanger* her forward main armament flashed brilliant white and another crash came over.

The clouds were lit by a second artificial moon, glowing hazily through, and the ocean was soon brilliantly illuminated by the two starshells as they emerged, drifting lazily, from the cloud base ahead of the forward screen. The Norwegian destroyer was stark white on a gentle swell, reflecting the light like black glass. Forward, *Watchful* was a geometric pattern of lines shining damply on her dark main bulk. As the lights sank down low on the water two more were fired almost simultaneously from *Stavanger* and a high-pitched, petulant yell came from an Oerlikon gunner above. 'Put that bloody light out!' Obviously others too thought the ship was an excellently silhouetted target against all that light.

The brightness revealed a figure coming down the iron deck on this side. Drawing near, the narrow features of the first lieutenant were plain under his fur hat. From his duffel coat pocket the top of an electric torch protruded. He was making his way aft to the stern, perhaps to inspect the torpedo men busy with the depth charges.

'Excuse me, Sir! May I ask what all that is about?' David ventured boldly. The first lieutenant paused briefly and looked back at the sinking flares. 'The U-boats are surfaced and making top speed to get ahead of us for another go. I'm afraid, laddie, it isn't finished yet. *Stavanger* hoped to catch a careless one a bit too near,' he added, with a touch of irony. 'They're very keen.'

'Yes, Sir, I've been told.'

'How do you feel, Freston?'

'Very nervous, Sir!'

In spite of the circumstances the first lieutenant smiled. 'That's a quaint way of putting it. Aren't we all? Never mind, lad, old soldiers say you never get hit in your first battle. You're our good luck charm.' He went on under the raft supports, taking advantage of the last flickering light. So we are not considered Jonahs after all, thought David.

Just after midnight George was sent down to take over the telephone point. He arrived in an unhappy frame of mind, more tersely phlegmatic than ever. For it was not agreeable to leave the relatively warm office and risk the upper deck – 'dodgy' was his word – to get to that chilly place. However, he did mention that the U-boat signals had died out for the moment.

Although the ship was still fully alerted, individual ratings and little groups were being permitted to snatch some sleep by their action stations. David carefully picked his way back to the main office and, sitting down in the corner behind number five set, soon fell asleep.

About three o'clock he was rudely awakened by the shivering rumbles of a depth-charge pattern exploding in the wake and found he had slid down to be fully stretched out across the deck of the office. Stiffly he hauled himself to a sitting position and noticed Pots smiling down at him. 'They're having another go,' he said, 'but you seemed so peaceful it was a pity to wake you up.'

During his sleep another merchantman had been torpedoed but now, although the escorts were dropping charges all round the convoy, it was likely they were beginning to outrun the submarines again and this was the tail end of the present attack. David realized he had been lucky. All the others present had been awake and therefore enduring the tension of the previous two hours.

'This is a pretty one-way affair,' said Streeter who was sitting on the deck opposite, by the main transmitter. He had taken a smouldering pipe from his mouth. 'Our people getting knocked off and we can't go after them.' He put the pipe back precisely at the centre of his mouth, letting it rest in his clasped hands, which in turn were supported by his right knee that was thrust up in front of him, the other leg being straight on the deck. He was of medium build but thinner than usual for a man of his years. His hands were soft, pale pink but had prominent veins across their backs. The nails of his bony fingers were kept remarkably neat, probably filed, but he had never been observed to manicure them. Behind the thin veil of smoke he seemed to prefer a gentle puff, not a veritable smoke screen; his face hinted at the essential skull beneath, but it was neither cadaverous nor obviously structured like Fred's. It was covered by strong, almost cordlike, muscular lines and at the side of his intellectually domed forehead the veins were again prominent, tending to give an impression of deep thinking. His remark drew an explanation from Robbie, turning briefly from the radio telephone. 'If we chased the subs too far it would suit them well. We can't go far from the convoy.' This remark was silently affirmed by Ginger and Pots with a nod.

The dry-mouthed sluggishness of half rest was giving way to the growing resurgence of fear. David strove to damp down its debilitating effect. He would be glad to get on watch again instead of sitting here listening to the grumbling deeps and curt speech in code passing between *Severe* and the other escorts.

At four o'clock he relieved Fred who, urged by Pots, went off with Robbie to make some coffee. It was the last of that bought at Akureyri. When it was served he was told to go down and relieve George and, going to the door, Fred made a grimace of dismay. 'Tell Corder he can get his head down on the lockers if he wants,' Pots instructed him.

The latest flurry of situation reports from U-boats was dying out. Bearings were not coming in very quickly and David, in spite of the coffee and his mental discomfort, might easily have dropped off to sleep over the bench.

15

Following the long, grim night, breakfast was a subdued affair. The bulkhead door near the canteen had been opened and ratings had access to the forward messes. Everywhere those not required immediately at action stations were snatching a little sleep, but the ship was in a state of acute readiness and the majority of the ship's company, jaded though they were, remained at their posts. Most forms, lockers and deck spaces had their quota of sprawled figures yet at the head of mess tables there was usually some indefatigable character making tea, even though those gathered around to drink were few and speaking quietly, if they spoke at all.

Robbie poured a mug of tea for David as he saw him carefully picking his way between recumbent figures on the deck. 'I've just been telling the others, Dave. There's another client in the sick bay,' he said.

'Who's that?' whispered David, settling down with the others, grouped like conspirators.

'Scouse Edwards.'

'What's he done? Fallen down a hatchway?' enquired Fred, with that eccentric, ill-timed levity to which they were getting accustomed.

'Got cramps on B gun platform a couple of hours back. Tiffy reckons it's the appendix.'

'That's bloody hard graft. I hope they get the poor bastard to hospital in time.' The leading signalman of red watch was genuinely concerned. Not small, but hardly of medium height, he was a fellow just into his twenties and indeed he, Robbie, Ginger and Streeter made the four who drew their rum ration. The front of his head was rather narrow and consequently gave a long, thin cast to his pink, bony features, which were sharp without hardness. Dark brown eyes without any trace of duplicity, were warmly candid, and his hair was very dark brown almost to blackness, but lacking that bluish lustre of truly black hair. It was parted indecisively more to the middle than the left side and usually sleeked down to glossy smoothness. When speaking he presented an impression of earnestness, cocking his head to one side and screwing up his eyes as though straining to read a distant and difficult signal.

He was, of course, not very much different in age to Robbie and Ginger but had entered the service after them. Yet he had a few months of seatime before this commission, in a frigate attached to a hunter-killer group. Why it had only been a few months had been a mystery. Now it was explained. 'I got appendicitis on the *Uphall* just as we were entering the North Channel,' he continued. 'Fortunately we were within a few hours of land and they got me into hospital in time. If we'd been a few days out it might well have been my lot.'

'What chance is there for Edwards then, Vic?' The leading signalman, Victor Bouveney, cocked his head and squinted closely at Robbie, 'It all depends, Rob mate, on now quick it's coming on!'

'How long have we got to go?' Fred asked at large.

'We should be in definitely late tomorrow or early the next day,' said Robbie.

Seven green bottles, thought David as he got up and found an unoccupied part of the deck near the hammock net out of the way of passers-by and lay down in his duffel coat. This unhappy thought soon fled for, in spite of his legs which were beginning to sting, he almost immediately fell fast asleep.

Three hours later thick yellow lentil soup, a standby in times of particular difficulty, was served to all messes for dinner. It was drunk – or eaten – by the cupful, with biscuits. After consuming his share David felt better but fear still lurked in the background threatening to overwhelm him if his defences weakened. He spent some time disentangling his hammock from the crammed jumble in the net, lashed it and stowed it properly. He expected to find the toilet gear left in its clews but when it did not come to light, had to probe in the scran bag among a lot of sticky towels and odiferous garments until he found the toilet bag rolled in the towel. He felt liverish, clammy and dishevelled and it was a relief to manage a tolerable wash, the water both hot and cold getting back in the washroom taps. Determined not to lose his toilet gear in the bag again he carefully shook and folded the towel, wrapped it round the bag and stowed them neatly in the locker.

It was just after midday when he arrived at the funnel club and there was daylight, but only just. More accurately it might be described as twilight which passed as day for two hours at this latitude. The ships were all in much the same positions to each other but the deplorable losses of the merchantmen were very evident in the general pattern of shapes they presented to viewers on *Watchful*. On the water there was a slight swell which was quicksilver smooth and lighter than the glowering sky. The wash from the ambling destroyer was now evident on the surface although they hardly seemed to be moving at all.

The ensign, stirred more by the motion of the ship than the light breeze was flapped away almost to the vertical red bar in its centre and another would be required very soon. The group about the funnel was quite small but it was surprising to find Ginger out there, well wrapped up, duffel coat hood over a head already crowned in a balaclava. Abstractedly he stared out over the ships, automatically drawing on a cigarette, with a tension and preoccupation uncomfortable to behold.

On the way back David looked into the office and asked Pots if he was wanted.

'No, Dave, get your head down lad while it's quiet, there'll probably be another long night ahead.'

From just before midday action stations had been secured and during the afternoon there was a return to cruising stations. At 1600 hours, during the first dog watch, it was clear no traffic had been coming in from mid-morning onwards. It suggested the enemy was resting through the hours of half light.

Next to David Ginger leaned back in front of the radio telephone and silently gnawed his nails. The finger tips were unpleasantly red and it was evident he was still tortured by that same fear David had managed to damp down into the background of consciousness. He wanted to say something to comfort him but was aware that it would be presumptuous to do so and that nothing utterable could bring him solace from that horrid trauma.

At supper the ship's cooks produced a cheering surprise for everyone. Taking advantage of the quiet afternoon they had prepared soya bean sausages and mashed potatoes. It was the best sustenance in twenty four hours of erratic feeding and particularly welcome for those coming off watch. After the meal there were far too many people eager to help clean and tidy the mess and it was likely everybody was trying to be as occupied as possible to put out of mind the coming night. The second dog watch was always, in some degree a rather sad time, with the prospect of the dragging night watches looming, when thoughts stealthily crept out of the subconscious and plagued one with supernatural horror and fantasies like spirits emerging from tombs and haunting familiar places and people in a grisly Hallowe'en.

Ginger got out his ludo board and looked enquiringly at David, who without a word, sat down with him. Fred, busy shaking his duffel coat over by the canteen – one wondered what he was expecting to find clinging to it – hurried over to get into the game. Vic Bouveney, stacking up the bulkier items of his topside gear on the locker close at hand, offered himself as the fourth player.

The game went along in an unenthusiastic manner. Ginger chewed his finger nails hard but the sharp commentary that was usually a concomitant of his play was lacking. About the two messes fellows were busy tidying their gear or going to wash. Finishing their little tasks, they began to settle down at tables or on the deck, dozing, reading and writing. The sway of the vessel was slight, her vibration soothing and the hum of vents pleasantly restful. It was as though the ship sought to ease the struggling thoughts that made the actions of everybody so detached and gentle; to recompense for the nerve-shredding conflict and calm their agitated anticipation of the coming night.

Now and again an indistinct voice could be heard in the TS, then getting on for 1900 hours a loud call up the voicepipe to the bridge came clearly out to them breaking the false sense of peace.

'Dark object bearing red five zero closing.'

'Oh Christ!' burst out Ginger. 'How long is this bloody thing going on?'

The others looked at his strained features, not daring to trust words past the choking sensation in their throats. An amalgamation of mind-freezing panic at the prospect of the re-engaging U-boats and compassion for the continuing agony of Ginger stifled any comment before its thought in the aching brain of David. 'I was at Dunkirk and Crete and I still can't get used to these bastard things,' he protested, an indignant moistness starting in his eyes. 'I try, I really effing well try, but they always get me down. It's the waiting. The effing waiting, that's what does me in. Oh Christ, roll on death!'

The others drew perceptibly away as though they would catch his abiding terror. Embarrassed, David picked up the dice and box and pretended to be busily rattling. He had no contempt for Ginger. How could he? This tortured man enduring the same mental agony as himself, or the others too, if they had a particle of imagination and common sense. The pity of it was that the world in its rottenness could let a young man suffer like this, not once or twice but again and again. The green years of his life blighted by the shadow of death. His feeling was an understanding for the suffering he had known himself, that this fellow, who had had no youth, had carried for years which must have been interminable. There was a dullness surrounding his own terror, fortunately, for nature had wrapped it in a psychological cocoon. His temperament must cease to torment itself or become demented, but for Ginger there seemed no panacea. The years of sadness passed slowly and sooner or later there would be one battle too many for the jarring discords of his mind.

Yet somehow, almost with a feeling of guilt, his own fear, that had become leadenly organic, not sharp, a more than terrestrial gravity dragging at his vitals, was numbed even more by his senior's frank admission and blunderingly he saw that his apparently particular pain of mind was not unique but common to all and that Ginger had a noble sort of courage to admit it.

Returning from the washplace, Robbie, as spruce and neat as was customary with him, witnessed the emotional outburst of his old shipmate. He looked gently unhappy, as much for his friend as himself. Putting his toilet gear away he looked up from the locker and said quietly, 'Ginge, why don't you get your postcards out?'

Ginger looked doubtful.

'Go on mate,' urged Robbie, 'Fred'd like to see them, wouldn't you?'

Fred nodded enthusiastically.

'Maybe, Dave too,' added the leading hand.

The ludo contest was forgotten. Ginger put the board away in his locker and drew out a packet about two inches thick, wrapped in newspaper printed in Arabic characters. He took off an elastic band and carefully unwrapped the cards. Robbie joined the group and one or two others as well. It was obviously not an unfamiliar diversion for them.

Ginger, on the other side of the table, took the top card and passed it to Vic, who smiled quietly at what was well known to him and passed it on to Fred. David saw it was some kind of photograph; but exactly what, was not clear. A smile wavered on the face of his opposite number and burst into a loud cackle which showed his irregular teeth. 'Cor!' he said, 'I've never seen anything like it.'

Robbie got it next and he gave a quiet snigger and it came – to the impatient annoyance of David – into the hands of a radar rating who had no business in their mess anyway but had parasitically joined them when he saw the packet being unwrapped. 'Bloody'ell,' he said in a strong northern accent, 'I wish I could get my missus to do that.'

It was impolitely grabbed from him by David, worked up in his curiosity, as he handed it on.

David looked. There were two figures. Both well upholstered Levantine types, a lady and a gentleman, largely undressed. At first he thought it was some kind of Japanese wrestling match. It was not possible. Nobody had ever told him people could contort themselves to that extent. His eyes glazed with concentration but not for long. In turn it was snatched from before his sight by the equally curious, stocky, young red watch signalman.

'Hold on, bunts,' he complained.

The signalman growled, 'There are a lot more, biff, don't strain yourself.'

Another card was on its way round the group, drawing giggles from even the experienced voyeurs. 'My life, a thing like that isn't possible is it mate?' asked Vic of Robbie. 'How do they manage it?'

'Celery,' was the reply.

By the time the next card reached David it was rather damp from many fingers. His tired eyes slowly focused and two more figures, a very large lady and a very small but not insignificant gentleman were confronting each other. He felt a flush run over his face. Fortunately the others were all eyes down on the chain of entertainment moving round the circle. Ginger, like some croupier at a casino card table, neatly stacked the returning cards on one side as he sent forth his artistic treasures from the other.

Fred was getting visibly disturbed. He was scratching himself hard, on buttocks, armpits and forearms. 'They're not real Ginger, they're waxworks,' he cried in disbelief.

'They bloody well are, Fred,' Ginger assured him through a babble of laughter. 'Reynolds offered twice what I paid for them, but I've had much better offers and I won't part with 'em.'

'Disgusting,' said David, without evangelical fervour, It's a good job Rowe's on watch, he thought. The card that lay in his moist fingers was of a lady whose only items of apparel were shoes and stockings, and who seemed surprised to find a totally undressed gentleman behind her. 'Oh, Ginger you are filthy,' he murmured.

The pile had been reduced to about half its original size when the first lieutenant and chief bo'sun passed by, going on rounds into the forward messes. They glanced with mild surprise at the cheerful group over in the communications mess. Later, as they came back and moved over to the starboard side, the second-in-command told them to sit easy as they scrambled to rise. He peered with interest at their amusement and grinned an aside to the bo'sun. 'I wonder if the Ministry of Information has thought of this for raising morale, Chief?'

'Young Ginger ought to go in the photographic business after the war, sir,' he observed.

The first lieutenant permitted himself the familiarity of picking up one to look at it closely. 'She seems to be exercising some kind of semaphore with all her limbs,' he said.

About this time David thought they were getting repetitious but continued to glance at them as they passed. By the signalman's watch it was getting near 2000 hours. It was clear Robbie knew well from earlier experience the therapeutic properties of the cherished photographs, bought, perhaps in the seedy bazaar of a Middle Eastern port. People seemed remarkably eased and Ginger, for the present time at least, was not biting his fingernails. It was just another of those instances that puzzled David so much, as to where evil ended and good began.

He was stretched out on the lockers when George came off watch and sat down on the other side of the table. All was quiet, he said, as he lit a cigarette. Nothing doing but the hourly routines. The lights were switched off in most places and when he finished smoking he lay back on the bench. 'I've written to the girl,' he said softly. 'Just as if I'd heard nothing.'

'Yes, chum, that's good,' David was getting drowsy. 'It's the best idea to let it alone for the time being.'

Other people were looking for places to settle down, but no hammocks were slung. Voices could be heard in the TS from time to time, but there was no urgency in them. Then a high-pitched call to the bridge stifled any hopes of a peaceful night. 'Asdic contact red two zero,' and the distant rolling reverberations of a depth charge attack came almost immediately from somewhere over on the starboard side and were in turn smothered by the rattling action alarm bells.

'Bugger it,' sighed George resignedly, nearly falling off the bench in his hurry to get up. 'Goodbye sleep. Here we go again.'

Once more the off-duty watches swept in a human stream out of the forward messes and down the TS alley, pulling on fur hats and gloves as they ran. Each closing door and hatch must have driven crucifying nails into the spirit of men whose duty was on the escape-sealed side of the clanging metal covers.

The bearings were starting to come in thick and fast from radar, asdic and HF-DF. The writhing course of the destroyer as she began turns that ended in targetless frustration was felt through the swaying deck and the tension grew as the roar and rumble of battle echoed round the convoy, but David, still nursing the dull pain of fear, was not dominated in his thoughts by it. No twisting thoughts of succour by a larger power came to him now. What was to be would be. One could only hope an end to it would not be messy. He tended to watch the others more closely as they took messages, decoded, received bearings and called the bridge. An objective interest grew in the development of an attack on a submarine that had tried to let the convoy slide overhead as it lay submerged and silent in its path. When detected it cleverly evaded attack and presumably got away too far to be chased by escorts closely tied to their charges.

'What we want is an independent group to go after these bastards,' Robbie said indignantly. 'It's all bloody take.'

Through the slow hours up to midnight the struggle waged fiercely round the convoy perimeter, the escorts at last fully getting the measure of the attackers and keeping them at a distance. What deadly shafts of explosive sped beneath the glassy surface and failed to strike a target would be only ever known in the secret records of the enemy. How near the merchant ships, heavily laden with guns, tanks, aircraft and other war fodder they came; or how close they skimmed to the warships crowded with men gazing at dials, screens and gauges, or staring into a vacuity of mind or darkness will never be known, but every dreadful second creeping reluctantly behind its predecessor, carried the aching threat of annihilation. The barrage of depth charges, to the innocent, might appear to herald the death of many a submarine, but the experienced knew only too well that U-boats took an awful lot of concentration to destroy. The sad countenance of Ginger as he turned occasionally from his work on the radio telephone said that though the firepower of the enemy was silent it was infinitely more deadly.

Fred tumbled gladly out of the chair at midnight to prop himself in the corner. His face twisted wryly as he mentally laughed at the obscenity of fear. 'I'll never,' he told a half-occupied David, 'see another effing Errol Flynn picture again, if I get out of this in one piece.'

The signals poured in as the baying sea wolves told their leader of their positions and tactics. It was fantastic to listen to the hubbub and impossible to comprehend the usefulness of so much signalling; the practice of writing the bearings on the relative message had long since been abandoned. Obviously the direction-finding operators must have been wearing themselves out trying to catch and telephone each bearing and they had stopped sending in those that were on the other side of the convoy and sent in only those of immediate concern to the ship.

About two in the morning Pots, now more parchment grey and haggard than anybody, having spent the best part of thirty hours in the office, called George down at the aft damage control to go and change places with one of the DF operators. By way of an explanation he turned to David. 'Those blokes'll be falling apart if I don't give them a break.'

At four o'clock George was called back to do his watch on the set and as Fred had slipped down into a quietly snoring escape from their predicament Pots told David to go and relieve one of the operators. George stepped over the coaming, bringing the cold in with him. He was quite frank. 'I'm glad to be out of that rat hole,' he said fervently.

Clutching his way down the iron deck to the nagging rumbles of conflict from the other side of the merchantmen, he got into the sick bay flat. X gun crew had been brought down from their exposed platform and sat around and on the hatchway to the HF-DF cubicle. They moved sluggishly and opened the heavy lid and he went down the steep ladder. One of the operators came out of the cubicle, nodded in a dazed fashion and slowly climbed to the hatchway. The gunners let it fall back with a loud clang and with a scrape of clips it was secured. He felt entombed alive.

In the cubicle Jumper Collins wearily grinned a welcome. 'Do you want to operate this thing? I'll go bonkers if I take another bearing!'

There really was no answer to this oblique appeal and David sat down tensely, put on the headphones and was just running his fingers over the controls to reassure himself he would not fumble when the squeaking and rush of atmospherics was broken by the squeal of a signal. He spun the pointer to a dip in the volume, pressed the switch and it went loud. It was the reciprocal; the true bearing was green five three. Leaning up by the telephone Collins said, 'Goodo, that's the other side. I won't send it up. That's where the uproar is now.' It was the same engagement he had heard coming aft.

Confident in David's competence, Collins sat down in the corner within arm's reach of the telephone and opened a book. Well into the morning watch they found this arrangement satisfactory, David developing his rapidity of operation and Collins using his discretion as to the bearings sent to the bridge. During intervals he was absorbed in his reading. About six o'clock the traffic began to decrease and there was a little, jaded, terse conversation. Collins showed what he was reading. It was *Sons and Lovers*.

'Never heard of him,' was David's uncouth reply. Wells or Conan Doyle were near his mark.

'Do you want something to read, Dave?' he was asked.

'Wouldn't mind. Could manage it now.'

'What about this mate?' Collins held up a book with *Of Mice and Men* on the front.

'That's one of those you were talking to Fred about isn't it, Jumper?'

'Yep. Interested?'

'I'll give it a go.'

The petulant frequency, of which he was heartily sick after six hours, was losing its quality of crisis. Collins got up. 'I'll do a bit now, Dave,' he said, 'I think I can manage both.'

David sat on the deck and opened the book. It was on poor standard, war economy paper and the print was rather grey for his strained, tired eyes. The soft card cover was in simple black, white and orange. He folded it round to the back. Gently he was eased away into a sunlit, dusty California, hot and pervaded by the smell of leather, hay, dung, horses and the sweat of labour. He escaped for a time from present grim reality into the world of sad and desperate working men and even into their fantasies. For two blissful hours the simple prose steadied thoughts and emotions and in company with the fading battle noise and wireless signals chased the demon fear away. At eight o'clock they were stirred from their quiet abstraction by the hatchway creaking open and a clatter of boots down the metal rungs of the ladder preceded the appearance of the other two HF-DF operators in the doorway.

'Keep the book for the time being,' said Collins, 'it won't take long to finish it.' Indeed, after two hours so concentrated had been his attention that he was two-thirds of the way through it.

The two arrivals noticed at once – perhaps a little refreshed by sleep – that which had passed unobserved earlier. The heading of the ship was now south-south-east. 'Looks like we're turned for the Kola Inlet,' one said.

Sleep was all David craved after a sleepless night and having quickly drunk a mug of tea, he settled down on the lockers between the messes. Despite painful shins and aching head, he soon fell fast asleep.

From this happy state, tormentingly insufficient, just before noon he was roused by the metallic thump of A and B guns firing. Shakily looking up in a bleary-eyed daze he saw the few people in the mess area remained unconcerned. Jim Streeter, preparing for dinner at the end of the table, said it was only a spotter plane, so David went down to the iron deck for a breath of fresh air before the afternoon watch.

It was full daylight. The low sun filtered brightly through a high, thin layer of cloud. The ships were steaming obliquely towards this southern glow. On the portside of the funnel a handful of loungers watched the shooting. The main armament of *Obstinate* roared and flashing pinpoints of light appeared in the fleecy puffs of earlier shells. These marked the flight of the enemy aircraft prowling in the northern greyness. The firing made the task unpleasant and difficult for its pilot, but the distance was too great to make it particularly dangerous. He leisurely counted the ships and perhaps radioed back the result of the attacks, then slowly the airplane turned for base disappearing in the gloom behind the convoy.

For dinner it was delightful to find corned beef, mashed potatoes and baked beans. The meal was very cheering but its effect was to make David unsuitably sleepy on watch. Fortunately, things were now very quiet and he had no difficulty in reading the book to its doleful end.

By now the destroyer was rolling almost imperceptibly and her crew were back at cruising stations. The charged atmosphere was easing, the talk being more lively between messmates and watchkeepers. During the dog watches David, with many others, dozed on locker and deck, changing his position from time to time as one part or another of his anatomy went numb. The first watch came round soon enough and it was silent on the frequency except for the hourly routine from control.

Just before midnight George came in, looking well-scrubbed and smelling strongly of shaving lotion. In the mess areas hammocks were slung and most occupied. David managed to get his slung and prepared without disturbing Fred, who was completely under his blanket. It was obvious everybody thought the present tribulations were over. Getting his toilet gear and a change of underclothes from the locker as quietly as possible, David went down to the funnel for a little air, joyfully relishing the prospect of several hours of unbroken sleep.

Outside the tarpaulin curtain there was a glow like moonlight on the superstructure. He looked up for its source but found the sky clear but moonless, with many stars glittering frostily across the void. High over the stern an eerie light-green glow was spread across the firmament. He was reminded of the drapes of a stage, illuminated by footlights, before they parted. An enormous, ethereal curtain, circular in form, spread in a shining ellipse from near to far, crowning the winter dark wastes of the polar regions. The exhaust heat from the happily quivering funnel flicked the stars into agitation, but of its own volition the halo of the world wavered and rustled silently as though stirred by a celestial draught from planetary space. The water, masking its impartial treachery, shone smoothly with the brilliance and it fell like a benediction on the thankful convoy emerging from its long seaway of fear.

Looking round the break of the fo'c's'le David was overjoyed to see a coastline. Low, snow-covered hills, undistinguished in outline, reflected the green luminosity from above. However, although they might be coming out of danger, over on the starboard bow others existed or died on their own particular Golgotha. The silent spurting flashes and flickering gunfire, the rising and falling of flares, showed plainly the grim, static battle front midway between Murmansk and Petsamo.

In the washplace there was still a lukewarm humidity when

David returned to indulge in the solitary luxury of a shower. He managed to get the water to a comfortably hot temperature and began to smother himself in lather. Very soon he was aware, beneath the caressing, warm rivulets of water, of a trembling sensation. This strengthened through quivering into a violent shaking that was impossible to control. The pent-up tension of days flooded out through rapidly relaxing muscles, and bitterly ashamed though he was of his craven, abject body it was tempered by relief that it was alone in the privacy of the night that the reaction occurred.

After the shower, standing in front of a mirror and shaving by half light, he felt better. The hot water seemed to have exorcized the fear that had gripped his body so long and driven it vigorously also from his clouded mind. There was a tremor in his hands as he scraped the growth and lather from his peaky face. On it there was a set hardness that made him see himself as a stranger. It was an expression remembered, in particular, on the face of another. It was like the stone hardness he had detected beneath the tanned features of a convalescent infantry sergeant they had met on a train a long time ago.

16

There were many cheerfully rested people around the mess tables at breakfast the morning the convoy arrived at Kola Inlet. Fred, in particular, was happy, not having had to turn out for the morning watch. The watch on the Arctic Series had ceased, both fore and aft, at two in the morning, according to George, for the ship had passed through the defence boom entrance at one and soon after a radio telephone message was received ordering a close-down. There were, however, many people still closed up to their posts. The gunners and look-outs, other communications ratings and engine-room staff kept the destroyer on a footing of instant readiness, because the enemy, not at present an underwater threat, was still within easy air striking distance.

During the forenoon those not watchkeeping were busy cleaning the ship, and if free, themselves and their gear. Once more George and David, with Fred this time, got the main wireless office to clean. At the outset there was a minor squabble about the cigarette-ash tins, and Fred was coerced into going to empty them as it was claimed by the others, Ginger as well, sitting majestically inactive in front of the radio-telephone set, that he was mainly responsible for filling them. He came back to say that they were alongside an oiler; that bread was coming on board and, most remarkable, it was getting light, though only just ten o'clock.

Going back for stand-easy, they found that the metal discs or deadlights, now free of the ice that had covered them for several days, were lifted up and the glass scuttles open. It was chilly, but a healthier, airy cold that helped refresh and dry out clammy corners. The atmosphere apparently aired the minds of those present for as the scalding cocoa was doled out they sipped, smoked and made flippant remarks increasing up to the old vivacity. Through the portholes a rising sun cast long tubes of cheerfulness across to the canteen side and as fellows came and went they were caught briefly in the rays.

There were a few more little jobs to be done. One of special interest was to go down the hatchway below the galley flat, passing the forward entry to the noisy, hot and oil-smelling engine room, then along under the fo'c's'le and down another ladder to somewhere near the bottom of B gun support into a little compartment, cold and silent as a tomb, near the magazine. From among stocks of stationery – it was surprising to see how much paper the ship required – they had to open a packet of message pads and get some log books from one already open. 'What a mountain of bumf. I wonder if anyone does a duty down here?' speculated Fred.

'Somebody must,' said David, 'the ammo has to be passed up from next door.'

In the privacy of the compartment Fred was very frank. 'Christ, sooner them than me. The huff-duff cubicle is bad enough. You go through two hatches and three doors to get to this hole.' The thought agitated Fred. Thoughtlessly, to David's horror he felt beneath the khaki jersey into his overall pockets for cigarettes and lighter.

'Hell, Fred you want to blow us sky high?'

'Oh yes; sorry mate, I forgot. It's working hours too!'

'Working hours? If they caught you at it down here it would be twenty years in Fort Darlan at least. Me as well.'

Just before dinner they were able to join the funnel club for a spell as the ship was beginning to get under way, going north along the inlet for Polyarnoe. They had been about half way down the forty-mile stretch of water to Murmansk, at a slight bend which formed a wide bay. Right down at the inner end there were grey blobs of buildings which suggested the outskirts of this one northern Soviet port, free of ice all the winter and not in the hands of, or besieged by the enemy. For most of its length it was at its narrowest about half a mile wide and here in the bay probably two miles. The banks were steeply rocky where bare rolling granite hills, not high but extremely broken, dropped down suddenly into the deep, dark blue water of what was more a sea fiord than a river estuary. The whole landscape was bright with sunshine from a clear blue sky and blanketed in deep snow. Dotted here and there were little jetties or huts, so although the whole length of the inlet presented a desolate aspect there was no stretch without a building of one kind or another. The eastern shore, the Kola Peninsula itself, suggested an empty ice-bound waste and though the western bank had a similar appearance it was most likely deceptive, for between twenty and forty miles from its edge the northernmost extremity of the fantastically long eastern battleline ran to the sea and in that area hundreds of thousands of men must have been on both sides of the hideously icy front.

The last, tardy cargo ships were creeping south to the cranes of the port, and astern the oiler had two destroyers refuelling. Ahead the *Obstinate* was already disappearing towards the inlet entrance and Polyarnoe. This smaller harbour was sheltered on its north side by a large island, on the outer edge of which was the defence boom and the open Barents Sea. It was a convenient resting place for the escorts as several could tie up at its long jetty and were well placed to take their positions as the homegoing convoy came down to the sea from Murmansk.

At dinner Robbie said to Ginger, 'Did you hear they took Scouse off in a motor boat as we came in last night?'

Ginger nodded. 'Pots said he was sent straight in for an operation.'

Robbie went on. 'There was no room for Eddie and Reynolds and they're being landed this afternoon.'

For Robbie the meal was something of a tour de force. He had made a meat pudding. It was dense but very eatable. Tinned peas and dehydrated potatoes completed the dish. 'You can make a first rate bit o' duff, mate,' admired his friend. Robbie took the approving grunts and murmurs from around the table with obvious delight. Dessert was tinned plums, yellow and sharp, their acidity countered by a lava-like dollop of custard. He had certainly taken advantage of the placid forenoon to put some vitality into his flagging messmates.

Having helped with the washing up, David and the others were in the fortunate position of being free during the afternoon. 'Let's go and see Eddie,' he suggested.

The upper deck was empty except for lookouts, the weakening light and grey desolate monotony of the passing shores having lost interest for all. The sun was sliding at a very shallow angle down below the darkening west bank, the opposite side catching its last sad glow. The awful frostiness of the Arctic night was already pressing down, as though to crack and splinter the metalwork of the destroyer. They were glad to enter the familiar shelter of the sick-bay flat.

Reynolds was asleep or unconscious when they went into the sick bay, but Eddie was awake, his large eyes, with their prominent, almost doll-like lashes, shining with pleasure when they entered. He was not well enough for much of a conversation but was anxious to see his gear was in safe hands. They agreed to pack everything and get it to the hospital after he had landed.

It was dark by three o'clock when they rounded the sheltering island and slowly approached the jetty of Polyarnoe. Several hundred yards long, it could accommodate at least four destroyers tied in line, one behind the other. They were surprised to see floodlights along its length, silhouetting several ships already cosily tied up, and as they drew near, tall buildings rather like blocks of flats materialized out of the general dark mass of the shore behind the lights. The illumination not only facilitated the business of tying up abreast two other ships but helped the coming and going between them and the store sheds at the back of the jetty. At the western end of the wooden wharf a large building was being constructed in timber, the workmen using a tool like an adze for almost every joint.

Before tea they cleared Eddie's locker and packed everything into his kitbag and case. They got his hammock from the net and put them together, ready with Reynolds' belongings. Seamen came through with Scouse's gear and there was a little pile of baggage causing an obstruction beside B gun support.

George went down to ask Pots about getting the baggage to the hospital, but came back sulky, having been told that watchkeeping started again at 1600 hours, because they were going out again. 'Why for eff's sake?' queried Ginger irritably.

'He's vague himself,' said George. 'All he knows is that the whole flotilla will be on its way out of the boom at 1700 hours. But we're coming back because he said there's no time to take the gear off now and we can do it when we return.'

By five o'clock the destroyers were slipping their lines and moving out round the island. The only one left behind was *Sentinel* which, under the floodlights by the building site, was busy, but rather shamefacedly, repairing its damage. There was just sufficient luminescence to perceive the ships as they formed up in line ahead and cleared the boom gate vessel. Out on the open sea there was a modest swell on the unruffled surface and the vessels quickly beat up to a smart cruising pace of fifteen knots.

By the funnel the dark figures, behind glowing cigarettes, fruitlessly asked each other what it was all about. There was, as they said, not necessarily in that precise, chaste term, no rest for the wicked. The only good thing about it was they were going along at a speed that did not make them an easy target for torpedoes.

When the white watch was called at 1800 hours the mission was at last general knowledge. David stepped over the coaming into the office to hear Robbie telling Ginger, 'Pots says we're going out to pounce on the Jerries before they can gang up on the second part. He reckons we'll be in their regrouping area by 2100.'

Ginger was not happy. 'You've got your bloody independent hunting group and we're it,' he said peevishly.

'Never mind, mate, at least we won't be creeping along asking for it. It'll be pleasant to get at the bastards.' As an afterthought, in a surprisingly mock aggressive way, he poked a finger at Ginger and said emphatically, 'We'll be fighting 'em!'

Fred handed the headphones to David. He pulled a long face as they heard the exchange of remarks. 'Do you remember what that two badge AB said on the depot ship, Dave?'

David scratched behind an ear thoughtfully as he put on the headphones. 'Yes, something about getting all the trouble.'

'"If there's any crap you'll find it," to be exact,' Fred mumbled. 'That bugger knew a thing or two.'

Down below the engines throbbed steadily. The ship rocked gently and only static came through on the enemy wavelength, but Polyarnoe and Admiralty were working themselves into a state once more. Evidently, their messages were not for the flotilla moving unalteringly north-west, but for the second part of the convoy now entering the danger area. Apart from logging preambles Rowe at number one set and Ginger at number four were unoccupied. Streeter was busy in the coder's place, writing a letter. Ten minutes before the end of the watch an announcement was made. 'Hands will close up to action stations at twenty hours.' Streeter closed his writing pad and Ginger leaned back in his chair looking pensively at his fingernails.

Anticipated as it was, the action alarm still jarred the nerves when it rang. The rush along the alleyway was not quite as frenzied and the other ratings arrived in the office almost casually compared with previous occasions. David handed over to George, but it was Fred who was sent to aft damage control, so David settled down in the usual corner and hoped the apprehension that lurked vaguely in the region of the lower spine would not grow into that monstrous fear he was resolved to try and smother. Everybody else was inactive as well. That the ship was manoeuvering there was no doubt because from time to time it listed one way or the other in turns and the tempo of the engines rose and fell constantly. Half an hour of the first watch had passed and nothing had happened. Nobody spoke. The tick of George's watch was very clear. Cigarettes were offered, taken and lit. The minute hand of the clock had moved at last into the second half of the hour. Then the door opened. It was Vic, bringing a blast of cold air with him, down for a quick visit to the heads. Pots did the talking. 'What's going on, Vic?'

'We're in line abreast now, combing their last known concentration area. The yeoman says that if we find them we'll be working with *Masai*. She's on our port beam.'

George's headphones squealed. Everybody looked in his direction as he took down the U-boat signal. The telephone buzzed. HF-DF said the bearing was starboard at seventy-eight degrees. 'I'd better be off,' said Vic and as he slammed the door an ill-tempered rumble of depth charges far away on the starboard side suggested that the submarine, which had warned its companions of destroyers in the locality, was under attack.

The radio telephone crackled into life. 'Hullo *Bouquet*, Hullo *Bouquet*, this is *Bluebell* – disperse and search – executive to follow – over.'

While Pots was informing the bridge, ships acknowledged tersely, When all had answered the executive signal was given and passed to the bridge. Instantly *Watchful* lurched suddenly to port and was presumably racing off to her own particular hunting zone in company with *Masai*. The submarine signals came in, but reluctantly, for now they could bring down persistent retribution. The thundering anger of the attackers was coming from every direction, far distant and near, as the ships in pairs made contact along the diverging fan-shaped lines. But *Watchful* and her consort were out of luck and it was getting well past 2100 hours. Suddenly the sound of rushing air came down the bridge voice-pipe. The captain's voice, high-pitched, called, 'Signal to *Masai* – Have contact – Am engaging.'

The ship eased her pace to get a more accurate fix by the asdic equipment, then up went her speed and shortly afterwards came the now familiar rattling roar of ten exploding cylinders. Somewhere astern guns crashed, soon followed by another roaring pattern of depth charges. *Masai* was obviously giving the contact another dose of misery. The aft damage control telephone buzzed. Fred's voice could be heard shouting excitedly. 'The *Masai*'s just crossed our wake, shot flares up and dumped another lot of crap. It's beautiful up here just like Guy Fawkes' Night!'

'Righto lad, calm down – the night's still young.'

'Bloody 'ell,' said Ginger, 'he's getting ecstatic!'

'It's better than the pictures,' said George with an unusual attempt at stolid humour.

Another half hour and several hundreds of pounds' worth of explosive later did not seem to bring any success to the prowling, darting, sniffing, listening sea terriers. Pots took advantage of the lull to send David down to relieve Fred. He did not refer to him as Fred or Windenham, but as Cecil B. de Mille, which raised a ripple of amusement in an office unsure whether it was afraid or excited. The walk down the iron deck was quite easy for right away to the south-west on the port bow, a very noisy and well illuminated contest was in progress. So many flares, such an uproar.

'If that isn't *Stavanger* I'll eat my pusser's boots,' David said dramatically to Fred when he arrived at the aft torpedo tubes. His opposite number stood between them and the sick bay flat entry, fascinated, in company with the sick berth attendant, his bony face under the duffel coat hood reflecting the starshells.

'What an effing ding-dong,' said Fred, 'I won't take you up on that remark, Dave.' He started off for the fo'c's'le, taking his time, stopping to admire the distant spectacle.

Going in to report the changeover, David had no need to inform Pots of his speculation. 'We know all right, Dave. They've started chattering like a couple of bomb-happy fighter pilots. It's *Stavanger* and *Obstinate*.'

The hunt was dispersing over a wide area of ocean and depth-charging although going on all round, was too distant to be of immediate interest. David went and sat in the sick bay with the attendant. He was a resourceful young man for somehow he produced a jug of steaming cocoa and offered a cup to David. It may have been imagination, but he thought there was a faint smell of antiseptic about the drink and maybe the hot water was obtained from the sick bay equipment.

The attendant was about twenty and of medium build. Strong enough, but not too thick-set for his height. His face was oval in shape and lacked prominent features, almost to the point of being distinctly oriental in appearance, an effect emphasized by a very yellow-white complexion. His hair, soft and limp, was more grey than blonde but this may have been due to the half light in the compartment. David was on the bench just by the door and the attendant on the lower cot opposite. The latter felt disposed to talk of his plans for when he left the service. He was going to study medicine, of that there was no doubt. He had left school at fourteen and until he was called up had worked first as a messenger boy and then as a warehouseman, doing civil defence first aid work in his spare time. He had been talking to Collins and felt the matriculation examination would not be such an obstacle as he used to think. In fact Collins was helping him with the mathematics and English already. All very fine, thought David, but here is another one tempting fate, like Eddie. If the faintest hint of speculation on a future peacetime existence crossed his mind he stifled it in almost superstitious terror. It brought a desperate yearning to see days of peace that after four years were only a vague, half-forgotten memory of sunnier times.

'What you going to do, Dave?' The question, full of casual, friendly interest, slashed at his nerves.

'I – er – be a miserable bloody clerk again, I suppose, Dick.' David tried to be off-hand, for he knew Dick Baker had sensed his discomfort. He looked up at the clock. It was nearing 2300 hours. 'I wonder how long we're going to be piss-balling about out here?' It was said harshly, an attempt to cover his embarrassment as much as to change the topic of conversation. Baker took the mugs and went over to a little hand basin on the other side of the cots, to wash them. It was where the hot water had come from.

'Well, they must give us a breather when we get back,' he said, turning round to dry his hands. 'It'll take time to organize the return trip.'

In dismay, their glances met at the sound of an exploding torpedo. 'Jesus,' said Baker, 'somebody's got a packet.' They rushed out the starboard exit but there was nothing but blackness. The light and sound of battle had faded over the invisible horizon. They went into the flat and waited by the telephone. There was a loud knocking on the hatchway to the DF cubicle. Baker went over and unclipped the lid and heaved it up. Collins looked out. 'What's up, Dick?' he asked.

'Don't know, mate. A tin fish somewhere.'

The telephone buzzed. Collins, half out of the hatch and Baker standing by it, looked across as it was answered.

'Listen, Dave, it's the *Masai*. She's copped it. We're going to take the blokes off. Tell Baker to get a stretcher ready that end and you and the spare huff-duffer make yourselves useful as best you can. The buffer and Jimmy'll be out shortly. All right?'

Poor Spence, thought David, hardly paying attention to what was said. Never mind, he was most probably on the flagdeck and would not have been caught below. He recollected what had been said and passed it on. 'What kind of a loafer does Pots think I am?' said Baker indignantly. 'Everything is ready. Come on, Jumper, give us a hand up here.'

Collins came up the last few rungs and put down the hatch

cover. They got the stretcher out onto the iron deck by the forward tubes as the destroyer raced across the undulating sea.

Somewhere out on the starboard bow was the torpedoed ship and the order 'Open shutters', was passed to the searchlight platform. The neutral blackness was pierced briefly by the sweeping blue-white light and the superstructure was momentarily a stark pattern of damp surfaces reflecting the sudden brilliance. The beam sped across the dark, slowly heaving surface of menacing water and caught the *Masai*, at a standstill, already wallowing in its failed strength.

There was just time for the bridge to assess the situation and the light snapped out as dramatically as it had come on. Slightly turning to starboard the racing destroyer slackened pace and closed up, more by its impetus than motive power, to effect a rescue.

They had been momentarily dazzled by the beam but, becoming accustomed once more to the dark, they could make out the darker bulk of the doomed vessel against the night. They were very close now, and the bo'sun was quietly but swiftly seeing the scrambling nets and fenders put down the side and the gangplank readied for pushing across, if it were practicable. Curiously, some residue of shaded light emanated from their ship which, as they closed, cast itself on the newly painted light-grey superstructure of the gently rolling vessel. She was already cold and still. Not a wisp of steam or smoke blurred her ghostly lines. The foremast was dimly seen to be bent at an angle away from them over the other side.

The distance narrowed to a few yards and dark forms were moving back and forth. Sometimes the flicker of shaded torch or red light clipped to lifebelts suggested that the crew were uncertain which way to get across to them. A babble of voices floated across and as helpers on the iron deck waited silently, the curt, businesslike voice of the captain, quietly spoken in the loud hailer, addressed the commander of *Masai* evidently a personal acquaintance. 'We'll take you off your fo'c's'le onto my iron deck, Charlie.'

Charles required no urging and immediately the officers and petty officers were organizing an orderly evacuation. His ship's company was directed up to beside B gun deck where the ship's side was now perilously low in the water but providentially only five or six feet above the iron deck of the hove-to *Watchful*. Soon men were tumbling over and falling on to her hard, freezing but welcoming plates. Mumbling, quietly cursing at their danger, breathing prayers of thankfulness and relief, groaning with some already incurred injury, sometimes stifling a cry of pain as they landed awkwardly unable to judge the height correctly, the dark torrent of humanity was grabbed, pulled clear and helped off to the galley-flat as quickly as the gloom and confusion would allow. A voice unsubdued by pain, repetitious in its agony could be plainly heard on the other deck. 'Thanks, Yorkie, thanks mate; we'll get across won't we?' And a special combined effort of many willing hands, some risking in the slippery darkness a fall in the merciless sea, carried a helpless form over on to the stretcher that had been brought up by Baker. The voice of pain was below them now. 'Thanks mates, thanks Ted.'

Turning to grab a handle, David was forestalled by the shipmates of the injured man who, blundering on an unfamiliar deck, carried it into the fo'c's'le.

The mass coming over had thinned to individuals; senior ratings, stout of build and cool of head, having seen their lads out of dangerous compartments and lethal corners, were heavily but nonchalantly jumping down, one or two even gripping little attaché cases containing their own particular treasures.

Presumably the captain could perceive his friend moving down from the bridge by way of the flagdeck and port Oerlikon platform for he urged, 'Hurry up, Charlie, it's time we were going,' and as the final lonely figure appeared darkly above them David realized with a spasm of terror that they had been motionless far too long. Yet whilst actual men before him had been in need of succour the general desire to help which had animated his shipmates for some time had pushed the instinctive passion for self-preservation from his mind.

Instantly the captain of *Masai* landed on their deck the first lieutenant telephoned the bridge from a point below the Bofors platform to say all were clear and the life pulse of engines revived and *Watchful*, as though desirous of putting distance between herself and her dying companion, from which came an ominous crack and muffled roar of collapsed bulkheads, moved swiftly away.

David, wanting to see Spence was comfortable, followed the last of the survivors into the galley flat. Over by the bridge ladder a group round the stretcher was frantically occupied by the light of emergency lamps. All round men were packed together. Some sat passively; some stood; some treating others for injuries, lighting cigarettes with shaking hands and all the way up the TS alley into the forward messes the murmur of voices. Baker moved urgently from one casualty to the next, bandaging legs and arms, putting them in splints. There would be a brief yelp of pain, or groan, but it seemed that the only critically injured rating was the one on the stretcher. The desperately concentrated group around him included the captain and and coxswain of *Masai* and its sick berth attendant.

Most upper deck men were in their heavy gear and David grew ashamed of wandering unhelpfully and peering into the faces of shocked men. He asked an older fellow in overalls and peaked cap if he had seen Spence. 'Sorry, lad, don't know him. I'm engine room.' A figure in white fur hat, duffel coat and sea boots looked as though he might be a signalman. 'D'you know Signalman Spencer – have you seen him?'

'I know the old ram, mate,' he said, 'but I was on the aft Oerlikons. Don't know if he got off.'

He must be all right David told himself emphatically. All the crew seemed to be here. Even the people down below got off. He was probably somewhere up in the fo'c's'le; there was hardly a square foot to spare up there. He would look for him later; for the present he had to get back to the telephone.

On the iron deck the bo'sun and his team were still busy securing equipment. There was no doubt as to what was happening now. The ship was speeding along at over twenty knots, headed for Kola.

Back at the telephone David reported to Pots. 'You'll have to hold on down there a bit longer,' the latter said. 'I've got George helping the *Masai* blokes at the moment.' It was odd, thought David as he went into the empty sick bay, how in this emergency it was not in use. The X gun crew came down from the cold and congregated round and on the hatch and the locker next to it, but it was still quiet and empty in the aft housing. All those people crammed together forward, it was good to be in this uncrowded space away from that sickening atmosphere. However he would like to satisfy himself that Spence was all right. In some curious way he felt a special obligation towards him.

Just before two o'clock George peered round the sick bay door. 'I'm right glad to get away from up forrard,' he said, being remarkably communicative. 'It's effing depressing. Some of 'em shaking like hell. Our tiffy was first rate. As good as a quack I'd say. They're doling out kai right now.'

Pushing aside the blackout tarpaulin at the fo'c's'le entry, David saw that it was now apparently empty in the flat. The first impression was not quite right, for in the blue lit quietness there was an enveloping sense of horror. There was somebody. A shivering figure, oblivious to the cold, in light-blue overalls with the blue and white propeller badge of a stoker on the arm. He sat on the deck with his back to the galley, smoking quietly, staring across at the bridge ladder. David followed his gaze. The stretcher was still there, in the deepest shadow, pushed up against the wireless office bulkhead. Its dreadfully still burden was totally covered in blankets. As David crossed the flat the stoker looked up, expressionless, and said flatly. 'He's my oppo. We came from the same place. His folks treated me like one of the family.' There was nothing worthwhile to be said in reply to such uncomprehending grief and feeling hopelessly inadequate David nodded, looked again sideways at the dead body and went up to the office. No wonder George had been depressed.

Fred was turned round facing the door when he entered. Leaning back in the seat, smoking, the headphones on the message pad. 'The bastards are keeping very quiet,' he said, answering what must have been a questioning look on David's face. 'Now and again we get a signal, but they're all back there. The others must still be persecuting them. They're running too much to talk.'

The mess deck is chock-a-block, Dave,' said Pots, who sat on the bench under the voice-pipes, '... you might as well stay here out of the way – oh, this is Bill Hopkins.' He indicated a *Masai* rating, in a dark blue jersey and overalls, sitting at number one set. 'He'll most likely be with us until base, doing Reynolds' watch.'

The new fellow was rather tall, or so it appeared as he lolled in the chair, but thin of build, He was about twenty-three or four. His narrow face, though fair-skinned, had pinky edges to it at nose, ears and eyes. It was not a very handsome prospect, for his nose was too long and hooked, and his lips too thin. Also his ears, thin and opened in contours, were unpleasantly close to the head. His soft and lank fair hair was already thinning at crown and temples. Moreover, when he spoke his voice was unfortunately a less vulgar reminder of the North Midlands' accent of Reynolds. Fortunately, however, appearances belied his nature for he was singularly amiable and remarkably unshaken by his ordeal.

He was telling the others what happened. 'As I was saying, it's a good job the torpedo hit the other side. The officers' heads, ship's office and one of two other unoccupied places took the full force of the blast. It bulged the bulkhead on that side but didn't bust through. Still, it's fair wrecked the office. I was sitting on the deck clear of the sets, but those at the bench were lucky to get off with bruises and bashed heads. The whole lot came down on them – it was a bloody grimocious tangle. The lights went out, we could hear the water pouring in somewhere on the other side of the bulkhead and the door was jammed. We had to take an axe to its panels to get out. By the time we got out most of the others were on the upper deck. The alleyway was buckled to hell, pipes and cables all over the place, but we had emergency lamps. And you know, just as we staggered out, the buffer and Jimmy went past as bold as brass, with lamps, into the fo'c's'le, checking everybody was out.'

David just had to ask him if Spence was unhurt. 'Don't know, mate, everything being in the dark till we got in here. But I should think he's all right. Some stokers got it in the explosion, it got the forrard end of the engine room, but I reckon everyone else is OK.'

The door banged open and Vic blundered in. With upturned earflaps to his brown fur hat, heavy boots and gloves, he was a latter day epitome of Genghis Khan. He pushed a piece of paper in the direction of Pots. 'The skipper wants this sent chop-chop.

Didn't they hammer the poor old *Masai*?' He noticed Hopkins. 'Got your yeoman up top with us,' he told him.

Streeter was in the coder's seat and with Pots coded the signal, not at all clandestinely, so that everybody could hear its content. 'Signal, to Flag Officer, North Russia – information of Admiralty and Captain D, *Severe* – time of origin 0220 GMT.' There was some murmuring as they worked out the groups. 'Estimated time of arrival Polyarnoe – 0500 – landing 23 injured 1 dead from *Masai*.' There was some more mumbling – '. . . most of complement safe.' There was another pause, in which Vic closed the door and made himself comfortable for a brief smoke.

'Righto, mate,' Pots said to Robbie, 'suppose the skipper thinks it doesn't matter now breaking silence, so here's your little billet-doux for Polyarnoe W/T.' So saying he turned to the switchboard and plugged a line into a socket and threw a switch. The main transmitter glowed with red light. Robbie unlocked the transmission key, tapped it a couple of times to be sure of power, looked at the message and called Polyarnoe. The sparks at the key were transformed into light in the transmitter, flashing on and off in time with the Morse pulses. On receiving an acknowledgement he began to click away till the message was sent, answered an enquiry about code groups and when he was finished Pots switched off the transmitter.

17

Watchful was inside the boom by the time white watch was due to be called so Pots did not bother to wake David, who had gone to sleep propped up in the corner behind Fred. At half past four, however, Fred clumsily woke him by kicking his foot. 'Cup o' char, mate?' he grinned cheerfully and handed down one with his left hand as he sipped another in his right. He then made himself comfortable on the deck and lit a cigarette. 'We're coming round the island. The *Masai* blokes are getting ready to go ashore. S'pose the fit'll be coming home with us.'

When they had drunk the tea David got up and put on his gloves and balaclava. 'Coming to see us tie up, Fred?' he asked.

'No bloody fear – it's too cold out there!'

The galley flat was empty; the stretcher had been taken out onto the iron deck. The same lights glittered along the waterfront as the ship drifted in and tied up astern of *Sentinel*. The boards of the jetty were covered in a surface of crisp, smooth snow that glittered frostily in the floodlights. Work was still proceeding on the building although the damaged ship below it was silent, with everybody getting a good sleep. Waiting nearby were three horsedrawn sledges or droshkies; the animals looked extremely thin and cold. With the drivers were several Soviet naval and military officials and one or two sentries armed with rifles or machine pistols. As the gangplank was put across an officer from the hospital, a naval surgeon came across and said to the first lieutenant, his breath clouding in the icy air, 'Hullo, old man, we've got a couple of droshkies for those who can't walk and the other will take that.' He indicated the stretcher. 'We'll take all the *Masai* chaps in the hospital, give them a quiet night until they're allotted ships for going home. We'll send down those who are fit enough to travel.'

'Are you ready to take them now?'

'Yes. The uninjured can walk. It's not far. Up those steps, round the back of that big block. The droshkies'll go round by the road at the end there.' He pointed to the floodlit end of the jetty. 'We'll see this poor chap is decently attended to. You've got enough troubles without that.'

The captain of *Masai* came down from the fo'c's'le deck and joined the conversation. 'We're just about to send them off, Sir!' the first lieutenant said.

'Good. He goes off before any of us,' said the captain, looking at the stretcher. The first lieutenant nodded to the bo'sun and the deck party reverently lifted the body and carefully took it over the gangway and onto the first droshky. Its handles were tied to the wooden frame of the sledge. Out of the darkness on the other side of the searchlight platform two figures emerged. David had seen both before. One was the engine-room artificer and the other the stoker, both now clad in duffel coats.

The artificer saluted. 'Excuse me, Sir. Request permission to go along with him.'

'Yes, all right. Permission granted, but be sure you go on to the hospital afterwards.'

'It's going to the hospital anyway, Sir,' put in the surgeon.

The driver made an odd rolling sound with his tongue and the poor beast wearily plodded off down the jetty, the sledge runners crackling softly on the snow. After it went the two sailors, oblivious of the stares from Russians and their countrymen.

'Shall I get the injured out, Sir?' the first lieutenant asked the captain. The erstwhile commander of *Masai* nodded. Those able to limp came along and sat on the droshkies; two had a helping hand from their shipmates. There were five on each vehicle and they too started off along the jetty.

David had not seen Spence, and thinking it would be a suitable time to look for him as they came off the ship, went back in and along the TS alley. He had still not found him among those who were filtering past on their way ashore. He looked around in the canteen area and was about to go into the forward messes when he saw a petty officer coming down the ladder from the mess above. There were crossed flags and a crown on the arm of his jacket. It was the yeoman of *Masai*. 'Excuse me, yeoman,' he said, not entirely suppressing the concern in his voice, 'but do you know if Signalman Spencer is all right?'

A fleeting unhappiness crossed the face of the petty officer. He shook his head. 'You one of his pals?'

David nodded. He knew what was coming. In fact he had probably felt it all along.

'It was the lousiest bad luck. He was over by the starboard signal lamp. It could have been me too. I'd only been talking to him a few minutes earlier. The explosion was right underneath. Wrecked the whole of that side. Carley floats, Oerlikons went completely. Blasted the flagdeck bulwark on that side. Must have had it instantly, before he ever hit the water. Him and gunners. What the tin fish didn't do the foremost gubbins and all that did. Fell that side mangled everything.' He pulled on a quilted alpaca jacket and zipped it closed at the front. He shook his head again. 'First rate bloke. Bloody pity. There's no damned sense to it.' He sauntered off to join the last of the survivors going out along the alley.

Taking off his boots and lifebelt, David lay down on the lockers.

'Call me up, Fres,' he heard a cheerful voice saying, 'I'll complete your education.' A genial, benevolent voice. 'Call me up, Fres.' See you in Smokes, Spence, see you in Smokes. He turned away from the mess, put his arm under his head and thankful for his utter, insensitive weariness, fell asleep.

Eight bells brought him up from his far too short rest to find himself on his back, mouth open and dry, limbs stiff with tension. He thought there would never be enough sleep again. A rubicund, kindly face came back to his mind's eye and a catch in the throat made him sit up sharply. George was making the tea. Others around were rising wearily, like some minor resurrection. 'I'll complete your education, old bean.' Every movement by him and the others was a reproach. He felt ashamed to have woken up, even to this bleak prospect. The tea smelt acrid and repulsive, but still he craved it. Pulling on his boots, he went to the end of the table and cut himself a slice of bread, another and a third,

'Bloody gannet,' grunted George, but not really in reproof.

Crouching down by the electric radiator, willing a browned surface on the toast, David said emphatically, 'I'm hungry. Fantastically bloody well hungry. I could eat ten breakfasts.'

Ginger had been prone on the locker behind the table. He heaved himself upright, propped elbows on the back of the seats and yawned heartily. 'Well, Dave,' he said through a rush of air from his lungs. 'I've got some news that'll knock the appetite out of you.'

Fred, rising up seedily from within the voluminous folds of his duffel coat that had been littering the deck near the hammock net, stopped in process, an anxious look on his haggard features, and a claw-like hand frozen in mid-air as it grasped for a mug of tea. 'The huff-duff officer is coming to see you before stand easy and after it at 1100, they're going to see us about the misbegotten Reynolds.'

'Blimey!' groaned Fred, almost as agitated as he was in the face of the enemy.

'What you getting in a panic about?' said Ginger. 'You were half asleep at the time!'

Fred's hand continued on its way and seized a mug.

'I don't give a tuppenny eff, if it's fighting Jack Burnett himself,' snarled David, aggressively spreading butter on the toast as thickly as he could.

Robbie had walked back into this exchange, freshly groomed from his early morning ablutions. Hearing the last remark he burst out laughing. 'You know, Dave,' he said, 'I reckon we've made a matelot of you at last.' George sat down on the bench, sipped his tea and was very thoughtful.

It was a relief to clean the mess for morning rounds and then change into full uniform for the official business of the day. Not long after nine the three special operators went down to the empty main office to await the arrival of the sub-lieutenant from *Severe*. They sat quietly, although Fred and George fidgeted a little, perhaps wanting to smoke. Round about the half hour Pots appeared in the doorway and, indicating they should stand up, made way for a short, slightly built officer in a duffel coat and carrying a peaked cap which in his small hands was absurdly large.

'Thank you Petty Officer,' he said, a trifle patronizingly and turning, took the door off the latch and closed it, leaving Pots very much out in the cold. He put his hat upside down on the bench, tugged off his gloves, slapped them together and put them in it. His hands were white, with blue veins showing clearly on the smooth, somewhat plump flesh of their backs.

'Well,' he said, with a trace of irony, as he patted back over a very high forehead the soft, thinning hair, which was a rich gold midway between ginger and yellow, 'you're not ashore raising hell this time.' As though disconcerted at the way the trio stared glumly down at him – even Fred had the advantage of several inches and George virtually towered above him – he ordered, 'I think you'd better sit down.'

His bland white face looked down through large tortoiseshell spectacles. His sight was most likely not very good without them and he had the introspective look that David, from schooldays, associated with what they used to call a swot. His studies had been advantageous to him, thought David. A nice bunk, collar and tie to wear and, still more, treated like a name instead of a number.

Delicately rubbing his fingers together, in a vaguely prayerful way, he began his lecture. 'Now, first I want to say that Captain D was pleased with the help he had from the whole of our organization, which includes you. It was very useful. You seem to have settled down quite well and to be doing a passable job. On the way back you'll be doing the same thing and you should know it is of utmost importance.' He paused, apparently not quite certain what to say next. It was hardly surprising. He was only months older than the ratings before him. They were quietly respectful. There was no option, but those three pairs of eyes were really taking stock of him most alarmingly. It would probably be advisable to let them talk, perhaps helping to dispel the disconcerting silence. 'I – er, if you've got any problems or questions I'm really the one to see. After all I know what you're doing.'

'I've a question, Sir.' Fred, urged on by his eternal curiosity, stepped in where the more circumspect feared to tread.

'Yes? Ah, let me see, you're ... ?'

'Windenham, Sir. About those messages that came and went. We've got a theory.'

The sub-lieutenant was cagey. 'Have you, what is it?'

'That it was a battleship out on a foray. We think it was the *Trebnitz*.'

Their superior seemed to squirm in a dilemma. George could recognize an advantage when he saw one. 'In fact we know it was. We worked it out.'

'Worked it out?'

'Yes, Sir, on a map, with the bearings. Alten Fiord and the rest.'

'Well now,' but the HF-DF officer was not too sure. 'I don't suppose it'll matter if I tell you. By the time we're back at base, there'll have been an official communiqué.' He stroked his hair again, thoughtfully. 'It was the *Trebnitz* and from the cross bearings she was making straight for us. Got within forty miles and turned tail back home. We don't know whether she feared a trap similar to the one that finished the *Schleswig* – she'd have been right – or it was just a pass to make the convoy scatter. That would have given the U-boats their chance, And just think of the pickings the next day for the aircraft.'

'With all due respects, Sir,' David asked deferentially, 'would they expect us to fall for that?'

'Unfortunately, it happened once. Before your time – and mine – the truth'll be known one day.' He picked up his cap and gloves. 'I'll send over the start time, but it's the same frequency and the same look-out for the unusual. Who's to say they might not make a real attempt next time? Taking the empties back may not be so attractive a target for such a risk but one cannot afford to ignore any possibility. That's all.' Taking the hint they stood up. 'Good morning, men.' The last politeness was rather too theatrical and incongruous. Putting on his gloves he left the office. It was something of an anti-climax, like the messages.

They wandered back to the mess as Robbie was presiding at the cocoa. The gathering looked up at them inquisitively.

'And what,' said Ginger, 'did young Clarence have to say?'

Fred, being foremost, answered for the others. He relished the centre of the stage. 'You'll be interested to hear,' he scratched inside his right thigh, pausing with great feeling for the dramatic moment, 'that the *Trebnitz* was almost within spitting distance before it had second thoughts.'

'How distant?'

'Forty miles.'

'Jee – sus,' Ginger moaned, 'oh, the glory of it!'

His racing imagination was directed from intense speculation as to what might have been, by Pots coming down from his mess, smartly attired in jacket, collar and tie. He came over to the mess. 'Everybody who was present any time during the well-known fracas be at the W/T office in ten minutes.'

The coxswain came down after him and they went off along the alleyway together.

The gathering, as ordered, was waiting silently, till Fred, unable to contain himself any longer, likened the proceedings to those that generally went forward at the Old Bailey. 'For Christ's sake, Fred,' grumbled George testily, sitting on the bench massaging the shine on the blue serge of his trouser legs, 'it's no joke!'

Pots came back and called out Ginger. 'Call the next witness,' Fred repeated, mimicking several kinds of voices. Five minutes later Ginger poked his head in the doorway and gave the thumbs up sign to George. Pots came and got Streeter. George felt for his cigarettes, then remembered where he was. 'Come on, Dave,' said Pots, beckoning from the alleyway, several minutes having elapsed since the coder had gone out. As he followed Pots round to the ship's office his legs got the same unpleasantly weak sensation that he had when going to see the headmaster at school.

The door of the office was secured open and he could see the first lieutenant, with a vaguely troubled look on his face, sitting at the writer's desk just two paces inside. He was in a jacket with the two gold rings of his rank on its cuffs, collar and tie, and his peaked cap was on the desk. In front of him was a sheet of paper and a pencil. Sitting beside him on the right, at the end of the desk was the writer, jacketless, but neat in white shirt and black tie, a shorthand notebook open in front of him. Standing just inside the doorway on the left was the coxswain, formally dressed, his cap in the crook of his left arm. He peered out enquiringly and Pots said, 'Telegraphist Freston.' The coxswain repeated the information.

'How many more, Coxs'n?'

'Windenham, Rowe, then Corder's the last, Sir.'

'Righto, wheel him in.'

'Come in, lad. Attention for the first lieutenant.'

David entered as smartly as possible, although the coaming had to be negotiated, and stood stiffly, thumbs in line with whatever side crease remained in his bell-bottoms.

'All right Freston, stand at ease.'

David relaxed in the first stage of informality.

'I'm going to ask you a few questions and you must realize that anything said now may have to be maintained under oath and detailed examination at a court of enquiry. In this instance it is for my report and we must have everything watertight.'

'Yes, Sir.'

'You should also know that an incident of this nature is not an admirable thing for our ship to admit to, and the depriving of the fleet of a rating's services at a critical time is a very serious matter indeed.'

'Yes, Sir.'

'Very well. Now. First, were you present in the main W/T office when Ordinary Telegraphist Reynolds received his injury?'

'Yes, Sir.'

'How did he receive his injury?'

'He fell back against his chair. It swung round as he tried to hold it for support and he slipped downwards to the deck hitting the back of his head on the edge of the safe in which the confidential books are kept.'

'How do you know his head hit the safe; hearsay since?'

'No, Sir. There was a sound like a box – hollow box – being struck.'

David mused that this was probably an apt description of the state of Reynolds' brain, but was not allowed to reflect on it too long.

'Now Freston.' The first lieutenant looked up from his notes, making a nervous pulling grimace of his mouth. 'How d'you suppose Reynolds managed to get himself into that unfortunate predicament?'

'Corder pushed him!'

'Well, that doesn't make things look very good for Corder does it?'

'Oh, no, Sir!' David vehemently asserted. 'It was self-defence. Reynolds made a very aggressive move to strike him and had got up out of his seat. It George had – Corder I mean – had struck him there'd have been another bump, on the front of his head, as well as the back!' He was quite confused by a wish to speak well of George and a sudden realisation he was getting too outspoken. He went hot and stirred with embarrassment. The second-in-command smiled secretly and glanced up at the coxswain. David's eyes flicked from one to the other and he could have sworn there was the hint of a smile too on the severe features of that total embodiment of discipline.

'That last remark has no relevance and should not be put in the typed transcript,' the officer said in a quiet aside to the writer. 'There is one other thing that could come up at an enquiry. The question of Corder's disposition. You and Windenham have known him the longest, what's he like?'

'Very easy-going, Sir,' said David. Then as a daring afterthought, 'Reynolds' been needling him ever since we joined. He took it jolly well, really.'

The first lieutenant cut short his advocacy for the defence. 'All right, Freston, that'll do for now.' He thought a moment, then went on. 'Now remember, this is an unfortunate as well as inconvenient episode for the ship. We could be the laughing stock of the flotilla. You understand me?'

'Yes, Sir.'

'Remember, don't keep chewing the fat with other ratings and maybe officially it will be kept in proportion. We've got enough to concern us without this kind of stupid incident.' He scribbled something down. His attention brought back by an officious cough from the coxswain, he looked up and said, 'Oh, that's all, Freston.'

'Aye-aye, Sir.'

''Shun. Turn right, dismiss,' said the coxswain briskly.

By dinner time the whole business was complete and, according to Pots, likely to be forgotten. He came into the mess area with George just as the meal was being served and evidently had said something encouraging, for Corder had a less downcast look on his face than earlier. Before he went up the ladder to his mess Pots spoke to Streeter, who was standing at the end of the table, one hand tucked in the waist of his trousers, the other holding his mug containing the rum tot, which he was sipping. The odour of the rum mingled with the smell of cooked food gave its unique bouquet to a naval dinner. 'Jim, there's transport coming at 1300 to take the baggage to the hospital. I'll want you to go and see it safely there. You can take young Dave with you.'

At the appointed hour there was a droshky waiting near the gangway and several people helped load the three bags, hammocks and cases. In the bright sun there was a great deal more of interest to be seen as they followed the sledge along the jetty and round a bend in the road that led off its end. At the back of the jetty, running its length, were low, wooden sheds in which, indicated by seamen carrying boxes and sacks back and forth, were located the naval stores so vital at the far end of the line from base. Behind these sheds rose a steep, rocky, snow-covered bank, which in turn was surmounted by a long, large building of several storeys constructed of red brick. A large, pretentious portico in white stucco was the main characteristic of its façade, this being a decorative feature rather than growing out of the structure.

As the road, which was surfaced with packed snow, treacherously coated with patchy ice, went upwards from the jetty, a view was revealed of the desolate landscape. A track led straight down to the waterside from hills which were higher than might be estimated from sea-level and they were rolling masses of granite and ironstone covered in deep snow and ice. To the right of the track there was one level patch of ground the size of a football pitch, as indeed it was, the goalposts at each end sticking out of the snow making that evident. The end of the pitch away from the waterfront was blocked off by a wooden bridge about twenty feet high which carried a road from the track at right angles up to another large red brick building, also with an imposing classical portico, that served as porch to the doors of what was later identified as the Red Navy Club. To the left of the track before it went into open wilderness were several smaller, two-storeyed blocks which looked like apartment houses.

The droshky continued round the back of the waterfront building into an area that was really a cluster of similarly large buildings. At closer range the havoc wrought by arctic frosts was apparent in cracked bricks and bare patches in the stucco. There were a few short streets but otherwise nothing else distinguished enough to be noteworthy. Behind the blocks was again a strip of Ice-Age terrain, then a huddled grouping of more traditional Russian buildings. This was Stary Polyarnoe, or as the boys of the mess called it, Dodge City. Everywhere were posts carrying not only telephone and electricity wires but also trumpet-shaped public address equipment. Wherever they went whilst ashore these loudspeakers were evident.

The horse stopped. *'Gospital zdyes,'* said the driver.

'Spasibo,' said Jim to the amazement of David. 'I'll wait here Dave, while you nip up and make sure we can bring the stuff up.'

Agog with interest, David went in the entrance which had two pairs of doors: one outside pair, then an inner couple with a space between for people to gather their senses after the numbing cold. Between them a Russian soldier leaned against a wall reading a book. His outfit was the usual observed on people out of doors. He wore a brown, rough fur-lined round cap with earflaps that tied up on the crown. A khaki canvas-quilted jacket increased the impression of bulk, being padded with felt. He also wore thick trousers in a similar material and grey-purple felt boots. On the front, upturned peak of the hat was a red enamelled metal star. His rifle, with bayonet fixed, was propped against the wall. His round, flat, pallid, Slavonic features grinned a welcome and he said. *'Zdravstvootye. Gospital?'*

David nodded.

'Tam,' the sentry pointed up the stairs, visible through the glass-panelled doors.

David went up one flight and at the first floor landing there were tall, heavy panelled doors on the right and left. They were closed and trying both sides he found they were locked as well. He went up the next flight to the second landing and a strong smell of carbolic told him he had arrived. There was a bench on the landing and three soldiers, much bandaged, sat on it, smoking cigarettes that had a heavy rich odour, incense-like, similar to the Turkish cigarettes once obtainable at home, but quite distinct in character from them.

He looked through the door on the left side of the landing. In a huge room the size of an assembly hall for a large school was a scene that struck not one but two chords of memory together. He went in. Away to the far end, except for several square-sectioned columns, the whole floor space was covered with simple wooden beds, which were little better than litters or stretchers. Apart from two aisles there was not more than a foot or two between the beds, and lying or sitting on palliasses, sometimes covered by a blanket, were soldiers and sailors in varying states of injury. They had bandaged heads, arms, legs and bodies. Some, where legs or arms should have been, had stumps. Here and there, a stomach-turning sight, blood seeped through dressings. The casualties and their clothes were clean; most articles of uniform had been washed, but many still bore the stains of battle, despite the cleaning. Some, a minority, had pathetic little bundles of personal belongings tucked in beside their beds. They had managed to cling to them through the process of evacuation. They were well cared for as much as the limited equipment and supplies permitted and white-coated men and women moved continually among them. But the scene reminded him of prints he had seen of the barracks at Scutari in the Crimean War and a scene from a recent colour film about the American Civil War when Confederate wounded were primitively treated in the market square of a Virginian town.

It was, fortunately for the patients, very warm, but far too hot for David. He began to sweat, felt a sickness which was aggravated by the moans of pain that arose from time to time above the generally subdued murmur. The flashing lights he had seen two nights ago were reaping a rich harvest. He pulled off his balaclava and opened his duffel coat, uncertain what to do next. A middle-aged, balding man, wearing gold-rimmed spectacles, in a white coat, a stethoscope round his neck, approached. He noticed the foreign uniform. 'Oh, you want English hospital,' he said pleasantly. 'Is next door.' He pointed along the ward. 'Sorry, not possible to go that way. Go in by next entrance.'

David thanked him.

'*Pozhaloosta*. Is nothing young comrade.'

David was not sorry to leave such a place before his stomach heaved and he clattered down the steps to tell Jim. The coder turned to the driver. '*Angliski gospital, von tot,*' he said pointing to the next entrance.

The Russian made the same curious rolling sound and the beast moved.

'Hiding your light under a bushel,' said David with admiration. 'Where'd you learn Russian?'

'I've been at it on and off for a couple of years.'

Whilst Streeter continued to exercise his Russian with the driver David, entering the next entrance which was identical to the first, went up to ascertain they were at the right place. On the first floor the doors on the left were open and several *Masai* survivors could be seen standing or sitting about. Just inside the door was a little room that functioned as office and dispensary. He enquired of a sick berth attendant the whereabouts of Eddie and his shipmates. They were on the floor above. He went up to make sure and through the glass doors could see Eddie sitting up in bed at the other end of the ward. They soon got the gear up to the landings where an attendant insisted that all the baggage except the cases was to be left in the office for the present and so they had very little to carry along the ward.

The room was about the same in size and fixtures as that in the Russian hospital but the accommodation was neat, white hospital bedsteads, with sheets, blankets and the ubiquitous blue coverlets embroidered with the crest of the service. There was a space of four to five feet between each bed, with a combined locker and bedside table between each. At the near end of the ward was a boisterous group of merchant seamen, unsubdued by the variety of injuries they shared; then a middle gap of unused beds; then the three most distant, occupied by the *Watchful* ratings.

Approaching they noticed that Eddie's right shin was encased in plaster, as was his right wrist. A neat bandage encircled his head above which curly, fair hair sprouted luxuriantly. As they came along the broad centre gangway, he beamed with pleasure. Behind him was Reynolds, fast asleep, and there was a screen round the end bed, in which Edwards was coming out of anaesthesia. Beyond the end doors was, they heard from Eddie, the operating theatre.

'Broken wrist, cracked tibia and a touch of concussion,' Eddie informed them in reply to an enquiry as to the state of his damage.

'But the doctors say I'll be fit enough to travel after a few weeks' stay here and will probably get the next convoy home.'

Reynolds apparently had a slightly cracked skull and severe concussion and would have to stay at the hospital much longer. The medical authorities did not expect any permanent disability but he would most likely be discharged the service with a pension. Happily for Edwards, the appendix had been taken out in good time and he would probably be going home with Eddie.

'I'm so glad you've brought my case. Now I can while away the time writing down all those notes I was too tired or busy to do on board. Even if I can only manage an awkward scrawl.'

This last was amplified by him lifting his plastered hand from which only the thumb and fingers protruded. He went on to enquire what they had been doing since he had entered hospital. Streeter mentioned going out again, the loss of the *Masai*, details of which Eddie knew from talks with other patients.

Attracted by an outburst of laughter from the merchant seamen David turned away, but heard Streeter murmur something behind him and, looking back, saw an addressed envelope being given to Eddie, who seemed astonished and puzzled. 'Why Jim? You'll be home before I will.'

Streeter bent over on the other side of the bed, looked embarrassed but extraordinarily sad too. 'Don't say that. You can't be absolutely sure and we might be sent anywhere but back to base, and I want her to have at least one letter written without the thought of a censor seeing it.'

With the letter in his left hand Eddie lifted it up in a gesture of acceptance. 'All right, Jim, of course, if you wish. I'm bound to get sick leave. I'll post it in Town for you.'

'Thanks son,' said Streeter in a husky whisper. 'My wife'll be very grateful to you. Very grateful.'

'Have you a family?' enquired Eddie, showing suddenly a lot of interest, perhaps not entirely owing to curiosity but maybe to dispel an uneasiness devineable in the situation. David was moved by the break in Streeter's voice as he tried to speak casually.

'Yes, two kids. Girls, four and seven. The younger takes after me. She's a tomboy. The elder is like her mother. I reckon she'll be a real beauty one day. Here's their photo. See for yourself.'

He took a wallet out of his jumper pocket. In it there was a thin leather case, not unlike a holder for a season ticket. There was a photograph of all three of them. His wife at the top of a pyramidal group of portrait heads and the two girls formed the base of the arrangement. His wife was a fine-looking blonde.

'Very handsome,' said Eddie, admiring them. David whistled. 'Your wife is a real humdinger.' Streeter stood looking a long moment, then carefully put the picture away.

The arrival of two surgeons, a chief and two other sick berth attendants at the bedside of Edwards brought the visit to a speedy conclusion. At the other end of the ward they turned and waved back, as Eddie gazed thoughtfully and somewhat regretfully after them. He put the letter in his case and fastidiously tidied the bedclothes. What a pity, he thought, to leave the others in this silly way. Still, better an accident by way of one's duty than the ignominy of Reynolds. Yet there was something odd about Streeter, an air of preoccupation. Forebodings too grim to utter. He leaned back drowsily. Still, it was to be expected, a reaction after danger, a common enough phenomenon and they were tired. He was tired too. All he wished to do for the next few days was sleep. Then he would start to write.

'Let's take a walk over to Stary Polyarnoe before we go back,' suggested Streeter as they came out of the hospital building. 'It's much more interesting than here. All the houses are built in the traditional Russian way, double log walls, and there are boardwalks on each side of the street and some of the shacks have overhanging verandahs.'

They went along a boardwalk, built on piles to allow for the deep snowfall and which followed the contours of the ground up and down steps. Their paces echoed on the planks as they strolled across the white dreariness, passing an occasional impassive Russian, padding quietly along in felt boots.

David was intrigued by his companion and wanted to know what he had been in civilian life. He ventured to enquire. 'What were you in Civvy Street, Jim?' he asked. The answer flabbergasted him. Streeter smiled defensively and looked rather sidelong at him.

'A schoolmaster.'

'I thought that was a reserved occupation.'

'For my age-group it was until recently. Then they decided they wanted us.'

'Oughtn't they make you an officer?' There was a certain residue of awe left over in David since his classroom days.

'Sometime, maybe,' the coder said drily, 'they'll discover that my talents are being misapplied.'

They went down a long flight of steps into the main street of Old Polyarnoe. The near end of the street came to an abrupt stop with a short street at right angles to it which had several low, but large houses in front, and behind could be seen higher wooden buildings like warehouses. That this was the waterfront was obvious because a few masts were visible above the rooftops. Here the Red Navy gunboats, torpedo craft and the occasional destroyer lay alongside. In the other direction the street, rutted with dirty frozen slush, stretched several hundred yards till it petered out in the wilderness. On both sides there were mainly small wooden houses of two of three rooms, but interspersed among them were larger wooden houses adorned with false façades and covered verandahs not unlike those associated with the North American West. Some, in better times, by the shape of the front windows, had functioned as shops, but now the shelves were bare, except for old cardboard displays gathering dust. It was a busy scene, people coming and going constantly, some on skis others on droshkies. A lorry of ancient-looking make clattered over the frozen ruts and rocky bumps. It was not much, but worth seeing, if only to step back into a picture book past for a little while.

The tour, however, was not quite over. 'I'll show you something really peculiar,' said Streeter mysteriously, and he led the way across the road and down an alley between two huts. They came out on a piece of open ground beside the water, with a view across the inlet, unimpeded by the island. It was a cemetery, but one with a difference. There were no crosses, angels or eulogious inscriptions on simple headstones. Instead there were either plain wood boards with names and dates on them or – quite often – little obelisks, painted in various colours, but all surmounted by a small red star. Impressed by the alien character of the place they almost failed to notice the line of ships moving up to Murmansk.

The second half of the convoy was serenely arriving as daylight waned.

While they walked back in the gathering dusk, through the newer part of the town, the loudspeakers came to life. There was a lot of crackling and whining, then a voice said, '*Govorit Moskva – vot izvestiya.*' This was followed by very martial music crashing through the atmospherics and resounding through the freezing air. 'What's that, Jim?'

'Radio Moscow – the news.'

The voice began to speak again and it was evident fascists and place names were involved. 'They're announcing the villages and towns liberated yesterday.'

Plodding carefully down the main steps to the jetty they wondered who bothered to stop in the cold and listen to these extraordinarily long lists.

Coming into the mess when tea was about to be served, David was delighted to hear the familiar voice of Johnny in a cheerful babble round the table. He was sitting on the locker with George and Fred and on the other side Rowe was a listener to their repartee. 'I've just been telling the others Dave, we only tied up at noon. We were after that sub for hours.'

Streeter came up to the group, with a cup and piece of bread and jam. 'What sub?' he asked.

'The *Obstinate* and *Stavanger* got one between them,' put in Rowe.

'Did they get proof?' George asked sceptically.

'The evidence of our own eyes,' said Johnny enthusiastically, his black orbs glinting with a cruel look of the hunter in them. 'I saw it go down. It skulked for hours and we made and lost contact over and over again. Then *Stavanger* put in a run that must have damaged it. It was about that time I heard our guns and as I wasn't on the set or phone, nipped outside to see what was happening. There were about half a dozen flares coming down and it was as good as daylight. I saw our pattern go over just before we crossed the *Stavanger*'s wake. The water was still boiling from her attack; there was the vapour shock on the surface from our charges and then a bloody almighty upgushing and what rises up at all of forty-five degrees but the whole arse of the U-boat. You could see the hydroplanes and even the turning propellers. Like an effing great whale it was stuck up for a moment at the top of the mound of water and everybody cheered and shouted like a cup tie. The signalmen and lookouts were jumping up and down with joy.'

He paused a little. Everybody in the mess was silent. 'Then it slid down almost vertically in a rumbling froth you could hear above the ship noise. It must have been breaking to pieces inside. It was a wily bastard, but the effing old *Obstinate* is wilier. Those blokes could hear a tiddler sneeze at ten miles. And you know what those buggers in *Stavanger* did? They came back over the spot and put down a deep pattern to help it on its way.'

Breaking the grim silence that followed Johnny's narrative, Hopkins said quietly, 'Well its evens for the poor old *Masai*.'

'Reckon that hunting trip paid off,' reflected Vic Bouveney. 'The yeoman says that the second half was completely unmolested.'

'How many ships in the second part?' asked Fred.

'Twenty-five merchant packets and an escort group from Western Approaches,' said Vic. 'I bet they're missing Lime Street.'

'You know what I think,' said Ginger, from the other end of the table, 'I think we were used as a decoy. Right out in front to attract Jerry's attention. Roll, bowl or pitch we took it all.'

'Go on, Ginger, you're exaggerating,' laughed Robbie, 'although – why two parts to the convoy?'

Streeter had been filling his pipe from a pouch. He pressed the tobacco down and put a lighter to it. Waving aside the smoke he said quietly, 'The Forlorn Hope.'

'The what, Jim? Sounds like a pub.'

'In olden times they put a line of skirmishers out in front of the main army. For obvious reasons they called them, "The Forlorn Hope".'

'That,' said Ginger decisively, 'was the situation in a nutshell.'

'Never mind, mates,' said Robbie, 'we'll all be one great big happy family on the way home.'

'How d'you know?' Vic had to be convinced.

'Heard the coxs'n telling the chief buffer. He said he'd heard the skipper telling his pal Charlie as they went ashore up to Navy House.'

This brought the matter of shore leave to mind. Streeter told the others what the pair of them had been doing whilst ashore in the afternoon. Most felt they had not missed much and there were remarks about their odd taste in tourist attractions. However, several looked forward to the evening at the Red Navy Club.

'Going to this do tonight, mates?' asked Johnny.

They all were, even Fred who, though duty watch, was absolutely unable to resist such an attraction and hoped to ingratiate himself with Pots into being allowed to go along in exchange for some future extra duty. He was determined not to miss the fun and splendour of the concert and grinned impishly as though ready to desert if frustrated.

Following supper those going to the show were busy in their messes, polishing boots, brushing clothes and trying to make themselves as presentable as possible. Called by the loudspeakers, they began to trickle down to the galley flat, where station cards were collected and a perfunctory inspection took place. It was strange to see the space well lit for a change.

'What time's this thing start?' asked Johnny. He was waiting on the jetty as they stepped off.

'Pots said 1900,' replied George. He looked at his watch. 'Plenty of time, twenty minutes.'

There would have been no need to ask the way. The libertymen, their breath trailing vapour clouds in the icy air, trudged up the track and along the wooden bridge, the way lit by the uncanny glow of the Aurora Borealis. Particularly difficult to cross was the open piece of ground in front of the club building, which was surfaced with well-trampled snow frozen into an ice sheet. To accompany their walk the public address system broadcast a lengthy news bulletin, punctuated with fanfares and marching songs, to the indifferent Arctic night.

They went up a short flight of steps below columns of the entrance portico, built of stuccoed brick and into the welcoming heat of the vestibule. Russian servicemen and women stood crowded into the area, smoking and talking animatedly. It was a contrast to their stolid demeanour out of doors, observed during the afternoon. They became acutely conscious of the sweet, pungent aroma of the papirosas, or cardboard-tipped Russian cigarettes. Red Army men and women alike wore a tight-collared, loosely-fitting tunic more olive green than khaki, gathered in folds at the waist with a buckled leather belt. They had tight trousers, tucked into jackboots of poor quality leather, reflecting dully the brilliant light diffused in the tobacco haze. Officers stood cheek by jowl with privates, some of whom, breasts decorated, wore a galaxy of medals in bronze and silver, enamelled with red stars. The dark blue of the Soviet Northern Fleet sailors was liberally spread through the mass of khaki, the officers and petty officers in a uniform of typical naval cut. However, the ratings wore narrow trousers and over a vest of blue and white horizontal white stripes, a short jumper also secured at the waist with a belt very similar to that of the soldiers.

Rather self-conscious in the relatively festive atmosphere they encountered, feeling boorishly unable to adapt after the past bruising weeks, they edged their way towards the theatre. They passed through double doors to the left of the vestibule into a long gallery decorated at the far end with a larger than life-size bust of Lenin. This effigy had many flags, service and national, as a setting, and at the near end of the long room an image of Comrade Stalin stood in a similar arrangement.

It was not these, however, which arrested their eyes, but the numerous paintings along the walls. Gaudily painted in a bogus realism, recalled from books produced in the Great War, they depicted heroic achievements of the Northern Fleet along the coasts adjacent to this extremity of the cataclysmic Eastern Front. Comrades standing bolt upright, unscathed in the most withering fire, made dramatic gestures straight from the days of the silent film. The enemy dead lay in heaps along the shores and in the background their ships sank by the score as water sprouted in the best picturesque tradition. No half tones, but strident blues, reds and yellows gave colour to an Arctic that never was, whilst reeling under the weight of impastoed paint, the enemy succumbed to the might of masses.

In the gallery people, standing about, were still numerous enough with their presence and densely pungent smoke to mute somewhat the effect of this visual propaganda, but not so many as to make it impossible to note individuals. Very occasionally, among the round, flat features of the women, there would be a woman of extraordinary beauty, wrapped in fine furs and simple but elegant clothes. And with charm and poise of such dazzling perfection, so exceptional it seemed to the life-tensed eyes of the sailors, that they felt that not all the old aristocrats had left with the last defenders of the monarchy a generation before.

Eventually they arrived at the door of the theatre, halfway along the gallery, and were delighted to see that it was still not full. Indeed it was half empty and as it was only a few minutes to the commencement of proceedings they went in and settled down in seats nicely situated in the centre of the auditorium. Soaking in the warmth of the building they relaxed, ready for an evening of choruses and dancing.

The doors soon closed, silencing the chatter in the gallery, the theatre still quite unfilled. It was puzzling. All those people outside, not anxious or intent, apparently, on enjoying the entertainment of the evening. The visiting sailors passed from mystification to amazement when the curtains opened, with the auditorium lights undimmed, and they saw in the middle of the stage a long table draped with the Red Navy ensign. Behind it, seated in the centre, was a commander, flanked on both sides by sailors and marines of various ranks.

To the left of the stage, seen from the audience, was a lectern, behind which was a bunch of the now familiar red banners of various kinds. The commander rose and opened a large book and solemnly read a passage, from which the names of Karl Marx, Lenin and Stalin frequently issued. He stopped, closed the book carefully and all those present stood, the embarrassed and reluctant foreigners included, whilst the Russians vigorously sang what appeared to be a patriotic song. In this, fascists seemed to get some sort of mention. The congregation sat down and it was the turn of a lieutenant-commander to introduce a petty officer, who walked, papers in hand, from the table to the lectern, arranged them carefully, paused, gently patted his not inconsiderable medals with the palm of his left hand and proceeded to relate some distinguished action against those same unfortunate fascist gentlemen mentioned in the hymn.

The lecturer returning to his seat; there was applause as energetic as the echoing condition of the hall would permit and once more all stood and some other inspiring theme was sung. The commander then read another lesson from the large book and so through a steady, and seemingly interminable cycle, lesson, thumping seats and shuffling feet; song, sermon, applause, thumping seats, song and lesson, a variety of greatly decorated servicemen from able seamen to commander enlightened their – Russian – audience.

Time dragged. George's blue Saxon eyes seemed heavier lidded than ever. From a slight twist in the corner of his mouth a murmur informed his companions he could do with a cigarette, whilst his weighty, powerful frame settled into deeper boredom. Fred's thin face only half struggled to prevent a grin of chagrin and self-condemnation on the one hand and amusement at the proceedings on the other, pushing away the mask of decorum. His slight body writhed in frustration beneath his overcoat, tortured by the vision of bliss conjured up by George's desire for a smoke. Johnny, his face getting sulkier in proportion to the length of the meeting, alternated between a curved, slumped apathy, low in his seat, and a standing bent sullenness during the songs.

Nevertheless David, at first stung by what he considered to be a piece of chicanery on the part of the Soviet authorities, began to look upon the pattern of the service as a kind of burlesque. Rather unneedful of the discomfort of his companions in the long periods they were seated, he relaxed, enjoying the warmth and luxuriating in the steadiness of the theatre, although his seat seemed to slide and push against a body attuned to the motion of the ship. Caressing him into a peaceful state of mind complementary to his physical comfort was the realization that for the present at least there was no need to steel oneself against the terror of annihilation.

At eight o'clock their stoicism was rewarded and the proceedings ended with the national anthem, a tune familiar to them already. The curtains closed, the doors opened and a veritable wave of humanity surged in, racing for seats. It was obvious that not all citizens of the Soviet Union were churchgoers to the state religion. The four ratings took advantage of the uproar to remove their overcoats, folded them and put them under the seats. By a quarter past eight when the lights dimmed, the hall was packed and the throng included a large number of men from the escort vessels.

The head and shoulders of the music director appeared over the orchestra pit. A hush fell and the first notes of music blared forth. The curtain parted to reveal a huge choir of sailors and they at once launched into a boisterous rendering of *Cantata to Stalin*. From time to time this big group came back to perform solemn hymns of valour, Mother Russia and correct political thinking. Between these broadsides smaller groups would sing with balalaika accompaniment and dancers demonstrated their agility in the crouching leg-kicking, folded-arms style of peasant dancing. Some, a glimpse of old Russia, wore costume.

A remarkable lapse from all this folk culture was the appearance, twice, of what might be generally considered – by the uninitiated – to be a dance band. They played syncopated dance-time numbers and received applause that was perhaps a little less enthusiastic than for the more indigenous performances.

Two hours passed all too quickly and the three smokers had completely forgotten their addiction for the time being. The end of the concert came with sustained and thunderous clapping and when the entertainers came on to acknowledge the tribute, they – an odd touch to alien eyes – joined in the applause themselves.

Fred and George had hardly left the building than they fell to bickering about the dance band. It was irritating enough to edge carefully over the ice-sheet and walk gingerly down the track – there was quite a drop on the left down to the football pitch – without hearing the spinsterish assertions and contradictions nagging back and forth. The lights on the jetty were observed to be out and work on the new building stopped as they came down the slope, but their way to the ships was lit by the soft green glow from above. Ten of the ships were alongside, tied up abreast each other in cosy groups of three and four. Wisps of steam curled upwards from them and as one approached they could be heard humming quietly, as though glad to be huddled up in each other's company.

Nevertheless, the public address system having at last fallen silent, there was no competition in the silence of the frosty stillness and the main themes of argument were reluctantly overheard. George, as would be expected, considered the music to be a quaint version of the current dance-hall swing music. Fred, on the contrary, maintained that it was an isolated backwater of the great mainstream of early Dixieland rhythms last heard twenty years before and developing its own idiosyncracies into a definite regional flavour. David, keeping his own counsel, being too pleasantly tired to chatter, thought the only thing required for the band to sever itself from the original source of inspiration was a violin. During the next day or two Fred worried the matter like a cat a mouse, mauling it and pushing it about with all who would care to listen. He had a particularly sympathetic listener in Jumper Collins who had been at the concert and took his part against George.

On board again, with the aid of a few lights left burning, they slung hammocks and turned in. Wriggling down into the depths of his hammock, Fred, showing powers of recuperation and resilience of mind that were quite admirable, whispered across to his neighbour, 'Dave, don't you think it was almost worth coming all this way to see that show tonight?'

18

From the very first call of 'Wakey, wakey, rise and shine,' coming harshly from the loudspeakers and the loud music that followed, so unsuitable for the cold early morning, it was evident that the day would be run in a very tight, routine naval manner. Living and working areas were cleaned for morning rounds and there was an urgency in the loading that was taking place from the jetty. By the time 'Up spirits' was piped everybody knew they would be going out before the short day ended, and by dinner there was no doubt about it. A note had come over from the HF-DF officer. Watchkeeping fore and aft was to start at 1200 hours.

David positively gobbled his dinner and was out at the funnel as the ships let go their lines and slipped away round the island. Each played their particular tune on their sound relay equipment and strange was the contrast as they faded into the distance. Some were martial, Others whimsical. *Watchful* seemed to have a choice too genteel for this brutal world, but another was ironically amusing *Any old iron, any old iron...* Captains and crew members waved across to acquaintances on opposite bridges and platforms. To see the yeoman lean over, shouting to his colleague on the *Opportunity*, which had been alongside, filled David with a pang of sadness. 'Call me up, Fres. I'll complete your education.' He watched the jetty recede, deserted now except for *Sentinel*, still licking her wounds until she was capable of crossing the dangerous waters. Polyarnoe, getting smaller over the widening water had been worth one visit but once was enough.

In the bright sunshine the destroyers, in line ahead, skirted the edge of the island and the boom gate ship made an opening through which they filed into the wide mouth of the inlet. Behind them, coming down from Murmansk, the so-called empties – though some were ballasted with pine logs – in their turn came out onto the estuary and began forming into their columns. The frigates were to make the close escort and the destroyers went ahead in a distant screen. As the snowbound shores slowly fell below the horizon the returning convoy, in contrast with the close intimacy of the outward, was distant, almost hull down on the quietly heaving sea.

The destroyer screen formed a rough arc moving north-west over several miles of water. *Obstinate* was on the south-western end, with the disappearing coast on its port side. Ahead and to starboard was *Watchful* two miles away. Thus forward along the bulging curve to *Severe* at its foremost point then on round and back to *Opportunity* over the horizon, at the end of the north-eastern extremity of the arc. Crews were shaking down into cruising routine, the radar beams span invisibly round the rim of the ocean and the asdic sound waves pulsed down to its bed, then echoed back to the equipment with monotonous pings. The vessels weaved back and forth on their zigzag courses but at all times stems were pointed north and west towards those terrible waters concealed in the week-long night.

Whilst they were drinking tea that afternoon Streeter mentioned the *Sentinel* being left behind and this evoked the general question from Ginger as to whether anybody had seen her damage. Most had seen splinter marks all the way up the starboard side on the stern superstructure and gunshields but no large hole. It was generally agreed that the torpedo had burst before striking the hull of the destroyer. 'How could that've happened?' wondered George at large to the others.

'Gnats,' said Ginger, not denying by the expression on his face that it was meant as a *double-entendre*. The less experienced members of the mess thought it was a joke at the expense of the countryman,

'And the same to you,' he said, rising waggishly to the occasion.

'No, you swede-bashing, plank-headed crun, I'm not joking. It was a Gnat.'

'What the bloody 'ell is that?' asked the little signalman of white watch, rubbing his bristles in perplexity.

'It's an acoustic torpedo.' This brief explanation was not enough for the slower brains present. Ginger got irritated. 'You tell 'em Jim. They're too dim for me.'

Streeter obliged. For a brief moment he seemed to be back in the classroom again. 'An acoustic torpedo,' he said heavily, 'is one that has a device to attract it onto the sound waves beaten out through the water by a ship's propellers. It has only to be aimed in the general direction of target and will home onto it like a kind of sound magnet. However, in the case of *Sentinel* some quirk of the vibrations exploded it before touching the hull, or perhaps water pressure triggered it off.'

George was aghast. 'Christ, whatever will they think of next?'

When David went into the main office at 1600 Fred tapped the message pad with his pencil and said, 'You know what today is?'

'What?'

'Sunday. So tomorrow's Monday, but we don't have to worry about that Monday morning feeling. We get it all round the clock on this tin can.'

Through that night and all the next day they moved northwest. The swell was getting heavier and a light wind fanned down bitterly on the starboard side. During Monday night, the term used to describe the hours usually associated with darkness, there being once more only a few hours of twilight, it began to snow. Shortly after dinner, for an hour, whilst the light held, all spare hands were out sweeping and raking the snowfall from deck and housings. It was not a pleasant task for the sea was more violent than when they had previously done it. They missed the close proximity of other ships, seeing only *Obstinate* on the one hand and *Stavanger* on the other as indistinct blurs in the twilight. Occasionally they winked their signal lamps mournfully to each other through the lonely greyness. The snowflakes were large and wet and advanced across the heaving surface in successive cloudy walls. The ships were continuing to push north and west and Ginger said, 'If we keep going in this direction, we'll hit the pack-ice.' He was very grumpy and bashed furiously at the stanchions below the searchlight platform.

For the listeners to the enemy all was quiet. The convoy was well into the area of high danger but the coast stations were mainly silent and also the submarines. In this weather there was obviously no concern about aircraft.

In the early hours of Tuesday David woke suddenly from an uncomfortable sleep, in which he had been hardly able to stay on the lockers. George sat on the bench opposite, head down on the mess table, asleep in folded arms. By his wristwatch David saw it was thirty-five minutes past three. Feeling unaccountably alert, he decided to wash before relieving Fred. Going towards the TS alley, he stepped carefully over figures sitting and sprawled on the deck. All, heavily wrapped in duffel coats and other heavy clothing, were mounds of khaki, blue and brown. To steady himself David paused by the ladder to the petty officers' mess. Around him the sleeping faces were innocent and child-like. It was not difficult to imagine his shipmates, of quite diverse origins and varied dispositions, as the children they once were, and how, on countless nights, through happy and anxious years parents had looked down on the same sleeping countenances as they grew through infancy and childhood. Now and again, disturbed by the tilt of the destroyer, one of other would stir, scratch himself and change to a less painful position under the mass of clothing, and then slip back into unrestful sleep. Ginger was rigidly prone on the lockers at the head of the table. The tautness was gone from his mouth where a quiet smile rested and closed eyelids contained his painful mind in the blessed solace of sleep.

Pausing against the TS door, he saw the green-lit face of a startled radar watchkeeper glance out at him as though conjured from a hereafter in which he could not now rest assured. If anything, that was the real sea-change he carried home from this voyage. The destroyer shuddered quietly as though unwilling to disturb the sleeping men she cherished in her body. He shivered too, for the alleyway was bitter cold and the sea sound loud as he went down to the washplace.

On the other side of the bulkhead Fred was sunk down in the swivel chair. It was not warm enough in the office for him and his duffel coat, hanging over his shoulders and untidily down the back of the seat, swung backwards and forwards with the roll of the ship. He lit another cigarette and glanced up at the clock. Three thirty-seven; not long now, this was the last smoke before sleep.

Roll on Dave. The watch had been totally inactive; even the Admiralty line at the end was silent. Perhaps they had gone home to bed down there in Smokes. He pushed up the sleeves of his jerseys and scratched at a bad spot. It was the diet, he thought. Nothing but stodge. When he got out he would eat properly, he hoped, after the war. Robbie turned from the magazine he was reading. It was a woman's journal. He smiled, moved away in mock repulsion and said, 'What's the matter, Fred, have you got 'em?'

Well astern of *Watchful*, high up in the HF-DF cubicle of *Obstinate*, Johnny, sitting before his motionless screen, also scratched himself. But it was through that peculiar irritation of the skin that assailed him when he was fighting to stay awake at this indecent hour. He had read the book Fred had given him, written a letter, and smoked far too much. Looking up at the clock he saw it was three thirty-eight, still twenty minutes to go. Then he remembered to draw. This was becoming a pastime. As soon as he got leave he would buy paints and see what he could do. What to do now? What about the jetty at Polyarnoe with all the ships alongside? Could he manage it? He tore a sheet from the pad. Deciding to have a go at it, he sketched in the eye level.

Far less agreeably situated than Johnny, above and forward of his cosy little office, the officer of the watch crouched in the lee of the wind shield on the starboard bulwark of the bridge and wondered if his mind would eventually go numb enough to be as useless as his limbs now felt. The wind, strong but not furious, drove curtains of snow almost horizontally across his very limited vision. Sometimes there were breaks in the showers and forward through the clear view screen in the general dim whiteness he saw the smooth, oily black swell. Out to windward somewhere there were the other ships, keeping company by radar. He bent down below the bulwark and pushing aside layers of clothing on his wrist, by the luminous face of his watch saw it was three forty; twenty more long, crawling minutes to go. The middle watch always seemed longest, the last hour of it endless. He longed for a mug of cocoa and his bunk. He retreated out of the disagreeable present into the mental pictures of his last leave in Town.

In the yet unfrozen depths of his thoughts he could see and

almost feel the warm curve of white skin beneath his hand, a fragrant perfume dwelt in his memory with a provocative laugh, and in his mind's eye there was a finely turned ankle he had first seen tucked round a bar stool in the Silchester. 'Hello, mouse,' she had said, puffing smoke in his face, as he came, the old salt, to get a real drink from under the counter. He had wondered what the hell she was talking about. 'We're mice,' she explained, 'and my cat is far, far away.' He was not shy about going to the mouse's flat. A nice enough nest he thought. She said there was some good whisky back there. Where it came from she did not trouble to explain – she was busy taking her clothes off – but there was an American label on the bottle. The ship jerked into the crest of a swell. He shook himself out of these pleasant recollections. At least they had helped to get his circulation going a little.

Below the absent-minded watchkeepers the shipless captain of the *Masai*, wrapped in a blanket, sea boots off, slept on the settee in the wardroom. It was not a healthy sleep, but a fitful half-wakefulness, where the explosions and the faces of men looking at him for orders plucked at his bowstring-taut nerves. His slumber was a no-man's-land of conflicting thoughts out on clashing patrols in the confused darkness of his mind. He twisted and turned, a still hidden, sub-conscious grudge disturbing his peace of mind. It had been a singularly useless commission. Six grinding months of hard work, nervous strain, no spectacular achievements and a wasteful, inglorious end to his first command. His friends were steaming to the next promotion whilst he had to start all over again. If they would let him. This, and other reluctant, forgotten thoughts, still to emerge boldly into his wakeful perception.

Johnny, in a creative splurge, was rising up awkwardly from his chair to get a rubber that had been mislaid behind the set, when the sudden, now familiar echoing boom of a torpedo bursting seized at his fearstruck bowels with icy fingers. Almost in the same minute the centre spot in the screen flicked in a twitching line as a U-boat crowed to base of its success.

That same grim instant, on the bridge, the evil night was momentarily rent by that blinding white flash ahead which, despite years of active service still struck the duty officer in his deepest soul with horror mingled with grief. It swelled with the following roar, only too dreadfully confirming a luckless ship. He groped to press the action alarm button and was calling down for full speed when the dark form of the captain loomed up from his sea-cabin to ask hoarsely, 'Who is it?'

'Don't know yet, Sir. Seemed to be in the direction of *Watchful*.'

The question was soon resolved. A whistle from the wireless-office pipe was acknowledged, then 'Wireless office to bridge – *Watchful* says she's torpedoed, Sir.'

'Tell them we're coming up.'

'Aye-aye, Sir.'

Down below, the former captain of *Masai* rose up on the settee, the turmoil of his sleeping mind confounded by his waking senses. That was a real explosion. Throwing aside the blanket he began to pull on his sea boots. Bleary-eyed, he reeled across to get his topside clothes, stacked on the table. The youngest steward, a scared look in his eyes and inflated lifebelt round his waist, burst into the wardroom to prepare it for emergency use. 'It's the *Watchful*, Sir,' he said, not waiting to be asked. 'Tin-fished. It'll be dead dodgy getting them off in this sea won't it, Sir?'

The lieutenant commander remained silent. The lad was right. Could he tell a stupid lie? 'We'll have to do our best, steward, won't we?' he said quietly, dissembling his own anxiety as he put on his fur hat. Yet he was sick at heart. Old Colin, poor bastard, he would be sweating right now. He tottered out of the wardroom and up the bridge ladderway.

Just as abruptly as the steward Johnny's two colleagues burst into the HF-DF cubicle and one gasped agitatedly, 'They've had it on the *Watchful* – poor sods!' The pencil snapped in Johnny's hand; he turned and looked hard at the screen, which was blurred in his smarting sight. An overlooked mistake and he could have been on the thing. Scratched out names then, on the draft list by a master-at-arms, and now, by something else.

'Oh, sorry chum. Your mates are in *Watchful*, aren't they?'

Johnny had written down the submarine bearing. He could not trust himself to speak. He handed it to the others to tell the bridge.

On the humming, freezing dark bridge as the asdic relay amplifier twanged despairingly into the night, the TS called the captain again. 'Radar reports *Watchful* stopped at green two five, Sir.'

The engines were vibrating furiously and through the snow showers they could see deck lights. 'I've seen them,' the captain answered tensely. 'Trying to get the rafts away,' he muttered as an aside to the captain of *Masai* whose vaguely lit features had appeared over the faint light from the binnacle. The whistle jabbed his nerves again. Answering, he learned that there had been no acknowledgement of the radio-telephone message.

The TS came back to say *Watchful* was still stopped at twenty degrees on the starboard side.

'Yeoman!' the captain called. He came forward in the gloom. 'Sir?'

'Try them on the lamp. Tell them we're coming up.' The petty officer signalman felt his way to the lamp on the starboard side and the tinny click-clack of its shutter was punctuated by the brief flashes of light.

There was no reply.

The pings of the asdic amplifier added their unceasing echoes to the urgency of the moment. For a few minutes a curtain of falling snow obscured the lights and when it passed there was only the blackness of oblivion.

'TS to bridge. *Watchful* disappeared off plot, Sir.'

'They can't go just like that,' protested the captain bitterly. 'It's impossible. Open shutters.'

The beam probed slowly back and forth across the sullen, heaving, dreadfully black water that had claimed their sister ship. There was nothing but the acid-cold sea and the ghostly snow. The light switched off.

The strident twanging of the asdic echoes had been increasing in pace and changing in tone and from below came, 'Large contact at red one zero, about half a mile, depth uncertain.'

The vessel turned towards the contact and as it slowed to gain accuracy, a further call said, 'Contact red zero five, below six hundred feet – unlikely submarine.'

'Christ,' whispered the captain, the echoes suddenly maddening to his ear. 'Switch that bloody thing off!' he shouted.

In the darkness he clutched the binnacle, face turned from its glow, glad only that the men on the bridge could not see the hot moistness that started in his eyes. The sub-lieutenant, also relieved that nobody could see him, punched his gloved right fist into the palm of his left hand. Leaning against the bulwark he gazed out into the shroud of night, swearing silently, uselessly.

The early train was making its usual way leisurely through the south-eastern suburbs of the city. The low morning sunshine of late spring glowed across the carriage, showing up its neglected shabbiness and the somewhat threadbare tidiness of its occupants. The man in the bowler hat was in his accustomed place by the outside corner window, back to the direction of travel. His newspaper, open on his lap, was unread as he looked out on the bright roofs. Opposite him was a large woman of ruddy complexion, in a brown woollen dress and grey cardigan. Thick-legged and heavy-shoed, she may well have been a cleaner or factory hand. Her hands, fat and red, were folded in a matronly way over a straw woven carrier bag. Next to her the middle-aged workman, cloth cap still well down over his forehead, read a newspaper as the veil of smoke rose from the damp, misshapen butt end in his lips. He was rather thin and overshadowed, for the ample figure of the lady perpetually knitting sat on his right. The younger woman in the corridor window seat, quite awake, was reading her newspaper as well. Across from her the young man in dungarees and jacket was dreamily staring into the corridor, a picture-magazine on his knees. Between him and the city gentleman, two schoolgirls fidgeted and bickered, giggling occasionally over each other's belated homework.

There were fewer people in the corridor; they and the undistinguished skyline went unnoticed by the young workman. A tall black American technical sergeant in a forage cap that was oddly pointed at front and back leaned down to chat to a young woman with fair, curly hair, rather tubby of figure, but clad in a red, two-piece suit and black patent shoes. She carried a handbag made in a similar shiny material. These articles, too smart for the austerity imposed by five years of war, hinted at their transatlantic origin, and confirmed by the nylon stockings that sheathed her not particularly elegant legs. A few soldiers and airmen were in the coach but no navy men. Indeed there had been fewer going and coming from the stations for the naval base as the year advanced. The regular passengers were not unhappy about that.

The endless smoker appeared to be now on conversational terms with the marathon knitter. 'Lost another ship,' he mumbled.

'What'sis name?' enquired the knitter, not taking her eyes from the fencing needles. He answered formally. 'The Admiralty regrets to announce the loss of HMS *Watchful* through enemy action. Next of kin have been informed.'

'Have you heard of it?' she asked, pausing to tug at the wool emerging from her bag.

'Nah! Don't suppose its very important. Still it's the second this week, there was one the other day. What was it called?'

'Massy weren't it?' she suggested.

'Oh, yer, the *Masai*, yer that's it.'

'Terrible though, ennit, for their relatives I mean?' confided the knitting woman.

The reply was as much a cough as a grunt.

The younger workman, stirring up from his abstracted mood, looked out on a brick wall beside a school playground they were slowly passing. On it, in large white letters, was daubed 'STRIKE IN THE WEST NOW.' He turned to stare at the oblivious knitter. 'It's nothing to what the Russians have had to put up with,' he blurted out. 'Look what they've done in the past three years and we just sit here doing nothing,' he added, heatedly. He was regarded from all directions with every kind of meaning: anger, embarrassment, incomprehension and astonishment. The two girls squirmed with surreptitious nudges and sniggers.

'It's true they done a lot, mate,' vouchsafed the smoking man, 'but we were at it before them, remember?'

'Why have we been waiting about years except to wear them

out?' What help are they getting? Sweet fanny adams! Our lot just lay about doing nothing.'

'Perhaps they're not trained properly yet, dear,' said the knitting lady in a motherly effort to mollify him.

'After three years?' he asked indignantly.

'I expect they'll go as soon as they're ready,' broke in the young woman opposite him, with some asperity of tone. 'My brother who's in the county regiment says it's only a matter of months.'

'Yes, after they're beaten anyway,' concluded the politically-minded young man scornfully as he took up his magazine to look at pictures of the Eastern Front.

The compartment settled down again into its early morning torpor and soon after the workman's outburst the travellers began to get out at the increasingly frequent stops. First the schoolgirls, then the knitter, then the young workman, soon followed by the smoker, and before the terminus the large lady in the corner.

The sun cast a moving beam through the dust and smoke drift. The man in the bowler hat glanced over to the young woman in the opposite corner. He folded his paper. 'My son . . .' he ventured, 'was killed in 1940.' A pause for recollection. 'When it was still an imperialist war. He was a fighter pilot.'

The young woman thought he looked older and more drawn in features than she had noticed before. Perhaps it was the brighter light. She smiled, compassionately. 'My husband's in the Air Force,' she said, rather lamely, she felt. She looked out of the corridor window, and the light reflected in her glance seemed too bright. They stirred up, self-consciously, preparing to get off as the train clattered across points, jerked as it slackened speed and slowly drew into the platform.

Further down the train there had been a naval rating with the other passengers, service and civilian who alighted. He was dressed in a standard issue uniform with a blue edged white fronted shirt instead of a blue jersey. Getting off the train after everybody else, with great care, it was evident as he came along the platform that he had a slight limp. A sartorially-minded observer would have noticed that he wore his hat neither at the rakish angle popular with the wartime sailors of his years, nor at the absolute level regulation manner, low across the eyebrows, the hallmark of a regular serviceman. It was level, but high on the forehead, in the manner of the raw recruit, still unused to the strange garb.

At the barrier, the ticket collector noticed that his right wrist was bandaged although he managed to carry a blue raincoat over that arm. He offered the ticket without raising his hand. In the other he had a little brown attaché case and a large paper parcel. He went across the concourse, the railwayman gazing curiously at his receding, oblivious back, to a waiting taxi. Emerging from the shade the sun felt warm on his blue serge.

'Where to Jack?' asked the driver.

'Dolphin Square, please, Cabbie,' said Edward Meecham. He fumbled at the door but there was no real strength in his right hand yet. There was a slow mending of injuries where he came from.

''Ere, arf a tick, mate,' said the driver, noting his difficulty and nimbly getting out of the cab and opening the door. 'You seem to 'ave 'ad a rough time,' he observed sympathetically. 'Where'd you collect that lot?'

'On the way to Russia,' murmured Eddie, sinking back in the seat.

'Blimey, son,' said the driver, as he slammed the door, 'sooner you than me!'

Eddie relaxed to enjoy the luxury of the ride alone. He would be by himself, except for his aunt and one or two friends for fourteen days. He could get up when he liked; eat when he wanted and go out when he felt like it. If his weak wrist would allow he would rewrite those notes he had scrawled almost illegibly whilst it was in plaster, and other things that might be of interest one day. There would be no bad language and his private functions would be done in private. He would not be jostled by men's sticky bodies or breathe air fouled by fetid stench and reek of fuel oil.

Yet there would not be fellows about like good-hearted, temperamental Ginger, absurdly cheerful Fred or pensive David Freston. Nor would there be steady rocks such as Robbie, taking the inanities of this world as though they were all beyond redemption; reserved Streeter, puffing his pipe and thinking of home, his wife and children, or George whose slow voice and manner had made him think of golden fields of wheat, when in the place where the only harvest reaped was that of death; and Pots, leaning against the voicepipes, smiling benevolently down on his argumentative team and unobtrusively rounding the more awkward corners of service routine.

Perhaps he would meet others like them when he went back, and of course there was Scouse Edwards. When he had seen him in the drill shed they had exchanged addresses. He was going to be at the depot gunnery school for a long time. 'I've got a cushy number at last,' he had said, unbelievingly. Wondering, perhaps, how the ball had stopped on the right number for him in the end. 'I reckon it'll see me through the duration.'

Eddie looked out of the cab window. It was already warm in the metropolis. The dust and traffic fumes were starting to build a haze in the night-freshened air. As they strode purposefully across the bridge to the city, under the blue sky and the sunlight dancing on the quiet river the workers knew in spite of the absence of weather bulletins that it was going to be a fine day. A day for strolling about at lunch time, in what remained of the ancient, narrow streets, or to sit in the little squares which violence had suddenly given new vistas. It was going to be a good day and they were cheerful because there was an air of expectancy. Things were on the move.

The bright sun caught the early weeds blossoming in the war-scarred gaps. People felt the warmth entering their long-shuttered, musty offices as the wan electric light lost the contest with the golden shafts from outside on desk and counter. The hands of antique clocks moved past nine o'clock and the pace of the capital quickened as clerks and typists followed commissionaires and cleaners in commencing their daily routine. It was a fine, warm day; a good day to be alive.